BETRAYED

Quantum Twins Series

RIPPED APART
HUNTED
BETRAYED
REBELLION

BETRAYED

QUANTUM TWINS

ADVENTURES ON TWO WORLDS

GEOFFREY ARNOLD

Matador
9 Priory Business Park,
Wistow Road, Kibworth Beauchamp,
Leicestershire. LE8 0RX
Tel: 0116 279 2299
Email: books@troubador.co.uk
Web: www.troubador.co.uk/matador
Twitter: @matadorbooks

ISBN 978 1789016 529

British Library Cataloguing in Publication Data.
A catalogue record for this book is available from the British Library.

Printed and bound by CPI Group (UK) Ltd, Croydon, CR0 4YY
Typeset in 11pt Goudy Old Style by Troubador Publishing Ltd, Leicester, UK

Matador is an imprint of Troubador Publishing Ltd

ACKNOWLEDGEMENTS

My continuing thanks go to my supporting team. Cecily Wheeler and Josephine Brand who type the stories the Twins tell my whilst we're on holiday, my editor Judith Henstra, Caroline Swain who proof reads and provides a detailed edit, and although this is 'self-published' I have a publisher - a great team at Matador. Gary Brown for his splendid redesign of the website. Stephen Ling and Pegggy Driscoll who read the books and give me invaluable reader advice and suggestions. Through it all there is my wife who gives me the space and the time it takes on holiday and then at home, and the continuing interest and support of friends and family.

WELCOME

In previous books I have written:
"Welcome to the story the Twins have told me. They do not consider this to be a work of fiction."

While we were discussing a scene in this book I challenged them to explain how they know what other people were doing or thinking. Their answer was:

'There is no Time in Timelessness.'

The Twins have gone on to live long lives and reached the ninth dimension where, as with Sigma-Space, they can turn the pages of the story of their lives. To be present both "then" and "now" means entanglement. When I see them, the superpositioning collapses (Hullo, Schrödinger's Cat) and they are present as they were in that part of their lives they are telling me about.

PRINCIPAL CHARACTERS

VERTAZIA
A Vertazian day equals 28 hours on Earth. That makes the Twins equivalent to seventeen and a half years old, Tamina and Xaala nineteen and a half. But Tazii live to be about two hundred and the children mature slower.

Qwelby & Tullia (15) their father: Shandur, mother: Mizena
Tamina (girl almost 17) & Wrenden (boy almost 14) sister & brother
Pelnak & Shimara (boy & girl 15) the not-twins
Shandur's Great Uncle Mandara (Gumma), Great Aunt Lellia (Gallia)

Ceegren, the Arch Custodian
Xaala (girl almost 17), his acolyte
Rulcas (boy 16) Xaala's side-kick
Dryddnaa, a Chief Readjuster (Psych or Psi Doctor)

FINLAND
Hannu Rahkamo (boy 15), father Paavo, mother Seija
Viivi (19) Jenni (16) Oona (14)

Miska Metsälä, Suojelupoliisi (SUPO) Finnish Intelligence Service
Chief Inspector Ulla Koivuniemi
Ivanova & Nicolai Rushailo, FSB
Sherwin and Farah Green, CIA

KALAHARI

The Meera Tribe

Tsetsana (almost 12) father Milake, mother Deena
Xashee, her 16 year old brother
Tomku, their 4 year old sister
Nthabe, their 7 year old sister
H'ani (boy 17)
Kou-'ke and Nlai, 16 year old girls
Mandingwe & N!Obile, 12 year old girls
Ghadi, tribal chief
Kotuma, his wife
Xameb, the Shaman
Xara, senior hunter
Tu, a healer

Police

Inspector Modisakgosi
Constable Ditau

RAIATEA

Professor David Romain
Dr Tyler Jefferson & Dr Miki Tamagusuku-Jefferson
Angélique (just turned 16)
daughter of Hokuao, the housekeeper and cook

SAN PRONUNCIATION

A reminder.

X Imagine the way the English say 'Gee up' to a horse, a click at one side of the mouth, usually the noise is made twice. The X is pronounced with that sort of click made at both sides of the mouth at the same time.

Ts A normal Ts movement but with the tongue pressed hard against the back of the top teeth and pulled sharply away. The sort of 'tsk' sound someone makes in a 'tut tut' expression.

! An explosive sound made with the tip of the tongue pulled from the top of the palate. A sort of 'tok' sound - without the 'k'.

' A glottal stop - made by closing and reopening the back of the throat quickly.

- A single 'gee up' click.

" Half way between ! and Ts

ÓWEPPÂ
THE TALISMAN

Tamina

Pelnak

Tullia

Qwelby

Shimara

Wrenden

CHAPTER 1

FREEDOM

THE KALAHARI

Qwelby jerked awake with his twin's scream reverberating through his head.

Why? She was in his arms.

She wasn't.

She had been.

In his mind as he wrapped his arms around her – in a prison cell!

Charging to her rescue, he hurtled out of his Form into the eighth dimension as he morphed into his Attribute of a powerful dragon and burst into her cell, rocking the building as he ripped all the doors to the cells from their frames. With a mighty roar he smashed through a solid metal door into an office where he saw his twin and tore out the door that was barring her escape.

'No. Kaigii. NO!' Tullia yelled.

Puzzled, Qwelby halted and smiled as he noted the confusion on the faces of the people unable to see him. Tullia knelt and tried to lift the door he'd just come through. Responding to her plea for help, he gripped the edge of the door and saw his arm covered in dragon scales as he raised it up. A tall slim young man wearing dark blue, who'd been lying to one side, crawled to the

1

door and dragged from underneath it an old man also wearing dark blue.

Qwelby let the door crash back onto the floor, raising a cloud of dust and making the young man cough. He recognised the three marks on the old man's clothing - a sergeant - of police. "The Authorities" he knew meant imprisonment, dissection and death as people on Earth believed all aliens were out to destroy them - and would destroy any alien they met. Here were two of them!

No. Kaigii. They good.

His twin's thoughts stopped his rising panic and were followed by her request to share healing energies. Qwelby saw the six fingers of their one pair of hands manipulate the vivid interplay of colours as healing wrapped around and through the sergeant's lungs and cracked ribs.

There was another presence in the seventh dimension. No. Two. He was tingling as someone was reading his energy spectrum. That one was inexperienced for there to be a tingle - a youthful male. And the other was contributing healing energy with a vibration that tickled a memory of the Space Wars of some eighty thousand years ago.

The twins opened to the cosmos and moved into Timelessness as Qwelby saw the energy flowing through them from Tullia's Uddîšû - the great healer from the time of the Space Wars. The bright colours muted as the sergeant's ribs were mended and his lungs healed. Their hands moved to his head, appearing to give him a thick head of golden hair.

With the sergeant finally restored to health, Qwelby looked around the room. Everyone's face was dark brown and the sergeant's wrinkled face the darkest of them all. On the other side of the desk stood a tall and well built man also in dark blue. From the silver badges on the shoulders of his uniform jacket, Qwelby assumed him to be a senior officer. This side of the desk, a well built teenage girl of average height was standing, wearing what he assumed was a school uniform of a red sweater over black trousers and boots. As well as her facial features, an energy link told him she was the officer's daughter.

The tall young policeman righted a chair beside her and helped Tullia get the sergeant to his feet and settled on it.

The girl was staring open-mouthed at Tullia, her energy field displaying a mixture of fear and wonder. He smiled at her startled look as Tullia placed a hand on her arm and infused her with calming energies, then saw her fear disappear leaving only a look of wonder in her eyes. Realising a conversation was taking place and not understanding the language, he slipped into his twin's mind.

I'm not using my compiler.

I understand, Tullia. Trust me. I've had to... dissemble. Switch compiler to second mode to translate their words and leave you free to speak your own.

Okay. But you must not let anyone know what we are.

Understood.

Using the little Afrikaans she had learnt personally, Tullia made a fresh start. 'I sorry I scream. Kaigii think I in danger. Kaigii strong here.' She put a hand on her chest between her two hearts. *Your arrival caused a landquake.*

She went on to repeat the story she had told the police the previous day when interviewed in the village. Then, she had spoken in a mixture of Afrikaans and Meera with the Shaman translating for her. Now, she spoke slowly and hesitantly as Qwelby made occasional and judicious alterations to her proposed words.

The upshot was that Tyua'llia, *The name given to me by the Meera, the local San tribe who know what we are and have adopted me,* belonged to a tribe called Tazii who believed they were the ancestors of all San. She came from a long line of powerful healers and she and one male were the only ones remaining on the planet, which was all true.

That fitted what the others were thinking. That Tyua'llia was a highly skilled N'om K"xausi or Sangoma, and Kaigii was the name both of a powerful elemental in the otherworld and her companion, or possibly they were one and the same.

Inspector Modisakgosi, who did not believe in elemental spirits, had not changed his mind overnight. He still considered that she and a very real companion were running away from whatever trouble they had caused. He had never heard of the name of her tribe, which was not surprising if she came from Namibia. And that was logical, because from her red hue he assumed her tribe was similar to the red-skinned Hiechware who were one of the oldest San tribes of Namibia, and that her height and build were probably due to one of her parents being a Himba, another Namibian tribe.

Tullia had remained standing in the group with the constable, the Inspector's daughter and the seated sergeant. Taking comfort from the energy of acceptance she was experiencing from those three, she looked across to the Inspector standing on the opposite side of his desk.

'Please, Sah, ceremony tomorrow. I become woman.'

Your Awakening?

Yes.

Me too.

<DragonsBreath/HornsFlute. Too fast!!>

'QeïchâKaïgïi… Know you are cared for.'

'Oh please Daddy, you have to let her go,' Akila said and turned to Tullia. 'You really want this, don't you?'

Tullia nodded.

Not wanting the traditional African ceremony herself, that her mother was determined she should have, Akila asked Tullia to explain why she wanted it. With Tullia's compiler rapidly building its dictionary and syntax of Afrikaans as they talked, she thought she understood the ceremony the girl was explaining, but that was not possible.

'Akila. You no mean... all that... cut off!'

'Yes...'

4

Tullia screamed.

'No. Kaigii. NO!' Tullia shouted as the building rocked and was again filled with the smell of plaster as more fell from the walls and a mug rolled off the desk to smash on the floor.

Staring fearfully at what, from her father's description, she believed to be an alien – an alien surrounded by a shimmering golden haze – Akila moistened her lips. 'I do not want that,' she said to a pair of twirling, purple eyes set in red ovals.

Tullia pulled Akila into a close embrace. 'Please, Sah. NO!' she said, looking at him over the top of his daughter's head.

Inspector Modisakgosi was taken aback by the power of the words that seemed to hit him physically. He was an educated man and did not believe in the stories of aliens in Africa or the superstitious rubbish talked about the powers of witch doctors. Yet he had just seen an earthquake happen in his own Station, plus some trick of illusion that made it look as though a young woman had lifted a heavy metal door, then restored his sergeant to health without actually having touched him.

And his own healing she had given him earlier that morning. The back pain was a minor but long standing problem. Gone. His shoulders had been getting increasingly rigid as the weeks of argument at home continued. He rolled them, amazed at the ease. And today's headache. The worst ever. Gone.

He saw the pleading looks in the eyes of his daughter and.... his prisoner. He could not think of the tall and well built young woman as the fifteen-year-old she claimed to be.

If he was right with the assumptions he had made yesterday, she and her companion were criminals on the run and he would soon receive arrest warrants from Namibia. He had the girl and would arrest her companion when he came looking for her.

But...

He walked around his desk, stood in the doorway and looked down the corridor that led to the cells. Through a film of dust and a smell that made him cover his mouth and nose, he saw the steel doors of both cells had been ripped from their hinges and the wooden door into the ablutions was smashed to pieces.

Qwelby was consumed with embarrassment. The attractive young woman clinging to him was producing the same exciting stirrings in his body he'd experienced kissing cute little Oona. Acknowledging Akila's fear, his mind slid into hers as he reassured her he meant no harm, whilst his lips sought her very kissable pair. As her eyes went wide and his hearts beat faster he remembered he was in Tullia's Form and, enjoying being naughty, controlled his twins' actions.

'Kai-ji?' Akila mouthed.

Qwelby/Tullia smiled and winked.

Akila leant forward and a kiss was shared that jolted all three with a brief, burning flare. The twins saw the look of amazement on Akila's face, lip-read her 'Thank you' that they had proved Tullia was an Extra Terrestrial, and understood her thoughts – Akila treasured the secret she was going to keep to herself.

Qwelby completely withdrew from Akila's mind and grinned at the mental slap Tullia gave him.

Modisakgosi turned back into the room and his daughter pleaded with him to let Tullia go, at least for the day of the ceremony.

'I promise, Sah...' Qwelby changed his twin's intended words to, '...I no run away.'

Qwelby suggested her "Little Girly Act", which he hated, but here and now... Tullia had seen the Meera girls do something different. She made her eyes go round, her ovals turn white and her purple orbs shine brightly, dipped her head a little and slowly lowered her long black lashes before looking back up at the Inspector from underneath them, sending a strong "please be nice to me" energy.

Still very innocent in such matters, she would have been appalled to know why the Inspector spluttered and hastened back around to the other side of his desk, his mind definitely made up.

'The cells are ruined. You'll have to go back....'

6

'Oh, thank you, Sah,' Tullia said as she stepped right up to her side of the desk. She couldn't help it. As her mouth broke into a big smile she again made her eyes go round and bright and this time fluttered her eyelashes at him, as she thought of herself as one metre ninety of sweet, young innocence.

Yay-oh! Kaigii. Qwelby thoughtsent the image of a laughing face.

'Sergeant,' Modisakgosi almost shouted. 'Get her out of here!'

'And you my girl,' he added as he turned to his daughter. 'You realise there's going to be hell to pay at home. My life won't be worth living!'

'Thank you, Daddy.' Akila threw her arms around her father for siding with her – no circumcision! 'And you Tyua'llia,' she said as she faced Tullia across the desk. 'And Kai-ji,' she mouthed as she winked and then her lips kissed the air.

CHAPTER 2

ON LICENCE

THE KALAHARI

Tullia was in a daze as the sergeant led her outside into another bright sunny morning. She didn't understand why the Inspector had suddenly become so angry, yet she was happy and excited. She was going to attend her Moon Day, she had saved the girl from being brutalised and for the first time since leaving Vertazia three tendays ago she and her twin had been vibrantly together.

She was so happy that she hadn't given her twin a slap for making her return Akila's air kiss. He had been looking after her. Normally she would fight him, but this time she had needed his help. 'Kaigii,' she murmured. He was Kaigii. She was Kaigii. They were Kaigii. The Tazian word embracing so much more than "Twin."

And that three-way kiss?

Receiving his '?' and not expecting their connection to last much longer, Tullia opened to her memory of that morning.

'QeïchâKaïgïi,' that voice whispered in her head in Old Aurigan. She felt as though she was being bathed in a smile. A smile that was as fresh as the morning dew and as ancient as the Tsodilo Hills.

She was brought back to Earth as the sergeant opened the door to the Land Rover. He slipped his hands inside his open necked shirt, pulled a pendant over his head and held it out to her. Dangling from a cord made from grass, she saw a small piece of intriguingly coloured stone bound around with fine copper wire. A typical Bushman necklace.

As she took it in her hands her whole body tingled and images of Auriga flashed before her eyes: the dying world her people had left a hundred and fifteen thousand years ago.

She saw him take it back, his dark brown eyes looking very seriously at her whilst she gawped at him. Bearing her twin's energy signature, an image appeared in her mind of a piece of rock about the size of a fist and with the same sort of colouring. *Three more*, she heard his thought.

Just then, the tall young constable came out of the Station with the blankets and other items that Tullia had been allowed to take with her when she'd been arrested. As he opened the back door and put them onto the seats the sergeant put the pendant back in Tullia's hand and closed her fingers over it. He gave the slightest shake of his head.

'My hearts sing,' Tullia said as they stared into each other's eyes.

Climbing onto the passenger seat Tullia slipped the pendant into a pocket of her tracker bottoms. Once again Ditau fastened the seat belt around her. She turned her head and smiled. He blushed. Now she understood – he liked her. She felt herself blushing and a warm feeling infused her body. Embarrassed, she dipped her head, then leant back with a big sigh.

Back in his bed in Finland, Qwelby entered his twin's memory. It started with her being led out of her prison cell into the Inspector's Office where she was introduced to his seventeen-year-old daughter. Sensing there was a particular reason for the visit, Tullia had slipped into Akila's mind where she discovered the girl believed Tullia to be a Siska – an ET well known in Africa.

Tullia noticed the Inspector's badly disturbed energy field and offered healing. Persuaded by his daughter, Modisakgosi sat down and Tullia set to work, but was unable to ease the extreme tension caused by a decision he had to make. When she discovered that the decision was about his daughter's circumcision, Qwelby was so horrified at the accompanying explanation that he nearly lost hold of the memory.

During the healing Akila had whispered to the sergeant that she thought she saw a shimmering golden haze around her father's head, which had lead to the policeman telling a story of "Old Tu". That had been so many years ago he could not believe it was the same Tu that Tullia knew, saying that Tu was a young child in nineteen thirty-six when the then government of South Africa issued the last permit to hunt the Bushmen.

Having been acknowledged as a Bushman, accepted into the Meera tribe and adopted by a family with young children who had named her their "Big-Big sister", Tullia had screamed in horror and it had been that which had brought Qwelby crashing in.

Still shaking from having heard about the appalling deformation of a girl's body, the shock on hearing about the killing of Bushmen that had been licensed by "The Authorities," was too much – he lost the memory.

It didn't take him long to recover it as he thought of what he'd done. Believing his twin to be in need of help and in a prison, he'd rushed to her aid. He'd not caused a landquake but his unconscious had acted on his knowledge, virtually destroyed the prison and caused Tullia to be freed. He was proud of himself. No pretending to be a Warrior, or relying on weird ancient memories, but himself – a fifteen-year-old Quantum Twin exercising his powers through the third dimension. 'Khuy! But I'm good!' he told the room.

He ran through what he'd personally experienced. The senior police officer had shown himself to be a caring and fair-minded man. Qwelby liked what he'd seen of the sergeant and the constable and had more than shared Tullia's desire to protect Akila. All the people he'd just seen were dark-skinned and that confirmed his plan to leave Finland and travel to his twin.

Sadly, he was soon to discover that his assumption that he and his twin would be welcomed by all dark-skinned people, was wrong. He had forgotten that the Azurii, the inhabitants of Earth, were as human as the Tazii.

CHAPTER 3

REFLECTING

EARTH AND VERTAZIA

Calmer, Qwelby reflected on all that had happened since he and Tullia had left Vertazia three tendays ago. He was now certain that life on Vertazia was based on lies, deceit and control. There was no real freedom. Everything was manipulated. But by whom? How The Shades was he supposed to know!

He rolled out of bed and stood looking at himself in the mirror. He had left home twenty-three days ago and had been on Earth for sixteen days. The Image that looked back at him was taller and more powerfully built. Liking it, he brushed his hair back where it was lying over his right shoulder. He stopped and stared, then repeated the motion. He was not looking at Mirror and seeing Image, but a reflection! I am an identical twin, so a well developed chest is not surprising. He ran his hands across his chest, found solid muscle and sighed with relief.

Feeling unsettled, he washed and dried then started to dress. A pair of Hannu's trousers he'd been wearing had become tight. He'd put that down to eating well and not a lot of exercise. Which he had to acknowledge was not true, with all the skiing and then the energy drain from transdimensional working. He was unable to pull the trousers up over his thighs.

He tried his own t-shirt and got stuck trying to get it over his shoulders.

Taking a deep breath, he returned to stand in front of the mirror, switched vision and put his right hand over his left heart. Image did the same, which meant that Qwelby saw the opposite movement to a reflection.

Warrior

Qwelby laughed as his mind deciphered the images. He stepped back and sat on the bed, helplessly giggling like a child at the off-beat humour of an Essence existing in a higher dimension. Then sobered as he realised the full implication of the message. Even with all the symbolic meaning contained within the Old, Living Aurigan, "Warrior." was a neat, self-contained energy construct. "Warrior" had no ending. Once again he was being told that he was a Warrior, but this time there was no end in sight. He had started on a journey, but to where, or to when...?

He swallowed, stood up and faced mirror. Holding his head up, he raised his right hand and placed it over his left heart. He ought to say something. What?

'Together, we will return home and tell the truth.' The mirror shimmered, became Mirror and he saw his twin's Image nod before once again all he saw was his own reflection.

Sitting sat back down on his bed, images swept through him of their thirteenth rebirthday. The whole family had gone to visit their father's cousins who worked with the Shakazii, the most liberal of all Tazii. They had been taken to a WingedMeet, a gathering of dragons and winged unicorns, seen them flying and learned how the symbiotic relationship that had existed on Auriga was still the basis of their continuing lives.

'We're like that, Kaigii,' he'd said, proud that the dragon's role was as a protector and happy that dragons needed the support of winged unicorns.

Tullia was relieved when the Land Rover turned onto the track to the villages. During the drive on the blacktop, Ditau had not only talked a lot but spent far more time looking at her than the road. Now, he had to concentrate on the tire marks, looking for any dangerously deep areas of sand, leaving Tullia both relieved and disappointed. She let her eyes concentrate on the track whilst she slipped into silent contemplation.

In the sixteen days that she and her twin had been on Earth, they had rocketed ahead with personal development so much so that both of them were Awakening – the virtually instantaneous equivalent of Azuran puberty that should not have happened for another eighteen months. That had brought with it disturbing insights into the reality of life on Vertazia.

Reluctantly, she confirmed her previous thoughts. Vertazian life was built on a lie. A lie that was slowly driving not just her race to extinction, but also depriving the inhabitants of Earth – the descendants of a mixture of the original Auriganii and an Earthly tribe of hominids – of their chance to restore the unparalleled beauty of what many millennia ago had been Aurigan life.

She and Kaigii had to be reunited, physically, to be able to return home and tell the Truth. Mentally she capitalised the word. Her lovely Meera had a plan for that. In a few days time a party of adult students was going to arrive. When they left she hoped to travel with them to the Republic of South Africa, the first stage of her journey to her twin. With the three powerful connections they had made, there would be a residual energy signature at his location. Easy for her to find.

Now Awakened, when she joined her power to his, their twinergy would be massively stronger than ever before. Energies coursed though her body as if her blood was flowing stronger, making her a little dizzy and reminding her of her Moon Day to come. An alarm sounded inside her and she switched her attention to her eyes. No rock!

'Stop. Deep sand,' Tullia said.

'No. It's all right,' Ditau replied.

'Please stop.' Tullia turned to look at the young constable as she put a hand on his thigh and sent energy through to his foot.

The Land Rover stopped and Tullia fumbled with the seat belt. Ditau moved her hand away, undid her belt, then looked up at her, blushing.

Happy that she understood it meant he liked her, Tullia smiled. He was cute. Ditau's face flushed a darker red.

They got out. Ditau took a long metal rod and thrust it into the sandy track. Safe for driving. He took a pace forward, still safe, then another pace and the rod went further down. On each of the next several paces the rod showed deep sand. Finally, shallow sand again.

A brief discussion and all Tullia was able to say in her limited Afrikaans was that she had seen the rock base deeper than normal. Ditau explained that with thick bushes on either side of the track there really was no option but to stay on it. Blushing, he said he might need a push. Understanding the sub text being about her weight, Tullia smiled ruefully. She'd got used to being a "Big Girl."

Ditau reversed a short way then drove forward at a slow and steady pace. Following behind, Tullia saw the front wheels sinking into the soft sand. The back wheels started to spin, Ditau declutched and called out, 'Push!' Tullia ran forward and threw all her weight into pushing as Ditau let the clutch out. Wheels spinning, Tullia digging her feet in the sand and pushing with all her might she fell flat on her face as the front wheels found firm ground and the vehicle shot forward.

An embarrassed policeman got down and had his apologies swept aside as Tullia brushed the sand away, happily smiling at her increasing abilities in the third dimension. Ditau cut several branches off bushes, stuck a few upright into the soft sand and laid the others across the track, explaining that was a warning.

Tullia watched as her mind wondered just why she was learning so much about so many different aspects of life that had never been relevant to her life on Vertazia.

Ahhh, little QeïchâKaïgïï...' An image appeared of the moon revolving around Vertazia.

Arriving at the village they were met by Ghadi, the tribe's chief and Xameb, the tribe's Shaman. Portly and of average height, Ghadi's obvious power made him seem much larger. Ditau passed on the Chief Inspector's message that, in view of the damage to the police station, he was releasing Tullia into Ghadi's custody and would question her further at a later date. Ghadi asked Tullia to translate into Meera to ensure he had understood correctly.

Knowing it was not necessary, Tullia took the opportunity offered to explain that her actual words had been, 'I promise, Sah. I no run away.'

Ditau was delighted to be asked about the damage and have to tell the whole story. Seeing Tullia's embarrassment as she started translating, the tall and rangy Shaman took over. That only increased Tullia's discomfort as Ditau embellished the story.

HornsFlute and DragonsBreath, Kaigii, by all The Shades, my time here is turning into the Flaming Tullia Show! She was puzzled by the obvious feeling of envy that came back.

CHAPTER 4

CONFUSION

VERTAZIA

As the twins ended their healing of the police sergeant, nearly seveneen-year-old Xaala found herself back in her room on Vertazia, full of confusion. Not only had the amount of caring the twins had displayed for the sergeant and the teenage girl been a surprise, enwrapped in their loving she'd contributed her own healing energies, stirring impossible memories of the Space Wars.

She'd seen the Twins' propensity for violence before – but only when attacked, a treacherous memory surfaced. Now, she wondered whether Chief Readjuster Dryddnaa was right – that the twins could be healed if they returned.

Unusually for a girl, Xaala had inherited strong male genes. Tall for her age, her slender form was toned to perfection from all the time and effort she had spent failing to build a muscular boy's body. Yet no matter how hard she'd tried in all other ways to be the second boy her parents had wanted, her life had been one of failure to win their approval. She wanted more of the Twins' healing love she'd just experienced. But she had committed to Ceegren, the Arch Custodian and her beloved Teacher, to ensure that the twins neither reconnected nor returned. Although, perhaps the girl...

'Aieee!' she lifted her head and cried aloud.

She, the best acolyte that Ceegren had ever trained, mentally and psychically superb, she didn't know what she wanted! What to do!

She cried waterless tears as she twisted the bedding in her hands, her mind torturing itself with conflicting images. Images that stirred conflicting emotions and sent unwelcome colours swirling through her energy field.

It was a shaken, short and stocky sixteen-year-old Rulcas who returned to his Form. Having been pulled onto Earth amongst violent Azurii, he should have been terrified, but Xaala's energy field had wrapped protectively around him and he'd been excited. The Ice Bitch was good. Very good. "One of them" as good as her word. He was amazed.

But something was all awry. Xaala had explained that he was to work with her to prevent the twins from mentally reconnecting and returning to Vertazia. Why? The healing for the man, then the concern about the cute Azuran girl. He didn't understand what that was about, but Tullia had helped the Azuran and the girl had been really happy. And the boy, bloody good blasting apart that Azuran building because he loved his twin.

If Xaala's big boss, the Arch Custodian, didn't want the twins to return? Nah. That wasn't right from what he'd just seen – and that meant getting the twins back had to be good. And that was what he'd been coerced into agreeing to do for Chief Readjuster Dryddnaa. Odd the bosses differed, but either way he got what he wanted – to go and live with his father amongst the freedom-loving Shakazii. And that was all that mattered!

CHAPTER 5

MUGGERS

KOTOMÄKI-FINLAND

Over a late breakfast Qwelby explained his plans to Mrs Rahkamo and how he was going to make the fruit machines deliver their jackpots. She was concerned about his safety on his own in Jyväskylä, relieved that he was expecting to be gone by the weekend, worried about what mistakes he might make as he travelled the world alone and, underneath it all, sad that he was leaving. He had become one of the family.

Telling him he couldn't walk around town wearing snow goggles, she took him to Tokmanni in Kotomäki where she bought him a pair of sunglasses large enough to cover his unusual eyes. As they approached the bus stop, Seija pressed two hundred markkas into Qwelby's hand, saying: 'If there's any trouble. Get a taxi and come straight home.'

Qwelby grimaced as he said his thanks, knowing how unpopular were people of his dark colour.

The small arcade where he went for his first try with "one arm bandits" was dimly lit. With the hood of his coat pulled over his head no-one took much notice of him. Carefully monitoring the machines as the dials rolled around, he soon understood how they worked and adjusted them to make occasional wins.

Eventually, he went for the jackpot and was the centre of attention by the handful of other players as the machine choked out what seemed like a never-ending flow of coins. Changing them for notes, he was unable to decide whether the cashier's bad grace was due to his colour or his having won.

Happy that his plan was working and that even in the slow vibrations of the third dimension the machines were easy for him to manipulate, he headed for another arcade. Again he was cautious, playing for a long time with the occasional small win before going for the jackpot. Aware that two lads had been watching him for some time, he was uncomfortable as a stream of coins spewed out. Changing the coins into notes, he left the building and stepped into the falling snow Mrs Rahkamo had forecast.

Qwelby was pleased. The quicker he could win more money, the sooner he would go to Helsinki. His plan was to book into a small hotel, buy some smart clothes and get into a casino where he would play cards. Practising with his friends, he had learnt to read the cards from their minute energy fields which showed their colour and power; although the Ace with its two values presented problems.

The snow was falling faster and thicker. Turning a corner, he lost his bearings and became disorientated as the thick snow swirling around the buildings took him back to the unpleasant time when he had been trapped between Vertazia and Earth. As the emotions of that time flowed through him, panic rose up and he was badly shaken when he saw two dark figures looming out of the snow, just as had happened on that occasion. Uncertain where he was and knowing that at some point he had to make a turn to the left, he swung down the next street and quickened his pace.

As he neared the end of the buildings, a figure came around the corner and stopped right in front of him. One of the lads from the arcade. He stopped, backed up a pace and turned around, only to be confronted by the other lad.

Trying to quell his panic, be aware of exactly where the lad behind him was and read both their thoughts, Qwelby only half heard the one boy's words. What did he mean that it was "Their money"?

'Make it easy on yourself Blackie. Gis' us that jackpot 'n, we'll let yer go,' the lad in front said.

'Leave yer 'nuff for a banana,' the other joked.

'What's a banana?' Qwelby asked.

'Finks e's a comedian, eh?'

'Yeah. Black 'n Black Minstrels.'

A slim black object appeared in the hand of the lad who Qwelby was facing. He heard a click and saw a glint of light as a blade slid from what he realised was a handle.

'Oh, no,' Qwelby groaned. He'd been attacked five times since arriving on Earth sixteen days ago. Coming from what had been a world of total peace, he was sick of violence. He dropped his head and shoulders in despair at the prospect of having to fight yet again.

'Oh, yeah, Blackie,' the lad with the knife said. 'Gis 'ere 'n I'll not cut yer.'

Minds and auras too muddled for searching or scanning to produce clear answers, Qwelby was still unable to get a clear sense that either lad wanted to harm him, as had been Arttu's very clear intention both times the thief had attacked him. Yet the threat was there.

"An Aurigan Warrior fights..." *'For Justice'* The end of his father's words which had been, "only in defence," were obliterated by that annoying voice. Who The Shades was it?

As he struggled to cope with looking down from a height of over three metres onto a scared Tazian youngster and two opportunistic Azuran lads he saw the Tazian youth – That's me! – lifting his hands in a gesture either of surrender or pleading.

'You don't want to do this,' he heard his own voice saying. Oh Shit! That's a challenge if ever I heard one!

'Nah, mate. It's you what don't,' one lad said and slashed with his knife.

Feeling a rush of energy as his inner warrior slid back into his Form, Qwelby stepped to the side and grabbed the lad's wrist. 'I said' he swung the hand towards him and up, 'you don't' slid underneath the arm, swinging the lad around, 'want' and sent him crashing into his partner, 'to do' violently wrenched the lad's arm and forced him to the ground, 'this.' The knife fell to the ground and Qwelby heard a yowl of pain as the lad's shoulder dislocated.

Qwelby stepped around the injured boy towards his partner who had slid half way down the wall as his mate had crashed into him. As the lad levered himself off the wall. 'Stupid!' Qwelby said as he punched him in the stomach. With a thick coat absorbing most of the blow, the boy sprang back off the wall, pulling his hand from his coat pocket.

Flaming knives! Qwelby thought as he swivelled on one foot and kicked the boy in the face with the other, slowing the speed of his leg at the last moment as he remembered hitting Erki and the grave warning that voice in his head had given him. Staggering back, the lad tripped over his mate and crashed down on top of him. There was blood on his face from a broken nose.

'Getting good at this aren't we, Dragon Lord.'

Yes

With pent up rage burning to be released, Qwelby leant forward, grabbed the bloodied boy by his shoulders and lifted him high up.

'Dragon Lord!'

Qwelby's eyes were burning red ovals with orbs as black as coal. Fighting for control, his arms were trembling, shaking the Finn like a rag doll.

'Bloody hell. The Devil 'isself!'

The youth's terror pierced Qwelby's Self. With a roar of rage for all the violence, pursuit and dislike of his colour, he half threw the youth on top of his companion to a loud cry of pain. Qwelby snarled and had the satisfaction of seeing both youths flinch as he turned and walked away.

He felt bad and good. Bad for the viciousness he'd let flow into his actions. Good that he'd fought swiftly and effectively and, more than that, without any time-slipping images of Space Wars fighting. It had all been from within himself in the here-and-now.

As the fugue passed, he stopped, turned and retraced his steps as he searched for the youths' mental signatures. In shock, they were easy to find around the next corner. He stunned their minds as he walked into view. 'Stop. Stay. I make good.'

Opening to his healer's genes and slipping into NoseBoy's mind, Qwelby soon had him holding ArmBoy in the correct position. Taking a deep breath, Qwelby pulled and rotated. A silent scream and ArmBoy collapsed. Qwelby grunted with satisfaction. He could do more. Should do more?

No. This was not Vertazia with its natural energy-balancing system. This was Earth and retribution, he savoured the word, relevant and appropriate. If he was wrong there would be consequences. He was not yet an adult, but he was a man and would deal with whatever recompense he had to make.

With the snow falling ever more thickly, Qwelby turned and forced himself to walk calmly away. After turning two corners he recognised where he was and made his way to the bus stop. He thanked the multiverse for looking after him as he boarded a waiting bus, then spent the next few minutes filling the youths' minds with images of a slobbering WereBeast.

Mrs Rahkamo was relieved to see Qwelby return in the early afternoon and happy for him as she saw the bundle of markka notes he produced as he returned her two hundred. As he started to tell her what had happened she made him a typical open sandwich: Ruisleipä, a dark rye bread, with sautéed mushrooms topped by Edam cheese. She was sliding it from under the grill as he got to where he was approached by the two lads. She sat down beside him at the kitchen table as he ate.

'The awful part is, I enjoyed the fighting. It's as though

skills I've learnt a long time ago are, well, just there. But that's impossible. I understand the genes running through my family for eighty thousand years might somehow carry memories with them, but actual skills. That, I don't understand.'

There was nothing Seija could say. However human he acted and looked – and she'd even got used to his strange eyes – he was an alien. She put a consoling hand on his.

'I broke one boy's nose. The other. I dislocated his shoulder. That was bad. I put it back in.'

Seija was stopped from asking any questions by the sound of knocking on the back door. Going though the rear lobby she opened the back door. 'Oh. Hullo, sergeant...'

'Pia. Please,' the smiling and out of uniform Sjöström said.

Qwelby was frozen in panic, certain she'd come to take him away because of the fighting. Not in uniform? Keeping it quiet for the sake of the Rahkamos?

It was surreal as the sergeant came in, removed her outer clothing revealing a multi-coloured sweater and jeans, and stepped into a pair of the ubiquitous slippers that all Finns kept for guests. She accepted the offer of a bottle of beer, confirming she was not on duty. She sat at one long side of the kitchen table opposite Seija, with Qwelby at one end.

Pia asked after Qwelby's health and the injuries from New Year's Eve. He was happy to pull down his sweater and show no signs of any cuts around his neck. Using the very limited Finnish that was all he spoke to anyone apart from the Rahkamos and Keskinens, he slowly relaxed as he answered the sergeant's questions about his time in Finland, the food, skiing and making friends.

When Pia asked if he was Dr Jadrovitch's son, Seija explained the misunderstanding that had arisen and how that had been corrected as Qwelby learnt a little Finnish.

Carefully choosing from his limited vocabulary, Qwelby answered all the sergeant's questions. He only told one direct lie, about his home in Turkey. Everything else he answered truthfully, albeit being economical with that truth and not correcting the misunderstandings he caused.

When the sergeant stood up, thanking Mrs Rahkamo for her hospitality and wishing Qwelby good luck with communicating with his family and, meanwhile, an enjoyable stay, Qwelby stood and offered Pia his hand. As they shook, he mentally reassured her that all was well and saw a faint glow of energy infuse her aura.

'Police nice people,' he said. 'You help me that night.'

'It's you and your friends we have to thank, Qwelby,' a smiling Pia replied, unable to take her eyes off the shining eyes of such a nice polite young man.

CHAPTER 6

ERKI IS RECRUITED

KOTOMÄKI-FINLAND

Professor Romain's telephone call to Erki requesting a discreet meeting had lifted the latter's spirits. There was an easy solution to the Professor's request and Erki had been clear with his instructions.

Romain drove up to the road bridge crossing Lake Jyväsjärvi early on Tuesday afternoon, turned down the lakeside road and parked far enough along to be out of sight. The tall slim Englishman in his fifties with a trim moustache walked back and stood on the middle of the bridge, looking around and checking his map. After his second meeting with Erki, Romain had taken the youth's advice and was now wearing a Parka, thick trousers, boots and a cap with earmuffs typical of any Finn.

Seventeen-year-old Erki was not cut out for the excellent and liberal Finnish schooling. His abilities lay elsewhere – in a large degree of natural cunning. His outlets denied at school, he had found satisfaction in the shadow life he had with Lokir, a minor gang boss based in Jyväskylä.

Erki, tall and well-built from all his time in the gym, had been waiting in the woods on the opposite side of the lake from well before the appointed time. He had a clear view of Romain's arrival and also the car that followed. The other driver had no option other than to cross the bridge and swing around and park on the edge of the same woods.

Coming down the side road as if from one of the houses, through a wing mirror Erki recognised the driver as the second visitor who had been around the ski slopes the previous weekend. As Erki crossed the bridge, Romain stopped him and the two talked for a few moments.

'You're being followed,' Erki said. 'Don't look now. Where I've come from. The car parked at the edge of the woods. He was skiing over the weekend. He was around that group of kids on Saturday. He seemed to be watching you on Sunday.'

Erki confirming what Soininen had said banished any thoughts Romain had as to whether the PI had dressed up his report to justify his expensive fee. He was brief with his instructions. He wanted the foreign boy watched and as much information as possible about him: what he did, who he was with, where he went. As he passed Erki an envelope that quickly disappeared inside the youth's coat, he added, 'This boy has something I need and it must not fall into the wrong hands.'

Romain took a deep breath in response to Erki's questioning look. 'I don't know what it is. Only that it gave off a brief signal that my equipment detected. That first time we met you said the family had spent a long time looking for it, so it must be small.'

Erki was intrigued. If he found whatever it was, how much would the Professor pay to get it back? Was this something that he should tell Lokir about? The decision was simple. Find it first, then decide. He would not have to tell Romain that he had it, only that he knew where it was, or that he could get it.

'So, it's vital to his research, eh?' Erki slapped a fist into the palm of his other hand. 'Must be worth a lot. At least to the Professor.'

Back in his hotel room Romain used his GlobeSynch to make a totally secure call to Franz Shosta in Geneva. When there was no answer he left his usual message: "Man from sunny isle."

Franz returned the call very much later and confirmed the usual conditions still applied for the provision of a false passport. When Romain moved on to tentatively enquire about the "Possibility of the delivery of a package," Franz was unable to keep the surprise out of his voice. Given that it was then the early hours of the morning they agreed a more suitable time for continuing the conversation.

As he settled back to sleep Romain was nervous but happy. He had come all the way from his laboratory home in the Pacific, certain he had discovered something that was going to validate his years of research – and a whole lot more. If all his other efforts failed, it seemed that "Plan B" was a possibility.

CHAPTER 7

DEPARTURE

KOTOMÄKI-FINLAND

When Hannu arrived home just in time for the evening meal he was met with the good news that his plan about slot machines had worked and Qwelby had a story to tell.

When they finished eating, they took their drinks into the sitting room where, carefully modulating his rich, almost musical baritone, Qwelby thoughtwrapped Hannu and his parents, Paavo and Seija, into his experiences in Jyväskylä. There was silence when he finished with the bus pulling away.

'Wow,' Hannu said at last. 'That was amazing. I was there. I was you. Every time you tell a story it's stronger. I still feel shaky from the fight.'

'There's more happened today,' Seija said. 'Qwelby, I think it's best if I tell this.'

Qwelby nodded, and Seija explained about Sergeant Sjöström's visit.

'It was strange,' Qwelby said when Seija finished speaking. 'There was one moment. I had said no communication with home. Pia asked if my father is under arrest. I said no. Was he in hiding? I said no. I started to panic at a trap she was making. She said...' Qwelby paused.

'"I'm sorry. I didn't mean to pry. It's... I'm... concerned about

29

you,'" Qwelby said in a way that made everyone feel it actually was the sergeant who was speaking.

'I saw her eyes change. She pulled a shutter down on... more questions. I saw her as a bubbling pot with a hand holding the lid on.'

'Yes,' Seija said, then gave a little laugh. 'Not as vividly as Qwelby, but I felt that Pia was skating around what she really wanted to ask.'

'If the sergeant returns, I cannot go on telling all the lies and half truths. It... hurts me. That's how it is with my people.' Qwelby kept to himself his discovery that the more he deceived people by careful use of words and thoughtsending a correct answer, the easier it became. 'What makes it worse is she's nice, and that makes deceit even more difficult.' And that is true, he added to himself.

'This is just like in American films,' Hannu said. 'There's a crime. The FBI comes in to take over. The local cops are pissed off. It's their case and they want to solve it. So they carry on. But they have to be careful. I bet that's what's happening here. Those two men over the weekend. Secret police... '

'Possibly Suojelupoliisi,' Paavo interrupted. 'Our intelligence service.'

'I must go,' Qwelby said in a tone of panic as he got to his feet. 'Tonight. Now.'

'I've been thinking about that since you told me what happened,' Seija said as she motioned Qwelby to sit down, then turned to her husband. 'As he was expecting to go to Helsinki before the weekend, I haven't phoned my friend Elsa. I'll do that now.' She went into the kitchen.

'That's settled,' Seija announced as she returned. 'I've said it's an emergency and we'd only be there for a couple of days. Elsa said we were welcome to stay until Saturday.' She turned to her husband. 'Elsa asked if I was leaving you. I said it was nothing of the sort but it was all too complicated to explain over the phone.'

Qwelby felt uncomfortable in the long silence that followed. 'I put my things together,' he said as he headed up to his room.

Hannu was fighting with himself. He was relieved that Qwelby would no longer be around Anita and he could at last have time alone with her. But he knew his mother. She would want to drive in the daylight and thus they would be back early Saturday afternoon, giving him plenty of time to be with Anita. In the meantime, he could have a few days alone with "his alien." When it was just the two of them together he never felt that Qwelby was talking down to him, as he sometimes felt when Anita was present.

'It's err... a long drive. And err... in the dark,' Hannu said hesitantly. He cleared his throat. 'You don't like that, Mum. And you'll be driving back. You'd like company. Especially in the dark. And, well, on the way back, by yourself.' He stopped, wondering if he'd said too much?

He saw his mother give his father a long look.

'Yes,' Paavo said, to his son's surprise, partially assuaging the guilt he felt at what he saw as betraying the trust Qwelby had placed in him, when on his first day in Finland the boy had collapsed in Paavo's arms. 'I'll square it with the school. Promise me to make sure that by Monday you'll have studied as much of this week's work as possible.' He fixed his son with a meaningful look.

'Thanks Dad. Yes. I promise. Anita's in the same class. She'll be able to tell me what I need to get done. And help me next weekend.'

'Good.' Paavo had a second motive for agreeing, not so much with his son but with his wife's unspoken request. They had become concerned at their son's reactions as Qwelby and Anita had formed a close relationship that had resulted in a major row the previous evening. This would give the two boys time together without Anita.

'Hannu. Go and help Qwelby pack,' his mother said and turned to her husband. 'He's grown so much he can borrow your spare ski suit. I'll sort that and one or two other things he'll need.'

Paavo nodded, smiling. His wife knew his clothes better than he did.

Taking after his father, Hannu was big for his age. Qwelby had been embarrassed at having to confess only that morning that he had grown out of Hannu's clothes. Lots of changes were taking place within him that he was not able to explain as he did not really understand them himself. It had been a great comfort that the whole family accepted a growth spurt as normal for a teenager and had laughed about the time when it had happened to Hannu.

Yet it was a disconcerting experience. The more Qwelby got to know the Azurii and accept how human they were in many ways, he saw this, which never happened on Vertazia, as more evidence of the falsity of life there. Once again he saw a way of living being imposed on all Tazii that was contrary to what was taught about the beauty of the Aurigan way of life. A truth that he and his twin had to reveal - when they got back home!

'Yes, Mum. And thanks again Dad.' A happy Hannu ran up the stairs. Bunking off school for a few days and having some fun with "his alien" was going to be good. And get Qwelby to tell him stories about Vertazia. Be there, meet his friends - and see Tullia again.

'I must say goodbye to Anita before we go,' Qwelby said, when Hannu told him what was happening.

'Of course,' Hannu replied, trying to quell the feeling of jealousy that arose as he thought of them having a "Goodbye kiss." He telephoned Anita.

When Anita arrived a few minutes later, Paavo explained what was happening as the others were still upstairs.

Qwelby was first down with a sports bag and his Tazian satchel, "Fill Me", over his shoulder.

Anita immediately pulled him into a hug. 'Be careful. Tullia needs you,' she said.

'I will,' Qwelby replied. 'And you look after him, Anullia,' he added, with a smile to Hannu as his friend came into the room as, more than once, he'd mentioned that Tullia always said she had to look after him "because he was only a boy".

Anita felt she had been taken to Vertazia by Qwelby's stories and seen his world and friends through Tullia's eyes. Like Hannu, she had seen Tullia on New Year's Eve and had even felt as though she had become his twin whilst tending to Qwelby's wounds. He had called her Anullia, making her feel that she really was linked with Tullia.

'I will,' she said tearfully. 'And you. Look after him,' she said to Hannu as she broke away from Qwelby, hugged and kissed her boyfriend.

Bags loaded and Qwelby comfortably settled out of sight in the luggage space of the Volvo CXR100, Hannu turned to Anita for a last kiss.

'Be careful,' she said. 'Come back safely.'

'I'm only going to our friends...' Hannu's puzzled protest was smothered by Anita's fierce kisses as she pressed hard against him.

With the door into the house closed, garage lights turned off and no-one waving, the big black Volvo left as inconspicuously as possible.

As Paavo closed the garage door, the door bell chimed. Opening the front door he discovered Professor Romain who asked to speak to Qwelby. Paavo took great delight in saying that the boy had gone back home. The people who had dropped him off had come to collect him. The boy had been happy and said he was going home. As to where home was, Paavo shrugged his shoulders and happily told the truth: that he spoke Russian, knew the boy did not speak any related language and did not understand a word of the boy's own language.

CHAPTER 8

PREPARATION

THE KALAHARI

Tullia was happy, excited and nervous. Returning from her imprisonment in Shikawe she had spent the rest of that day learning the practical side of "women's duties." She was happy to have helped Deena, her adoptive mother, prepare the evening meal and excited that by becoming a woman in the tradition of the Meera tribe she would really be seen as one of them and no longer a Goddess or Alien Ambassador. She was very nervous from the teasing about a woman's "other duties."

Seated with her Meera family around their little fire she thought of seventeen-year-old H'ani, their kisses and that he was going to ask her to walk with him one evening. She felt her hearts beating fast and knew she was blushing at the thought of more kissing. Now she understood why her girlfriends enjoyed the kissing games played at home. She had never joined in. With Qwelby in her mind, kissing a boy would have been like kissing him. She shuddered at the thought.

She smiled as an image came into her mind of the look of almost shock on sixteen-year-old Xashee's face when she had kissed him. Eleven-year-old Tsetsana had said "We don't do that," and, blushing, had added, "It's just that what you have done is... very friendly…" Tullia had only given Xashee a quick kiss. If that was "very friendly…" what on 'Tazia were her long and hot kisses with H'ani? Especially the one after the transdimensional battle when, in a desperate need for comfort and not fully aware of what she was doing, she'd crushed him to her as she'd dug her nails into his back. She recalled how willingly he had responded. Her stomach turned a somersault at the prospect that H'ani was expecting more than just kissing. She wasn't ready for that.

Please Cagn, don't let H'ani ask me to walk with him tonight, Tullia thoughtsent to the only God the San acknowledged.

As the family finished eating, Milake, her adoptive father, and Xashee got up and took the two young girls, Tomku and Nthabe, by the hand. Each of them said to Deena, Tullia and Tsetsana, "Two sunrises," and all four headed out of the village.

From the next sunrise to that of the following morning, the whole of the tribe's area would belong to the women, the four about to be initiated into womanhood and a handful of the oldest men, including Xameb, the Shaman. That area included the village itself and the large area to the West where all their celebrations were held. Well out of view to the South the land dipped down to form what looked like a large crater. During the day the centre of that had already been turned into a temporary base for the all the other members of the tribe.

As the families finished eating, the girls, young boys and remaining old men made their way into the centre of the crater. Overseen by Ghadi, the tribe's leader, all the other men were taking up positions in a large circle around the crater, the village and the area outside where the ceremonial fire was held in order to guard against the many wild animals that roamed this corner of the Kalahari.

The men were spread wide apart around a very large perimeter. They had to be out of sight of the women's area as it was forbidden for anyone to look on a woman during their Moon Day. Just as it was forbidden to any woman to leave what was to become their sacred area.

The older boys acted as runners both between the men on guard and between them and Ghadi. Supervised by the oldest girl, the older girls were carrying out the women's duties of cooking and looking after the younger children.

CHAPTER 9

RUNNING AWAY

FINLAND

It was some time before Seija was able to pull onto the side of the E63. Even then she waited until there was no passing traffic before allowing Hannu to get out and open the tailgate. Qwelby was glad it was dark as he was sure his face was very pale. Although he'd not been in the storage compartment for very long, it had given him an unwelcome taste of being imprisoned. He could not imagine how Tullia had coped with that for a whole night.

Deliberately keeping his mind busy he'd been thinking through his plan for getting money and travelling. That had led to images of Tullia, their two brief meetings and wondering how they'd been able to access the eighth dimension and their Attributes of dragons and unicorns.

'Consciousness,' he muttered to himself. 'The so-called fourth dimension. It runs right through to the ninth, where Auriganii existed as pure energy. It must work both ways. So, with our "twin gene" operating at the quantum level, that's why my Awakening has confirmed me as the boy I consciously want to be.' Qwelby slumped back against the seat with a great sigh.

'You okay?' Hannu asked.

'Yeah. Great.' Using the back of the front seats, Qwelby

pulled himself forward. 'Big understanding. Explain later. And Hannu?'

'Yeah?'

'Help me with Oona. Please.' He gripped his friend's shoulder. 'I'll explain that as well.'

'Okay,' Hannu replied, intrigued, as all Qwelby had said was that he and the girl had a nice day together and had spent more time talking than skiing.

Settling back, Qwelby continued trying to understand his mixture of feelings for Anita, Oona, Tamina, the unknown Tazian who grabbed hold of him the night he'd travelled to the Kalahari and even his twin. And still worrying about what he had done that had caused Oona to suddenly throw him out of the house when she had been very happy with the kissing.

He consoled himself with one important fact. His natural Tazian energy constructs were working well. From his first evening with them he had realised that there was a strong energy connection between Hannu and Anita. No matter how much he liked Anita and how important she had become to him, he did not feel about her the way he did about Oona. He could not leave Finland without doing something about what had happened with the cute, cuddly girl and felt relief now that he'd made the decision to ask Hannu's advice.

Recalling his time with her in his arms he drifted into a fantasy. Oona was Tazian. Unique, with her fair skin, blonde hair and blue eyes. Out of shame, she was kept prisoner by her extreme traditionalist Kumelanii family. He was training to be a DragonRider. As he was exercising one day he saw her through a window and heard her anguished mental cry for help.

Qwelby was not bothered by his story's lack of plausibility. It got him into the action. A challenging flight, a daring rescue, feeling Oona's arms around his waist as they flew back to his home and he was rewarded with passionate kisses.

The trumpeting of his dragon awoke him. Startled, he looked

around. His mind replayed the sound and he realised it had not been his dragon but a car horn.

In response to his question of, 'Are we nearly there yet?' he was told there was about an hour to go.

Daring DragonRider, huh! he said to himself. I'm a cowardly boy running away. But... if I'd stayed in Jyväskylä.... police, arrest, orange suits, chains, interrogation, torture, dissection... and Tullia, without me, half a person for the rest of her life. But...

'Strategic withdrawal.'

He nodded. Of course he knew that after two thousand years of on-off space warfare it was the sensible course of action. But the young boy he also was didn't know.

He set to thinking about an alternative story to explain who he was and why he was in Finland. Using his mobile to display a virtual tablet, Hannu had been reading a spy story where the hero had been on a mission in Turkey involving some sort of hidden government. Hannu had called to Qwelby, spoken his requests and a few moments later the virtual tablet had displayed a series of entries from the internet.

The more Qwelby thought about a possible Turkish identity, the more he liked it compared to the Chechia story. He'd be able to say more about his home and family and friends. Truth, albeit not the whole truth. Coming from a race where, at least at his age, telling lies was impossible, even speaking half truths hurt emotionally and mentally. But as he had slipped into a routine of "game-playing," he had actually started to enjoy the mild deception.

He was working through what words he would use to answer various questions to keep it all simple as he pretended to speak little Finnish, when he leant forward and grasped Hannu by his shoulder. 'I'm going to stop using my compiler. At least with other people. It speaks perfect Finnish. That's not right for a boy from Turkey. I've learnt some myself. I think enough to be simple. I switch off compiler and try now.'

Qwelby slowly explained to Hannu and his mother why he, a Turkish boy, was in Finland and afraid of the authorities.

'Confusing, muddled, brilliant,' Hannu declared, swung around in his seat and the boys exchanged a knuckle-punch.

'I'm lost,' Mrs Rahkamo said. 'After two weeks with you I should understand better. So, tell me again, slowly.'

Qwelby did that, adding that he was not telling any lies.

'That's very clever, Qwelby. Yes. I understand what you're doing now,' Mrs Rahkamo said.

Qwelby continued practising as they discussed plans in more detail. 'I like to speak like this,' he declared when they finished. 'I have to speak slowly. Time to think and I know what I say. Even if I say wrong. I know words I have used. Compiler uses my thoughts and pictures in my mind so I not know if what it says is correct.'

It was late by the time they arrived at their destination. Apart from Elsa Korpijaakko, Mrs Rahkamo's old school friend, the rest of the family was in bed. The two women had agreed over the telephone that Seija would sleep downstairs on the sofa-bed, whilst Qwelby used the guest room on the top floor and Hannu shared with Riku as usual. Although at seventeen Riku was eighteen months older than Hannu, the two boys got on well together.

Asked by Mrs Korpijaakko, Hannu took Qwelby up to the guest room where he set down his bag and the two boys headed downstairs to get drinks. They heard raised voices and as Hannu opened the door into the sitting room, clear words.

'But you didn't say he was black,' Elsa said.

'He's not,' responded Seija.

'Well he's not white is he?' was the tart reply.

Qwelby was shocked. He had become so comfortable with the Rahkamos and the Keskinens and Hannu's group of friends that he had put the incidents with Erki and Arttu to the back of his mind.

Seeing the look of distress on Hannu's face as his friend turned to him, Qwelby gritted his teeth, shook his head, turned around and walked back up to his room with his shoulders slumped.

As he entered the room he was immediately hit by the heat. Previously all he had done was to drop his bag and kick off his shoes. Without turning on the light, he crossed to the window, opened it and turned off the radiator that was underneath. Slipping out of his clothes he sat on the end of the bed and gave way to despair.

He was a brown boy in a country of whites, most of whom did not like him because of his colour. To reach Tullia he had to travel through countries full of white people, not only who did not like him but were on the lookout for terrorists; dark-skinned terrorists. And his eyes! No-one on Earth had eyes like his.

Each border crossing, passport control, ticket purchase, hotel booking; could he mentally convince everyone that Hannu's passport really contained his own picture and that it wasn't a photo glued on top of Hannu's? He buried his head in his hands. One slip. One mistake and... the end of everything.

CHAPTER 10

INITIATION

THE KALAHARI

The women were spending the day together naked, honouring their bodies, reaffirming their connection with life-giving Mother Earth, celebrating their ability to bring forth new life and ensure the continuation of their race. Used to swimming, sun and moon bathing naked, not wearing any clothes for the whole day was not an issue for Tullia.

She was amused at how cold the others found the day, everyone with one or even two blankets draped over their shoulders and keeping close to the embers of the big fire. By mid morning she had thrown off her blanket and was basking in what was, for her, hot sun. Enjoying her whole body tingling as the sun fed her Solar Energy Quotient she was unaware of how energised she had become and how a golden haze surrounded her.

By midday her nervousness had gone. The means of living amongst the Meera were unlike anything on Vertazia, even camping at home bore little relationship to the life she was now living. But, Life, people, relationships - the underlying energies were similar.

She had discovered that between what she had learnt at college, working on both families' farms and all the duties she undertook at home helping her mother, plus over two weeks with the Meera, there had been nothing surprising in the morning's learning about women's duties of plant gathering, cooking, child rearing and many other practicalities.

She was disappointed that all four girls were not together. As Tu explained, it was a special day for the whole tribe and all the women wanted to partake by sharing the four girls amongst themselves. Thus Tullia found herself constantly being moved around amongst different groups, although seventeen-year-old Ungka was constantly at her side. It was a comforting similarity to being at home when, in a situation like this, her BestFriend and elderest, Tamina, would have been with her.

After a light lunch the day's learning moved into a new area and she found herself in a group with Kotuma, the tribe's Senior Woman, and Deena. She explained that arriving on a strange world and without her twin for the first time in her life she'd been desperate to make friends and even more than that, had wanted to be seen as what she was: a young teenager and not some all-powerful alien goddess.

She was covered with embarrassment when told that everyone had taken her to be a mature young woman and seen her actions as indicating she wanted more than friendship – and many young women found that threatening.

Living and working on two farms, Tullia had not needed much college learning to know about sex and babies. But now she was blushing at the intimacy, the ribald humour and the disparaging remarks being made about men. H'ani's name was mentioned and Tullia's blushes deepened. As she was teased, her blushes spread from her face across her body right down to her belly, to the delight of the others who teased her even more.

As she confirmed that she liked kissing him, but was adamant that she was not ready to do more, she noticed tensions that had arisen were slowly subsiding. She was heartened when Ungka put an arm around her and gently stroked her back, saying that she wanted babies one day but didn't want to do those things with any man.

The Moon Day was a time for the women of the tribe to come together. Ungka's actions at the Melon Dance had created a rift and the tribe knew. Taking courage from Tullia's acceptance of her contact, Ungka said 'Tyua'llia. That day at the Melon Dance when you saved Tsetsana from a nasty injury. That was my fault. I put Kou-'ke up to it. I didn't think that a mere girl was suitable company for you and.' She lowered her eyes. 'I desired you the first moment I saw you walk into the village. Too much.'

Shocked by the words, Tullia slipped into Ungka's mind and saw genuine contrition. Breaking all the rules of life on Vertazia, she followed the thread through to the beginning and saw Ungka's red hot desire followed by intense jealousy and a very recent softening. She withdrew and waited.

'Can you forgive me?'

'I didn't need a woman's advice then. I do now.'

Tullia sensed a mixture of relief and approval from the older women who were part of their group.

Ungka rose to her feet. 'I must apologise to Tsetsana for that trick with the melon.'

The sun was sinking close to the treetops as Ungka returned to say that all was well with Tsetsana. The older women moved away and Tullia found herself with only two young women – Ungka and seventeen-year-old Ishe, her hut mate.

It was the warmest part of the day. The sun had not yet lost any of its heat and had had almost twelve hours to warm the thick, red sand. As Tullia sank back into the joys of being, there was a touch of sadness that Tamina was not with her. Not as she'd last seen her BestFriend as a coruscating column of fiery salamanders, but as herself, tall and slim with a coppery cast to her skin and her golden highlighted hair so long she could sit on it.

As her new friends embraced her with their hands and lips and tongues, she felt as though she had become a musical instrument.

Her purring music stirred a volcano. She pulled the girls tight against her as the volcano erupted, shooting through her body, firing her breasts and exploding in her head. Tears trickled down her cheeks. Lips kissed them away.

'I love you, Tua'Tu,' Ungka murmured.

I am me. A woman. I am loved. 'I love you, K'ah.' Tullia burst into tears as faces paraded through her mind. The incredible beauty of her heroine Rrîltallâ Taminûllÿâ, Tamina, Tsetsana, her twin. I love you all. She kissed Ungka fiercely, revelling in the young woman's responsiveness.

CHAPTER 11

PASSPORTS

SIILINJÄRVI-FINLAND

Qwelby awoke feeling as though all energy had been drained from him. Last night he'd felt despondent. Now, he felt hopeless. Lethargically, he went down to the bathroom, washed, returned to the bedroom and dressed. Breakfast. He didn't feel like eating. Hannu. He didn't want to talk with his friend. What did he have to say, except... he couldn't do it. Any of it.

As he opened the door a picture on the wall caught his eye. Set in the countryside, a ruined building, a crumbling stone wall half covered in greenery. That's what he felt like! As with the irresistible force of nature, energies he was unable to control were pulling him apart.

A stone wall.

Tullia's police station!

He'd destroyed it! Well, not quite. But he had ripped several big metal doors from their frames.

Yes! He smacked his right fist into his left palm, then ruefully shook his left hand. I can bring eighth dimension energies through into the third dimension. But no. That was the two of us together. Our twinergy. Because her scream fired me up we linked automatically. Yeah, but, only for that. But look what we did together! Healing the police sergeant and then feeling that girl in my arms. I WAS there, in Kaigii, our identical genes at work. All more powerfully than anything we've ever done at home...

My plan WILL work. With Kaigii in my mind adding her power to mine, I will travel safely. Oh, Kaigii, we can be together. He sighed. And then we can go home.

With his confidence restored he went downstairs to greet Hannu with a happy smile. Johan Korpijaakko was at work, Riku and his sixteen-year-old sister, Jenni, at school.

Elsa, blonde, blue eyed, short and a little dumpy, had taken time off work in order to be with her old school friend. She and Seija had had a long talk the previous night when Seija had explained Qwelby's Turkish origin. Elsa was taken with the idea that, as a member of the former Imperial family still held in great esteem in Turkey, Qwelby might actually be a prince. Seija felt a little guilty at deceiving her friend, yet there was a clear advantage. Her friend was happy with the thought that she might be helping a real prince to be reunited with his family.

Over a late breakfast Elsa explained that arrangements had been made for the four children to meet up after school at the skating rink. She had also agreed to Seija's request that the boys be allowed to use the family computer and printer.

Qwelby and Hannu settled down to change the Finn's now rather old passport. Together with Anita they had previously experimented with Hannu's identity card, using the Czech names she had invented. Those had soon been changed as they needed names with the same number of letters as on the identity card: Hannu Rahkamo. Qwelby had been puzzled to discover that Hannu's surname was the same as his father's. Discovering how Finnish names worked, he had asked why Anita had invented a surname for him rather than using Jadrovitch, when the story had then been that he was that man's son.

Anita had laughed and explained that there was no way with

his colouring that he really was Dr Jadrovitch's own son. Hearing the different surname, anyone would assume that he was a son of a second wife, a stepson.

Now, Qwelby chose the names Qenco Sofuoğlu. The boys thought that with the slight link with Osmanoğlu, the family name of the large family of Imperial descendents, it added to the implications in Qwelby's deliberately vague cover story, and Qenco helped explain his "nickname" of Qwelby.

The original photo taken with Hannu's mobile was replaced with one taken in a photo booth. For Qwelby, that had been one of those weird in-two-worlds experiences that was happening from time to time. Although the booth was nothing like anything on Vertazia, entering something of a similar size, sitting on a stool and looking into a mirror so as to get his head in the correct position was like being fitted with a helmet before entering the StroemCavern.

They had not stuck the photo or names on Hannu's identity card, merely placing them carefully on a table for people to look at as a trial for Qwelby's mental skills. This time they worked on the passport until they were as satisfied as possible that it would stand being handled. Qwelby explained that to get through a full check where the passport was scanned, he needed to merge with Tullia. He needed to be in the mind of whoever was examining the passport so that they did not detect the alterations, his twin also to be in that person's mind, convincing them that any electronic copy of the photo on Hannu's real passport that might be displayed was that of Qwelby. Mental hazing in the third dimension of the Azurii's less well organised minds was not easy. When they were mentally reunited he would simply borrow his twin's mind and anything was possible

'I still don't understand how you do it, Qwelby,' a puzzled Seija said when she had examined what she knew had to be her son's passport, yet could only see it as Qwelby's.

'Please do not worry, Mrs Rahkamo. If I am caught.' He licked his lips and took a deep breath. 'I will say I stole it. Hannu needs it not in Finland as he has his identity card.' He turned to Hannu. 'Now, the internet. I learn some Turkish and find another home.'

Along with Tazian, his Great-Great Uncle Mandara had installed Reduced Aurigan in the compilers to provide two comparators. When Qwelby had discovered how quickly it had mastered Finnish, his friends had tried him, or rather it, with two languages that most Finns spoke to some degree, English and Russian. With four different language bases the compiler rapidly mastered the syntax and grammar of Turkish together with a basic vocabulary.

Hannu explained that there had been so much in the news about the latest troubles in that region, Qwelby had the perfect reason for leaving Turkey for a holiday.

'And remember. Not a word about the passport. For everyone else, you're here on holiday.'

Hannu used the remaining time they had until leaving for the rink to show Qwelby short clips from science fiction films on his virtual tablet, choosing Star Trek because it was largely non violent.

When the four youngsters met in the reception area it was obvious to Qwelby that his colouring was a surprise. Having met their mother he was not surprised that Riku and Jenni were blue eyed blondes, but he had not expected them to be tall and slim. Later, he was to discover that they took after their father.

As they paid and exchanged shoes for skates, Hannu made the introductions and explained that Qwelby came from Turkey, was staying with his family for a holiday and spoke very little Finnish. Qwelby tapped his large shades and Hannu added that Qwelby's unusual eyes were a genetic oddity that affected all his family and he had to wear his shades a lot as his eyes were sensitive to the light.

Having learnt how to handle skiing on Earth, Qwelby lost himself in concentration and quickly mastered the differences in skating from Vertazia. Deep in the exhilaration of being one with the skates and the ice, he was surprised when he was told it was time to go.

As the four youngsters made their way to the exit, they were jostled by a group of older youths. In the confusion as they all spilled out into the thick snowfall, Qwelby was thrust heavily against someone small.

'Watch it!' He heard a female voice from half behind him.

'Ghilusawena,' Qwelby said as he half turned and grabbed at her to stop her falling over.

'What the devil?'

Qwelby found himself with one hand gripping the outstretched arm of a small policewoman. 'Stupid!'

'You calling me stupid?'

'No. I no say.'

'Like hell you did.'

'I mean, no mean...' Forgetting he was towering over her – and "black" – he raised both hands in an apologetic gesture.

'Stop right there!'

He was looking down the barrel of her pistol and felt her fear.

'Easy, Inari,' the older sergeant said to the young probationer. 'Cuff him and put him in the car.'

As the rings snapped tightly around his wrists Qwelby grunted from the satisfaction that Hannu had been as correct about how they worked as he had been about the pistol – which did not have "one up the spout." His mouth went dry as images came back of the morning – Tullia with police in what had to be a prison...

'Move,' came the harsh command as the woman pushed Qwelby the few metres to the police car, opened the back door and thrust him none too gently inside.

Satisfied with seeing the black in trouble, the group who'd jostled the friends had slipped away whilst Qwelby and Inari had been facing off.

Having calmed the others and listened to their explanations, the sergeant walked over to Qwelby whose mind was whirling as he sorted out what identity he needed. He was carrying a Finish passport! "Just in case," Hannu had said. Qwelby agreed that he had said "Stupid," but that had been to himself for speaking his own language instead of Finnish. He also apologised for frightening the policewoman, saying that he had been pushed onto her.

The sergeant nodded. He'd noticed the black had been jostled from behind. A quick word with Inari and she reluctantly accepted Qwelby's story, backed up as it was by the three Finns. Reaching into the car to pull the black man outside, she stopped, staring at the handcuffs Qwelby offered her.

'What the...?'

'Fell off,' Qwelby said in what he thought of as "GamesPlay" as he got out of the car. He had spoken the truth. Merely omitted to say that he had used his mind to open the simple locks.

'Papers,' she growled as she folded the cuffs into the pouch on her belt, then gestured to Qwelby to remove his shades. With the snow still falling heavily, she bent over to shield the passport as she opened it at the photo page, carefully checking the picture against his face. 'You're fifteen?'

'Yes. All my family very tall.'

'Bloody giants,' she muttered as she held the photo page up to her videocam for a moment then handed it back.

Having discovered that the black man was spending a few days at Riku's home, the sergeant had done the same with Riku's identity card. 'Right, Inari,' he said. 'Let's get out of this snow and have a coffee. Time to introduce you to the rink's management.'

Almost collapsing with relief at the sight of the doors closing behind "The Authorities", Qwelby reached out a hand, grabbed Hannu's arm and stood staring at his friend. Moments later a broad grin split his face and his eyes twirled and sparkled. 'It worked!' he exclaimed as they shared a high five.

'What worked?' Riku asked, as he gestured to the others to follow him as he started walking towards home.

Qwelby looked at Hannu, desperately wondering what to say about the passport.

'The handcuffs. He's practising to be a magician,' Hannu said, shooting Qwelby a look of daggers.

'Games arcade,' Qwelby said.

'Yeah,' Hannu replied and turned back to Riku. 'The arcade's much nearer than your home. Qwelby wants to go there.'

'Why the hell d'you do that trick with the handcuffs?' Hannu hissed as he and Qwelby followed brother and sister.

'Was afraid. Needed to keep mind busy. Sorry,' Qwelby said trying to conceal a smile which turned into a grin when Hannu thumped him, just as Tullia would.

Later that night when the policewoman's videocam was processed, it was assumed that there must have been an exceptionally heavy flurry of snow just when she was filming the black boy's passport. She knew the difference between snowfall and electronic interference and wasn't buying that. But she was a probationer and that explanation was better than being accused of not knowing how to work her own equipment.

When they reached the arcade, Hannu explained what Qwelby wanted to do with the fruit machines.

'You no think I win,' Qwelby said, as Riku rubbished the idea. 'You play with my money. You see. You win.'

'We keep what we win?' Riku asked.

'Yes.'

'If we lose?'

'You no lose,' Qwelby was adamant. 'But. You lose. I pay.'

'Okay. Money,' Riku said, holding out a hand and grinning at his sister.

Forty minutes later Qwelby's machine clunked and clunked as it poured forth a stream of coins. Jackpot garnered – time to go home. Qwelby smilingly accepted the return of his stakes from the others, each of them only too happy with their own winnings.

As brother and sister went to change tokens for cash, Hannu

held Qwelby back. 'When the machines paid out and I was holding your arm, I saw coloured lights shining on the fruit machine symbols,' Hannu whispered.

'Lamane qinqolo thalawena,' Qwelby said with a grin. 'You are real Tazian brother.'

It was several months since Riku and Hannu had been together and as they left the arcade they walked side by side, deep in conversation, leaving Jenni alongside Qwelby. He was concentrating hard on answering with his limited Finnish and at the same time sending out his energy asking her to accept him and not think about his words. Once again he was entranced by a pair of blue eyes in a pink-cheeked face and it seemed very natural when Jenni slipped her arm through his.

Back home, all four youngsters piled into the sauna. Now Awakened and physically looking like any Azuran boy, and with his pale brown skin showing it was only his suntanned face that was a dark reddish brown, he explained his eyes as a family trait.

Over a dinner of traditional Finnish food, Qwelby confirmed to Johan what Seija had said to Elsa about his being Turkish, which Elsa had passed on to her husband over breakfast that morning. Deliberately getting confused with his Finnish, Qwelby left it to Hannu to explain how he proposed to get the money to return home. Challenged by a doubting Johan, Riku and Jenni explained Qwelby's success in the arcade.

Whatever doubts Elsa had about having the unusual looking boy with his strange story in her home, they were dispelled when Qwelby said, 'Smell good, taste better,' as he tucked into Kaalilaatikko, a mixture of beef, cabbage, onions and rice. Then a little later he declared the Mustikkapiirakka, blueberry tart, 'Is better than good,' and added, 'Sorry my Finnish no good,' as he happily accepted a second portion.

Johan tackled Qwelby about his decision to return home when he had been sent away for his safety.

'I must go. I must be with twin. Must be one,' Qwelby said almost vehemently. 'No casino here. More jackpots. Go to Helsinki. Two, three days.'

Johan shook his head. The boy was mad. And that made him feel even more uncomfortable as he looked into the shining eyes. If he didn't know better he would have said the purple centres were actually revolving. 'Good luck,' he muttered as he turned his attention back to his meal.

He could not forget those eyes. It was as if the boy was reading all his thoughts. He needed to get away and think. A beer would be very welcome. He thrust his chair back from the table. 'I'm going for a drink with Olavi.'

No-one spoke. The sound of the outside door closing broke the strained silence that followed Johan's abrupt departure. Elsa rose and started to clear the table. 'We'll do this,' she said, indicating Seija as everyone else got to their feet.

The four youngsters left the table and headed upstairs. As they reached the first landing, Riku ushered Hannu into his room and followed, closing the door behind him. Qwelby felt a stab of pain. He had been so happy immersed in the warm feelings.

'You have a twin?' Jenni asked.

Qwelby turned to her. She was standing half inside her room, holding the door open, looking very attractive in a short-sleeved peach blouse over a short black skirt and brightly patterned leggings.

'Yes.'

'Tell me about her,' she said as she stepped back into her room and beckoned. 'Ssh.' She put her finger to her lips as Qwelby started to speak.

As Qwelby entered the room Jenni closed the door gently. 'We must talk quietly. I'm not allowed to have a boy in my room with the door closed. Mother will think you're with the others.'

As Qwelby puzzled over the reason for such a prohibition, Jenni sat down and patted a place on the bed next to her. 'What's her name?'

After talking for a few minutes about Tullia in his limited Finnish the frustration became too much for him. He switched on his compiler and told her that he and his twin came from a parallel world which occupied more or less the same space and time as Earth.

Jenni gazed at him open-mouthed. Was he mad? Should she tell him to get out, or... what he'd done in the arcade?

Qwelby smiled and held his finger to his lips. Removing his previous mental interference, he proceeded to thoughtwrap her into a visit to his world to meet Tullia and their friends.

When he came back from what was for him a visit to Vertazia and opened his eyes, he found Jenni cuddled up against him, her energy field shining and vibrating. She lifted her head and a pair of bright blue eyes gazed at him with wonder. He lowered his head and their lips met.

Later, they became aware of the sound of knocking at the door and the urgent tone in Hannu's voice as he said it was the second time that Jenni's mother had called up about bedtime.

Quietly closing the bedroom door behind him, Qwelby grinned at his friend as Hannu shook his head in disbelief.

Still thinking of Jenni, Qwelby did not hear Hannu's words, but he sensed their meaning of 'bees clustered around a flower' and marvelled that it was true. In spite of his colour, all Hannu's friends had responded to his energy requests for friendship.

Johan returned after having enjoyed several beers with Olavi. He was particularly pleased with his success at the pool table. The two men were evenly matched and Johan had won by a large margin. Feeling mellow, he decided he could cope with the weird stranger in his house for a few more days.

Meanwhile, back in Jyväskylä, Qwelby's luck held and his mischievousness went unpunished. The dungeons of what was still referred to as The Old Palace in Jyväskylä were not the responsibility of the caretaker. By the time he'd remembered the incident of the appearance and disappearance in the Palace's torture chamber of a dummy of an overlarge black man, it was late on Friday and the maintenance man who looked after the dungeons had gone home. Deciding it was better to be able to show his boss the evidence, he'd asked Giselle, his niece, to send him the photos she'd taken.

Kids being kids and work being work, it was late Tuesday afternoon before he and the maintenance man went down to the dungeons for a double check on the absence of the dummy. They had been surprised to find that in the adjacent display of Duke Villnäs celebrating a victory, the sword always held aloft in his hand was in its scabbard. The caretaker had been forced to accept that it could have been done by one of the youths who'd accompanied his niece on the tour of the dungeons, otherwise closed to the public.

He telephoned Giselle and, although he believed her protestations of innocence, what was the alternative to accepting that both had been pranks she and her friends had carried out? Tell his boss, a man paranoid about blacks and terrorists – nearly a week later? Lose his job? With a shrug of his shoulders he agreed that it had all been a prank at his expense. An agreement later sealed with the maintenance man over a few beers.

CHAPTER 12

SHADOWS

VERTAZIA

The family's attempts to contact the Twins had effectively been paralysed by the speed of the decisions taken through the MentaNet two days ago to prohibit any attempt to rescue them. Their father, Shandur, together with his Great Uncle Mandara had returned to their attempts to research Aurigan science. Mandara's wife, Lellia, was focussing all her energies on her principal duty, that of Orchestrator of the First XzylStroem. The six XzylStroems linked the two parallel worlds together and had all been unsettled by recent events. The First was responsible for ensuring that all six worked in harmony and had been the most disturbed following its failure to save Qwelby.

The twins' mother, Mizena, a motherly looking woman with her dark hair full of what the twins called her "Worry tangles," was descended from the healer-heroine Rrîltallâ Taminûllÿâ who had flown her Winged Unicorn alongside the DragonRiders in the thickest of the battles throughout the centuries of the Space Wars. Those strong genes had enabled her to fight her way through the psychomental barrier preventing contact attempts. By calling on her Great Aunt's heroine, the Mystic Kûllokaremmâ, the two women again tried to reach the twins on the afternoon of that second day. This time they were driven back as a dark miasma engulfed Lellia's ancient crystal, Shannarah, with a nauseous stench of putrefaction.

'A slumbering evil has been awoken,' Lellia said as all colour drained from her face and her chair wrapped warming arms around her. The slightly short woman with a long thick strand of white in her otherwise black hair closed her eyes and rested the fingers of both hands on the orb of pure Adularia. 'It is not of the Dark Denizenii that exist in the NoWhenWhere between dimensions. Quite the contrary. It is Tazian in origin. Millennia's worth of suppression of thoughts and feelings.'

Lost in thought, Mizena leant forward and placed over the crystal a cloth made from the fine silk spun by a BlackNight butterfly. 'Fewer Healers and more Readjusters,' she said pensively. 'That's been going on for a long time.' She thoughtsent to Cook for a jug of hot restorative Chay as the two women looked helplessly at each other, acknowledging that penetrating the miasma emanating from what had to be Dark Denizenii was impossible.

CHAPTER 13

ATTACK

THE KALAHARI

As the last rays of the sun left the sky, more wood was added to the fire which was soon blazing its welcome warmth into the cold night air. Tullia threw a blanket around her shoulders as they settled down to eat and then listen to the women's sagas of good times and hard, sorrow and happiness and finally a joyful celebration of the cycle of life represented by a girl changing into a woman.

Heart swelling, Tullia stood up with Tsetsana, N!Obile and Mandingwe as they acknowledged their acceptance as women – and was engulfed with embarrassment at the teasing all were given about carrying out their duties to ensure the tribe's survival.

As the laughter died away, Neame stood up to announce the order for the final part of the Moon Day. Each new young woman was to portray an event from their lives, starting with Tullia.

Tullia had thought hard about what she was going to offer. Her two previous saga-tellings had been serious: being taken hostage and the hunt. With the kudu meat shared for that evening's dinner a reminder of her part in the hunt, she was happy that her decision had been for humour. Casting aside her blanket, she portrayed her first walk around the village with Tsetsana, when she had discovered a large hole in the ground where a nut the size of a rugby football had been dug out.

Whisper-singing in Tazian as before, this time she overacted the whole event. The hole was so large that she was unable to climb out by herself, but she was not going to give the nut to Tsetsana. It was hers! The scene eventually ended with Tullia, having pulled Tsetsana into the hole, climbing out on her friend's back, then lifting the nut out with the young girl clutching onto it, Tsetsana swinging herself onto Tullia's shoulders and the two of them returning to the village with Tsetsana triumphantly holding the nut above her head.

As Tullia made an extravagant bow, the laughter and ululating from the older women covered the fear and hatred emanating from several young women as the flickering flames reflecting off her sweat soaked skin and the golden haze around her whole body once again proclaimed her to be a powerful alien goddess – intent on stealing their men.

Tsetsana portrayed the sorrow of the death of her great grandmother, ending with showing how she kept the old woman's teaching in her head and her spirit in her heart. The applause revealed how much she had touched the women's hearts.

N!Obile and Mandingwe worked together, varying between being two young women, two young men or one man and one woman. Ungka leant over and explained to Tullia.

'They're at a big annual event when San from all over Botswana get together to celebrate. It's a special time to meet other tribes and find mates. It was very important in olden days when we lived in small family groups with no fixed homes, roaming the land as we wished. They are carefully saying that the people they are portraying come from other tribes.' Ungka laughed. 'You'll recognise our people. But they'll claim it's accidental!'

As the portrayal continued there was lots of laughter with women calling out various names to show they knew exactly who was being made fun of. In true San spirit, the girls also made fun

60

of themselves. Tullia laughed and at times tears flowed and she shared nudges with Ungka as she recognised herself, Tsetsana, H'ani and Ungka.

'I think I've learnt more about boys and girls and dating than I did this afternoon,' Tullia said to Ungka as the girls finished, causing more laughter as they parodied Tullia's bow. 'Those two have really brought alive all the uncertainty and shyness and, well, everything.' She put an arm around the young woman and pulled her close. 'Thank you for being with me today. At home my BestFriend would have been with me. She's nearly two years older than me and helps me through the changes in my life. Ungka. You've been like what we call an Elderest.'

Tullia found a pleasant stirring sensation filling her as she shared a long kiss with Ungka, which was interrupted by a growing clamour for her to portray her visit to the Tsodilo hills. She did not want to. Tsetsana and her sixteen-year-old brother, Xashee, had done that days ago. She was happy being a young woman and did not want to portray the powers that made people think of her as a Goddess.

The women had been moving around in between the portrayals and Tullia now found herself surrounded by her Meera family, mother, two grandmothers, two great grandmothers and Tsetsana on the opposite side to Ungka. Unable to resist the persuasion of her Meera family, she got to her feet and moved to a clear space a little distance from the fire.

With years of performing in LiveShows on Vertazia and now several enactments for the Meera, her natural talents took over. She slipped on a path, Xashee grabbed an arm as she fell over the edge and ended up dangling down the cliff face. He pulled her up and on top of him, his arms firmly around her.

Those few days ago she had been an innocent girl, saved from death by a lovely young man. Since then she had Awakened and enjoyed passionate kisses with H'ani. The demands her body was making from that long kiss with Ungka made her flush with embarrassment at how she had lain on Xashee and clung to him, and what she now realised was the message he must have thought she was giving him.

Carefully controlling herself, she continued to portray the injury he had sustained to his inner thigh, how she had helped him down the rocky path and then healed his wound. She finished as she had done that day: straddling his body and bending her head over as she poured healing into him from her forehead, unaware that it was being channelled by her unicorn's horn and that Tsetsana had seen the flow of golden light.

It did not need the day's learning and ribald humour for her position to produce giggles and nudges as some saw that as enacting a very different scene from what it truly had been.

Engrossed in the energy of that day, Tullia was puzzled by a sense of discord and jagged edges as she received the women's thoughts, very different from the soft appreciation following her previous performances. Tired and with her head swimming from all that had happened, she rose to her feet and started walking back to her family group.

Sixteen-year-old Kou-'ke was seething. The so-called Goddess had captivated her long time boyfriend, Xashee, the very first moment they'd met. She'd seen it in his face. How could any man or woman fancy the overlarge clumsy woman with the ugly face? Yet they did! Then she had stupidly fallen off the path. Stupidly? No! It had been deliberate. And then what had she done? Thrown herself on him as he lay wounded on the path. And now, the arrogant man-eating bitch, she was showing everyone how she had followed that up to steal her man!

It had been bad enough when Xashee and Tsetsana had enacted that day's events. Then it had been an eleven-year-old girl kneeling alongside her sixteen-year-old brother. But now, here, in front of all the women, the cursed bitch was showing that she had straddled him in the most obvious manner possible. Healing be damned! A flagrant display of what she really had done.

Everyone knew what had happened at the Melon Dance. A Meera would kick sand over a boy to show her interest. But she had to wait and see if he chose to follow up on that. Oh, no, not this bitch. She had clearly marked H'ani as hers, and then made that doubly clear by kissing him with passionate fervour in front of the whole tribe. And now she was showing that she'd already taken Xashee. Totally humiliated in front of all the women, Kou-'ke felt pain as if a knife was thrusting into her heart and being churned around. If the bitch goddess wanted to pretend to be Meera...

Tullia heard a scream of rage behind her. Still lost in the energy of the day on the hills, she slowly turned to see what was happening. 'Kou-'ke?' She spread her arms in a gesture of incomprehension.

Shouting words Tullia did not comprehend, Kou-'ke slashed at her.

Tullia cried out as pain shot through an outstretched arm. She stepped back raising her arms in defence and cried with pain at a cut across her other arm.

Backing away, sidestepping, trying to catch her attacker's arm, Tullia felt more pain as Kou-'ke's wild slashes cut her and some of the words started to make sense. 'Hate.. bitch.. steal.. men.. ruin..' then 'Goddess' said with such venom that comprehension dawned. Kou-'ke hated her for stealing Xashee!

'No!' she cried, shocked at the young woman's false reason for the attack. The knife flashed in the firelight, swinging towards her. A sharp pain in her lower abdomen made her bend over, grunting as her hands grasped her sides. She cried out with pain, staring at a line of blood across her belly. Then cried out again as a backswing from Kou-'ke left a second red line across her belly.

The tableau froze as Kou-'ke stopped to see what she had done.

Tullia saw blood starting to drip down from the two deep cuts. She was frozen in shock, realising how very deep the gashes would have been had she not bent over at exactly that moment.

'Bitch!' Kou-'ke screamed as she lunged forward aiming the knife upwards under Tullia's ribs.

Galvanised into action, Tullia stepped back and to the side. Her right hand grasped her attacker's wrist and swung her arm up and around, twisting her wrist so the knife fell and Tullia caught it with her left hand. As Kou-'ke was forced to swing around, Tullia kicked her legs from under the young woman, sending her crashing onto the sand on her back.

Tullia's arm swung above her head, the blade of the knife in her fingertips as her eyes focussed on her attacker's heart, a little to the right of centre. As her arm swung down, her screaming healer's mind overruled the warrior within.

Trembling at the thought of what she had so nearly done, Tullia stared at the knife buried deep in the sand between Kou-'ke's thighs. What had started as a move from a BodyDance routine she had practised with Tamina had segued into a fighting move. Now she understood how, following the death of the kudu, she had been out-of-body as a man, looking down on her physical woman's body. She had the same genetic inheritance as her twin, yet she had always concentrated on her healer's genes, deliberately ignoring her warrior inheritance.

Never before had she called on her warrior genes. The day she won her freedom from her captor, that had simply been a logical calculation of vectors. Kicking him in the face had been an accident. She had only meant to knock the gun from his hand.

She took a deep breath, relaxed, gave Kou-'ke a curt nod, turned and started walking back to her family group, only to stumble as a mental blow struck her mind. Hatred, rage, humiliation and DEATH. Hearing the faint thudding of feet on the thick sand she pivoted to her right, partially ducking and flinging her right arm backwards, bent at the elbow. She felt a knife graze across her back a split second before her elbow struck her attacker on the side of the head.

Kou·'ke crashed to the ground as Tullia swung around and stepped firmly on the wrist holding the knife. Bending down she took the knife from her attacker's inert hand, stood and once again swung her arm above her head with the blade in her fingertips. She trembled with pent-up fury at the sense of betrayal. She had won the brief fight fairly, yet again been attacked from behind, this time without the slightest warning. The faint crackling of the fire only made the women's silence more obvious and the pattering of the mixed thoughts assailing her mind seem very loud.

She would have her revenge! Tensing her arm she felt the alarm running through the tribe. Her arm swung down straight towards the unconscious woman. The knife flew from her grip to land quivering exactly where she had ordered her inner warrior to send it – into a log at the edge of the fire.

Awareness returned to !Gei-!Ku'ma, Goddess of The Red San. Awareness of a diagonal of pain from right shoulder to left hip and of sharp pains across her belly and forearms hit her. Looking down, she saw two long lines of dark red blood seeping across her stomach and a long runnel down each thigh. She gasped and bent over but stopped herself from placing her sand covered hands on the wounds, turned and walked back to her family, aware of the colours of shock, disbelief, outrage and relief flooding through their auras.

As she reached the group she sat down on a blanket between Tsetsana and Ungka with one of the grandmothers holding her shoulders from behind. Tu appeared, carrying her medicine bag and added one of her plant remedies to a bottle of water before washing Tullia's several wounds. Having gone to her hut, Deena returned with a clean shirt which she draped over Tullia's back before encouraging the young woman to lie back with her head on her lap.

Tullia held out her hands to the other young women. 'Please, I need your energies.'

Tullia sank back as Tu continued to apply healing balm to the

65

deep cuts across her belly, and relaxed into the feeling of love that was coming from Deena and her two companions.

Dancing around the fire started, and Neame approached the family. 'What is between you and Kou-'ke must be ended by full sunrise,' she said to Tullia.

'I will not fight her again,' Tullia replied.

'She has challenged you. She has used a knife. That is the only weapon you may have.'

'I've been wounded.'

'Another may fight for you.'

'NO!' Tullia lurched up. 'Owee!' She sank back as pain flared through her belly and both young women gripped her hands.

Neame let her eyes roam around the family before leaving. They all knew the traditions.

'I will not fight, nor will I let anyone fight for me,' Tullia said in a soft voice.

'Tullia. Are you Meera?' Deena asked.

'Yes?'

'Are you my daughter?'

'Yes.' Tullia answered in almost a whisper. 'Yes,' she added in a strong voice.

'I will fight...'

'NO. Multiverse thank you.' Tullia was quick to silence both Tsetsana and Ungka who had spoken together. 'Now. Help me heal,' she asked as she smiled at each friend in turn and she sank back onto her Meera mother's lap.

Ungka started stroking Tullia's skin, marvelling at the velvet like feel. 'You're purring again,' she said.

Tullia smiled and as Tsetsana also started stroking her, she let the gentle energy carry her deep into her Kore and the welcome healing energies from Rrîltallâ, her Heroine from the Space Wars, whose genes she had inherited. She slipped into DeepMemory, looking for a way to end the feud with Kou-'ke without hurting her – more than necessary, she sadly added.

Killing was totally out of the question. It would prevent Tullia reincarnating and thus prevent her being alive when the time came for her people to restore the incredible beauty of their original Aurigan way of life. Identical Twins - it would also destroy him.

CHAPTER 14

CHALLENGE

THE KALAHARI

'I need to dance,' Tullia said a lot later. 'I will be careful.'

As she and her friends joined the dancing women, Neame walked up to her. 'Dance ready. Fight ready.' She led Tullia a few paces away to where Kou-'ke, holding a large and vicious looking knife, was standing with her best friend, sixteen-year-old Nlai.

Tullia felt a hand take her wrist. 'From our mother,' Tsetsana said as she proffered a smaller knife. Tullia recognised the knife with its pointed end. Much smaller than that held by Kou-'ke, it was very sharp.

Tullia had learnt from Tamina that BodyDance was a way of keeping alive Aurigan self-defence. Her Elderest had told her that her father belonged to a group that practised an Extended Form, which was effectively Aurigan Unarmed Combat. Using the experience with the kudu, she contacted her inner warrior and told him that Kou-'ke was not to be seriously harmed. Rather than see the slim male figure she had been that time, her warrior looked like her twin as she had last seen him clad only in a loinskin. *I understand knives. Trust me/my/our warrior genes,* he seemed to thoughtspeak.

Neame stepped away and the fight began. The slender Meera

was quick on her feet, darting in and out as she tested Tullia's reactions. Tullia's big advantage was her much longer reach, but she was not sure-footed on the thick and uneven sand. After a lifetime of living in the Kalahari, Kou-'ke had no such problem.

Tullia refused to use her mental skills to read her attacker's mind. She had said she was Meera and would behave like one. Aware that in comparison she was clumsy, she made some feints herself, slowly building up a picture of what she thought of as The Dance.

Ouch! Careless! Tullia felt a quick slash across a forearm, spun, stepped and slashed at the twirling Meera. She heard a faint cry and saw a line of blood across one of the girl's buttocks. Satisfaction. Not a deep wound, but a hit. And painful for sitting down on sand or coarse blankets.

The watchers saw an unbalanced match. A large woman who was slowly turning around almost in a circle as a much smaller woman danced in and out as she tested the defences and reach of her opponent. The deadly dance continued, firelight glinting off the knives and the two dark brown bodies shining with sweat.

Tullia was hurting and getting tired. Once again dodging the swinging knife, a stab of pain made her glance down at her belly where the wounds were reopening. She yelped as she felt the slash of a knife across a buttock and knew it had cut deep. She must end the action and soon.

Sinking deep into her Kore, and with the reluctance of a healer, she acknowledged her inheritance of DragonRider genes and recalled a furious fight on the HomeSphere when attackers had penetrated the very shell of the innermost third dimension where she and her fellow healers were fighting on foot.

From three metres above the sand her eyes looked down on the young and inexperienced fighter. *'Blazing Novas. In the future am I going to stagger around on stumpy legs like that!'* The Aurigan warrior laughed at the explosion of affronted anger from her Tazian descendant and slid into the youngster's mind.

A litheness entered Tullia's body along with an unconscious understanding of movement. She took the fight to the slender woman as she sternly ordered her inner warrior to obey her. Her opponent was not to be killed or even badly hurt. *'An Aurigan Warrior fights only for Justice.'* That was not completely reassuring.

Pressing hard and forcing Kou-'ke to take evasive moves, Tullia saw her whirl away in the wrong direction. A big step, a slash and a scream as Tullia's knife carved a deep gash down the other buttock. Raging, the wounded woman threw all caution to the wind and swung back the opposite way.

A scene unfolded in Tullia's mind as if a video was being played. She had a split second in which to act and had to trust her inner warrior: her Self. Throwing her knife away, she grabbed her attacker's arm with both hands and kicked her legs from under her. Taking the smaller woman down to the ground, as she landed on her side she rolled over the woman and pinned her left arm under her right knee.

Holding Kou-'ke's right arm high and keeping the knife away from her face, a harsh twist loosened the woman's grip. With her right hand Tullia wrenched the knife away, with her left she forced that arm to the ground and pressed it into the sand with her other knee. Breathing heavily and with sweat clouding her vision as it dripped into her eyes, Tullia rested the point of what had been Kou-'ke's knife against her throat.

'I do not want a man,' she said, and in a loud and carrying voice added the words she hoped would solve the problem – for everyone. 'I have my man. We were born to be together for life.' *Sorry Kaigii, I don't mean it the way I want her to think.* She lifted the knife away from the throat and rested it on Kou-'ke's chest, pressed hard and drew it down her body leaving a clear line of blood. 'You may have Xashee.' She dug the knife in just past the end of the woman's rib cage, watching her wince as blood welled up. 'If you live.'

Tullia searched Kou-'ke's mind – and was shocked. Tullia

loved her time with the children and being a "Big-Big Sister" and knew that she wanted her own children – one day in the far distant future. What she had learnt that afternoon, where her lack of interest had distanced her from what had become a new and close group of friends; the woman pinned to the ground enjoyed doing all that with Xashee. And wanted babies now!

Tullia had thought a lot of what the women had been talking about had been jokes. Jokes at her expense, winding her up as they realised she had been getting increasingly uncomfortable with what they were saying about men. But what they had said was true! Tullia shook her head. What would Kaigii say if she told him? He'd never believe her! Stunned, feeling sick at the thought of doing those things, needing to distance her head from Kou-'ke's in a pointless attempt to separate their minds, Tullia eased back and rose to her feet.

'She wants babies,' she said to Neame who was now standing alongside,

Neame's gaze flickered between the two women. Kou-'ke had not answered the challenge of Tullia's knife drawing blood from her chest, and now Tullia's withdrawal meant she was backing down. But was she? Did she understand that the fight was not yet over?

Tullia bent over and offered the recumbent woman a hand. After a moment's hesitation Kou-'ke took it and let herself be pulled her up on to her feet, glancing at the faces of the two silent women.

Still trying to get her head around what she had just discovered, Tullia was unaware of the tense silence, but did become aware that she was holding a large knife. Silently, she offered it to Kou-'ke, and wondered at Neame's sharp hiss of indrawn breath.

Kou-'ke looked at it, then at Tullia with blood trickling from cuts across her belly and forearms, remembered with satisfaction the deep cut she had made across the big woman's buttock and thought of Xashee. The big, clumsy, ugly bitch had not had the courage to follow through on her threat. Kou-'ke had won the fight and had established her claim to Xashee in front of all the women.

'That's not mine,' she said.

'I'll, erm, ward it, then,' Tullia said, knowing that the San had very few personal possessions and objects such as the large and useful knife would be passed around the tribe as was needed.

Neame let go a long-held breath. A strange outcome, but the matter was settled.

'I can heal the...'

'No.' Kou-'ke cut short Tullia's words.

Tullia understood the flicker of pride that ran through the young woman's aura. She had fought for her man, was alive and could say that she had won him. She felt goosebumps spring up all over her body at her warrior's satisfaction. For the resolution? For fighting well? For accepting him, her Self?

'Ah, not so little QeïchâKaïgïï,' chuckled the irritatingly unhelpful inner voice.

Nlai walked around the fire to help Kou-'ke, only to be roughly brushed aside as her best friend walked back to where she had been sitting.

Nlai remained staring at ... the flickering flames dancing over the tall woman's heavy body ... the daughter of the Sun Goddess. She feared losing K'dae to Tullia. How could anyone compete with a Goddess? Was she going to have to fight for her man as her best friend had just done?

Yet she was also remembering the good parts of their time together on the hunt, especially the feeling of being loved when she had awoken in Tullia's embrace and the sweet, soft kiss they'd shared. She noted the blood that was steadily trickling from the several cuts.

'Will she be alright?' Nlai asked, half looking at Tsetsana who had walked up as Kou-'ke had walked away.

'Yes. She is a healer,' Tsetsana spat out the words in anger. An anger that was directed as much at herself as Nlai. She was cursing herself for having been so over-awed with her relationship as servant, guide and teacher, that she had only been aware of the envy from those who resented that relationship.

As the oldest girl it had been her duty, which she enjoyed, to share a hut with the youngest girls. Thus she had not participated in any of the nighttime sharing of the unmarried young women and not heard the growing fears of many of them that Tyua'llia might steal away their men. In her beloved friend's moment of need, she had failed her.

A stab of pain low in her body made Tullia gasp and bend over. Once again she saw the dark lines of the cuts on her belly and blood trickling from both ends. She made her way back to her family and lay down as before with her head on her Meera mother's lap. 'I'm cold,' she said, and gestured to the two young women. They understood and cuddled up to her. Others of the family ensured that blankets covered the backs and legs of her two companions.

A deep pain stabbed through Tullia. Ahhh! It was what she had always feared. *Kaigii. I need you. Here. Now.* Then it struck her – was it more than that? At home they fooled even their BestFriends by pretending to be each other. Was this what their identical genes were all about? Some sort of weird body-swapping? His mind in her body and her mind in his? Pressure was mounting inside her.... she... a boy... here on Moon Day... Kûÿ-maó-lâš'tûn labirden kûlwââ khuy!

'I must go!' she cried out, thrusting her two companions aside and rising to her feet. 'DO NOT follow.' She stared at Tsetsana as she thoughtsent *Compliance!* and saw her friend recoil from the power. Bending over and seeming to be clutching her belly, Tullia turned and followed a broad track as it curved around, taking her away from the fire and where the rest of the village was spending the night.

All who watched her heading for the privacy of the trees nodded in sympathetic misunderstanding.

She stumbled through the trees and down the slope into a

73

more open area of bush. She knew she was safe as there was a ring of men guarding the women's area. Sharp pain shot though her loins. She dropped to her knees, gasping at the unwelcome sight of a male organ appearing between her thighs. Removing a clear sticky covering that had come with it, she noticed blood trickling from her reopened wounds.

Her head throbbing, she peered through the bushes and thought she saw movement. Reaching out with her mind she became aware of attention focussed on her. There. A large animal, slinking low. A leopard.

Assuming it was on the way to the small pool that lay some way behind her and to her left, she remained motionless. A faint breeze cooled her back. Bending her head she sniffed. Khuy! Blood and something else. She saw bright eyes staring at her. The leopard was smelling her as a wounded animal!

Panicked, she leapt to her feet and started running across an open spit of land towards the thick clump of trees that surrounded the pool, hoping to force her way in between them and be safe from attack.

Hearing the twang of a bow she looked over her shoulder and saw the leopard running towards her, further back a man standing behind a bush, throwing his bow to one side. Sprinting on with all her senses on fire Tullia heard the soft thunder of the leopard's paws, the heavier thud of the man's feet, his shouts, the hiss of a thrown knife – then a deathly silence. She stumbled and fell to her knees, heard a yelp and something dug into her right shoulder forcing her face into the sand. She pulled herself onto her feet and dived behind the trees.

'All is well,' Xashee called out. 'Leopard. It's gone.'

Nursing her bleeding shoulder, she watched through a screen of branches as a boy ran up to Xashee and an animated conversation took place.

A little while later, Xameb approached the trees and Tullia called out, telling him not to approach her. When he tried to reassure her that it was all right for him to see her, she shouted denial, saying she would explain later.

There was uproar when Xameb returned to the women and explained what had happened and what Xashee had seen. Kou-'ke screamed in despair and collapsed, her sobbing was heartbreaking to hear.

Xameb called out to Tullia when he returned, saying he was going to wait.

All Tullia's senses were awhirl. Neither her eyes nor her mind were clear. She knew she'd started to turn into a boy. But how far had it gone? She tried to contact her twin, but wasn't sure if she'd done that or – the fear that had driven her into the panic that robbed her of any clarity – turned into him.

She'd come to accept that Mandingwe had been right – she was a "Big Girl." She grimaced. Now, she was a "Big Boy!" Her belly was covered in blood. She started to wash herself. The cool water was helping to calm her and her vision cleared. She squealed with joy as she saw her breasts. Had they been there all throughout this second Awakening? She didn't care. Whatever had happened, she knew she was becoming herself again.

She'd been worried at her initiation with the girls when her breasts hadn't produced PassionMilk. How could they, when she'd been turning into a boy!

Lying down, relaxing and meditating, she recovered her composure and, oh joy of joys, her male organ withdrew and the rest of her body returned to normal. Happy, she called out to Xameb and waited a few minutes for two old men to arrive with blankets.

She heard Ghadi instructing the men on guard to turn their backs as she was escorted back to the women's area, completely wrapped from head to toe.

As she reached her family and handed the blankets to the old men, Kou-'ke flew at her, trying to scratch her eyes out. Tullia sharply ducked her head forward in self-defence. The two women's foreheads crashed together. Stunned, both fell to the ground as the top of the sun climbed over the trees.

'Take them both to Tyua'llia's hut and cover the entry with blankets,' Neame ordered, then turned to the two groggy young women. 'You will stay there until... either both of you come out, or only one. Your Moon Day lasts until then.'

Kou-'ke refused to share Tullia's bed of blankets and two more were brought for her to spend a cold night alone on the floor.

Tullia smiled weakly as Tu attended to her various wounds, sighed with relief when Kou-'ke's taut body sagged as she fell asleep, set a mental alarm should she be attacked and surrendered to her own exhaustion.

CHAPTER 15

SUBVERSION

VERTAZIA

Tamina awoke, pulled Shimara from her bed and dragged her into the room where Wrenden and Pelnak were sleeping.

Wrenden at nearly fourteen, together with his nearly seventeen-year-old sister, Tamina, the twins and the fifteen-year-olds Shimara and Pelnak, were BestFriends and years ago the six had formed what they called XOÑOX. There was a marked contrast between the two pairs. At one metre ninety-five, Tamina was the tallest of them all. Slim and with a perfectly toned dancer's physique, her auburn hair with its natural golden highlights fell in wavelets to mid thigh. Recently Awakened, she had at last become comfortable with her large breasts. Like his sister, Wrenden, was slim and tall for his age, sharing her copper toned skin colour, but with dark hair cut en brosse on top.

Both were wearing the currently fashionable tight fitting bodysuits, slashed with many pockets that looked like flames or leaves depending on the patterns and colours. Badly missing Qwelby, Wrenden was wearing his elderest's favourite colours, but the opposite way round – red with green flames. Struggling with her emotions following her Awakening, responsibilities and sorely missing Tullia, Tamina was wearing a two-tone blue outfit, the pale blue pockets looking like ice flares.

Shimara and Pelnak, often referred to as the not-twins because they acted more like twins than Qwelby and Tullia, were short for their nearly sixteen years of age, round in build, had a stronger red cast to their skins and identical page boy hair cuts. Quieter in character than the others, they had chosen pastel colours for their soft long sleeved tops over baggy slax. Aquamarine over rich cream for Shimara, rich cream over aquamarine for Pelnak.

'I had a Dreamstate about Tullia last night,' Tamina explained. 'Well, not about her, really, but with her.' She opened her Privacy Shield and waited for the others to get a feel of what she was trying to explain. 'She was different. Warm and strong, bigger and happy. Yet also... I sensed a warrior.'

Slipping back into the Dreamstate, Tamina became hot as she recalled the long kiss they'd shared – stronger than anything before.

'You're blushing, Sis?'

'Yeah, Eeky,' she said to her young brother, then looked at Shimara and Pelnak. 'I'm certain Tullia's Awakened. And been celebrating.'

Shimara put a comforting hand on Tamina's arm. The latter had shared that her moodiness since her Awakening was largely due to a confusing mixture of feelings for the twins and especially Qwelby. She wondered if he had also Awakened, and again became hot as another memory slid through her mind – of the love she'd sent him as she'd dived into his Pit of Depair. *Need your support, Shimmi. If you...*

Sisters.

Thanks.

'We've got to do something,' Tamina declared.

'Talk over breakfast,' Wrenden said.

They asked House to have the House Carls deliver the meal to the XOÑOX suite, while they settled down to planning. Unbidden, the colourscopes on the wall took the forms of an ocean and rivers, overlapping each other with a mixture of blues, greens, hints of whites and magical turquoises. House was keen to aid the youngsters with their plans to rescue the twins.

'I've got an idea,' Shimara said in her quiet voice as she reached for Pelnak's hand. He gave an encouraging squeeze to the quietest member of the group. 'We can choose any college for our tendayly attendances. So, starting now, in our pairs we go to a different one each time. And we can go more than once a tenday.' Mentally receiving the others' interest, she took a deep breath. 'With kids of our ages we talk about philosophy and co-ordination, saying we're preparing study papers for a group thesis.'

'Philosophy of the treatment of the twins,' Pelnak said.

'Co-ordination. The way in which agreements are reached for all Tazii,' Wrenden added.

'And an attack on the disastrous decision that's been made that stops the adults acting and us using CuSho,' Tamina summarised. 'Brilliant, Shimmi!'

'Divide a tenday in two,' Shimara continued. 'Four days split between here, our homes and colleges. One day all together here.'

They leapt to their feet and hugged. 'Subversion,' Wrenden said.

'SUB-VER-SHUN!!!!' they all chanted. The twist in the Tazian spelling making their intention clear.

'Tell the adults?' Shimara asked as they separated.

'They need to know,' Tamina answered as the boys nodded, thoughtsharing reluctant agreement. 'Mizena'll not let them stop us,' Tamina added and, much to Wrenden's embarrassment, she thoughtshared her Big Sisterly feelings for him to show how certain she was about Mizena's feelings for her children.

Diversions on their way to where the adults were finishing their breakfast enabled the youngsters to add support to their explanation. The Stroems were swirling positively and CuSho had said that the Cosmic Holograph showed that a concatenation of events appeared to be forming. 'TriUne indeterminacy,' Wrenden said. Which Qwelby was to tell them later was known on Earth as the Heisenberg Uncertainty principle. 'It can see a "where" in the Holograph but not a "when".'

CHAPTER 16

DECISIONS

SIILINJÄRVI-FINLAND

The morning after the skating, Jenni told her mother that with an upset stomach, pain in her back and a headache, she didn't feel well enough to go to school. Elsa gave her daughter a long hard look, then agreed her daughter could have a day off.

Qwelby and Hannu slept late. The three youngsters shared breakfast, after which Jenni said she felt a little better. Exchanging a knowing look with Seija, Elsa said Jenni was allowed to go out as long as she did not overdo it.

As the youngsters went upstairs to get ready, Seija took Qwelby to one side, saying she'd received a telephone call the previous evening. Then, she hadn't wanted to interrupt Qwelby when he was having fun with the boys.

The smile on Qwelby's face rapidly disappeared as Seija told him what Dr Keskinen, the quantum scientist father of Hannu's girlfriend, had said. Thanking Hannu's mother, Qwelby put the disconcerting message to the back of his mind to think about later.

Qwelby was happy. Yesterday, not wanting to repeat whatever mistake he'd made with Oona, he'd kept a tendril of his mind in Jenni's, making sure she was happy with everything they were doing. During breakfast he'd searched her mind and scanned her mother's energy field. He knew Jenni was not ill and her mother knew that. He felt certain that both knew what the other was thinking.

It was all very different from Vertazia where people's thoughts were very open and their energy fields easy to read. Communication amongst the inhabitants of Earth was subtle. As he put on his large sunshades and followed Hannu outside he wondered how much he was missing.

Jenni closed the front door, pushed in between the boys and linked arms with both.

Qwelby grinned at her. He preferred non-subtle.

Lost in chatting happily as they walked into town the youngsters were startled when someone spoke to them.

'Excuse me,' a man said in English as he looked from one to the other. 'I believe I'm addressing Qwelby and Hannu – and Jenni?'

Stunned, the youngsters stared at the man.

'Let me introduce myself. I'm David Romain. Professor Romain. Did Dr Keskinen pass on my message to you, Qwelby?'

Qwelby was in panic. He recognised the man who had been around Muurame over the same weekend that two other men had been watching him and his friends. Men that were thought to be from Finnish intelligence.

Dr Keskinen had been trying to find a way for Qwelby to communicate with his friends on Vertazia by piggybacking a message onto a satellite broadcast of a programme they liked to watch. What were called Flikkers on Vertazia because of the poor quality of the few transmissions that slipped across to the fifth dimension.

Qwelby had been taken aback by the content of Dr Keskinen's call to Hannu's mother, saying that, without giving anything away, he had listened to the Professor and had agreed to suggest to Qwelby that it was important he should return to Kotomäki and meet Romain. The Professor was one of the world's leading experts on quantum mechanics and believed that Qwelby had seen or found something that could help him with his research into other dimensions.

Qwelby didn't trust the energy he saw in the Professor's aura. Shaken by the encounter, he stepped back. He wanted to walk away, yet at the same time he didn't want to let go of the reassurance of Jenni's arm holding his.

Romain took Qwelby's reaction as confirmation that his message had been passed on. 'You will know that I believe you have information that could be vital to a major piece of research I am conducting.' He fixed Qwelby with a level gaze. 'Research that could help you.'

Sensing Qwelby's distress, Hannu intervened. 'Erm, Professor. Sorry but we're meeting some friends. And we're late already.' He looked at his watch.

Romain smiled, guessing that was an excuse, yet content that he'd at last made contact and sown the seeds for the future. 'I'm delighted to have met you, Qwelby. There's a lot I would like to talk to you about. And I think you know that you need to talk to me.'

'You have a mobile?' Romain asked Hannu as he produced his own.

'Yes?'

'I'd like to give you my number.'

Hannu pulled out his phone.

Romain thumbed a button and a virtual tablet hovered in the air between them. The Professor touched an icon and to his surprise, Hannu's phone rang. 'Please open the message and follow the instructions.'

Hannu glanced at Qwelby. Although loath to reveal too much about himself, the alien nodded as he read the electromagnetic signatures and discovered all that was going to happen was the establishment of a secure link. Hannu did as instructed then restarted his phone, Romain explained.

'A call on that number will be relayed to me anywhere in the world. But only with that mobile. All communications are secure. And Qwelby. Please do call me.'

'We must go, err, Professor,' Hannu said.

'Especially about the day you arrived in Kotomäki,' Romain continued, stepping to the side and swivelling round as the youngsters walked away. 'Hyvää päivänjatkoa,' he added as he raised his cap and hoped that "Have a nice day," was the right thing to say to teenagers.

'You've gone really pale,' Jenni said to Qwelby.

'That happens,' Hannu said. 'It's err....'

'She knows. I told her last night,' Qwelby said.

'What!' Hannu exclaimed.

'Coffee,' Jenni said in a firm tone. 'Let's go to Fontis, my favourite café. They have the best Nissu Nassu in Siilinjärvi.'

'You must try Lusikkaleivat,' Hannu added, turning to Qwelby and laughing at the expression on his face. 'Can't translate that either, eh!'

Qwelby shook his head and smiled faintly.

'Spice Cakes and Marmalade Cakes,' Jenni explained.

As soon as they were seated in the café with their drinks and traditional Finnish pastries, Qwelby asked the burning question: 'How did the Professor know how to find me. Us?'

Hannu and Jenni discussed the question. Their conclusion was that that their two mothers had grown up together in Kotomäki and been best friends since meeting on their first day in school. Kotomäki was a very small town. It would not have been difficult for Romain and whoever else to find someone who remembered that friendship and that Jenni's mother had moved to Siilinjärvi on marriage.

'I bet that was Erki.' Hannu said. 'Suckering you into the black run you'd not skied before and then threatening to get back at you when you hit him? He's a nasty piece of work. Lets it be known he's got some dodgy contacts.'

Qwelby felt as though he'd been punched in the stomach by a level of double-dealing beyond his understanding.

'That Professor must have been waiting for us,' Jenni said. ' I noticed him leaving the bar.'

'Hannu. Your mobile. Romain was really surprised to see it. Why?' Qwelby asked. 'It looked just like his.'

'Yeah. It is. A RonaldsonQ. Got to be the best phone in the world.' He took a breath. 'Long story short. December before last I'm skiing. Awful cry. Man's broken a leg. I'm there first. Sometimes work with Dad, unofficially. Know first aid and what to do. Anyway. This rich American, first day on holiday. Bad fracture can't ski for the whole holiday. On crutches right across Christmas and the New Year. I end up helping to look after his two children. Bit younger than me. Nice kids. Wife can't ski. Had a great time. Evenings out, day trips the lot. He's over the top grateful and gives me this phone.

'Now get this. It comes with a sort of docking station. A pyramid. Russian discovery he says. Last October received a message. Put the phone in the pyramid. Take it out twenty-four hours later and I've got the latest model. Molecular reconstruction. No shit!'

'Wow!' Jenni exclaimed. 'So, Qwelby, why don't you speak to him?'

'I've learnt from Dr Keskinen...'

'That's my girlfriend's father.' Hannu interjected.

'That Earth scientists know nothing of other dimensions. The best way back home is by uniting with my twin and then working with our BestFriends through the sixth dimension.' He took a deep breath. 'And I don't trust him. There's something dark in his energy field. Your auras are difficult to read at anything below a surface level. But I see, sense, a twist deep inside him. It's like a... I don't know. Nothing like I've ever seen on Vertazia. But then.' He sighed. 'I am only fifteen years old and we can live to two hundred.'

'Won't your family try to rescue you?' Jenni asked, putting a hand on Qwelby's where it lay on the table.

'Yes. But the violence our rulers are using to stop me and Tullia joining is so much, so unlike anything that's ever happened before on my world.' Qwelby glanced at Hannu. 'That tells me they fear that a lot. And they must see that as our best way home.' He responded to the caring energy coming from Jenni's hand by turning his over and holding her hand while he smiled, unaware of the effect his lopsided smile and twinkling eyes were having on her.

When Miska Metsälä, the SUPO agent, had discovered that Romain had left his hotel in Jyväskylä saying he might be away for a couple of days, he had spoken with Penti Harju, the Chief Inspector in Kotomäki. Pia Sjöström, his Sergeant, had not needed to make any enquiries to be able to tell her boss that the Rahkamos went to Siilinjärvi every year, so perhaps...

Metsälä's luck held. Harju had trained at the Police College in Tampere with Ulla Koivuniemi, who was now a Chief Inspector in Siilinjärvi. It had not taken her officers long to trace Romain to his hotel: the Spa Hotel Kunnonpaikka. She had put an officer on watch at the hotel with instructions to call her and follow Romain until she took over. She and Metsälä had taken over the surveillance in time to witness the encounter with Qwelby and friends.

Metsälä explained to Koivuniemi that his briefing had been decidedly lacking in useful facts. The Professor was a renowned Quantum Physicist and inventor of cutting edge technological advances whose applications were used in many countries around the world. Metsälä's instructions were to watch Romain in the hope that his actions and/or contacts might reveal why he really was in Finland. Whilst his explanation of being interested in strange weather events was considered dubious to say the least, care and caution had been impressed on Metsälä, not the least because their Russian neighbours were interested in Romain.

Now, it seemed that the Professor was interested in a teenage boy. Why? What possible connection could the youth have with the reason Romain had given for being in Finland? Having lost sight of Romain, Metsälä and Koivuniemi entered Café Fontis, took a table by the window, ordered coffee and pastries and watched for Romain passing by, whilst also keeping an eye on the youngsters.

As the youngsters left, the two officials got up and Ulla paid the bill. She was putting her purse back into her handbag when the youngsters returned in a group, jostling in the doorway and laughing. Ulla looked up and noticed a bag on the chair where the girl had been sitting. In the confusion, somebody bumped into the clothes stand. It started to fall and as the policewoman grabbed it, her handbag slipped off her shoulder, spilling its contents on the floor.

Jenni bent down. Picking up a pass she exclaimed: 'Police!'

Having righted the clothes stand, the policewoman took her papers as Jenni stood up. 'Thank you, yes. But I am not on duty,' she added hastily. Then held out a hand. 'I'm Chief Inspector Ulla Koivuniemi.'

'I'm Jenni Korpijaakko.'

As they shook hands, the Inspector noticed Jenni's eyes looking over her companion and a faint smile appear on the girl's face. Ulla felt herself blushing and thought how convenient, the youths would see her spending her off-duty time with a handsome friend and accept her presence as being accidental.

As the youngsters stepped outside the café, Qwelby turned to Jenni and said in a quiet but urgent tone of voice: 'Please. We go home.'

'Why. What's the matter?'

'Those two watch me.'

'How do you know?'

'I...' He switched on his compiler. 'Energy like at home and I'm playing HideNSeek with Tullia and my friends. When we search for somebody, that person feels it – and tries to stop that feeling sticking to them. You understand?'

'Sort of.' It sounded exciting, but a bit scary as she wondered how much he knew of what she was feeling and thinking.

'No,' Qwelby said. 'It has to be strong.' Then he grinned, Jenni blushed and Hannu laughed.

Linking arms with Jenni in the middle they set off for home.

The two officials stepped outside and watched the youngsters walk away. 'A nice bit of luck,' the policewoman said. 'Korpijaakko's an unusual name in Siilinjärvi. Given we know the direction from which the youngsters have come, finding where the boy is staying will be easy. And chance of a double check if the Rahkamo's car is outside as I've got the number of its licence plate.

With no sign of Romain, Miska suggested a beer at the Professor's hotel. Ulla agreed. She knew he meant for surveillance but he was pleasant company – and a connection with Finnish Intelligence was worth cultivating. Walking in the opposite direction to that taken by the youngsters, they failed to see Romain following.

'The Professor. He follows,' Qwelby said a few moments later, tapping the side of his head. 'He stays behind. Looks.'

'He wasn't in the café.' Hannu said.

'I guess in the bookshop opposite,' Jenni said.

'Let's lose him,' Hannu said. 'If all he's doing is following us, will be easy. Once we leave the centre, it's very open. He'll have to stay well back.'

'Hannu's right,' Jenni said, looking into Qwelby's twirling eyes and squeezing his arm with hers. He was more than cute.

As they rounded the last corner before Jenni's home, they sprinted along the road, round to the back of the house and threw themselves on the floor, laughing in between panting for breath.

Carefully checking that Romain was nowhere to be seen, the youngsters went into the kitchen. Jenni heated the pot of Lohikeitto, a rich salmon soup that her mother had left for them, whilst the boys buttered thick slices of rye bread. Cans of pop and packets of crisps finished the meal. Fortified and keeping a watchful eye for any followers, they returned to town to meet Riku at the arcade, as Jenni had arranged before speaking to her mother that morning.

Telling him it was no different from the laser shooting game Qwelby had happily played on New Year's Eve, Hannu persuaded the alien to have a go at the shooting games.

Shooting at targets was fine but when it came to soldiers and the gory sight of blood spurting from their bodies, it was all horrifyingly real for a boy from what had always been a non-violent world. As he explained when he stopped, the laser game in the woods on New Year's Eve had only been shooting at targets and the flash of light and screech of a hit was fun. No-one was hurt.

They returned to playing the fruit machines and, as before, everyone won a small amount and Qwelby claimed a jackpot. 'More jackpots and I leave Saturday,' he said with a grim smile whilst his mind tried to grapple with the idea that he was a Warrior who was unable to fight a real battle.

Back home and the four youngsters again piled into the sauna.

Dried and dressed they had started to answer the two mothers' questions about their day when Johan came home. Hearing a babble of voices as he entered the house, he stepped into the living room where he was confronted by everyone talking at once. He restored order and bit by bit the youngsters explained the day's events.

'You've got to leave,' Johan stated bluntly into what had become a tense silence. 'I can't have this Professor and the police following my family around.'

Elsa bit her lip and glanced apologetically at her friend.

'No. Those people. All of them are after me. I must go.' With an effort, Qwelby contained himself, remembering he was on Azura. To say that he could see Johan's fear was the sort of thing he had learnt was not acceptable. On Vertazia no-one would have to say anything like that. Everybody would be able to see the colours and vibrations in his energy field.

'Lainio!' Jenni exclaimed.

All heads turned towards her. 'I've been trying to persuade Dad to take us to the snow castle at Kemi. It's not open yet but Lainio is. If you've got to get away, why not go there? It must be just as fantastic even if it's not so large. We could all go and hide from these nasty people. Take a taxi to the airport, leave your car here, they'll never know where we've gone!'

'No, no, young lady. You have to go to school. And you,' Johan added as he looked at his son.

'I cannot afford that,' Seija said with a sorrowful look at Qwelby.

'It'll be fully booked.' Elsa said.

It was the definite tone in Elsa's voice as if slamming a door that struck Qwelby. 'I try something,' the alien said, getting up. 'Hannu, Jenni, you help?' He smiled and led the way up to his room. There, Qwelby asked them to sit on his bed, hold hands and think of him so he could borrow their energy and journey... "Out there."

'You mean explore, like the quantum stuff they teach as at school?' Jenni asked.

Qwelby nodded. 'The quantum world, the sub quantum world, underlie the whole of all the universes, the multiverse. They're very difficult to reach here in the slower vibrations of the third dimension, so I forget.' He grinned and held out his hands. 'Now, I remember.'

Later, when Qwelby squeezed the others' hands and they opened their eyes he smiled at the amazed looks on both their faces. 'Kabona. Umganerimiti. Thank you, my friends,' he said, translating the Tazian. 'I saw a rowing boat gliding along an underground river.' He turned to Hannu. 'Like in the tunnel under the Old Palace in Jyväskylä.'

'But you said that didn't go anywhere,' Hannu protested.

'We have to make this one go,' Qwelby replied.

'By phoning Lainio!' an excited Jenni exclaimed.

A few minutes later Seija used her mobile to call reception at Lainio and reported that they were fully booked.

'We wait and see what the multiverse will do,' Qwelby said to his disappointed friends. 'There is no time in the quantum worlds.'

Five minutes after the call to Lainio had finished, GCHQ in Cheltenham, England sent messages to Langley, Lubyanka Square and Suojelupoliisi HQ in Punavuori, Helsinki, where the joint command had been established. The message was simple – the telephone number of reception at Lainio. Thirty minutes later the only quantum computer in the world totally dedicated to interception provided the text of the call "with a ninety percent probability." GCHQ fowarded that to the same destinations.

CHAPTER 17

PUZZLES

SIILINJÄRVI-FINLAND

In his hotel room, Romain was idly glancing through the photographs in the Land of a Thousand Lakes book which he'd bought in the bookshop whilst keeping an eye on the youngsters. He was a brilliant scientist and now knew he was a very poor spy. Hannu had produced a RonaldSonQ. That model was very expensive and not available through normal mobile providers. If he'd been thinking clearly he'd have pinged the phone, bypassing the otherwise impenetrable security, and thus enabling him to record calls to his own phone. He would also have been able to activate the locator. Now, he had to wait for one of them to call him to do all that.

The boy having a RonaldsonQ was a puzzle. He didn't consider it significant but he didn't like loose ends and there was too much "weird" surrounding what he believed to be the alien. At least he had the identification number and could trace its history from his database on Raiatea.

Romain was certain he knew where the youngsters were staying. As he'd rounded a corner, they'd not been in sight. The suburb was very open and he'd been able to see a long way, meaning they had to have gone into one of the four houses in the short stretch of road facing him. Alongside the first house a snow covered Volvo CXR100 was parked to the side of the driveway, which had been cleared of snow. He assumed it was the Rahkamo's car and had made a note of the number. He might check with Erki. He might not. The less he involved that unsavoury youth the better.

But he had his uses. Erki had been able to tell Romain that the Rahkamos' friends lived in the Ahmo area. Backing a hunch that Qwelby and his friends would go skating, Romain had settled into the Café Konditoria on Kasurilantie. Just as he was beginning to wonder if it was a waste of time and could he drink any more coffee, he'd been relieved to see the trio walking by.

The man of the pair who'd been following him was the same man who'd been on the ski slopes the weekend that Soininen, the Private Investigator he'd hired, was there. The PI had said he was certain the man was an agent for the Finnish intelligence service, the Suojelupoliisi,

On the Saturday of that weekend, he and those two men had been skiing the same slopes as the boy and his friends. On the Sunday, Romain had skied different routes away from the youngsters and the PI. The supposed agent had been skiing the same routes as himself, and it was the same man who had been in the car by the bridge when Romain had met Erki. The conclusion was simple: the agent was following him. Why? My questions around Kotomäki. Did they see me meet the boy and his friends? I must be very careful.

Taking a small bottle of Chardonnay from the fridge, he poured some into a glass, took a large sip and let it swill around in his mouth. As the mixture of cold yet soft sharpness settled him, he thought back to his conversation with Dr Keskinen and once again about the blatant fiction concerning Dr Jadrovitch. Why?

Because he had been in a desperate hurry, Keskinen had thought of something that was close to the truth – a link amongst scientists? If the boy was not an alien but escaping from some deep plot his family was embroiled in, having him kidnapped...

In spite of Keskinen's laughing denial, I must talk to the boy and be sure one way or another. If he is what I believe him to be, I will give him the chance to agree to accompany me to my laboratory on Raiatea. If he is not willing and I go with previous thoughts and have him kidnapped? Right now I have to hope my guess about Miki's Doctoral thesis is correct and that will give me the strong hold I might need over her and her husband. Two bridges to cross, one at a time.

Romain continued to savour the wine whilst planning his next actions, including sending an update to his assistants on Raiatea and a request for more information about the boy's RonaldSonQ.

CHAPTER 18

ATONEMENT

THE KALAHARI

Warm, comfortable and still half asleep with a head resting on her chest under the blankets, Tullia wondered why it was so dark. And where is the other one of my twins? A little light was coming into the room from the floor. She lifted her head and saw that it came from the bottom of a large opening covered by something, and the bottom of that something was being kept away from the ground by a few sticks.

Memories flooded in and panic siezed through her. Very slowly she ran a hand down her body and between her legs. Her maleness remained safely inside and the swellings that had accompanied its emergence had completely subsided. She sighed with relief that her second Awakening had not turned her into a man overnight. In the frighteningly real Dreamstate from which she'd just awakened she had been herself in what she knew was her twin's body. Was that what had happened last night? A stronger version of the time they had been together in two places at once?

He'd said he was Awakening. Now she knew that for them it was in two stages she wondered how far he'd gone. As she tried to reach out to him with reassurance she was disturbed by her baby twin moving. She lifted the blanket. Of course it was not one of her twins, but Kou-'ke. And *I don't have twins!*

'Oh, ho, little QeïchâKaïgii?'

Leave me alone. I've got a lot of thinking to do, she thoughtspoke the annoying and now chuckling voice.

She slipped into Xashee's mind and found him in a tortured sleep. She froze as a memory surfaced. *It meant death for a man to look on a woman during the Moon Day celebration!*

Forcing herself to relax, she focussed her mind and replayed her internal video. *Xashee first saw me when I was running with my back to him. Good. Identical twins. We look the same from behind.* She licked her lips and swallowed. *A careful choice of words and he saw me-as-Kaigii. Well... I was. I think. But me? A woman who leaves the sacred space is ejected from the tribe. But a man who is within the sacred space faces death. The timing of my change into me-as-Kaigii must be exact if we both are to live.*

Kou-'ke stirred, opened her eyes and tried to push herself away, but tangled in blankets and with one of Tullia's hands trapped under her, she was stuck. 'I was cold,' she snapped, angry at herself. After a few moments of struggling, she got free, rolled out onto the floor, grabbed a blanket and wrapped it around herself as she stood up.

'I will kill you if Xashee dies,' Kou-'ke snarled. But her voice lacked venom. It was all her fault. She should've killed the man-stealing bitch when she had the chance. She had given in to her despair and had slept badly. Had awoken wanting to kill Tullia while she slept, but lacked a weapon and was too stiff from cold because Neame had provided only two blankets. She had got into bed intending to wake up later when warm and suffocate the big, ugly, murdering whore.

'He did not see me.' *In a way that is true,* Tullia thoughtspoke her twin.

'Lying bitch!'

'He only thought he saw me.' *Well...*

'You left the sacred area!'

'Yes, but...'

'He saw you!'

'No. He saw a man.' *Sorry, Kaigii. Depends on your definition.*

'What?' Kou-'ke's voice rose in incredulity.

'Sit!' Tullia swung her legs around as she gestured to Kou-'ke who sat at the far end of the bed. 'When a Meera girl has her first period she becomes a woman. For my people it is when the mouth to her woman's place opens. We call that Awakening. Until our hormones make that happen, a girl's body cannot have sex.'

'I didn't know.'

'No.'

'I assumed...'

'Yes.'

'We all thought... And at the Melon Dance...'

'Yes. Ungka told me. Yesterday!'

'But Xashee? You're a woman.'

'I am an identical twin. A boy has his Awakening when his male organs emerge out of his body. That is what happened to me last night. That is why I ran through the trees. By the time I was in the valley I was a man.' She impressed on Kou-'ke's mind an image of her twin, overstating the size of his manhood. *Sorry, Kaigii, but...* She thoughtadded a smile. From what she'd learnt yesterday, he might like that.

'I stayed hidden for a long time until I changed back.' Tullia rose, dropping the blanket from around her shoulders and using her hands to flatten her breasts. *A little deception. I don't want her to ask and have to tell an outright lie. But for a while... I thought... I did lose sight of them...*

'He'll know I attacked you. He'll never want me.'

'Explain to him.'

'Why didn't you kill me!'

'I cannot. It would mean total removal from the Cycle Of Life. And would destroy my twin.'

Kou-'ke slowly shook her head.

'Peace between us?'

'You tell truth and Xashee lives.'

'They will believe the Daughter of the Sun Goddess.'

Kou-'ke nodded. She'd become so focussed on seeing Tullia as an overlarge, ugly, man-stealing bitch, she'd forgotten who she really was.

'Right. Let's go do it.' Tullia swung round and picked up her new loinskin. 'I've got one for you to wear. You leant it to me.' She threw it across.

'That's only for celebrations.'

'We are celebrating. A peaceful end to our Moon Day.'

Kou-'ke nodded grimly, untied the extension to the waistband that she'd added for Tullia, and tied the band around her waist.

'What's that?' Kou-'ke asked, pointing at Tullia's loinskin with its letter "O" drawing attention to her woman's place and then a letter "T", which surely represented the male organs.

'This is the first letter of Kaigii's name, !wel'by, Tullia explained as she ran a finger around the letter Q. 'And this is T for Tullia, or Tyua'llia.'

'You stupid, stupid bitch!' Kou-'ke yelled as she strode up to Tullia and hammered her fists on the big woman's breasts.

'What in all The Shades!' Tullia exclaimed as she gripped her attacker's arms and stopped the onslaught.

'Don't you see? You're showing you've dedicated your womanhood to your twin. Oh why didn't you wear this before! Stupid, stupid...'

Tullia was staring in disbelief. All she had done was to decorate her loinskin in pleasing patterns that fitted the different shapes front and back, affirmed the at-one-ment with her twin she was desperate to restore and celebrated their BestFriends. Explanations tumbling through her mind were stopped as she saw an advantage, a big advantage to such a ridiculous misunderstanding. Grimacing at the deception and once again thoughtsending her Twin an apology she said 'Now you know and so will everyone.'

She took hold of one corner of the blanket covering the opening and gestured to Kou-'ke who reluctantly took hold of the other corner. As they stepped out into the midday sun Tullia took hold of Kou-ke's hand and heard a collective gasp run though the tribe.

Apart from the women, none of them knew of the fight and were startled to see the several bright pink lines across Tullia's arms and her belly and another down Kou-ke's chest. Drawing the obvious conclusion, Tullia heard the men's soft murmuring. She had not fought as an invincible Goddess but as a woman – a Meera woman.

The acknowledgment and the acceptance by all the tribe gave her strength. She stood erect, pulled her shoulders back and took a deep breath, but that did not stop the hot flush that started at her face and spread all the way down to her belly as she heard their thoughts that her loinskin was saying she wanted a man there. Not just any man, but by All The Shades, her twin!

She glanced to where Deena was sitting with Kou-'ke's mother, then across to Neame. As the two young women started walking towards Neame, Tullia pointedly used her eyes to indicate Ghadi and Kotuma.

Sensing Kou-'ke's gaze, Tullia looked to where Xashee was sitting between his father and a grandfather. There was a look of shock and horror on his face as he deduced what had happened. He dropped his hand to his thigh where he bore the faint scar from the healing that Tullia had given him that had saved him from bleeding to death after he'd saved her life. Tullia tightened her grip on Kou-'ke's hand as the young woman stumbled, preventing her from falling.

All five arrived at the Chief's hut at the same time as Xameb and Tsetsana, summoned by the Chief. The newcomers sat at his gesture, except for Tullia who dropped to her knees, crossed her hands over her two hearts and lowered her forehead to the ground. Lifting up, she settled back on her heels as the others had done.

Deliberately pitching her voice low so that it carried throughout the tribe, she explained. 'I am sorry, Great Chief. I did not know. When I came here I was desperate to be accepted as what I was, in my world, a child. A child with no interest in boys except as friends. The night of the firefight I kissed not H'ani, but Kaigii in... an in-between world.' Blushing she glanced at the tribe's Shaman.

Xameb nodded his understanding. 'Starting your Awakening.'

Tullia nodded, then repeated what she had said to Kou-'ke. That she had left the sacred space as a woman and by the time she was well clear of that and seen by Xashee she had become a man. *I really thought I was you, Kaigii.*

Ghadi told the two young women to return to their families. Seven pairs of eyes focussed on a very tall human figure with long black hair walking away from them. Identical twins. They were easily watching a handsome man. As the figure reached a hut, turned to the side and sat down, a woman was with her family.

The murmuring around the tribe died away and there was palpable tension in the ensuing silence.

Ghadi leant across to Xameb.

'I saw him clearly that night during the fight around the fire,' the Shaman said in a voice so low it did not carry past the group around the chief. 'Similar build. Same face. Identical eyes. Long black hair.'

Ghadi grunted. He did not have the same degree of sight but that also had been his impression. He looked around at a sea of faces staring at him. In his heart he was certain that with Tullia's extravagant gesture of submission she was saying that for this she was Meera and he her Chief. It was his decision alone. He stood up.

'Xashee did not see !Gei-!ku'ma. He saw !Kwe-!ku'gn.'

The tribe heard the sob that escaped Kou-'ke's lips.

Ghadi held up a hand. 'When Xashee told me what he'd seen. Or thought he'd seen. He did so with his hand on his heart.' A ripple of murmurings ran through the tribe. 'Xashee is a true warrior.'

The men whooped and the women ululated in celebration.

Ghadi sat and leant across to speak with Neame.

'Tyua'llia,' Neame called out,

Tullia rose and walked up to her, with hands clenched so tight her nails were cutting into her palms. *If they only throw me out of the tribe, at least I will have a chance of finding another tribe who might take me in.*

'Tyua'llia. You left the sacred space.' Neame glanced to where a group of the oldest women were sitting. She saw softness in their faces. 'You will be taken into the bush.' Neame slowly looked around the whole tribe, seeing the tension in their faces. 'You will not be seen or heard by anyone before the sun sets tomorrow.' There was a collective sigh of relief and the slightest of nods from Tu.

Tullia stared, her mind a whirl.

'You may take with you one item. Spear, knife or bow and arrow. Choose,' Ghadi said.

Surely that was not her punishment? Wild animals aplenty, but...

'Tyua'llia!'

'Err...' She replayed the Chief's words. 'A...' She swallowed. 'Knife.'

'Choose.'

'Err...' *'Get a grip!'* her mind said. She took a deep breath. 'The one I killed the kudu with.'

As if her answer had been expected, Xara walked up and handed it to her. She gave him the briefest of nods.

When Tullia emerged from her hut a few minutes later, once again her own necklace was completely covered in dark brown cloth and she was wearing the plain loincloth that Nlai had worn for the hunt, with an extended waistband added to it.

Xara held up a thick scarf and tied it around her head. She felt him take her hand and lead her away. From time to time he stopped, gripped her shoulders and spun her around until she was dizzy. From the hot sun on her body she continued to calculate the heading each time she was guided along.

She smiled to herself. Xara would expect that of her as a Bushman but did not know that it was natural for any Tazian to learn at a very early age how to navigate by the sun. Finally, the scarf was removed and Xara handed her the knife. He took a pace back and gave her a long, appraising look, nodded then turned and soon was lost to sight in the bush.

Tullia remained standing for a long time staring at the spot where Xara had disappeared. Trembling legs gave way and she collapsed to the ground. A wry smile crossed her face as she wondered. Quantum Twins. Had she really changed into - if not him - what? His brother?

'Hmmmm, QeïchâKaïgïi.' An image appeared of the two TwirlyPoles that linked their attic suite at home with the main house merging into one.

Breathing deeply, she settled down in the hot sun for a heart to heart talk with herself. A glance at the sun, a check with her internal clock, a rerun of the path she had taken and she knew in which direction the village lay. Her immediate plans were simple.

First, she would choose a stand of trees with thick sand for a comfortable bed in a semi-enclosed area which she would protect with cut down thornbushes - after checking for scorpions or any other inhabitants.

Next, she would dig up maramas, white, juicy, potato like tubers, to provide her food and water, and then for additional taste and nutriments pick the scarce winter berries. Finally, she would add to her shelter as many branches as possible with their desiccated winter leaves for cover against the cold night.

Later, having lit a small fire just as the sun sank below the horizon, she sat cross legged on the sand, so thick it felt like a cushion, and examined the fist sized stone she'd discovered as she'd been impelled to dig for maramas in what had to be the wrong place. The stone was vibrating and filling her mind with images of Auriga, the world her people had left over one hundred and fifteen thousand years ago. Images so real it was as though they were her own memories.

Needing to focus on the present, she eventually set it down and breathed in the faint apple smell of the almost imperceptible smoke and reflected on her almost two tendays on Earth. She'd learnt a lot from the Meera, a lot about herself and extended her own Tazian skills. She'd had disturbing insights into life on Vertazia, very different from what she'd been taught, believed or experienced. Because she was a youngster? Because she was shielded by her loving family? Or because the falsity could only be seen from outside and because of the reaction to her and Kaigii being what they were? That voice smiling in her head without speaking any words was such a Tazian normality that she knew her last thought had been correct.

'I'm not a Bushman,' she confided to the flames of her little fire. 'I'm a Tazian with Bushman skills, Healer and Warrior genes.' She looked up at the great snake of the Milky Way, imagining that Vertazia was there. 'I need Kaigii. I don't need Kaigii. Kaigii plus Kaigii makes Kaigii. I could live forever here as long as we are one. But I, we, can't. We must go home and tell the truth about life on two worlds and because......'

Energies stirred within her newly awakened genes and again the confusing sensation arose of wanting to nurture her own twins – a boy and a girl...?

'Ahhhh… QeïchâKaïgïi. Such beautiful memories.'

CHAPTER 19

SWEET DREAMS

SIILINJÄRVI-FINLAND

After dinner, the four youngsters went up to Riku's room for another gaming session. From there they heard the doorbell, then Mr Korpijaakko's voice raised in anger as he harangued Romain for accosting the children and told him in no uncertain terms that if it were to happen again the police would be contacted. The door slammed shut.

Qwelby got stuck into games-play with gusto. It was good being with friends and putting aside any thought of all the other stuff that was going on. Four people made for a squash. A comfortable squash as, when he and Jenni looked over the shoulders of Riku and Hannu as they played, it was natural for each to put an arm around the other. Qwelby squeezed her waist and she rested her head on his shoulder.

It was late when Seija's mobile chimed and she confirmed that she was the Mrs Rahkamo who had telephoned a few hours ago. When the call ended she sat for a few moments staring at her phone in disbelief before looking at her friend.

'There's been a last minute cancellation. The manager said it's not worth his while trying to contact people on the waiting list at such short notice. He's checked and there are vacancies on tomorrow morning's flight which is why he's called me. We can go to Lainio for five nights. For free! Well, except for a small administrative charge.'

'Amazing, but how?' Elsa asked.

'Cancellation so late Lainio doesn't make a refund. But as it's due to ill health the family who'd booked will be covered by the insurance built into the holiday package.'

'Nice for you. But what about school time?'

'I'll have to talk with Paavo. But.' She smiled. 'First, I'll book the flights. There's something about that young... man that... Well he just seems to attract... I don't know what. People. Things. Happenings.'

A few minutes later when Seija put her head around the door to Riku's room to say that the three of them were to leave soon after breakfast the following day to fly to Lainio, her news was greeted with a mixture of joy, sadness and envy.

Qwelby was surprised at how disappointed he was that Jenni would not be going with them. He knew that after Awakening all Tazii were driven to explore their new hormones but hadn't expected that to happen so soon. It was very unsettling. He didn't feel ready. Yet he liked the sensations she stirred in him and wanted more.

All too soon Mrs Korpijaakko was calling out that it was bedtime.

There was an awkward moment on the landing saying goodnight as Qwelby and Jenni just stood looking at each other.

In bed with the duvet pulled up to his shoulders against the cool air, Qwelby remained sitting up as he listened to the noises die away until all was quiet. He knew Jenni wanted a goodnight kiss as much as he did. Mentally feeling for her, he knew she was not asleep. Would he be heard if he went down to her room and knocked on her door? Could he mentally alert her and then just walk into her room? He remembered what she had said about not being allowed to have a boy in her room with the door closed.

He was staring at his door in indecision when it opened and Jenni's head poked round. She smiled, entered and quietly closed the door.

'It's cold in here.'

'Yes. No heating.' He reached for her and their lips met.

Jenni shivered. Her lightweight pale blue dressing gown and nightie were designed for hot Finnish houses. 'It's freezing.'

'Come and get warm.'

Jenni had dropped her latest boyfriend because he kept on pestering her for sex. She liked him but didn't love him. He'd never said that he loved her. She wanted better than that for her first time. She gave Qwelby a long hard look. They had spent a lot of time in each other's arms in her room the previous night and he hadn't tried anything on. Then she'd been disappointed, but now... She shivered again.

Qwelby lifted a corner of the duvet and Jenni slid in. He wrapped his arms around her, they kissed and Qwelby became embarrassed as he grew hot and his body reacted to being pressed against her.

He winced. Then a little cry escaped him as pain stabbed though his loins. The kissing stopped and a concerned Jenni questioned him as more pains struck. He needed his twin, or really Tamina who'd achieved her Awakening a few moons before they'd left Vertazia. But... Jenni was there, holding him and caring for him.

He found himself telling her how boys and girls looked the same between their legs until their Awakening. For him that had been six days ago when his organs had emerged from his body. For a girl, it was when her LoveMouth opened. Answering Jenni's questions he was amazed to discover that an Azuran girl produced an egg every month. Jenni was fascinated by the idea of a girl's body only having to produce an egg when she wanted a baby.

He explained his big fear was that with identical genes, his well developed pectorals might grow and produce PassionMilk and he'd turn into a girl. His twin's fear was that she'd end up looking like him.

His pains increased and talking stopped as Jenni held him close, reassuring him that she was holding a big strong man in her arms.

Finally, breaking out in sweat all over, he groaned as fierce pain spiralled up his spine, spreading out through the whirling wheels of his power centres into his belly and chest and finally into his head. As the pain eased, something deep inside told him that all the changes had finished. 'What's happened?'

Surprised at being so calm, Jenni slid her hand down his body. 'You're still a man.' She slid her hand further back between his legs. 'Your... LoveMouth has opened.'

'My male bits. They're all right?'

'Oh, yeah.'

'Jenni,' Qwelby sighed. Exhausted and aching all over, he cuddled up to her and fell asleep.

Dizzy, hot, disappointed, relieved, Jenni ran her fingers through his long hair, watching the green lights flickering as she explored the weird sensation that she had just given birth to an alien baby boy-girl.

Waking in the morning, he stretched and soaked in the new feelings running through his body and mind. Ever since his Awakening, 'My first Awakening,' he corrected himself, there had been a niggling awareness at the back of his mind that something was missing. That feeling was gone. He was happy at the change with what he thought of as his Inner Tullia firmly in place. And he was still a man.

Tullia had thoughtshared she was Awakening. He was filled with an urge that was stronger than ever to be with her and reassure her that after both stages she would still be herself. Yet different.

He felt much more vibrant and in a way he was unable to describe, more himself. That was good. Why, was all part of The Mystery of Quantum Twins that he and Tullia had to solve.

Hearing noises and checking with his internal clock, he leapt out of bed, flung his clothes on and rushed downstairs. There, he sat at the breakfast table feeling awkward and exchanging glances with Jenni as they ate, neither daring to speak in case they let anything slip about the previous night.

Not soon enough for his liking she got up to finish getting ready for school. He followed her into her room and quietly closed the door.

'I woke up. You were gone. I missed you. I...'

Jenni's lips stopped any more words.

'Jenni!' her mother called.

'You look like Tullia with your hair loose,' Jenni said as the kissing stopped.

Standing there, holding hands and staring into her eyes, his heart was racing, his head pounding and he knew he was sweating. He would never see her again. What words to say?

'Be careful,' she said. 'Look after that soft inside.'

'Jenni! You'll be late,' her mother called again.

Letting go his hands, Jenni turned and looked at herself in the mirror. 'Look what you've done!' she exclaimed as she grabbed a brush and quickly ran it through her hair before putting it down and picking up her bag.

Qwelby smiled. He knew all about girls and their hair and waited for the thump that Tullia usually gave him.

Slinging her bag over her shoulder, Jenni opened the door.

'You heartswarm me,' Qwelby blurted out, wishing he knew what words the Azurii used. He saw tears start in Jenni's eyes as she turned back, grabbed his arms and gave him a quick kiss.

He stood there feeling sad and happy. She'd understood his meaning. And he'd got a kiss. Grabbing a rubber band from Jenni's chest of drawers, he tied his hair back into what had become his usual pony tail and ran downstairs to find Riku just about to step outside and join his sister. The two boys embraced and Riku wished him all the best for the future. Inside, Qwelby was one, big, aching, empty space. He forced a smile on his face and lifted a hand in salute to Jenni as Riku stepped outside and closed the door.

CHAPTER 20

HOMEWORK

SIILINJÄRVI-FINLAND

Qwelby, Hannu and Mrs Rahkamo left a few minutes later in a taxi. It meant a longer wait at the airport than necessary but everyone wanted to avoid another encounter with Professor Romain.

Sitting in the small café at the airport, Hannu said he was certain that no car had followed them. Qwelby called up the mental signatures of what they considered were the two police officers, searched and advised that there was no trace. They were neither very near him nor further away and focusing on him. Opening fully to his sensing, Qwelby then swept the café and declared that no-one was watching him with any particular intensity.

Hannu put an arm around his friend's shoulders and pulled him close. 'That's great. We can have a few days fun. Just the two of us.'

'I like that a lot. You very special to me.' Qwelby's sensing told him that Hannu would not welcome the sort of kiss that men on Vertazia shared, so he squeezed the hand that was on his shoulder.

Seija's mobile rang and she took the call. 'Good news,' she announced. 'That was Elsa. Professor Romain called at the house asking to speak with Qwelby.'

'What she did tell him?' Hannu asked anxiously.

'That she didn't know who he was and would not speak to him. As she closed the door, he thrust a business card at her and asked her to tell Qwelby he wished to speak with him.'

'We've got away!' Hannu exclaimed as he turned to Qwelby and they shared a high five.

The boys got up and went to stand at the windows. Sensing Qwelby's mood, Hannu put an arm around his friend. A few moments later Qwelby did the same and the two boys stood in companionable silence watching the occasional plane take off or land.

Once they were in the air, Qwelby declared it similar to being in the nearest Tazian equivalent, called an Isotor. All he could say was that it flew by balancing the lines of the planet's magnetic field with the descending gravity waves and utilising an electro-gravitronic jetstream effect, which Dr Keskinen had said Earth physicists knew as the Coandă effect in air and liquids.

When Hannu protested that gravity didn't work like that, rather than say that he was able to switch vision to see both the planet's magnetic field and the pattern of gravity waves, Qwelby settled for an agreement that gravity worked differently in different dimensions, then looked out of the window to enjoy the views as Finland passed beneath them.

He recalled what Mrs Rahkamo had said in the taxi on the way the airport. Although Romain had followed them to Siilinjärvi, she had assured Qwelby that there was no way he or anyone else could know that they were going to Lainio. She had then reminded Hannu that, as part of being allowed time off school, he was going to have to write an essay explaining what he had learnt during that time. And that did not include how to trick fruit machines!

'Yes it does!' Qwelby had said, laughing as he turned to Hannu. 'A statistical exercise. The percentage of markas that are diverted down the back of the machine as the owner's takings. The number and type of symbols on each wheel. The various statistical chances of individual wins. How many markas before the machine is full so a maximum jackpot can be won...'

'Whoa!' Hannu had exclaimed. 'I don't know how many symbols there are on a wheel.'

'I do. How you think I win?'

'But, how...'

'To prove it?'

'Yeah?'

Qwelby thought for a moment. 'You Azurii must have something like a very fast action camera. Lots of photos of several different machines and lots of spins.'

'But I don't...'

'Say you have a friend who has a Dad who has one... Riku.'

'Yeees, but...'

'The maths is easy. I've done all that. What you say? Sorted!'

Seija shook her head as the boys shared a high five.

Now, Qwelby left his brain to record what his eyes were seeing as the conversation reminded him of college. Until they became adults, every Tazian attended college one day out of every tenday. The first session of the day was always to hand in work completed since the previous visit, with a focus on what each one had chosen to learn and why. That set him to thinking about what he had learnt since leaving home twenty-five days ago and arriving on Earth eighteen days ago.

He was maturing much faster than at home, physically, mentally and emotionally, and so was Tullia. Along with that went greater power and skill at handling transdimensional energies. He was completely confident of fulfilling his plans to get money and travel to Tullia. No-one was going to prevent their total reconnection.

His first night in Siilinjärvi he'd fallen into despair at the thought that he was not strong enough to face what lay ahead. Then, he had put that behind him. Now, he knew he had the ability. Outscoring both Hannu and Riku on the shooting games and, without drawing on group energies, he had thoughtwrapped Jenni into seeing life on Vertazia through Tullia's eyes. 'I have the power,' he quietly addressed the forests and rivers far below.

He was fed up with running away, even if he called it a strategical retreat, and now no-one was following him. He muttered words in Tazian that would result in his having energy privileges removed for galaxies knew how long if his parents heard him. *I have warrior genes. It's impossible, yet I feel like I remember times when I was the Dragon Lord. And further back in time...*

'QeïchâKaïgïi,' that voice whispered in his head.

This time with the words in the Old Living Aurigan, came a tumbling series of images, colours and feelings. He was enjoying "being real" as he called it when speaking the Finnish he had learnt for himself and not using his compiler. Now, even without the Reduced Aurigan that his Great-Great Uncle Mandara had built into his compiler the message was clear.

He smiled at the phrase used by boys and girls on Vertazia. His hair had grown fast and was much longer than the shoulder length affected by most boys. He undid the band holding it in a pony tail and shook his head, letting his hair settle down to his shoulder blades, then turned to Hannu as he switched on his compiler.

'At home we have a saying, so, when we get to Lainio, I'm going to "tie my hair back and go do it,"' he said as he made the quotation marks with his fingers. 'Xzarze! It's about flaming time I stopped acting like a frightened scuttlemouse, accepted my warrior genes and had some fun. More than just undoing a pair of handcuffs! You up for some serious fun, Lamaannu?'

'Hell, yeah. BroQ,' Hannu replied as he was engulfed by the alien's excitement.

After his Awakening following the terrible transdimensional fight that Hannu and Anita had witnessed, Qwelby had needed to reach out to his friend in a special way but was too shocked to do more than call him "Taziaannu".

A boy's Awakening was very different to that of a girl's. The emergence of the male sex organs was a special occasion. For Qwelby as an identical twin, the confirmation of his masculinity had been a very powerful event. Happening eighteen months earlier than expected and in such a manner that he had had no forewarning had deepened his shock. Hannu had been there and had helped with what seemed like a birth.

As he had explained to Hannu, had his Awakening taken place on Vertazia he would have had time to prepare and, as well as his father, Pelnak and Wrenden would have been with him. When he'd recovered from the shock he'd decided that he wanted to do more than acknowledge Hannu as AlienFriend. Delighted at the name of Lamaannu, meaning "Brother Hannu", Hannu had said that "Brother Qwelby" was too much of a mouthful, so he'd call him "BroQ", pronouncing the "Q" as a "K".

Sharing a high five in the aeroplane was a bit awkward so, grinning all over their faces, they settled for a knuckle punch, Qwelby remembering at the last moment to slow down the speed of his fist.

Sitting across the aisle, Seija smiled at their enthusiasm. Whatever problems Qwelby had been causing between her son and his girlfriend, she was happy at how Hannu was rapidly maturing, especially since Qwelby had arrived. Her son's days of shyness and awkward, bumbling speech were gone. She was certain that, once back home and without Qwelby around, the problems that had arisen between Hannu and Anita would soon fade away.

Arriving at the airport in Kittilä they picked up the Volvo V45R that Mrs Rahkamo had hired for the short drive to the Snow Village. Some twenty minutes later the trees parted to reveal a stunning view. They were looking down two double rows of chalets, set wide apart and narrowing further away like a curved funnel, drawing their eyes to the far end where the Snow Hotel and Ice Bar were sparkling in the bright sun.

The following day when they visited the hotel they were to discover that one and a half million kilos of snow and three hundred thousand kilos of crystal clear natural ice had been used in their construction.

'We've nothing like this at home,' Qwelby was to say, shaking his head. 'For all our technical advances there's more fun on Earth than on my world. I'll persuade Gumma to make an addition to Lungunu's programming. It will look totally real.' The experience was to add to his growing list of what he considered was wrong with his world and remind him of what his Great-Great-Aunt Lellia had said about the declining state of his race, the overall lack of energy and innovation.

Mrs Rahkamo pulled up outside a large chalet that was marked as the main office. They got out of the car and Hannu opened the door to Reception for his mother. Looking around, Qwelby nodded to himself, removed his shades, put his hair back into his usual pony tail and walked to the door. Hannu stepped inside and tried to close the door before Qwelby got there. The two boys struggled with the door until Qwelby lurched back, surprised. Seeing the puzzled look on his friend's face, he smiled and shook his head as he tapped the fingers of one hand against his temple.

Hannu nodded, understanding that his alien friend had switched off his mental searching. "Being real" as he called it, he had not detected Hannu's intention to let go of the handle.

The walls of the Reception were a pale blue and the furniture the ubiquitous light coloured pine. Behind the counter, with its imitation stone top, a conservatively dressed middle-aged man and woman were standing in conversation with another middle-aged woman.

The woman was of average height and build and casually dressed like most folk Qwelby had seen in a parka, trousers and fur lined boots. But there was something about the way she was holding herself and the energy dynamic of the threesome that told Qwelby she was not a relaxed tourist. It seemed that she was trying to sort out a problem with the accommodation.

Mrs Rahkamo was standing at the counter, completing the registration process with another man. Qwelby looked around with a touch of disappointment. Although with fair complexions, everyone in sight had either dark or light brown hair and brown eyes. Where were all the blonde haired, blue-eyed people he was used to seeing around Kotomäki and Jyväskylä?

A door behind the counter opened and a young woman appeared. Smartly dressed in a long-sleeved white blouse, black trousers and shoes, she had blue eyes and long blonde hair falling below her shoulders. As she came around the side of the counter Qwelby realised he was staring. She was so much like an older and bigger built version of Jenni. Embarrassed, he smiled and wondered why she blushed, completely unaware of the effect of his bright eyes and slightly lop-sided smile.

'Welcome to Lainio,' she said. 'My name is Viivi and I'm the manageress. The man talking with Mrs Rahkamo is Irro, the assistant manager. He is explaining that the holiday that was cancelled was a fully-inclusive package, all tours and entertainments included. But we do need you to book in advance as many of them have limited numbers.' She handed several leaflets to Hannu. 'I'm sure you'll find lots to do. For this evening.' She flashed a smile at Qwelby as she handed him a leaflet. 'I really do recommend the Sleigh Ride.'

'Kabona. Thank you,' Qwelby said softy as, free from the restraints of anyone following or watching him, he let his eyes twinkle and enjoyed the sensation of the still new stirrings caused by looking into the eyes of an attractive girl. He guessed she was about his Earth equivalent age of seventeen and a half and liked the rosy flush that deepened on her cheeks.

Registration concluded, Mrs Rahkamo joined the boys and decisions were soon made for several tours and events, with Seija happy to leave the boys to go clay pigeon shooting and Snow Karting by themselves.

The woman talking with the couple left the office and the man and woman stepped around the counter. 'I'm Mr Perälä and this is my wife.' They shook hands all round. 'We're two of the owners. We're very happy to welcome you to Lainio and do hope you'll enjoy your stay with us. We'd like to invite you to a small reception in the Ice Bar this evening before the Sleigh Ride and to meet the other guests who arrived today.'

'An unusual name, Mr Sofuoğlu,' Mrs Perälä said. 'I hope I have the pronunciation correct.'

'Please call me Qwelby,' he replied and spelt it out.

'So that's the man the Ministry is interested in,' Mrs Perälä said as the door closed behind Seija and the boys. 'But where the devil does he come from? And those eyes!'

'Would have helped if the Ministry had been correct about who was coming,' Viivi said as she turned to Mr Perälä. 'You said they told you it was a Mr and Mrs Rahkamo. I naturally assumed it was husband and wife so left the usual two double beds in the chalet.'

'Mrs Rahkamo was not bothered about the boys sharing a bed. She was only too happy that she only had to pay a small admin charge,' Irro said.

'Yes. Cancelling three holiday bookings is not good,' Mr Perälä said. 'But I've made the Ministry pay through the teeth for that. Charged them for well overpriced all-inclusive holidays plus heavy compensation for unhappy clients. We had quite a row when they telephoned the second time wanting three more cancellations. I refused to make it for a single official and insisted she had one of the staff rooms. Viivi. You'll see that our two girls who are having to share are all right?'

Viivi nodded. She was already looking forward to the reception that evening and the opportunity to get to know the tall handsome young man with the compelling eyes.

CHAPTER 21

ROMAIN ACTS

SWITZERLAND

Romain had timed his visit to where Qwelby was staying on the basis that the man, and hopefully his wife, would be at work and their children at school. He was taken aback by the vehemence of the woman's response and lying denial. He had already noted that the same Volvo was parked alongside the house, leaving the driveway clear for the family's car. The boy was still in Siilinjärvi.

Discreetly followed by Metsälä, Romain drove back to his hotel wondering why so many diverse people were sheltering the boy. Everything he was doing appeared to indicate that he had a hold over them. So why had Keskinen agreed to recommend a meeting? Ah. That suggested the boy's influence only worked when he was near the people concerned. Logical, and he needed to be very careful when close to the boy.

As Romain had returned the previous evening from his abortive journey he had caught a glimpse of the same policewoman in the hotel. Why were the police following him? And what if his interest in the boy made them focus on him? If he was an alien, why after more than two weeks had he not been rescued? The ghost image. Rescue was not possible without the "lifebelt" in Africa?

Romain nodded to himself. It all made sense. His own

enquiries around the electromagnetic disturbances had resulted in the authorities being interested in him. Although the boy was still in Siilinjärvi, Romain had to stay away from him. He would speak with Dr Keskinen again. Meanwhile......

Back in his room he took a deep breath, looked at a receptor on his GlobeSynch and a moment later was speaking with Franz Shosta. How Franz had ever managed to be a senior maintenance engineer at CERN for so many years when his skills seemed to lie much more in that area of life that bordered on, or dived into, the illegal, was a puzzle.

To the surprise of his fellow scientists the two had become good friends. Franz was an excellent engineer with a surprising interest in philosophy. Romain had been delighted to discover that Franz had an interest in the then newly emerging Noetic Science. Challenged over a beer as to how he could square that interest with his illegal activities, Franz's answer had been, like the man, an amalgam. "Consciousness, superconsciousness exist. Thoughts are powerful. People's thoughts act upon me and I supply the services they think they need."

Arrangements made to meet later that night at Bar Minge in Geneva, Romain felt a nervous shiver run through his body. Whatever his plans had been, they had been just that, thoughts of future action. Now he was committing himself. He felt sweat break out on his forehead and his hands became sticky with sweat.

Bar Minge was run by Pierre Kovich. He knew that neither man's surname was genuine. Taken from the surname of the famous Russian composer, Shostakovich, it was their way of saying that they had each other's backs.

CHAPTER 22

HUNTED

THE KALAHARI

Tullia woke just before the sun rose on her full day in the bush by herself. As the first edge of its orange disk rose above the horizon, as a Bushman she greeted its fiery presence and silently thanked the Mother for giving Life. Her Aurigan genes greeted the effulgent orb of salamanders of Šem-eš-a, The Shining One, who she called sister.

Clarity!

All the thoughts and wonderings that she'd packaged for herself to dream on were answered.

She knew that no event was ever truly random. All could be explained. Even human events tracked back to the "bits" of data that in-formed the inevitable result. She felt tension drain from her whole Self as she accepted that her own and her twin's departure from Vertazia and their arrival on Earth, she in the bush, and her twin as Xameb believed at the southernmost end of the Americas, was not an accident, but in the quantum sense, predetermined.

There would be fighting on Vertazia. Her knife fight with Kou-'ke had awakened her Warrior genes but she wanted to be and was, a healer. Back home she would need to find and train youngsters to be healers and find - how? - young Unicorns for them to ride in partnership. And once again be in the thick of battle alongside her beloved twin, attending to the wounded and defending herself and her healers.

By midmorning, content with her understanding of why she was where she was and that all her experiences were for a future purpose, she was settled on the sunny side of another small cluster of trees a good distance away from her night-time home. She had adopted the lotus position for a deep meditation and was focusing on the almost imperceptible sounds of the bush when the sound of a lorry intruded. Puzzled, because she had carefully chosen both locations well away from any tracks used for tourists, she moved cautiously and looked through the cover of the trees to see the normal open-backed lorry with its raked seating carrying tourists.

It was a long distance away, near where Xara had left her. It slowed and a figure dropped off. Picking up a little speed the lorry drove on, slowed and another figure dropped off, the man facing her as he landed. Although still far away she recognised one of the hunters. Focusing, she saw at least two more Meera in the back with the tourists. Hunters. She shivered.

Of course a night and a day by myself in the bush is neither a punishment nor a challenge. I'm now being hunted. If seen…? I may only be a pretend Bushman but I am a Tazian and will use my seventh sense. She flicked to her twin's corner of her mind. Nothing had changed. He was there but there was no contact.

'I have my own and strong Warrior genes,' she told the wide expanse of the bush.

'Ahhhh, QeïchâKaïgii.'

This time the irritating voice carried a sense of reassurance. More than that, Tullia saw that being her Tyua'llia self was an important part of her and as a Quantum Twin, their futures. Tullia-Tyua'llia spent the rest of her day in barely controlled terror, playing HideNSeek for what she feared was a deadly consequence.

CHAPTER 23

TROPHIES

LAINIO — FINLAND

The boys carried the bags into the chalet and they had a quick look around. The door opened straight into a small lobby that led to the living room. To the right were doors to the two bedrooms. Past them was a corridor leading to the back door. The bathroom was to the right and the kitchen to the left. The living room and bedrooms were furnished in the standard light pine with a two tone green carpet and brightly coloured curtains and cushions for the chairs.

The inspection completed, Seija chose the second bedroom and suggested they went to the Ice Bar for a quick drink, because with the sun setting just after two o'clock, the clay pigeon shooting the boys had booked on started at midday.

Permanently maintained at a temperature between minus two and minus five degrees centigrade, the Bar was made entirely of ice, including all the furniture, the several beautiful sculptures and even the drinking glasses. Everything was back-lit in a variety of colours, creating a striking effect. They sat at a clear ice table underlit in blue, set alongside a red backlit sculpture of a polar bear, each of them thinking how romantic it would be if their chosen companion was with them.

Xzarze! Tullia. Why you here? A shocked Qwelby stilled his angry thoughtsending as he realised that it was his own mind that had produced an image of his twin whilst he was deep in imaging being with Jenni. A jumbled mix of memories he had experienced since being on Earth cascaded through his mind. Through them all one feature stood out clearly. A pair of eyes. Rich purple orbs set in vibrant, pale blue ovals, all finely rimmed in silver. And a love that surpassed anything he felt for Jenni. A love he had known... knew...?

His thoughts were interrupted by the arrival of a waitress taking orders for drinks.

Later, as the two boys left the Ice Bar in silence, each enjoying the togetherness of holding the other's hand, they were watched by five pairs of eyes, two Americans drawing conclusions not shared by the Continentals.

As the boys reached the little hut that was the HQ for the shooting they were joined by five others, all wearing dark coloured parkas over equally dark trousers. A sombre contrast to the bright red parka and blue trousers that Qwelby was wearing and Hannu's co-ordinated bright green outfit.

The elderly man running the shoot asked if everyone spoke English. Qwelby turned to Hannu and raised his eyebrows. Free from all surveillance and sinking into what he called "Being real", he had toned down his mental searching as much as possible and was not using his compiler. When all the others confirmed they understood English, Hannu said he would translate.

Introductions were performed. The very dark skinned man with his close cropped black hair and his fair haired wife, both of average height and build, were Americans, Sherwin and Farah Green; the tall and well-built man and woman were Russians, Nicolai and Ivanova Rushailo. Except for Sherwin, they all spoke Finnish. Maija, the casually dressed woman the boys had seen at Reception, was Finnish.

Qwelby was startled when he heard Hannu introducing him

as coming from Turkey. He realised that he had been staring at Ivanova. He had become accustomed to pale skin with rosy cheeks and blue eyes - but not her bright green eyes. 'Sorry,' he said, shaking his head to clear the vision of the last time he'd seen green eyes - which had been hurling lightning bolts at him. 'Memory.'

The organiser explained that the shoot was a new venture installed that year as many foreign guests had requested it. There were twelve stations along the edges of the forest. Clays were launched in pairs. The first two stations were for practice, with the other ten for a small competition. The winner would receive a small prize and, if anyone destroyed all twenty clays, a bottle of Mali, Finnish Brandy. He went on to explain the scoring system. Two points for a destroyed clay, one point if a clay was "winged", meaning that it remained intact but with a small piece knocked off an edge.

Having explained that the only shooting he had ever done, mentally adding 'On Earth,' had been on video games, no-one commented when Qwelby missed the first two clays. A little later at the second station Qwelby hit both clays and was congratulated by Nicolai as the Russian gave him a searching look.

Walking to the next station the Americans and the Russians, who had each destroyed all four clays, challenged each other to a bet and dragged the reluctant Maija into an agreement of one hundred American dollars each.

Understanding what was happening, Qwelby asked how much that was in Markas. 'I play,' he said when told, and was deluged with protests. 'It would not be fair,' Nicolai said in fluent Finnish. 'We are all experienced. You have just had, how you say? Beginner's luck.'

'Thank you,' Qwelby replied. 'I understand. I like challenge. I have money.'

'Let the idiot lose,' Sherwin almost snarled. 'I'll take his money.'

Although he did not understand all the words, Qwelby was puzzled by the obvious antagonism.

By the time the party reached the tenth station, Qwelby and Nicolai had each scored the maximum of thirty-six points. The others' scores were clustered close behind, except for Hannu who was trailing with twenty-five, but was happy as he had never fired a real gun before.

The organiser warned them that the last station was the most difficult. 'As you can see, the gap between the trees where you can sight and shoot is not as wide as at any of the other stations, so the clays come out at a higher angle.'

The five experienced shooters had drawn lots as to who would shoot first at each station, with the result that it was Sherwin's turn at the tenth. 'Just my luck,' he muttered to Farah, already angry that he was losing, and especially to the boy who had disrupted his long awaited holiday in Florida with his family. 'Everything's against me today.'

Something was, as he missed the first clay as it arced high into the clear blue sky, leaving him with a score of thirty-seven.

Qwelby was happy to be third to shoot as Ivanova went next and missed the second clay. 'Perfect,' he muttered to himself, now having seen the full trajectory of both clays. He stepped past the Russian into the firing position as his brain rapidly processed the new set of calculations. He loaded two cartridges, closed the weapon and raised it to his shoulder.

'Pull!' he called, and the two clays arced into the sky.

Bang!

The first missile disintegrated

Bang! Had he left it too long? It was an agonising wait with the smell of cordite at odds with the lazerpulse slowly headed towards the missile. He started to groan as he saw the pulsar about to pass behind... but no! The missile seemed to hang in the air, the pulsar closed and the missile broke into a shower of tiny pieces.

Once again reflexes took over and, heaving a big sigh as he came back to Earth, Qwelby lowered and broke open the shotgun before turning to grin at his open-mouthed friend.

'I saw it,' Hannu almost whispered. 'A bolt of lightning. And the clay. It seemed to.... well... just hang there... and then I saw it break apart!'

Qwelby's grin spread the width of his face as his revolving eyes sparkled. 'I not thoughtwrap you. You thoughtshare! Lamaannu, you almost human!'

'Huh!' Hannu barked a laugh at their private joke.

Glancing over his friend's shoulder, Qwelby noticed Ivanova giving him a strange look. He winked at her as he put his shades back on and stepped aside for Hannu to take his place.

Bang! Bang!

'Likâbâlkitâ-Eh!' Qwelby punched his fist high into the air in salute to his friend as both clays disintegrated.

'What's that?' Ivanova asked, once again the almost musicality of the words sounding nothing like the clips of Turkish she'd pulled up on the Russian's secure MiniComp.

'Errm...' Qwelby felt his whole face heat up as he looked into her piercing green eyes and Tamina's face flashed across his vision. 'I think you say... errr... Hell yeah!'

Ivanova looked amused as she smiled and raised an eyebrow. Entranced by the vibrant colour of her eyes as he scanned them, Qwelby smiled. She was accepting a polite translation of a colourful expression but had no idea that: "Despicable troglodytes of lower dimensions," was the polite ending to what was contained within the Old Aurigan expression from the time of the Space Wars.

The boys were soon heading back to their chalet, Qwelby richer by two thousand five hundred markas and carrying a bottle of Mali and the winner's trophy.

As they headed for the chalets, the five adults discussed Qwelby and what they had gleaned from the brief conversations that had taken place as they moved around the stations. Maija, Deputy Director of the Suojelupoliisi, was amused at how carefully the two CIA agents and the two FSB agents were sharing opinions.

They all agreed that they believed Qwelby was telling the truth when he spoke of his home, family and friends and, from his brief explanation of why he was in Finland, accepted his refusal to say more as justified caution.

Sherwin later shared with Farah that he had been closely watching their target whilst English was being spoken and was sure the boy understood some.

When well out of earshot of the others Hannu demanded to be told how his friend had shot so well and what had happened to his eyes. He explained that after each shot as Qwelby had turned to him, his ovals had been completely purple but returned to normal as he'd put his shades back on. Qwelby steered them to sit down on one of the long seats that were dotted around the site. Hannu waited.

'I go mad,' Qwelby said eventually as he activated his compiler. 'The spray of the little pellets was wrong. It had to be like in the woods on New Year's Eve. A single beam from the gun... because that is what I used to shoot down missiles from spaceships attacking the HomeSphere. When I knew that, I saw that. I was there. Somehow the clays became missiles and I saw a single lazerpulse, like a bullet of light, from my gun.'

'And your eyes?'

'Eyes totally purple for me, and Kaigii, when we are... Venerables. Very old... very... what say? Experienced?'

'Dragon Lord,' Hannu said.

'But I wasn't. That's my ancestor...'

'You have his genes.'

'Yes, but...'

Qwelby was in a tunnel, fighting against humans half his height. Then under blue skies on a battlefield he was wielding a massive two-handed sword.

All went dark.

Arms around him. Strong, comforting arms. Kaigii? He looked up from where he was slumped over. Pink cheeks, blue eyes, blonde hair. Hannu. Grinning sheepishly Qwelby sat back up. 'Too many ancestors. Too many memories.'

Having presented Mrs Rahkamo with the Mali and shown her the trophy, all three made their way to the Ice Bar for a late lunch. Now that it was dark the variety of coloured lights made the Bar and the Hotel even more amazing.

Qwelby explained to Mrs Rahkamo how he had managed to shoot so well by calculating trajectories of clays and pellets. He turned to his friend. 'You tell me how you hit two on last go. Very difficult.'

'Don't you know?!'

'No.'

'You willed me to do it. Like you were in me, telling me what to do.'

'Sorry.'

'Sorry?!'

'Oh, Lamaannu, I wanted you to finish good. I...'

'Hell Yeah! BroQ,' Hannu said with a big smile, deciding not to try and copy the alien language.

As they tucked into their meal, the boys told Hannu's mother more details of the shoot, totally unaware that the mobile phones on the two tables where the Americans and Russians were sitting well apart from each other were picking up their conversation.

'Dragged away from my wife and kids on the first holiday we've had in years,' Sherwin was complaining. 'Sent to this frozen waste because I speak Russian and Czech only to discover that snidey git is Turkish and says he doesn't even speak English. Now that woman is telling him to call her Aunt Seija. You don't do that to a stranger do you? This is another cock-up those idiots at Langley have made.'

At their table, the Russians were having difficulty in concealing their amusement at how Sherwin was impolitely described and that both boys had noticed Farah frowning at his comments. Naturally, they were pleased to hear what a good impression they had made, that Qwelby liked what he described as Nicolai's warmth and how he was intrigued by Ivanova's green eyes.

'There's no way he's fifteen. More like nineteen,' Ivanova replied with a calculated look in her eyes.

'False passport. False everything,' Nicolai stated.

'I've an idea for the Sleigh Ride tonight. A chance for a good long... talk. Explain later.' Ivanova's eyes indicated the Americans with their phones on the table.

'We make a good team,' Nicolai said as he lifted his glass. They clinked their glasses of Vodka together and downed the fiery liquid in one.

Back in the chalet Qwelby took a deep breath. 'Oona,' he said to Hannu. 'We were kissing. I no in her mind but I know she was happy. Then she tell me leave. Fast. No explanation. Help me?'

Hannu checked his mobile. 'She should be home by now. I'll text her and say you want to speak to her.'

'What I say?'

'Tell you like her. That you miss her. That you wish she was here with you,' Hannu advised, as that was what he had been texting to Anita. 'And say you're sorry.'

'But I not know what I do.'

His expertise with girls at an end, Hannu shrugged as he said 'Oona.' Seconds later his mobile played her melody. 'Oona,' he said as he handed the phone to Qwelby.

'Hullo Oona,' Qwelby said as he stepped outside, where he could be seen walking up and down the veranda, talking animatedly and waving his free hand about.

When the door opened, Hannu and his mother saw a big smile on Qwelby's face. 'I no do anything. Her parents came home. She say big problem if they discover us together.' He handed the phone back to Hannu. 'She say she misses me and wishes be here.' Looking sad he added, 'She wishes we meet again.'

'Oh, BroQ.' Hannu pulled his friend into a big hug, having learnt that was a way of giving the alien the energy-feed he needed when feeling down.

'Also I speak to Jenni. Never see her again and... she special.'

'How d'you...?'

'Said her name.'

'But the phone's locked to my voice.'

'Quantum phone.'

'You cheeky sod!'

Qwelby laughed as Hannu thumped him.

'I'd like to explore the Ice Hotel and the Snow Village,' Seija said as the boys stepped back from each other. 'Plenty of time before the drinks party and the Sleigh Ride.'

'Okay, Mum. But time for me to call Anita first. I err...' A guilty feeling made Hannu stop speaking as his mother smiled and nodded.

While Hannu was in the bedroom talking with his girlfriend, Qwelby explained his plans to Mrs Rahkamo.

'I need more money for long journey to Tullia. Her tribe in corner of Botswana. Use many planes and hotels. Now I have enough for plane from here to Helsinki, good hotel for tourists so my colour no problem and good clothes to make me look older for Casino.' His face creased into his lopsided smile. 'And for playing card games!'

Seija nodded. She wasn't sure that it really was the right thing to do when he had demonstrated how he could tell what each card was by what he called its energy signature.

When Hannu came back into the living room they used his mobile to check on flights. Qwelby booked onto the first available flight to Helsinki, on Tuesday morning. Having hoped to return home on Sunday, Mrs Rahkamo shrugged her shoulders at the inevitable consequences and booked two tickets on Tuesday's flight to Siilinjärvi, saying she would phone her husband later that evening.

CHAPTER 24

SLEIGH RIDE

LAINIO-FINLAND

Qwelby was enjoying himself at the evening drinks party, smiling and nodding and saying little as he explained, truthfully as he was not using his compiler, that speaking so much Finnish was tiring his brain. Mingling with the guests as always, Viivi's rosy cheeks, blond hair, blue eyes and the soft warm colours shading through her aura stirred his own new responses. He was aware of a change in himself. A mature confidence that made him eat more than his share of the hors d'oeuvres she was serving so as to keep her close to him.

After a while Viivi asked the guests to follow her to where they were to be briefed for the Sleigh Ride and allocated their sleighs.

Speaking with the Russians, Qwelby accompanied them as they walked several metres into the forest to get into their sleigh, positioned immediately behind that to be used by the group leader. From the back of the line Farah saw Viivi walk to the front. After a brief discussion, Nicolai got out of the sleigh and Qwelby took his place alongside Ivanova.

'What's going on?' Farah asked. 'No idea,' Maija lied. 'Viivi is supposed to be driving our young friend in the last sleigh.'

'Last sleigh has a broken seat,' a disgruntled looking Viivi said as she walked past Farah and Maija. It was not broken. As Maija had required, Viivi had removed some nuts and bolts so that the seat of the last sleigh had collapsed when she'd sat on it.

Qwelby was enjoying the journey through the trees, happily establishing contact with the reindeer he was steering. Images slipped though his mind. How it would be if he was on Vertazia, and the time he was squashed against Oona when they'd been sitting on the sofa. Liking Ivanova's friendly energies, he put the reins in his right hand and slipped his left arm around her.

'Let me show you how we do this in Russia,' she said as, leaning over to take one of the reins, her right hand rested on Qwelby's thigh and remained there.

Ivanova was happy to answer Qwelby's question about where she lived and then continue talking about her life in Russia, pleased that she was building a good rapport.

Being part of a race where physical contact was as normal a part of communication as reading someone's eyes and energy field, Qwelby was happy with the touch that added to the gentle friendship that was growing as the ride continued.

When they reached the clearing where dinner was to be served, two Lapps gave the guests lichen for the reindeer and demonstrated how to feed them. As Qwelby fed the reindeer that had pulled their sleigh, he felt sorry for the Azurii with their limited experiences as, thanking the animal for the enjoyable ride, he was rewarded by nose blowing and face licking.

Wiping reindeer slobber from his face with the sleeve of his coat, he returned to the clearing where he sat between Ivanova and Hannu with Mrs Rahkamo on the other side of her son. On the opposite side of the oval the two Lapps were now sitting a little back from the others, half into the surrounding trees.

The two small, slim men with dark brown wrinkled faces from Lapland had been introduced as experts with the reindeer. It had been they who had shown the guests how to drive and feed the animals. Their faces reminded Qwelby of the Bushmen he'd found whilst using Hannu's computer to search the internet, looking for where Tullia was living.

'Tell me about the Lapps?' he asked Ivanova.

'They're also called Sami and live across several countries up here in the far North. They are the original inhabitants of this area and their sagas tell of their coming here as the last Ice Age ended. In some of their sagas they call themselves the First People. They are disliked by most other Finns.'

'My people were the first people seventy-five thousand years ago,' Qwelby replied without thinking.

'Many races, or tribes, have stories of how they came to be on Earth. I am not an expert, but in my reading I've only come across one other that says they were put on Earth that long ago. The Bushmen of the Kalahari.'

'Kalahari!?' Qwelby exclaimed as he leapt to his feet.

'Yes.'

'I... err... errm.' He turned to Hannu and made a gesture indicating a male need, grabbed his friend by the arm and pulled him into the forest.

'Tullia. I so happy when I found her, I not look more. Bushmen. Seventy-five thousand years ago. Kalahari. Auriganii. My ancestors. Our ancestors. Oh Hannu. If we not go home, we live there. You come. Bring Anita.'

'Whoa! BroQ. Talk about this later. Right now I smell food.' They returned and joined everyone tucking into the food being served from the several pots suspended over the fire: green beans, sugared loganberries and Finnbiff stew made of reindeer meat, cream, mushrooms, bacon and dumplings.

When everyone had finished eating, with the stars twinkling in the oval of black sky above and the crackling fire turning into bright embers, the Sami told stories of ancient times. All too soon the fire was extinguished and buried and everyone returned to their sleighs.

As Qwelby reached the one he was sharing with Ivanova, he stroked the reindeer and gently blew into its nostrils. Nuzzling and slobbering over him, the animal returned the greeting.

'Animals like you,' Ivanova said.

'I live on farm. Work with animals.'

Ivanova was delighted. She'd just been given an easy opening for her questions and would work her way round to the Bushmen.

They travelled as before, with his arm around her and her hand on his thigh. Enjoying the warm contact that was so much part of Tazian life, Qwelby was happy to talk in more detail than during the shoot about his home and family, and use the conversation as a practice for what he might have to say to all sorts of people during the long journey to Tullia.

CHAPTER 25

PRIDE

THE KALAHARI

A chill spread over Tullia-Tyua'llia's body as the lower rim of the sun reached the tops of the trees. She refocused her concentration. The last moments of any game were the most dangerous. Ease up and ... Death? She heard the high pitched "ewohw" of a lapwing a long way off, then another a lot closer, then two more. She breathed deeply and silently. That was almost certainly the call to end the hunt. But it was not yet dark. She remained where she was until the sun had set, then spent some time easing her aching joints before making her way back home under the stars shining in all their glory.

Clearing the last of the trees, she strode toward the village looking neither to left nor right as she walked in through the main entrance with her head held high and her shoulders pulled back. As her gaze took in the many little fires with families grouped around them she became aware as never before of the mixture of emotions swirling around her. Fear, envy, resentment, desire, pride, honouring and a new one. 'Worship,' her mind said and her vision switched.

The little fires were spread as far as the eye could see across a great verdant plane. Less than a league away were darker green foothills and rising from them the soft creamy yellow walls and towers of the Citadel. Today she, Zeyusa, would lead yet another assault on those walls as she endeavoured to prevent her twin, Anananki, from his crazy plan to energise the Great Crystal. Ninurtan rose to greet her as she reached her fire. But something was wrong with his face. She sat down and one of her twins climbed onto her lap.

'Big-Big Sister come back,' four-year-old Tomku said.

Tullia smiled. Yes, she was a Warrior, but right now was what she wanted to be: a teenage girl with her family, and Ninurtan was Xashee, her Meera brother.

At the edge of the fire was a bowl of milimili. Deena added a few purple !kerri berries to Tyua'llia's favourite breakfast food and offered her the bowl. Tullia grinned at the symbolic gesture of the welcome to her new life as a young woman of the tribe.

When Tullia had finished eating, seven-year-old Nthabe snuggled up alongside as Tullia put an arm around her, lost in the feeling that she had her twins with her and all she wanted for perfection was to have Qwelby at her side, making their family complete.

That want slowly turned to desire and that turned into need. As soon as the younger children had settled down for the night, Tullia told Tsetsana that she had to make another attempt to connect with her twin. She needed to do that as gently as possible. And she knew how. The very large lulwanulay in her twin's favourite colours of red and green, that Tsetsana had told her was known as a dragonfly, had previously led her to Xameb's hut to make contact. She would send her thoughts on gentle wings, hoping for her twin's subconscious to produce the right image for him.

On the evening of the firefight when they had nearly connected, he and his two friends had worn loinskins and had created a little fire in what had looked like a big tent. He must have found out where she was and seen images of the San around fires wearing traditional loinskins. Tonight she was going to recreate that energy in a gentle way, by lighting a small fire, wearing her new loinskin and asking Mother Tree to wing her thoughts to him. Tsetsana was happy to be asked to remain fully clothed and warm as she guarded her friend from wild animals.

Arriving at Tullia's favourite group of three tall Mongongos and well out of sight of the village, Tsetsana lit a small fire from a brand she had brought from the family fire. Tullia stripped down to her decorated skirtlet and eased her way back into the cave-like opening at the foot of the biggest of the three trees. Instead of allowing herself to become absorbed by what she called Mother Tree, this time she retained conscious awareness of where she was and thoughtsent an image of a white barn owl lifting off from a branch and flying along the winding snake of the Milky Way.

Drifting in her meditation she did not know how long it was until she sensed a slight connection, then it was broken with the faintest impression of...? She tried to refocus but was prevented by something fluttering against her body. Annoyed, she opened her eyes to...

'Lulwanulay,' she cooed. The dragonfly flew up to be an arm's length in front of her eyes and its wings beat as impossibly fast as a bee's. She saw the patterns. 'Ah, fractals! The underpinning images of everything. Oneness. Me and Kaigii. One. Of course.' She looked at Tsetsana and grinned. 'It's working.' She held out her hand and the large red and green insect settled on her hand with its multifaceted eyes staring hypnotically into hers. 'Oh yes, Kaigii,' she whispered in Tazian. 'I'll wait.'

As the dragonfly lifted off and disappeared, Tullia lay down in the space which, for her, marked Father Tree in another dimension.

CHAPTER 26

LISTENERS

LAINIO-FINLAND

As each pair of sleigh riders unharnessed their reindeer, Nicolai appeared from amongst the trees. When Ivanova said that Qwelby had been an excellent escort and how much she'd enjoyed talking with him, the big Russian took one of Qwelby's hands in both of his and thanked him for looking after her.

The boys were happy to agree with Mrs Rahkamo when she said she preferred to have a hot chocolate in the warmth of their chalet rather than go to the Ice Bar with the others. Qwelby switched on his compiler as they walked and explained how useful the evening had been. Although he liked Ivanova and was a little sad at the deception, he had enjoyed practising his Turkish story.

'I told only one lie. That I come from Turkey. Everything else was... well. Leader of Aurigan Warriors, the Dragon Lord, here is General. So I say my grandfather a General, thoughtadding eighty thousand years ago. Great-Great Uncle Mandara is the Arch Discoverer, so I say he's the Chief Scientist. My Great-Great Aunt Lellia, I say her job to keep balance of all people. Ivanova say Minister for the Interior. I not know words. Is right?'

'Very clever,' Hannu said. 'And not much pain for you?'

'No. Like rehearsing for a LiveShow.'

Declining the free drinks, the Russians and Farah hurried back to their separate chalets. Throwing their heavy Parkas onto the sofa, Ivanova got out a bottle and glasses while Nicolai went into the bedroom and emerged holding a small electronic unit. As they placed everything on the table, Ivanova poured the drinks and Nicolai switched on the unit's tiny speakers. Almost immediately they heard the sound of a door opening and people entering.

'Dangerous,' Hannu said. 'If anyone...'

'Yes. I know...'

'So why do it?'

'Ivanova. Well. It's not like with Oona and Jenni, but... she's nice. And her green eyes. Tamina's are green and... I like her, and I got talking and... had to answer her questions.'

'BroQ. You must be careful. Please. You mustn't get caught.'

Nicolai raised an eyebrow at the triumphant look on his subordinate's face.

They heard the door close and the sound of clothes being changed. That was followed by a general and inconsequential conversation about the evening. Hot chocolate was served and all they heard was the sound of sipping and sighs.

'Well, Major?' Nicolai asked.

'I'll explain details later, Comrade Colonel,' Ivanova replied with a smile. 'I had a useful conversation with our target. Amongst what I'm sure is true, he's definitely hiding something.'

Tap, tap, tap.

The sound of staccato tapping, as of a pencil on glass stood out clearly from all the other noises.

Tap, tap, tap.

'Look,' Qwelby exclaimed. 'A baby Horned Snow Owl.'

'Yeah. Just like on New Year's Eve,' Hannu said. 'Except it's not a horn. It's just a tuft of hair. I checked on the internet.'

The Russians heard the sound of movement, then silence except for: tap, tap, tap.

'Ahh... It is a miniature horn. Just like on a unicorn. Qwelby! You don't think?'

'Tullia.'

'But where? How? What...'

'A signal. She's waiting for us.'

In between bursts of static the puzzled Russians listened to a confusing conversation about the boys wearing loinskins and a girl called Anita guiding a meditation, then heard the sounds of furniture being moved.

'But the danger,' Hannu protested. 'Fighting your government each time you've tried to reach her.'

'We were fighting our rulers.'

'But...?

'My family is part of what you call the government. That wasn't who we were fighting.'

'What about that girl you fought?'

'Yeah. That was good. I wanted to...'

A screech of static, then Hannu's voice was heard.

'... she did that night in the Kalahari.'

Silence.

Tap, tap, tap.

The listeners heard a deep exhalation of breath.

'Now, Lamaannu,' Qwelby said. 'Think of Tullia when you last saw her.' Guessing what Hannu was thinking about Tullia, Qwelby gritted his teeth, but making a strong contact with Tullia was far too important for jealousy to interfere. Besides which, his twin was half a world away. He relaxed and recalled how amazing she'd looked – and been. 'Ignore all the fighting. Concentrate on her with the flames dancing all over her body. You said she looked like a beautiful Amazonian Warrior Queen...'

An ear shattering screech of static came through the unit. The LED indicating transmission from the living room went out and there was total silence.

Nicolai picked up the receiver and pressed controls. The

LED refused to light and there was no sound from it. 'Yanks,' he commanded.

Picking up their Parkas, Nicolai took the receiver and Ivanova a ready-packed bag of equipment and they made their way to the American's adjacent chalet. Farah let them into the living room.

The layout was the same as all two bedroom units, again with light pine furniture, bright curtains and cushions and this time a two tone green carpet. Like the Russians' chalet, the room was dimly lit and no curtains had been drawn. Their two chalets were on the inner row at the wider end of the funnel like shape, giving them uninterrupted views across to their target's cabin on the opposite side.

Nicolai placed his receiver on the table alongside that of the Americans. Farah shot a look at a surprised Sherwin. How had Nicolai got into the target's cabin without being seen by Sherwin?

'Have you...' Sherwin asked in a threatening voice.

'Nyet. Have you?' Nicolai asked.

'No.'

They exchanged brief nods, each knowing the other would be sweeping their own chalet on a regular basis. They went on to say where each had located their miniaturised transmitters in the living room and both bedrooms, grimly acknowledging that they were not brilliantly concealed. Nicolai had had little time after Sherwin had left and both had placed them where they could easily be removed, Maija having made it clear that the use of "bugs" had not been authorised by the Interior Ministry. Intercepting mobile phone communications was, of course, a different matter.

They discussed how and why both transmitters might have failed at the same time and what that said about their target and the equipment he might have with him.

'They're leaving,' Farah announced as Qwelby and Hannu stepped out of the front door, turned around the back of the two rows of chalets and headed along the road that lead around to the service area at the back of the Snow Hotel. They were going in the opposite direction to the Ice Bar and the facilities of the Snow Village.

'Two fags been dancing around in their underwear and now off to the woods. Sickening. Let's grab the little shit and sweat him,' Sherwin demanded.

'Wait until we see what they're doing,' Nicolai said in a firm tone.

'What about our comrades, Nicolai?' Ivanova said, her tone sounding like a genuine question whilst using the sarcastic description for the SVR. The Russian Foreign Intelligence Service most definitely was not their comrade.

'Think what they will say, Major, if we let the Americans steal the prize!' he replied with a smile.

Ivanova smiled and nodded. By addressing her by her rank he'd said that he was taking full responsibility.

'If we don't go now we'll lose them,' Farah said sharply.

'Grab them now. I'm not watching their dirty little games,' Sherwin said, scowling as he pulled on his boots.

'No. Remember our briefing. We need to know what that boy's all about. If it's what you say. More than egg on our face if that darkie has family in high places. Ours or theirs.' Farah nodded to the Russians, who were looking concerned about Sherwin's belligerent attitude.

All four argued tactics as they finished dressing for the outside. Agreement reached, the women left with Ivanova carrying the Russians' ready-bag and headed to the road that ran along the back of their double row of chalets. Sherwin carried the Americans' bag as the men headed diagonally across the open area to the road the boys had taken.

CHAPTER 27

TWINS CONNECT

LAINIO-FINLAND

The connection had lasted only a short time. As Qwelby had sensed Tullia in the open, he'd decided also to be outside. Led by him, the boys left the road and started trudging across the snow towards the forest. They walked in silence as they followed a curve in the tree line to a place where they could no longer see the lights of the Snow Hotel.

'Here will do,' Qwelby said as he stopped and removed his thick clothes, placing them on a big bin liner he'd put in a pocket, until all he had on was the suede loinskin he'd worn for the meditation in the chalet. He grinned at his friend who was wearing the same – underneath the clothes he was not going to remove.

'Bloody hell, BroQ, you'll freeze,' Hannu said as his friend lay down on the thick snow.

Sinking into his Kore, Qwelby focussed his thoughts on the baby owl and followed it as it flew away, skimming close over the planet's surface. With a jolt that shook him, twelve streams of energy sped forth from his fingers, like plasma flows ejected from a Black Hole.

Fearing the power was going to alert whoever on Vertazia was monitoring him and his twin, he tried to rein them in. Without success. Bright and hot rivers of lava swept him along. He was riding all twelve simultaneously and experiencing every twist and turn as the rivers sought the fastest path through the Earth's swirling energy currents.

He was feeling dizzy from the increasing speed then lost all control as he was jerked through a switchback series of climbs and descents over mountain ranges.

Gently focussing her thoughts on the lulwanulay, Tullia saw it lift into the air and hover for a moment, its whirling wings reflecting diamond sharp points of red and green light. *I'm coming* she thoughtsent as the dragonfly headed out into the night sky. Twelve streams of blue and green shot from her fingers, speeding rivers of the Waters of Life.

The streams met with a blinding flash and a deafening crashing roar of a dozen waterfalls pouring into a dozen volcanoes.

Qwelby's hearts burst open, he spread gigantic wings, tensed thighs like massive tree trunks and launched himself headlong, gathering all twelve rivers into his Kore. He opened his chest wide enough to swallow a planet and roared his love and need for his twin as he burst into a coruscating explosion of multicoloured light, sound and emotion as Tullia welcomed him into her hearts. He was home! They were together!!

Blackness. Silence. Hissing.

Hissing?

'Aaaaargghh!' he yelled as his body stiffened and arched, only his head and heels touching the ground.

Whole, complete, at one with herself and her twin, Tullia leapt into the star spangled heavens. The sounds of tumultuously rushing rivers and the rhythmic beating of a massive pair of wings carried her forward. Like a herd of winged Unicorns in the great waves crashing onto a sea shore she swept towards her twin and was swept into his hearts as a golden-maned, silver Unicorn was embraced by a mighty red and gold and turquoise dragon.

The Twins hugged, laughed and cried. Holding hands, human six fingered hands, they leapt up and down like a pair of six-year-olds, beyond caring what anybody thought. They were one. They were whole. It was time to start living again.

Hoo, hoo, hoo.

Qwelby opened his eyes to find himself lying on a patch of grass free from all snow, the hissing of steam rising all around him.

'A Horned Snow Owl!' Hannu exclaimed.

Qwelby rolled over and shakily got to his feet.

Hoo, hoo, hoo.

Qwelby hooted with laughter and the sound of saxophones, trumpets and tubas rolled across the snowy landscape. He threw his arms around his friend. 'Tullia! At last. We're totally reunited. I'm whole. Complete. Did you see her?!'

'She's fucking gorgeous!' Hannu felt the tension in the air and wanted to say something, but no words came as he saw the tears trickling down his friend's cheeks and the purple orbs of his eyes disappear as his ovals turned violet.

Taking a mental pace back, Qwelby replayed his internal video – and was stunned. His twin looked so different. She'd lost all her teenyfat, was taller and bigger and disconcertingly desirable. Uncomfortable with the stirrings in his body he slipped into Hannu's mind to check out how his friend had seen her. Staggeringly beautiful and... His anger was stopped in its tracks as the strength of his feelings for his twin hit him. Confused, he pulled away by switching his view to the cute little girl standing alongside his twin and discovered she was as important to his twin as Hannu was to him. Calmer, he switched his attention back to his friend and the reassuring comfort of strong arms around him.

'Yes.... she is,' Qwelby said slowly as he clenched his fists to stop his anger erupting. But was that directed at Hannu or himself?

'Ah, QeïchâKaïgiï.' With those words came a sense of the mouth of a whirlpool opening.

Trembling, he gripped his friend and was comforted as Hannu held him tightly. 'What else did you see?' he asked as he stepped away and started dressing.

'I saw loads of streaming colours racing across the planet. Then I was with the cute little girl I'd seen from the ringside seat that Anita and I had at the firefight in the Kalahari. I couldn't believe it. I was standing by three tall trees in the Kalahari with her at my side like we were old friends. We watched all those colours collide in a massive explosion. What had to be you and Tullia turning into a great, pulsating intertwined column of every colour imaginable. Including some I've never seen before and can't describe.'

'Oh, Lamaannu.' Qwelby knew his eyes were twirling as he looked into Hannu's. Receiving the permission he sought from his friend's subconscious, Qwelby linked with his twin and kissed Hannu on the forehead. A long kiss and as he watched what looked like fine rivers of fire run through Hannu's body

'Wha?'

'Become more Tazian,' Qwelby said in a voice that sounded deeper and older, then finished dressing. Qwelby was happy that neither dragons nor unicorns had been mentioned. He was still uncertain about what part they played in his and Tullia's present lives and was relieved that however much "sight" Hannu was developing from their close friendship, he was not yet seeing that deeply into the eighth dimension.

Whirr, whirrr, whirrrr.

Tullia opened her eyes to the sound of the dragonfly's wings and saw Tsetsana standing and staring down at her, her eyes and teeth shining white in the starlight. Filled with unbelievable joy, Tullia leapt up, stepped forward, picked up her friend and whirled her round, squealing with happiness. Realising she was crushing the slightly built girl, she put her down.

'Kaigii! At last. We're totally reunited. I'm whole. Complete. And so much more than before. Did you see him?!'

Winded, gasping for breath, Tsetsana nodded, unable to find mere words. She knew beyond a doubt that however Tyua'llia tried to explain that she came from a world like Earth, that just wasn't possible, not after what she'd seen tonight. And her big friend was no daughter of the Sun, because the Lord Kaigii she'd just seen had to be the very Sun God himself. So big, so strong, so beautiful with the energy flowing from him making the stars look dim. And she was in love with him, helplessly and hopelessly. And he'd even brought a special friend to be with her as the Dragons and Unicorns became one. She hadn't been afraid but his presence had been nice.

Tsetsana had seen cave drawings of Shamen transforming into animals of all sorts so as to travel to other worlds. Now she knew that one day she was going to be a Sangoma and travel like them. 'Takawena, Twana-Udada.' an echoing voice said inside her head, and she understood that she, Little Sister, was being welcomed into that world.

Ahhhhh
At last
At soonest
So young
So old
Memories premature
DNA initiation chaotic
One Essence
......Hope

The whispering was so faint that it went unnoticed by each twin's consciousness and slid into Deep Memory.

Holding hands and laughing, Tullia and Tsetsana ran back to the village and into Ungka's hut, where she together with Ishe, her hut mate, Mandingwe and N!Obile were waiting. The blanket was dropped back over the opening and soon followed by squeals of joy.

Sitting with Ghadi and his wife, Kotuma, Xameb nodded as all three sensed tensions draining from the atmosphere. Tyua'llia was still a Goddess and a desirable woman, but no longer in her own hut like a spider waiting to trap a man, instead she was now sharing a hut like a normal young woman and, most of all, everyone knew she was dedicated to her twin.

CHAPTER 28

A BLESSING?

VERTAZIA

Xaala writhed on her bed, cursing. She'd sensed wings, flying, two pairs. The Twins reaching out so gently that their vibrations had only triggered her receptors as they were close to linking. Blazing Novas! That had to be prevented. She needed help. Rulcas... a degenerate boy. Impossible! Ceegren, her beloved teacher, see her like this? Never! Dryddnaa? Humiliating, but... Wrenching herself into the eighth dimension her thoughtsending for Dryddnaa had become unfocussed as she'd screamed with the pain of her last mental barrier against Awakening being ripped away.

Wings. White, red, green, gold and silver sped towards each other. Stop. How? Devour. Devour? She morphed into her hated Attribute of a snake with its jaws wide open hurtling towards.... Scorching lavaflows, sparkling oceanrivers, thundering, roaring, crashing, merging. All through her elongated body the sublime energy flowed. Desire. Love. Joy. Fulfilment. Deep inside, the wounded child begged for more.

She roared her denial. She was mentally and psychically perfect and had no need of that revolting emotional and physical mess that was.... Yetch! She'd programmed herself not to achieve her Awakening for at least another two years, had every intention of outlasting the period of exploration, totally deny the change and remain as she was - a pure balance of male energies in a female Form. But now, now of all times, her weak female Form had betrayed her!

Hurled out of the eighth dimension and back into her body she squealed at the stabbing pains ripping all through her torso, rolled onto her hands and knees and was locked in place with her head hanging down as she watched runnels of sweat coursing from her body and soaking the bedding. She railed against her weak mind that had not controlled her emotions, even as her hearts beat fast with the memory of the love that had flowed through and around her.

Again, she roared denial. She was never going to accept that a beautiful Unicorn loved an evil Dragon, or that a Dragon was capable of anything except death and destruction. She sensed a head shaking and hissing. Her Attribute. She yelled at it to go away. Even more than dragons, snakes were the epitome of evil. That was not her Attribute! With sadness in its eyes, the snake shook its head, its forked tongue sending a message she refused to hear.

She sobbed as pain repeatedly pulsed through her breasts as though punishing her for denying them. Awakening was not supposed to be like this! Deep inside she knew it was her fault for trying to override her Self, her Kore. Her stomach heaved and she was sick. Tears fell in profusion and she collapsed on the dry side of the bed as the physical pains eased at last, leaving her to face the fact that she'd failed in her duty to her beloved master to prevent the twins connecting. The shame and horror engulfed her in darkness and mercifully dropped her into unconsciousness.

The following morning when Xaala confessed to the Arch Custodian she was knocked back by his ferocity. In his rage his self-control slipped and Xaala saw that his anger was directed inward to himself. For more than six years Ceegren had encouraged the development of her strong, male, Uddîšû genes, the same as his own inheritance.

After decades of training boys, she was his first female acolyte and he'd seen her boyishness as what he understood to be a common teenage phase and not a denial of her essential female nature. The baggy tops to her tunics and other clothes she'd taken to wearing as she grew older he'd assumed were a natural shyness at her developing bust, not a denial of her femaleness.

From a very young age and at each stage of her development she'd shortened her tunics to the same length as that worn by her older brother. Having seen sibling rivalry between boys, he'd thought nothing of it. When she'd reached the age at which she was entitled to wear them to mid thigh, which she was already doing, he had been surprised when she had shortened them even more, but had accepted that as a mixture of rebelliousness and a statement of her individuality.

After the death of her brother several years before, he had been hoping that she might develop the personality to become the youth leader he sought. The rebelliousness and individuality were welcome signs of the necessary strength of character. Then a little later, the hair style she'd invented that had become a unisex fashion; he'd seen that as making a statement of the integration of her male genes and female Form. How could he of all people have been so blind!

Lowering the level of his anger a little and shielding his fear of how easily the twins had accessed the eighth dimension whilst on Earth, Ceegren dismissed his stunned acolyte with a flick of his fingers.

Back in her room and still trembling from his ferocity, Xaala realised just how strong the Power Play was between some of the most important people on the planet. Her Form went cold from fear as her insides went hot from excitement at the danger and thoughts of what she could achieve if she ensured that only the girl twin returned. For different reasons, both Ceegren and Dryddnaa would be in her debt.

She took a deep breath and grinned as something inside told her that, now Awakened, she'd have a more instinctual idea of how to manipulate that devious little MUUD, Rulcas. She turned to look at herself in the mirror, spread her legs apart and put her hands on her hips as she imaged wearing her DarkSuit. 'Yeah... Bitch!'

Come. Ceegren's harsh thoughtsent command turned her to quivering jelly. He never actually punished her for her mistakes. Instead, she was required to redeem herself for her failure to apply The Teachings. At times that redemption had been harsh. Was her failure this time so gross that she was going to be really punished?

'As the twins have reconnected, I need to stay at the centre of our operations at IndluKoba,' he said in a tone so severely attributing the fault to her that Xaala almost wet herself. 'Apart from attending to my personal needs, you will work as a Senior Apprentice.' He thoughtadded an image of the tunic he'd given her for the meeting of the Custodians following the battle around the fire on Azura. Ultra-short as usual, it was a swirling mix of blue-greys with streaks of black, the same as her crystal of Xalulan.

'Tibor will transwarp with me. You will take your twistor. Go.'

Her mouth dry, Xaala lowered her eyes and glided from the room. Six years of intense training and she read him better than he realised. Behind his anger and disappointment in her, from the slight colours shading through his aura she saw he was disturbed by something more... personal... of wider import than the twins having reconnected. She slid that deep behind her Privacy Shield, to explore when she was safely in her shielded quarters.

CHAPTER 29

SURVEILLANCE

LAINIO-FINLAND

By the time Sherwin arrived at their chalet, complaining about having to lie face down in the snow to try and see what was happening, Farah had put the percolator on and changed from her outdoor clothing. She set four glasses together with a bottle of Southern Comfort on the table alongside the two cameras and video recorders.

'We've got good results,' Farah snapped at him, fed up with his persistent moaning.

A still grumbling Sherwin had just finished changing clothes when Farah put four mugs of coffee on the pine table just as the Russians knocked and entered, with Ivanova carrying a bottle of Vodka and four shot glasses.

The two women smiled at each other. Whilst watching the boys, Ivanova had mentioned that the trick she'd played over the Sleigh Ride had resulted in her gathering information she would share when they were all together. Farah had explained Sherwin was always complaining because of his interrupted holiday and being sent on the mission because he spoke Russian and Czech when, as the English speaking Romain had not come to Lainio, Sherwin was left with a target who spoke Finnish and Turkish.

Ivanova had sympathised with her and a professionally wary friendship had developed.

The men's view had been hampered by the trees and their camera and video recorder had not worked until after the boys had left. They were relieved to discover that the women had had an excellent view and their equipment had worked. When Farah played the video using their MiniComp to display it on a wall, the women confirmed that was exactly what they had seen through their night vision optics.

'Zilch,' Sherwin said. 'Bloody waste of time. Fags. What about the Sleigh Ride?'

'He said it had taken seven days from his leaving home to reach Kotomäki,' Ivanova explained. 'He is in hiding which is why he's moving around Finland. He's been attacked more than once by his own people and is horrified by that. All he said about getting there was that he used his family's special experimental equipment. He's very proud of his inheritance, particularly because it comes from both his parents and goes back for countless generations, as do his unusual eyes. His original people had travelled a long way. The journey had taken a long time and with many stops. He now lives in a remote and mountainous area in the East of Turkey. His name? He's very proud of that, saying the man was an important ancestor. And now we've seen his body, his overall colour fits with people from Eastern Turkey and his reddish brown face is clearly sunburn.'

'One thing is clear from tonight,' Farah continued the briefing. 'The Finnish boy not only saw this Tullia but also a girl who was with her, and he's seen them before. We know from what our bugs have picked up that they're in the Kalahari, some ten thousand kilometres away. Very powerful mediumship, suggestion or hypnosis.'

'Pair of New Age weirdoes!' Sherwin sneered, then jerked as Farah kicked him hard on his ankle.

'There's a lot more in so-called New Age stuff than just your weirdoes,' Farah snapped at him. 'He's probably descended from a family of mystics and been sent away as next in line of... what... head of a religious sect, perhaps?'

'I asked about religion,' Ivanova said. 'His reply, and I quote: "No what you call religion. I seek to discover truth of Old Aurigan Ways."'

'Aurigan?' Farah asked.

'He claims his people were the first on Earth, seventy-five thousand years ago,' Ivanova replied with a smile.

'Bloody nutter,' Sherwin said forcefully to his partner.

'No,' Nicolai said, firmly. 'You Westerners are hung up on religion, blinkering your views of life. There is a lot in what you mistakenly call the esoteric part of life that is demonstrable and provable. You should read the many papers our scientists publish on the internet. In Russian, of course.

'Just look at the work we have done with pyramids built without any metal components. Difficult, but worthwhile. The power they generate for good. Healing wounds, clearing radioactive land, increased crop growth. and your satellites can see this for yourselves: in an area above any one of those pyramids, closing the hole in the ozone layer.' Nicolai's tone of voice was so aggressive that the Americans were leaning back in their chairs as if they had been attacked.

'I agree with Farah,' Ivanova was quick to follow. 'The boy has strong psychic powers. We've been assuming that when he refers to "his people" he means his tribe. That last comment we heard about his friend becoming Tazian makes it clear. He's referring to his group of psychics. And that puts into context the disputes we heard him talking about. He's not fighting the Turkish government but the "rulers" of his tribe.'

'That Finnish passport the policewoman saw giving his age as fifteen. He must have a brother or cousin living in Finland,' Farah added to nods of agreement. 'Younger, I guess, as he looks eighteen or nineteen and that age fits with what we've seen of his connection with this Tullia. Ivanova and I assume his intended and a love match.'

'Bloody nuisance the snow prevented a picture of that passport. And why didn't someone tell the staff here to take a photocopy. Damned Schengen Agreement. All they asked for was a credit card for incidentals. I say pull him in and question him,' Sherwin declared.

'No,' Nicolai said firmly. 'You know the pressure we're under to play this carefully.'

They all knew what Nicolai meant. There was a new incumbent in The White House. Looking West he had been concerned about the possibility of China overtaking the USA to become the world's leading power both economically and militarily. Looking East to his supposed allies in Europe, he had seen their continual internal bickering and persistent failure to meet their share of defence costs, except for the British. Free to cock a snoop at the EU's embargoes, the British economy was booming because of its trade deals with a revitalised Russia.

Not wanting to face economic and military adversaries to both East and West, the American President had offered his Russian counterpart a new deal of friendship and cooperation. Equally uncomfortable with being sandwiched between East and West, the Russian President had cautiously accepted.

Exploring the electromagnetic disturbances that had affected a large area of Finland and reached across into Russia on 27 December, was the first serious test of that accord and a joint American-Russian-Finnish command had been created to establish the cause. The Americans were keeping NATO in the loop, as were the Russians their allies in CSTO, the Collective Security Treaty Organisation.

Farah took a deep breath. 'From our monitoring of Romain's work on Raiatea we know he has nothing to do with any form of weapon.'

'And the French agree with that,' Nicolai said.

From the rapidly concealed look of anger on the Americans' faces, the Russians deduced that the French had not shared that knowledge with NATO and hence the USA.

'Best guess?' Nicolai asked. The others nodded. 'Chinese weapons test. The disturbances on three January, a refining of the first test. We're wasting our time here. It's the science gurus who're going to find whatever it was. Romain has been "chasing the wild geese" and now he's going to Geneva to visit old friends at CERN before going back home.'

As the men continued talking, Ivanova picked up the bottle of Vodka. Farah held up a hand as she picked up the Southern Comfort. The two women smiled as each poured out two shot glasses, then pushed them across to the other.

'You're FSB,' Sherwin said. 'Internal security.'

'Yes,' Nicolai confirmed.

'So how...?'

'Initially, we all thought he came from Czechia.'

'And Finland?'

'Neighbours.'

'Turkish?' Sherwin insisted.

'Ah.' Nicolai smiled. 'The SVR. We'll be out of here. Shame. End to a nice warm holiday.' Both brought up in Siberia, the Russians laughed and lifted their glasses of Southern Comfort. 'Nostrovia,' they said. All four clinked glasses together and downed in one, coughing and spluttering at the bite of the unaccustomed drinks.

As the Russians returned to their own chalet, Ivanova reminded Nicolai what she had omitted to say to the Americans about her conversation during the Sleigh Ride: that Qwelby had been very excited about the Bushmen and there had been a sense of urgency about his desire to go the Kalahari. Both pairs reported to their headquarters. Neither was surprised at the responses endorsing each pairs' suggestion that they had witnessed very advanced distance viewing, almost certainly enhanced by the Torc the boy wore and that alone was worth exploration.

Nicolai was pleased at the approval from Lubyanka Square of his request for a Mil-39X StealthCopter to be stationed close to the border and ready to fly on his command. He told Ivanova that, if they sensed the Americans were going to act, she was to drive Qwelby to the local safe house and wait there. Meanwhile they were to use the following day's Karting and Fire Ceremony to obtain as much more information as possible. A mistake and they would be lucky to get away with an enforced holiday in Siberia.

An American extraction team had already flown into North Germany along with NATO's latest and fastest StealthCopter – the Eurocopter X5S. Langley approved Farah's request to alert the team for a possible extraction on Saturday night. Wanting a successful outcome which she hoped would confirm her promotion to the next available Assistant Director post, she approved Sherwin's plan to use the following day's Karting to have a "nice quiet talk" with the youth.

For his part, Sherwin was determined to ensure the boy provided the right information to warrant an extraction and thus be able to resume his interrupted holiday with his family.

Both pairs of agents then settled down to enjoy a brief period of relaxed holiday time, knowing that everything that was detected by their remaining listening devices in the bedrooms was automatically recorded and at regular intervals compressed and sent in burst transmissions back to their HQs.

LEDs on the receivers flickered between red and green as the agents heard the sound of doors opening and closing, brief snippets of conversation and the normal noises associated with people getting ready for bed. The LEDs for the boys' bedroom remained green.

'Tullia thinks you're cute,' Qwelby said with a smile.

'Wha?' Cute was for girls like Oona, not boys.

'Rosy cheeks, blonde hair, blue eyes, pink lips. She's never "met" anyone like you before.'

'But...'

BestAzuranFriends. Tullia's thought reached him, along with an image of the girl who'd been with her and a picture of Óweppâ. Qwelby took hold of one of Hannu's hands. 'Will you be our BestAzuranFriend?'

'Like your four BestFriends?'

'Yeah. As long as we all live. Somehow we'll all make it work.'

'All...?'

'Yeah. Our BestFriends at home plus the girl from tonight.'

'Wow!'

Images tumbled through four minds.

Ear-piercing static followed by silence from the receptors ended the agents' listening.

CHAPTER 30

TURMOIL

VERTAZIA

It had been five days since the planet wide embargo on contacting the twins had been agreed with such speed and totality of support that it was impossible for any adult to go against it, even those on whom no inhibitions had been imposed on achieving their adulthood. As senior members of what was the nearest Vertazia had to a government, it was especially true for Elders Mandara and Lellia. Even the youngsters were oppressed by the all-pervasive energy blanket, yet they continued to try to reach the twins using Óweppâ, their talisman.

Tamina's mind knew it was correct what she had said to Wrenden, her young brother, that they had not really failed to save Qwelby because it was essential the twins were together. But her heart did not agree and blamed her for not only failing to save Qwelby but also, because the twins had always been inseparable, failing to save Tullia.

Unable to bear the pain, needing to do something and spurred on by her mother's denial of the family inheritance, four days ago she had gained entry to the SubNet culture with one clear goal in mind: to discover as much as possible about the Uddîšû.

When she eventually found a woman who was prepared to

deal, a young man took her to one side. He told her that, against all the unwritten rules of the Shadow Market, the exchange had been set at a level so high that the woman knew a sixteen-year-old was bound to refuse to deal.

Fire flared through Tamina's belly, her eyes flamed and bolts of lightning singed the air where the man's head had been nanoseconds before. Although shocked at her reaction, Tamina had seen that as proving the strength of her inherited genes and the depth of her love for Tullia and, shaken by the realisation, Qwelby.

She was still spinning from the shock of her discovery of how the the heroine of the Space Wars, Léshmîrâ Kûsheÿnÿ, usually referred to as Hîaûlettâ, Reconciler, had actually succeeded in reuniting the Auriganii. Now Awakened, she was not really surprised at another description of Ÿenlûmâ, choosing to summarise the Aurigan as Befriender. It was how the Uddîšû had achieved the epithet of Kûÿ-maó-Lâš'tûn that had sent her reeling. However she tried to interpret the complex Aurigan, there was only one, bald summary: DeathDealer. At first in denial, then as she found the strength to explore all she'd learnt, she'd become angry at the discovery of yet another distortion of the truth of Aurigan times.

She'd been withdrawn since her discovery, not only as she struggled to cope with what she'd learnt but also because she could not share with her BestFriends. They were too young. But not to tell them was to perpetuate the deception. How could she do that, especially to her own brother? But he was the youngest of all of them and her "Little Eeky." She must not tell him.

Why not? She sensed his often repeated words. In Tazian that was pronounced "Eeknot," which had earnt him her nickname for him of "Eeky."

In turmoil, she left her friends and retreated to the bedroom she shared with Shimara. Looking around, eyes half focussed, waiting for inspiration to jump out at her, a bright colour on a shelf caught her eye. Focussing, she looked at Óweppâ – and stared.

'They're together again!' she shouted as she ran into their gatherroom, holding the talisman aloft. 'XOÑOX!'

Folding in on itself, the four dimensional game of BlackHoleEvasion slid into a niche in the local space-time continuum as, with cries of delight, the others leapt up and passed Óweppâ around, exclaiming at how the twins' colours were brighter than ever before.

'House. Lift. Four to the main gatherroom. Tamuchly,' Tamina commanded. Seconds later the four friends tumbled out onto a thick layer of soft moss that House had spread to save bruises. The bewildered expressions on the faces of the four adults rapidly changed into smiles of delight as they understood the excited babbling from what were for a few moments, four very young children.

In all the hubbub Wrenden grabbed his sister's hand and tightbanded behind their Privacy Shields: *What's up Sis?*

Nothing. The thought was never sent as she turned to her young brother and saw the look of concern on the face... of a tall, young man with the genes of an Adventurer and Explorer, and was reminded of her earlier thinking. She ruffled the top of his head where his hair was cut en brosse. He used to hate that but with their new relationship he'd come to like the gesture of fondness. She let her hand rest there for a moment as she tightbanded: *Later.*

O...kay.

Permissions granted, Pelnak and Shimara went to commune with the transdimensional Stroems, and Tamina and Wrenden went to speak with CuSho. The adults were left discussing the inevitable consequence that brother and sister would want to travel to Earth and should they, even if it was possible, prevent that.

'We cannot prevent that,' Mizena said as the family's Living Statues nodded sombrely. Mentally for the others it was like trying to walk through a swimming pool full of thick, dark molasses as they sought to grasp the challenge her "cannot" was posing to the planet wide consensus on not helping the twins.

The youngsters returned. 'The Stroems were steadily swirling with lots of blues and greens and stronger than last time,' Pelnak reported.

'CuSho told us that the warp, weft and wrule of the Cosmic Hologram has developed new colouration,' Wrenden said.

All four youngsters agreed that although the indications continued to be positive, once again there had been no indication of time.

They all made their way to the dining room where they were joined by Cook and her three young assistants for a quiet celebration over the evening meal.

It was Tamina, looking as though she'd aged several years over the last few days, who said quietly and assuredly. 'The twins are together and,' she blushed, 'from the energy I'm receiving from Óweppâ, they are Awakened. Now, nothing can stop XOÑOX.'

Tears sprang to Mizena's eyes. Once again it was inevitable that the fate of her offspring was in the hands of four, all far too young, children. The other adults sighed. "Cannot" had been resolved – in both interpretations.

Back home after dinner, thinking on how hard the youngsters were working and how much they loved her children, she smiled to herself at how much the four were building good energy quotients. Her children! What was happening to theirs? She never had to worry about that aspect of their lives and for several years had only checked their balances at the time of their rebirthdays.

Using her parental authority and feeling as though she was invading their privacy, she accessed their records – and was stunned. Their quotients had increased substantially over the last four months. Wanting to be sure, she thoughtspoke her husband to join her, and was reassured by his surprise as they studied the colours and vectors together.

The energy system was a complex Aurigan inheritance. When work was undertaken for an individual in a personal manner such as out of love or compassion, that person received a "bonus." Thus, as they expected, there were small additions from the adults and larger additions from their BestFriends' efforts. But the main increase over the two tendays since they'd left Vertazia was due to the twins themselves. Quick calculations showed that it was as if each of them had been going to college every day for the last tenday.

A question to their Great-Uncle Mandara produced the answer. 'We call ourselves Tazii, in honour of our new home of Vertazia. But that only happened when the two worlds parted thirteen thousand years ago. Remember, we are still Auriganii. Original, one hundred percent Auriganii. Sadly restricted to living in the fifth dimension. The Azurii are our descendants with mixtures of Auriganii genes, however latent.

'You know that we need and hope one day to reunite with the Azurii to regain our full Aurigan heritage and live through to the other dimensions. All that can only be possible if the essential Aurigan essence survives in the Azurii. What you have discovered. What your children are doing for all Tazii, I should say Auriganii, is show that essence exists, the Azurii are as human as us, and the dream can become real.'

Mizena and Shandur spread the news around family and friends; happy the children were protected as that level of personal information did not impact on the MentaNet, yet also sad that the significance of what they were doing would not be known.

CHAPTER 31

PLANNING

SWITZERLAND

Late on Friday night Romain took a taxi the short distance from Geneva airport to the Crowne Plaza. He entered the hotel and took the side stairs down to the underground car park. There, he slid into the back seat of a Mercedes SX675 with darkened windows. Some time later, having made certain that he was not being followed, the driver eventually turned into a less salubrious area of the city and stopped outside Bar Minge.

In spite of what he was about to do, Romain felt relief as he got out of the car and walked down the stairs to the basement entrance. He knocked and a little window opened. Hard eyes stared at him through the grill. He returned a level gaze. The window closed and the door opened. He stepped inside to be hit by a fog of smoke and alcohol. As he choked on the atmosphere, he gave a grim smile at the thought that, given all the laws the customers probably broke on a regular basis, that banning smoking in enclosed premises had to be bottom of the list.

Conversation stopped as the people nearest to the door turned to inspect him, then made way for a big, burly man with a thick head of dark hair who pulled Romain into a bear hug. Released, he staggered and Franz laughed as he said, 'Good to see you again, my old friend. Sehr gut. The man who followed you from the airport went back to his hotel after the car swop.'

After one of Franz's dubious deals had led to him being dismissed from CERN, he had worked for several months on the construction of Romain's laboratory on Raiatea. Now, he wanted to catch up with how the premises looked and what was going on.

Curiosity satisfied, he changed the subject. 'A delicate matter, Herr Professor?'

The following morning Romain stood at the window of his room in the Scandic Hotel enjoying the view over Lake Geneva. Under a clear sky, the blue water was a pleasant reminder of his island home. The "Jet d'Eau", soaring seventy metres into the sky, linking with the fountain in lake Jyväsjärvi, spoke to him as a good omen, for the night had gone well.

There had been a very pleasant reunion with two old friends, especially Franz who'd accepted what Romain had described as the youth's link with the study of Noetic Science. And business had also been good. Pierre had said that since the first discussion with Romain they had made enough checks to satisfy themselves that they were not going to upset anybody important by delivering a package to a suitable European destination. Romain had nodded, guessing the sort of people in the criminal fraternity to whom Pierre was alluding.

A French passport was to be provided as Raiatea was a French Overseas Department, together with a Visa waiver for entry to the USA. Arrangements had been made to deliver the package – if necessary. 'A lot less risk than in former times,' had been Pierre's dark comment. In case Qwelby returned to Kotomäki, Romain had given them Erki's name and number as a useful local contact.

Romain's next step was to return to Jyväskylä and make a final attempt to get Dr Keskinen to convince the boy to go to Raiatea.

CHAPTER 32

MORNING

THE KALAHARI

Tullia awoke in a state of total bliss. She felt both more relaxed and energised than ever before. All her fears of Awakening had been banished. The sensation of her own twins' heads resting on her breasts was the final confirmation she needed that she was a woman. She sank back into the magic of having been everything and everywhere, even for a time her twin with a tall blonde girl.

Her twin? Last night? She opened her eyes. The heads pillowed on her were not her twins but those of Ungka and Ishe, and two more girls were cuddled up behind them. Where was Tsetsana? Ah, yes. She vaguely remembered her leaving at sunrise to attend to Xameb.

Last night as they'd snuggled together for warmth, N!Obile and Mandingwe had been fascinated by her velvet-like skin. Ishe had stroked her, she'd started to purr and the sweetness of Ungka's lips on hers had taken her back to her Moon Day. Her discomfort as her body revealed why she'd fled the sacred space had been swept away by the girls' desire to explore. Her breasts had swelled, she'd dared hope, had asked – and her PassionMilk had set them all on fire, including an excited Ungka.

She and Qwelby had never been together as richly as they had been last night. No longer was she a female Quantum Twin – she was a powerful Quantum Woman.

Fire ran through her, or rather it was running through the young lass lying at the feet of the over three metre tall Aurigan who was smiling with joy as this other half child endured the full experience of *Thala llangaany ZhālāwaVezâGhi.*

Tullia was burning from the multicoloured streams of energy running through her body and sparking a myriad of bright firepoints of light. She knew more of her DNA was awakening. A disembodied face looked down from high above the hut, compassion in the heavily slanted eyes with their purple orbs set in bright blue ovals and all limned in silver. 'May there be unity in the bringing forth of your own birth,' a voice whispered in her mind. As she tried to grasp the meaning, sounds and movement brought her awareness back to where she was. She gentled her friends back from a night of riding comets amongst the stars and journeying through a multiplicity of exploding suns and erupting volcanoes.

As they washed with cold water and home made soap and dressed, she kissed each girl in turn, mentally reinforcing her request: 'Very special friends. Please. Keep my secret.'

Not only was she reunited with her twin more powerfully than ever before, she was about to spend her first full day as a woman of the tribe and, like all young women, spend her nights in a hut with a group of girlfriends.

CHAPTER 33

KARTING

LAINIO-FINLAND

Where am I? Qwelby looked around. There was a window through which he could see night-time sky with millions of twinkling stars. A lot of light? Of course, winter, reflecting off snow. But where? Ahh. A wooden chalet in northern Finland. Last night? Tullia! Where...?

He rolled over and saw pink cheeks, blonde hair and blue eyes. Hannu.

'Tullia says you're not bad at kissing.' Grinning, Qwelby leant towards his friend. 'But you need more lessons.'

'Gerrorff!'

Qwelby fell back laughing as Hannu pushed him away. Hannu leapt on him and pounded on his chest. 'I'll give you trying to teach me to kiss!'

The boys wrestled and fell off the bed, crashing onto the floor where they lay laughing until a draught on their bare skin from the slightly open window made them get up and put on dressing gowns. As they headed for the bathroom they passed Mrs Rahkamo standing in the doorway to her bedroom, where the agents' receivers recorded the conversation from the two remaining listening devices.

'What was all that about?' she asked.

'Tullia in my mind. No professor, no police, no-one spies on me. Three more days fun then.' He shot his fist into the air. 'Toolleeaa!'

Later, Mrs Rahkamo remained behind when the boys left to go Karting. Whilst they had been clay shooting the previous day she had explored the Snow Village. Now she was content to stay in the chalet and read a magazine. Something she seldom had time for at home.

Qwelby was lost in thought. He knew he'd not really become a dragon or Tullia a unicorn. All that imagery had been advanced, eighth dimension, energy manipulation of Attributes. But it had all been an unconscious, instinctive drawing on the power of their inherited genes. And that fitted with his two theories. The first was the repressive nature of life on Vertazia that inhibited growing-up. The second was that he and his twin had to have more active DNA than the normal Tazian twenty-five percent and, in spite of their Forms being in the third dimension, that DNA was being activated now they were free of those restrictions.

Maija and the agents had met that morning in the Russians' chalet to share the latest information they had received.

'The Foreign Ministry has reported that we have never issued a passport with either of the names Qenco or Sofuoğlu,' she said.

'Illegal bloody immigrant,' Sherwin snorted. 'That's why he's on the run. That Professor has spooked him. Sodding wild goose chase all right.'

Maija reported that Romain's flight to Geneva had caught everyone off their guard and their agent had lost him. They all grimaced. The downside of this new cooperation had been that the Russians had had to go to Helsinki to be briefed along with the later arriving Americans, when they could have already been on the ground in Siilinjärvi. Maija confirmed the boy and the others

169

were staying for the whole period of their planned stay as flights had been booked for Tuesday morning: Qwelby to Helsinki and the Rahkamos to Siilinjärvi.

She explained that three EM disturbances had affected the Snow Village last night. Two had occurred at the times that the bugs in the target's chalet had ceased to work, the other at the time the agents had been filming the two boys. When staff had spoken with guests they had discovered that for the first and third events, the interference had reached as far as several chalets to the sides of the agents' and in the row behind them. At the time of the filming, interference had spread across a much wider radius.

All the agents professed that they were content to accept the theory that the Torc was some form of enhanced communication device and had to be the source of the localised interference, but not the widespread disruption on twenty-seven December: that was down to "the boffins" to determine.

The fact that Qwelby was an illegal immigrant reopened all the unvoiced concerns the Americans and Russians had about possible connections with either the Dark Government supported by Russia or the American backed Alternative Government, whose members had been massively purged following the failed coup attempt or, especially as he said he came from East Turkey, a Kurdish liberation movement with whom both countries had ambivalent relationships. They agreed they needed more information and the next opportunities were the morning's Karting and the evening's Fire Ceremony.

Urgent messages to Lubyanka Square and Langley sent desk bound agents into a flurry of research.

A total of fifteen people had gathered for the Karting. Four Karts on the track at any time was considered optimum and Maija arranged for Nicolai, Sherwin, Qwelby and Hannu to be placed in each of the initial four races. With each of them finishing in the first two, and Maija again speaking to the Karting organiser, Qwelby and Sherwin met in the first semi.

On the first circuit Qwelby spotted Sherwin trying a dangerous overtaking move. The American had driven up the hard bank on the left and was coming down, forcing Qwelby to brake, pull to the right and helplessly watch as the rear of Sherwin's Kart clipped the front of his own, sending him spinning off the track into a bank of thick snow as his engine stalled. Qwelby was livid. Having searched the American he knew the collision had been deliberately planned. Free of surveillance and reunited with his twin, he had been really enjoying himself.

A satisfied Sherwin turned off the engine and got out of his Kart. 'Hey, buddy. Sure an hell am sorry. Hang on. I'll come and help.' Although shallow where he'd stopped, the snow was iced over making walking treacherous. Qwelby's feet had a good purchase against the hard packed snow and he was steadily pushing his Kart back onto the edge of the track.

'Hang on, Buddy. Don't injure yourself,' Sherwin called out, trying to sound good-natured as he pulled the thick outer glove off his left hand and slipped it with its thin, insulated glove into his coat pocket and felt the reassuring weight of the heavy Colt forty-five. He was right-handed but the way the seat belt fitted meant he'd had to put the gun in his left pocket. Perfect, Sherwin thought to himself. Now we'll see how much English you really do speak with my Colt pressed against your balls.

Sensing dark energy not just around Sherwin but actually reaching out to him, Qwelby was in a panic as he leaped into the Kart and the starter motor whined uselessly as a smell of petrol filled the air.

'Flooded the engine,' Sherwin said as he gripped Qwelby's shoulder with his right hand and started to draw the gun from his pocket. It caught on the edge of the lining. Qwelby didn't know what the American was doing but a dark grey energy shot through with dirty ochre surrounded whatever was in his pocket.

A memory surfaced. The energy was similar to but darker than that around the policewoman's pistol.

"Flooded." Qwelby stopped pumping the accelerator. *KAIGII!* Without thinking he reacted as he would do at home, reached for his twin's energy and sent his fortified mind into the engine, mentally screaming for help from the Multiverse. He saw sparks. The engine fired and the Kart leapt away, spinning Sherwin around to fall face down into the snow with a grunt of pain as, trapped between gun and body, his wrist bent awkwardly.

Qwelby tried his hardest to overtake the two who had driven by while he was stalled. It was all so different from Vertazia. 'Labirden Xzarze!' he swore as he spun off the track on his third lap right by the start line. Out of his Kart almost before it had come to a standstill, he strode away across the snow, pulling off his gloves, parka, sweater and shirt and throwing them to the side before throwing himself face down in deep snow.

Hannu followed, picking up the clothes and stood watching his friend, remembering New Year's Eve when he had done something similar to cool off.

Qwelby sat up. 'I want to terminate the Lifeline of that man without a father,' he ground out between teeth clenched to stop him from shouting.

Hannu stared at his friend. Then burst out laughing.

'What's funny?' Qwelby growled.

'Stick to swearing in Tazian,' Hannu said as he tried to stop laughing. 'Why? What happened?'

'The American. He tried to ram me. Pretended it was a mistake in overtaking. I know it was deliberate.' Qwelby tapped his temple. 'He has a big gun and he was going to... I'm not sure.'

Further conversation was stopped as Viivi approached, calling Hannu for his semi-final. Hannu thrust the bundle of clothes into Qwelby's arms and set off walking back to the track.

'You're all wet,' Viivi said, looking at the clothes Qwelby was holding and added, 'Here. I'll dry you.' And started rubbing his arms with the towel she'd been carrying.

'You all right?' she asked.

'Yes. Was very hot. Had to cool off.'

'People say that, but I've never seen anyone do it so literally.'

The towel rubbing across his chest was nice, arousing strong stirrings inside him. The hood of Viivi's parka had fallen back. He was looking at rosy cheeks, blonde hair, bright blue eyes and soft, warm colours flowing through her aura. He lent forward but was stopped as Viivi dried his face with a smile on her bright pink lips.

'Must watch race,' he said as he heard the sound of engines revving. Viivi took his bundle of clothes and handed him garments one by one as they walked back to the track.

Although Hannu came last in the second semi, he was happy to be greeted by Qwelby telling him he had gone round in a faster time than before. Nicolai was content to come second in the final to the youthful Canadian woman who had won Hannu's race of three Karts and this time really showed her skill by setting that day's fastest time.

Trophies were presented, photographs taken and the group broke up with most people heading for the Ice Bar.

Viivi approached the boys. 'Are you all right after your... accident?' she asked Qwelby.

'Yes. Snow very different at home.' He smiled, pleased at how he was learning to manipulate words so that he told the truth, yet conveyed a different impression.

Looking up at him, once again the hood of her Parka fell back. Qwelby leant forward.

'Not here!' Viivi said, putting a hand on his chest.

'Oh. Where?'

Those eyes! That smile! And it felt as though her hand was vibrating. 'There's a tour of the Ice Hotel this afternoon. Meet at the Ice Bar at four.'

Qwelby placed his left hand over his right heart and made a little bow as Viivi stepped back and walked away.

'You cheeky sod!' Hannu exclaimed as he punched Qwelby on the arm. 'How d'ye get away with it?'

'Don't know! All so new. And... bloody great!' He grinned as he tried what he thought was a Finnish swearword and Hannu didn't laugh. There had been a brief moment when, after receiving his twin's energy, he had realised that their joining had made him much more powerful than ever before on Vertazia. The exciting feelings spreading through him at the thought of kissing Viivi pushed that awareness into Deep Memory.

CHAPTER 34

PLANNING

LAINIO-FINLAND

That afternoon, Maija joined the agents in the Americans' chalet. Sherwin ruefully explained the Karting "accident" and had to admit that his plan had not given him the intended opportunity to "have a quiet chat" with their target. He did not mention his gun having got stuck. That had not been part of the plan he'd outlined to Farah. Ivanova and Farah said that their plan to have a friendly chat with Mrs Rahkamo had failed as she had not left her chalet.

Both pairs of agents shared the latest briefings they'd received. Not surprisingly, they were different. The Russians focused on the psychic nature of the communication, the Americans on group hysteria. Both dismissed the EM disturbances as being due to the Aurora Borealis, the officially given explanation for the widespread disturbances on twenty-seven December and the much smaller effects on three January. Except for "Qwelby", names the boy had used or was using were on databanks, but none related to any individual of his apparent age and certainly not with eyes like his. Both Lubyanka Square and Langley had provided various interpretations of "Government" and "Rulers" and were keen to know more.

Knowing how quickly the Russians were able to whisk the target across the border, the Americans emphasised the need for further fact finding. Nicolai agreed. He would have anyway, but inside he was seething at having his hands tied by an obvious power struggle in Moscow. He had received another message that morning. The MGB, the Ministry of State Security that had overall command of both the FSB and the SVR, had stepped in and Nicolai's authority to order an immediate extraction had been revoked.

'What's the Finnish take, Maija?' Sherwin asked.

'I agree with what the scientists have put together in the papers you have. As far as the Torc is concerned, its short range effects cannot have anything to do with the EM disturbances on twenty-seven December or three January. When he arrives in Helsinki, we expect him to get another flight to take him to this Tullia. We will ensure that goes smoothly.

'The original agreement was for you to monitor the Professor. You're only in Lainio because it was assumed that Romain was going to follow the boy. The Minister has agreed that you may continue to keep a "protective eye" on the boy until he catches his plane on Tuesday. We'll obviously monitor at the airport in Helsinki.

'The variety of reports we all have received indicate that Romain has nothing to do with any weapons developments. He is a highly respected scientist and businessman. He is no longer a person of interest. The answer to the EM disturbances lies elsewhere with, as we have previously said, the scientists.

'You must be careful. There must not be any more rash actions as with the Karting. We still don't know who the boy is and what his connections are. With words like "Government," "Rulers" and "Fighting" against one or the other being bandied about, my government does not want this surveillance turning into an international incident.'

All four agents sanctimoniously agreed.

As they went their separate ways, both pairs of agents were of the same opinion. If no-one else, Professor Romain believed the boy was somehow related to or a witness of whatever had caused the EM disturbances. Each pair needed to ensure the others did not take any precipitate action and would watch them carefully.

When the Americans returned to their chalet, Farah was both relieved and delighted at the message from Langley authorising an extraction and, as Agent-in-charge, empowering her to initiate that when the conditions were right. She agreed with Sherwin that a celebratory drink was in order: for him, now able to return to his interrupted holiday with his family; for her, another success to chalk up towards a future promotion.

Mrs Rahkamo joined the boys for the afternoon tour of the Ice Hotel where, like the Ice Bar, the temperature was kept at between minus two and minus five degrees centigrade. When the tour finished and she and Hannu were walking back to their chalet, she asked why Qwelby wasn't with them, and decided not to probe her son's smiling reply that Qwelby was checking arrangements with Viivi for the Fire Ceremony.

CHAPTER 35

BURGLARS

LAINIO-FINLAND

Not liking to arrive early for an event, Mrs Rahkamo was embarrassed when Viivi directed herself and the two boys past the other people already assembled to places in the front row and close to the Sami presenting the ancient ceremony.

'Have I done it how you want?' Viivi asked Qwelby as she removed the "Reserved" signs from a chair and three thick cushions.

'Kabona, Vii. Perfect,' he replied with his eyes twinkling and his smile turning into a grin at the pretty picture of her cheeks reddening.

'I take it she's joining us on the ground,' Hannu said. 'Why?'

'Closer to the energies of the land.'

Hannu shook his head in wonder. So many people didn't like Qwelby because of his colour yet he had no problem with girls. And it wasn't only girls. Hannu himself really liked the alien and his group of mates had accepted Qwelby as one of them the very first time they'd all met. 'Magnetic bloody personality,' he muttered under his breath. Then wondered if he might ever really meet Tullia. And hoped.

A few moments later Qwelby looked up in surprise as he saw Viivi removing the Reserved sign from the cushion next to him and indicating that Farah was to sit there. His hurt that Viivi was not sitting by him as arranged disappeared, to be replaced by curiosity as Viivi's look and gesture of helplessness confirmed his quick search of her mind. Yet he saw Farah was not happy as she glared behind him. He turned his head and smiled at Ivanova where she was sitting by Maija.

After an introduction and explanation by the Sami, which Viivi translated into English, the ceremony commenced with the induction of the guests into the world of the Sami. Then the drumming started.

Hannu was enthralled as he watched the ice melting and the edges of the glaciers swiftly retreating north. Great herds of animals of the many different kinds that had been grazing between the southern edge of the ice and the northern side of a great inland lake moved ever further north, followed by several tribes of humans. Finally, as the glaciers ceased shrinking, the floods dissipated and the large lake had become an inland sea, the great herds of reindeer settled and the Sami set up their present day homes.

There was a long silence when the drumming finished. Qwelby forced himself back to the present and opened his eyes. Turning to the side he saw a look of amazement on his friend's face.

'What did you do?' Hannu asked.

'Nothing.' With the heat building inside him, Qwelby had unzipped his parka and his fingers were resting around his pulsing crystal. 'Drumming take us into energy of land, and land show us. You are close with me and Tullia. So you saw what I saw.'

'But there aren't any records of the Sami until much more recently. I know because we had to study that in history lessons.'

'What you saw is true. I was there... errm... my genes.'

'Well, how did it start then? That day at home you said a war. But bows and arrows and spears did not do that.'

'We used more...'

The conversation was interrupted by a Lapp asking everyone to stand for the conclusion of the ceremony.

179

Qwelby was very happy to force back into Deep Memory the images of the events thirteen thousand years ago that had precipitated the ending of the last ice age. Sinking back into the memories that he assumed were encoded in his genes made events totally real. Reliving a life as the Dragon Lord was one thing, but to experience that fight with his twin that had caused the separation of the two worlds. That was far too painful a memory.

He was pulled out of his memories by the leading Sami walking around, marking everyone with a Fire Sign, then he was surrounded by a curious group of people, including Farah asking penetrating questions. Eventually, pleading that he was too tired to continue speaking a foreign language, Mrs Rahkamo took his arm, and with her son on her other arm the three set off for their chalet, Mrs Rahkamo saying she preferred a hot chocolate to more of the sub zero temperatures of the Ice Bar.

The sight of the jewel pulsing in the boy's Torc and the discussion with Hannu that Farah had overheard were all she needed. As she made her way to the Ice Bar to meet Sherwin, she sent a brief text. Shorn of all the coding were two words: 'Extraction immediate.'

Seated in the control centre in the specially adapted C17 parked at the edge of Germany's Hohn Air Base, a little south of the border with Denmark, the colonel heading up the American extraction team barked her orders. The XS5 StealthCopter was pushed out of the hangar and a few minutes later was in the air and headed North East above the Baltic Sea.

Now seated in the Ice Bar, Farah's phone pinged and she showed her colleague the code word indicating the Chopper was airborne, followed by the expected time of arrival.

Sherwin confirmed that during the Fire Ceremony he and Nicolai had planted more bugs in the target's chalet to replace those that had been destroyed.

'Good. We'll stay here and look as though we're drinking,' Farah said. 'We can see the Russians' chalet from here and they can see us. I want them to think we're relaxing. Nearer the time we'll go back to our chalet, get ready, keep them quiet and afterwards be very apologetic.'

'Please, Aunt Seija,' Qwelby said as they reached the chalet door. 'I need to stay here under the stars.'

'With my son?'

'Kabona. Thank you.'

Qwelby led Hannu a short distance down the road until there was no-one nearby. 'Something's not right,' he said as he switched on his compiler. 'I asked Viivi to arrange the seating so we three were close to the Sami, as we were, and with a cushion next to me for her. But she put that American woman there. I could see she had to, so I searched her. The American. She was like that police sergeant in Kotomäki, but it was like her questions were harder.'

'More difficult?'

'No. More needed. The sergeant wanted to know. This American had to know.'

'Why?'

'She started during the tour in the Ice Hotel. At first I thought she was just curious. But her questions about me. She was trying to build a picture.'

'But you said the Russian woman asked questions.'

'I'd asked about her life. And my reaction about the Bushmen. It was over the top. I got out of that. But she's nice. Warm. This American. I don't know. Then there's her husband. How he looked at me as we arrived. Strong dislike. The clay shooting, he was really nasty. Then that deliberate crash with the Kart. Stupid. Energies not right. Why me? I must find out.'

'Search him?'

'I searched his wife. I didn't learn enough. At home I would know, but here, reading you Azurii, it's not like at home.'

'Ask Viivi.'

Qwelby shook his head. 'I've been scanning my memory. I don't think she was telling the truth about the damaged sleigh. That hurts. I thought she was nice. Well, no, she is, but...'

The boys stood looking at each other.

'Hannu. You Azurii tell lies easily?'

'Well, yeah, but...'

'If you don't want to. You're made to?'

'That's... well... not good.'

'Got it!'

'What?'

'Viivi was going to sit next to me tonight. I've let her think I'm nineteen. She's nineteen. Her first big job. Mr Perälä's her uncle. Tonight. I know she was made to let Farah sit by me.'

'So what now?'

'We'll take a look in the American's chalet. They're in the Ice Bar.'

'What?'

'The back door. It's not got a card slide lock.'

'But...'

'Come on.' Qwelby grabbed one of Hannu's arms and they started walking back towards the hotel complex as he explained how they would get in. As soon as no-one was in sight, Qwelby pulled his friend off the road and behind the cover of the chalets.

Reaching the back of the Americans' chalet, Qwelby went to work on the door whilst Hannu watched in the direction of the Ice Bar. Using Hannu's pocketknife to put gentle turning pressure on the lock, Qwelby slid a hairgrip into it. He slowly and carefully raised each tumbler in turn, keeping them raised by the slight pressure of the pocketknife. A careful press with his shoulder and the door swung inward. He whistled to Hannu and stepped inside, smiling. It had taken a lot more concentration than on Vertazia but no alarms had sounded.

Hannu checked the lock. Finding it didn't need a key to open from the inside, he let the door close and followed his friend down the short corridor into the living room. He stood well back from the window as he again looked towards the Ice Bar.

Qwelby went into the principal bedroom and found the safe in the same place as in their own chalet - in the wardrobe. With energy signatures all over the keypad with its ten numbers, he flicked into the corner of his mind that was Tullia's. She was there and so strong that he asked to borrow some of her energy, receiving a definite whiff of her sweat along with a draw on her Solar Energy Quotient. He grinned at the restoration of their normal life. The smell was her way of making him pay for the energy.

Cursing the slow vibrations of the third dimension, he placed his hands on either side of the safe and rested his forehead against the front. Very slowly and with a mixture of feeling and seeing, he identified the four numbers most recently used. His luck was in as, with twenty-four possible combinations, the safe opened on the seventh attempt.

Having learnt his several languages from CD's, YouTube and speaking Finnish, he had not learnt to read much of any of the scripts. The few names or words he needed to know he recognised from their shapes. He called Hannu and between them they closed the bedroom door, drew the curtains and switched on the bedside lights. At the bottom of the safe, underneath a few papers and small wads of money of different currencies was a white envelope. Hannu carefully removed and opened it.

'It's a letter from the Interior Ministry,' Hannu said. 'Says ... "requested to give all assistance to... CIA... and comply with requirements of any officer of... SUPO." That's our intelligence service. Bloody Spooks!'

'Ghosts?'

'No. Spies. We're in deep shit! Let's get out of here.'

With trembling hands, Qwelby carefully replaced the envelope in exactly the same position, closed the safe and then the wardrobe door. As Hannu went to switch off the lights he caught sight of a black metal box on the dressing table with LEDs glowing. 'Hey BroQ, look at this.'

The boys examined what looked like a miniature speaker set. The oval shape had five small grills. By each one were a red and a green LED, a circular depression that looked like an on/off switch and a short rectangular screen. By one grill a green and a red were glowing, reds were also glowing by two other grills. By all three the small screens were lit. 'Volume controls, I guess,' Hannu announced. None of the other LEDs or screens were lit.

'I bet the Yanks are bugging the Russian's chalet.' Hannu said, then explained what he meant as they switched off the lights, opened the curtains and allowed time for their eyes to accustom to the faint, star-lit room.

Qwelby opened the door into the living room and was blinded by a light shining right into his eyes.

'What the hell!' Sherwin exclaimed, having expected to see the Russians.

Qwelby's eyes saw a two-tone, sand coloured carpet, a figure half crouched in a firing stance, wearing khaki trousers, a tan sweater and a dark brown, leather jacket. A large pistol was pointing at his face. His mind saw another planet, hard sand baking under a bright sun, a man swathed from head to toe in sandy brown robes with only his piecing black eyes visible and aiming a long, projectile firing weapon at him.

Qwelby grabbed each side of the door frame and launched himself forward and down and head butted his assailant in the stomach. Sherwin staggered back. A low table catching him just below the knees, he flailed his arms, lost his balance and crashed down with a loud bang as his gun went off.

'Stay right there!'

Qwelby heard the command from another warrior to his right and saw a long, brown weapon with a shiny end being raised to point at his WingRider. He swung to his right and grabbed the hand holding what he thought was the end of the weapon as he threw his left arm around the man's waist. He straightened up, lifted the man off his feet and swung him around.

Crack! The gun under Qwelby's hand fired.

'Yeow!' Sherwin cried out.

There was a thump as the feet of the man in Qwelby's arms hit the wall, then he slipped in Qwelby's grasp. As his mind cleared, Qwelby realised he was not holding a man but a woman, where he was and who he was fighting.

Seeing Sherwin using his gun hand to push himself up, Qwelby swung Farah back. Throwing up his left arm to guard his face, Sherwin fell back as there came another loud crack from Farah's gun followed by a sharp, double-crack as the double-glazing shattered, an expletive from Sherwin, the boom of his forty-five and a crash as a wall light was smashed.

Farah was nearly jerked out of Qwelby's arms as she caught her foot in the sling supporting her colleague's sprained wrist. Qwelby's mind flashed up one of Hannu's explanations. His thumb was on that little lever. He pressed it forward and squeezed Farah's trigger finger. As Farah tried to wrench the gun away, Qwelby emptied its magazine in an ear shattering series of reports, thuds of bullets striking walls and furniture, sounds of tinkling glass, a yell from Farah and a stench of burning from all the cordite.

'Don't move,' Sherwin grunted as he tried to bring his gun hand around his colleague's struggling body, pressing on his chest. 'Don't move!' Sherwin shouted over Farah's stream of invective at having been shot with her own gun.

Qwelby lashed out with his left foot. Dizzy and with his ears ringing, his aim was off. Instead of kicking the barrel of the gun, the toe of his boot smashed into Sherwin's wrist. The loud report of the forty-five almost covered the American's shout as the gun was ripped from his hand and went sailing through the air to smash into the television monitor. Qwelby remained transfixed, staring at the two struggling Americans.

'GO!' his WingRider shouted. His hand was grabbed. 'COME ON!' He was pulled along the corridor.

'I've shot two people!' a horrified Qwelby exclaimed as he threw away the now empty pistol.

'You think I don't fucking know!?' Hannu tugged the alien out of the back door and round to the end next to the Russians' chalet. 'Quiet,' he hissed. 'Look.'

Peering round the corner they saw Nicolai crossing to the Americans' chalet, his Parka flapping open and holding a large gun out in front of him. A few moments later they heard a brief shout in Russian but were unable to make out the words. They heard the door to the Russian's chalet close and Ivanova appeared with her Parka zipped up and carrying a black holdall.

His whole body vibrating, a dazed Qwelby felt his arm grabbed as he was pulled to the back door of the Russians' chalet. 'Open the lock,' his WingRider commanded. Qwelby slid the penknife into the keyhole. Puzzled that he was being given the orders, but aware he was dazed, he complied. The Solid's locking system was so simple. He slid his mind inside it, pushed the door open and was pulled into a chalet where all the lights were on, and through into a bedroom. As a door was opened he saw a keypad with four energised numbers, which faded one by one.

'Open it!'

Qwelby depressed the four numbers in the same sequence as they had faded and the safe door clicked open.

Pushed out of the way, Qwelby staggered backwards and sat on the bed. Senses returned and he saw... Hannu opening the door wide and, after a moment's hesitation, easing part way out a dark blue folder with red lettering. 'Federal'naya Sluzhba Bezopasnosti,' Hannu read slowly. 'FSB. Russian intelligence!' he exclaimed.

'Look Lamaannu,' Qwelby said in a hollow sounding voice, pointing to a unit that looked similar to the one in the Americans' chalet. One green and two red LEDs were glowing, whilst the other three pairs remained unlit.

'Shoulder holsters!' Hannu exclaimed, pointing to the headrest where leather contraptions were hanging from the ends. He slid the folder back, closed the doors to the safe and the wardrobe and the boys ran out though the back door, not stopping until they were behind a chalet in the second row.

Breathing heavily, they heard the sound of footsteps and peered around the corner of the chalet. They heard the door to the Russians' chalet open, then a few moments later it was closed and Ivanova walked from her chalet back to that of the Americans.

'Oh, Hannu. I thought she was a friend. I liked talking with her. And Nicolai. At the drinks, then clay shooting. Both of them. All lies. What a terrible world you live in.'

'You've said yours is not so good,' was Hannu's tart reply.

There was a strained silence as, through the paths between the chalets, they watched several people arriving at the Americans' chalet. First came Maija running up from the direction of the staff accommodation at the back of the Ice Hotel, followed moments later by Viivi and then from the direction of the Snow Village, Mr Perälä and two medics.

As the last person disappeared inside the chalet, Qwelby heaved a big sigh. 'You're right,' he said in a sombre voice. 'The Americans wanted to shoot us and thieves wanted to steal from me. That's easy to see. But my world. It's mental, emotional and psychological oppression. And so deep in our way of life we don't know it's there. Only now I'm on Earth I see it. Having sex in The Shades! Hannu. We think your world's terrible. But mine's worse.'

Deciding Qwelby's attempts at swearing in Finnish were both too funny to correct and that it showed his friend had recovered, Hannu led the way as they jogged down the back of the double row of chalets and up the other side. As they came alongside their own chalet, Hannu stopped Qwelby from going inside, saying, 'I've been thinking.'

The once again quiet night was pierced by the warbling sound of sirens, followed by the strobing red and blue lights of two police cars.

They saw Maija and Nicolai come outside the Americans' chalet and talk with the police. Nicolai was showing them a piece of paper and Maija was on her mobile. A policeman pulled a handset from his car and started talking into it.

With the sirens turned off, the boys clearly heard raised voices. After what was obviously a long argument the officer put the handset back, all the police got into their cars and drove off whilst Mr Perälä walked away in the direction of the office.

The boys looked at each other in amazement. Then Hannu grinned. 'It's like what I said about that sergeant questioning you. Same as in American films I love, where the local cops are told to butt out by the FBI. Well here it's our SUPO.'

A clattering in the sky, a bright searchlight piercing the night and a yellow helicopter ambulance descended. Two paramedics entered the chalet. Several minutes later, steadied by the first two medics who'd arrived, a limping Sherwin emerged with his left arm in a bigger sling and his right hand swathed in bandages. He was followed into the helicopter by a stretcher with Farah on it. As soon as the chopper had left everyone else came out of the chalet and stood talking for a few minutes before dispersing.

'There's a lot to be said for the good old-fashioned ways of espionage.' Nicolai's laughter filled voice reached the boys. 'Seeing those two Yanks taken out with their own gun, and by a kid. Much better than shooting down a bloody drone.'

Maija accompanied the Russians into their chalet and the original two medics headed back to the Snow Village, leaving Viivi to walk back to her apartment by herself.

'I find out what said,' Qwelby said and set off running along the service road behind the chalets.

As soon as Maija had left, Nicolai sent an urgent message to Lubyanka Square detailing what had happened and urging in the strongest possible terms that the boy be extracted immediately.

CHAPTER 36

VIIVI

LAINIO-FINLAND

'What happened?' Qwelby called out as he caught up with Viivi as she was about to close the door to her apartment.

'Come in.' She closed the door behind him. 'Join me when you're ready.'

Apart from kicking off her shoes she didn't bother removing her parka before opening the inner door. Barefoot and wearing shorts and a t-shirt, Qwelby followed a few moments later into the bed-sitting room, the perfumed smell reminding him of Jenni's bedroom. He realised why Viivi had been in a hurry to get into what was for him the very overheated room when he saw that all she was wearing under her now open parka was a black t-shirt and leggings.

'You don't drink, do you?' she asked as she took a large sip from a glass of Mali.

'No.' Hannu had told him about the effects of alcohol, which were very different from what was drunk on Vertazia. He wanted to try it but feared losing control and giving himself away.

Viivi sat on a chair and gestured Qwelby to the bed. She took another large sip of brandy and swilled the rest around in her glass before looking back up at him. She had been briefed in the strictest confidence about who he was and that the Americans and Russians were there to protect him. 'Didn't you hear the announcement over the tannoy about security preparations for an important visitor?'

'No.'

'The Americans were cleaning their guns when they accidentally shot each other.'

'That's a lie!' Qwelby blurted out before his mind was able to stop his mouth. He'd been too engrossed in remembering their passionate kisses in the Ice Hotel and hoping for more.

'What?'

Qwelby heaved a sigh and told her the story of what had happened in the Americans' chalet, omitting any mention about opening the safe. Inevitably he spoke in his rich musical baritone and thoughtwrapped Viivi into being there as if she were him.

As she returned to awareness of her room she found herself clinging for safety to a big, strong man. 'How did you do that?'

Qwelby leant forward and their lips met. Both were hungry for more. Kissing Oona and Jenni had been lovely. This was exciting and a new throbbing told him he wanted more. But what to do?

Viivi grasped his t-shirt and pulled it over his head. Her arms went around him as their lips met again and she felt skin like velvet. She ran her hands over his back and a soft rumble started in his throat. He was purring! She moved her hands to his chest and pushed him away. 'Who are you?'

'I show you,' he said, breathing heavily and slipping into her mind. 'First, we have to fly there on my dragon...'

Viivi opened her eyes and saw a brown face with very kissable dark red lips. Soon he was purring again. She was very aware of his hard masculinity pressing against her. He was a great kisser, knew exactly what she liked, but... something was wrong. She'd been to his homeworld, met his twin and amongst his friends two more definitely human-looking girls. She pulled away and searched his face.

'Have you ever been with a girl?'

'I'm with you.'

'I mean sex.'

'Oh, no.'

Viivi smiled. He was blushing. This big hunk of a man she'd fancied at first sight had turned into a shy boy! Alien customs? 'You want to?'

'Oh. Yes.'

She guided him, saying words like 'There' and 'Just like that.' But it was over all too fast for her. She'd expected that and waited for his breathing to steady when she smiled and said, 'Again. This time slowly.'

He proved to be a quick learner. Apart from an occasional 'Not so hard!' she let her hands and sighs guide him.

His pectorals were swelling. Only a little but the pressure was too much. He was a Quantum Twin. He guided her head. 'Do the same for me.... Harder... Bite me.'

His roar carried them amongst the stars. She locked strong legs over his thighs and together they plunged into the fiery heart of an exploding sun.

'You make my hearts burn.'

'You're heavy.' Viivi grunted and unlocked her legs. As he rolled off onto his back, she cuddled up to him, rested her head on his chest and told him the story she'd been given about him. 'Your father is very important to the peace process in a war torn area. Not specified. He's afraid you may be kidnapped and used against him. So you've been sent away for safety. Both the Americans and Russians want the warring to end so are here to protect you. They wanted you to stay here as it's much easier to protect you here than in some big city.' She moved her head to look him in the eye.

'The Americans and Russians hate each other. My purring Tiger, you're not safe now the Americans have gone.'

Having noticed the jarring energies passing between the two

191

couples, Qwelby was not surprised at her last comment. He was not going to spoil the wonderful feelings coursing through him by thinking about that now. Gently, he stroked her and listened to her mental purring. She hadn't needed to guide their second time. When she'd started his lesson he'd slipped inside her mind and learnt what to listen for. Still joined and swamped by both their sensations his mind was totally blown.

They dozed.

A harsh ringing sound intruded.

'Shit! My business phone.' Rolling over him Viivi picked it up and answered in a brisk, professional voice.

Qwelby felt his chest. His pectorals were back to normal except for her bite marks and some tenderness. PassionMilk had jetted and the cosmos had whirled around them. He sighed with relief that his latest discovery of what it meant to be an identical twin was... all right. In fact... very all right. His biggest fear was now totally laid to rest. He grinned. He wasn't just a Quantum Twin, he was a powerful Quantum Man.

Fire ran through him or rather, it was running through the young lad lying at the feet of the nearly four metre tall Aurigan, who reached out a hand in comfort – and stopped. He could not, must not deny to his... this half child, the full experience of *Thala llangaany ZhālāwaVezâGhi.*

Qwelby was racked with pain as he watched multicoloured streams of energy running through his body sparking a myriad of bright firepoints of light, whilst a disembodied face looked down on him from above the ceiling. Compassion was in the heavily slanted eyes with their purple orbs set in bright blue ovals and all limned in silver. 'May there be unity in the bringing forth of your own birth,' a voice whispered in his mind.

As the pain and the image disappeared, his brain continued to feed him Viivi's words. However long that experience had lasted, it had been in another dimension as he hadn't missed a single word. He lay there, running his hands over his body, arms and legs. It had all been inside. He was certain it meant more DNA was awakening.

Hannu! How long ago had he left his friend in the cold? By the time Viivi had finished speaking, Qwelby was in the lobby and about to zip up his parka. Totally spaced out as though he was everything and everywhere at once and wondering if that was what it was like to live in the ninth dimension, he watched Viivi walk up to him and take hold of both of his hands. Too amazed at all that had happened he'd not recovered enough to think of ending the mentalink and knew how much she cared for him. And how much he felt for her. 'My... You... I...'

'Now, scoot,' a smiling Viivi said as she placed her hand on his chest and gave him a gentle push. 'I must see to the guest that phoned.'

Outside in the cold with the star spangled sky shining on the snow, once again he was overcome by the sensation of being everything and everywhere and Tullia with a group of slender dark-skinned girls. And a Quantum Man.

'Wha?' Qwelby jerked as he heard a voice and a hand grabbed his arm.

'Away with the bloody fairies!'

'Eh?'

'I said, what took you so long?' Hannu demanded, wondering at the bright rainbow colours that had replaced the usual blue ovals of the alien's eyes. 'I've been freezing my butt off waiting for you.'

'Getting good news.'

'And you had to snog it out of her!'

Qwelby's smile turned into a grin as he shrugged his shoulders and avoided eye contact.

'I hope it was worth it?'

'Yeah.'

'Well?'

'She not believe Americans shoot themselves. So I tell truth.'

'Fuck's sake, BroQ. You can't....'

'I did all myself. Not memory from life I not had.' He gripped Hannu's arms. 'Me. Me! Labirden Xzarze. Exciting!'

'What about me? You standing there bleating about shooting people. I took command, led you out and then into the Russians' chalet. I must have been out of my mind. Fuck's sake, BroQ, I'm not stupid. I know if you mess with badass guys like that you're dead meat. And we nearly were!'

Qwelby stepped forward and took hold of Hannu's shoulders. 'I love you.' He pulled his friend close and kissed him full on the lips. Heat rose within and passed into Hannu as he held him for a long and firm kiss.

'Warrior,' Qwelby said as he stepped back and watched a range of emotions chase themselves across his WingRider's face.

'Yeah, well, I've been thinking and talking with Anita. You know those leaflets of the various events Viivi gave us when we arrived?'

'Yes?'

'Well. In the chalet there's a folder with all sorts of stuff. You get one in hotel rooms. It's got a timetable of events. Totally different from ours.'

'So?'

'Don't you see? It's been done specially so there were lots of events whilst we're here so those spooks can follow you around, watch you and question you.'

'Vii must have known,' Qwelby said sounding very disheartened.

'Of course. She works here. She's got to do what she's told. Now. I went outside to talk with Anita because of those listening devices we saw. They must be bugging us. You've got total recall haven't you?'

'Well...'

'What've we said that might give you away?'

Hannu felt a different sort of cold as Qwelby's eyes went black.

After a few moments they returned to normal. 'Vertazia, Tullia, names of BestFriends, talk about firefight in Kalahari. Not said alien. Have said human. Talk about here and what we do. No talk about Turkey or my story.'

'I had a lot of time to think while you were gone,' Hannu said pointedly.

Qwelby's eyes twirled.

'Listen!' Hannu thumped Qwelby's shoulder.

''Kay.'

'It's like this. That Professor thinks he knows what you are. P'raps other people do. Those two men at Muurame that day and then the police in Siilinjärvi. If they thought you were an ordinary illegal immigrant. Well. Ask for your passport. But no. So Yanks and Ruskies have an idea of who you are. You look like a, well, nineteen-year-old boy. What if you're an alien scout in disguise and your invasion fleet is, say, behind the Moon. Or in outer space with warp drive or something to get here in a few days. Or. You said about not fighting your government but the rulers. What if the spooks think you're a terrorist? A Turkish freedom fighter or something. But they don't know which side you're working for. Both of them either protect you from the other, or kidnap you, or even eliminate you. See what I mean?'

'Khuy! Vii said I not safe now Americans gone.'

'Yeah. Right. I guess we have to stay one jump ahead of them. Now to do that...' Hannu explained about listening devices and asked if Qwelby had anything that might detect the transmissions. Qwelby said he had a box that opened when matched to one of either his or his twin's eyes. Inside were a variety of disks and a complicated dial. He had no idea what it was for but as it had been made by their Great-Great Uncle Mandara and they weren't supposed to have found it, it was worth a try.

The boys walked on, lost in thought. Qwelby was remembering the exciting feel of the pistol jerking in his hand, the sharp crack of the bullets and the smell. It was so different from laser rifles or sleepdart projectors. He was finding it difficult to focus. The deeper than ever before sharing with Tullia had started when he was with Viivi and he was still being pulled into his twin's world of celebration, walking on thick sand and then inside a grass hut with a group of slender dark-skinned girls. He took off a glove. Hannu removed one of his and they held hands. Qwelby needed the contact with his Azuran friend to anchor him in Finland and think about the situation, yet at the same time he was pulling Hannu out of his world and into a connection with Tullia.

He knew what his friend was thinking about Tullia and he minded, but... he and Tullia were one. Kaigii. Two Forms, two halves living different lives who had always been and always would be – one. And now, both twice Awakened and far more powerfully together than before.

'Hannu. Fighting the Americans was exciting. Not mean to shoot them.' He took a deep breath. 'I find truth about lies on Vertazia. Big lies. They want stop me and Kaigii. Teenagers at home not affect MentaNet, so must be, what you say one time? "In their face." The rulers. There will be fighting. I cannot do that to real Tazii. Dissipating the projected energies of strange beasts. You say killing. But Tazii who send not have Lifelines terminated. Hurt yes and that bad, but...' He turned to his friend, blanking his mind and hoping for an answer from somewhere. 'Nicolai. Focused energy. He looks for me.' Qwelby tapped the side of his head. 'HideNSeek, Tazian style.' He tapped his head again.

The two offset rows of chalets provided excellent cover as the two lads made their way to their chalet.

CHAPTER 37

"BUGS"

LAINIO-FINLAND

Frustrated at having walked all around Lainio and not having seen either Qwelby or Hannu, Nicolai returned to the chalet to be greeted by Ivanova saying that there had been no further messages from Moscow about the requested extraction.

'MSG, KGB, change their names but the dithering incompetents at the top don't change,' Nicolai almost snarled. 'Still, at least with the Americans gone we can relax until our bosses stir themselves.'

'What's this do?' They heard Hannu's voice as the LED for the boys' bedroom turned green.

'Gumma made it. Some sort of communication device, I guess. Doesn't work.'

'Can I see?'

That was followed by what was for the Russians an unhelpful discussion consisting of comments like 'What does this do?' 'Try that.' 'A faint tingle.' Interspersed with occasional bursts of static that had happened several times previously and the agents guessed were when Qwelby's Torc was very close to a transmitter.

'Turn the volume up?' Hannu suggested. Moments later

there was a loud screech, silence and the LED that indicated the transmitter in the boys' bedroom went dark.

'Try a longer distance.' Qwelby's faint voice came from the transmitter in the living room, followed by a brief conversation of where to stand. Ivanova looked at Nicolai, raising an eyebrow as they heard faint static.

'Behind the picture near the door,' Nicolai said. 'Assuming it was the boy's Torc that had burnt out the others, we placed the latest ones where he was not likely to sit or lie down.'

There was another screech, silence and the LED for the living room transmitter went dark.

'Chyort voz'mi!' Ivanova exclaimed.

'Now nothing from the woman's bedroom,' Nicolai said as he sat staring at the speaker unit and drumming his fingers on the table. 'Damn her for keeping her door closed.'

In their chalet Hannu and Qwelby took Mrs Rahkamo into their bedroom and showed her the four burnt out listening devices. The plan the boys had discussed on the way back to the chalet had worked. Qwelby had been delighted when he'd opened what he and Tullia called Soloc, which Wrenden had referred to on the night of the firefight as EyeBox, the red crystal in his Torc had glowed gently.

Using mental communication only, he'd asked Soloc if it was capable of detecting variations in the energy spectra. When his Torc tingled with confirmation, he'd then asked if it was able to compare those variations with what he was seeing and advise any discrepancies. Another confirmatory tingle, he'd linked his mind to Soloc and looked all around the room. As two of the Aurigan symbols had glowed he'd discovered that what he'd originally seen as one inner ring was in fact two. By turning the rings so the symbols came together, then setting them opposite one another, and each time sweeping the room, the green disk had eventually brightened.

Asking more questions requiring only a confirmatory tingle, he'd rapidly established that behind a picture were two transmitters and, finally, a burst of amplified energy on the same wavelengths had resulted in no more transmitting. Behind the picture the boys had found two burnt out transmitters. They'd then repeated the procedure in the living room, again finding two dead transmitters behind a picture.

Hannu was in his element, explaining to a shocked mother all about listening devices and sweeping for them and, in the process, confirming her decision to leave Lainio. He explained that although the really super RonaldSonQ he'd been given made totally quantum secure communications, they were being watched. The spies had arrived in Lainio almost at the same time as they had and that must have been because their flight bookings had been detected. His mother reluctantly accepted her son's logic about not making any advance bookings of an hotel or flights.

The boys packed and all three went into Mrs Rahkamo's bedroom.

In the Russians' chalet the LED indicating Mrs Rahkamo's bedroom turned from red to green and Nicolai increased the volume just in time to hear Hannu say 'Aw, Mum, do we really have to stay in all tomorrow?'

'Yes,' his mother replied in a firm voice. 'Anita has sent you a mountain of schoolwork and you promised your father.'

'We help you,' Qwelby said.

'We?'

'Yes. Get Tullia.'

Nicolai and Ivanova shared an "Oh, no!" look and a deafening screech issued from the receiver as yet another LED went black.

His mind made up, Nicolai reached for the MiniCom unit and sent a short message to Lubyanka Square. Shorn of its "Immediate Maximum Priority General Commanding" coding, the message was simple: 'All listening devices disabled. Recommend immediate extraction by StealthCopter already in position by the Finish border. Repeat immediate.'

'Until the ditherers in Moscow act,' Nicolai said. 'We will take turns in watching and... enjoy our time here.' Both agents smiled at the memory of a previous joint assignment.

Qwelby opened his eyes, blinked, saw concerned looks on two faces and grinned. 'Tullia very happy, much energy. I borrow. I send patterns to Russians' minds for tomorrow. They accept.'

Mrs Rahkamo had packed after the transmitters had ceased working and the boys took all the bags to the car park. The two rows of chalets were staggered, providing a perfect screen and making it easy to stay out of sight from the Russians' chalet. There, they switched number plates with an identical Volvo V45R parked behind theirs. Hannu explained to an intrigued Qwelby that what he was doing came from several films he'd watched, as they searched for and discovered first, then a second, of what Hannu was certain had to be miniature tracking devices fitted underneath their car.

They both detached just like the one he'd seen in the last film, with an almost invisible lever deactivating the magnet. Hannu then lay down alongside the car whose number plates they'd switched. The magnets were so powerful that each time he moved the lever, the tracker was pulled from his fingers onto the same place on the rear sub-frame as each one had been on their car.

Leaving Qwelby to load the car, Hannu returned to the chalet and walked back with his mother. With the hand brake off, the boys rolled their car forward. Mrs Rahkamo watched as they heaved mightily and moved the other car into the space she'd just vacated. Saying it would look suspicious if the car was seen travelling without any lights on, she switched them on and quietly left Lainio, heading for Ylläsjärvi via the Lainiotie.

Having dealt with the client who'd telephoned, an unsettled Viivi spent some time walking around the Snow Village, exchanging a few words with guests and stopping for brief chats with staff. On her way back to her room she saw activity in the car park. The pony tail on the big man was a give-away.

She blew him a kiss. His head turned and his bright eyes seemed to stare at her. Of course he couldn't see her. Feeling like a silly young girl, she waved - and went weak at the knees as she saw his big grin and felt her lips being kissed.

Her heart flipped as emotions tumbled through her. Happiness for him escaping from the Russians, sadness for herself robbed of another night with him, sweet memories of having met his twin, a flash of jealousy - and a memory of his rainbow eyes as...

'Oh you stupid girl! "You make my hearts burn," didn't mean he had indigestion! And those rainbow eyes. It was his alien way of saying he loves me.' Smiling and shaking her head she set off to walk back to her apartment, suffused in a warm glow.

Qwelby relaxed in the car and thought of all the knife fights and shooting the Americans, and the thrill of it all. Amongst all that had been fun and friendship, discovering girls and getting a big handle on the "What" of Quantum Twins. The big question was still "Why?"

Getting home and revealing the good side about life on Earth and the dark side of life on Vertazia was going to take a lot of courage. At least he was being prepared for that. And perhaps it was only after that, because of that, that he and Kaigii could discover the "Why" of being Kaigii?

A picture played before his eyes as for a moment he again saw himself as the big sergeant from the last arcade game he'd played. Supposed to lead his soldiers into battle across an area of scrub and sand littered with abandoned vehicles but unable to cope with the blood and gore, he'd stopped playing. If he'd ever been a DragonRider, and those apparent memories weren't just fantasies from so often playing Dragons and Unicorns, he'd killed Solids, as the Auriganii termed people who lived in the third dimension.

The viciousness of the very first attack on himself and his twin, then the extent of the attack that night in the Kalahari, there had been so much fear in the background that it was pointless to hope they wouldn't be attacked if they ever managed to return home. Khuy! His mind in a whirl, he started to reach for Tullia and again experienced the happiness in her hearts as they'd reconnected. He shook his head. Quantum Twins, yes. He was also a Quantum Man. He'd not burden her now.

He was aware of a discussion just below the threshold of hearing and recognised the energy as that of the irritating voice. Then came a sense of cool relaxation intention-alising him.

Schrödinger's Cat yet lives

And was aware of the speaker joining in the chuckling as the other eleven picked up on the reference to an Earth scientist. Although he had no idea what that meant, he felt the positive energy, and that was so typical of life on Vertazia that he chuckled. Relaxed and thinking happily of his beloved Tullia, he slipped through levels of consciousness to be with a group of slender fun-loving and almost Tazian girls.

At Germany's Hohn Air Base, the American colonel in charge almost squawked with incredulity at the news that the two CIA agents had been shot by the teenage target – and with one of their own guns. The earlier coded abort signal that Farah had sent had been received just as the X5S had been about to leave its flight path along the Gulf of Bothnia and turn inland for Lainio. It was now headed back to Hohn. The Colonel was advised by Langley that a US military jet was on its way to Hohn to take the two agents currently on board the C17 to Kittilä, expected time of arrival there was late on Sunday night. Extraction by the X5S was now to take place on Monday evening when the target had returned from a day long Husky Drive.

CHAPTER 38

ELDEREST

LAINIO-FINLAND

Luck was with them when the three arrived in Kittilä. Hostel Hullo Poro had two rooms available on the ground floor. Using false names and Qwelby's money, Mrs Rahkamo took both rooms and Hannu helped Qwelby into his twin-bedded room through a window. Qwelby was both sad and grateful that Tullia had fallen asleep, thus so could he. But that was delayed by Hannu talking.

'In the car you said how wonderful it was to be able to use your mind to talk with that gadget. Just like being on Vertazia. Well. That made me think. Those bugs were so easy to find. If we'd searched the room by hand we'd have found them dead easy. But in all the films I've seen those sort of things are always carefully hidden. In light sockets, telephones, behind air conditioning vents and so on. Are you sure there weren't any more?'

'Oh, yes. When the symbols lit up it was another confirmation of how much I've developed with my two Awakenings and now being reunited with Tullia. Linking my mind with Soloc it was like I was it. So, yeah, I'm how you say? "Dead sure".'

Qwelby reached out a fist and they shared a knuckle punch. 'Hannu. You said Tullia was like an Amazonian Warrior Queen. What she look like?'

Hannu pulled out his mobile, asked for the virtual tablet and appropriate images. As the screen filled, he explained that there were tribes who lived in the Amazon but what Qwelby was seeing were totally different fantasy ideas. Qwelby stared, then laughed. 'Hell, Yeah! That's Tullia.' He pointed. 'And that one. Look at the eyes.' He pointed to another and laughed. 'She wore a little more than that! Oh, Hannu, I love you.' He gently thumped his obviously puzzled friend on the shoulder, and took a deep breath. 'I explain. No. Better. I take you there.' Carefully modulating his voice, Qwelby started talking and took them back thirteen thousand years to when most of the planet was covered in ice.

In the highest room of the Citadel's Grand Tower he, Anananki, wearing the long robes of a Venerable, was supervising a team of Auriganii who were setting up Shadow Energy projectors around a multicoloured spherical crystal as tall as an Aurigan which was slowly rotating in mid air. Zeyusa, his similarly garbed twin, was arguing that more work needed to be done on the EnergyWeb or the planet would be destroyed if the crystal was activated now.

He was contending that they had to leave what was still known as Azura Yezi to find a planet closer to the centre of the Galaxy, where there was a supermassive Black Hole continually ejecting a flow of Shadow Matter to enable their race to continue to extend through to the ninth dimension. Leave it any longer and the race's vibrational level would have fallen below the critical level, they would never leave and no Auriganii would ever again reach into the ninth dimension.

He was jolted as the scene shifted in space and time and he was outside the Citadel where yet another battle was taking place. His twin had raised an army from the group of Hominids that later came to be known as Homo Sapiens. His army was largely made up of what later came to be called Homo Sapiens Sapiens, the offspring of Aurigan-Hominid mating.

Casualties mounting amongst the non-Auriganii, both sides drew back. Anananki signalled, a trumpet sounded and an arrow from either side whistled through the air to thud into the churned up soil. Into the strip of torn land between the arrows he strode forward to meet a tall and lightly armoured figure. As a display for their "Sapiens", minimal armour highlighted to perfection both of their muscled and toned bodies, their real protection being their mental skills. Anananki was puzzled at a whisper of "Amazonian Warrior Queen" and wondered how he knew it was perfect for his twin.

The twins hammered and hacked at each other with massive double handed swords until, eventually and as always, their fight ended in a stalemate. Exhausted, battered, bruised and bathed in sweat but never bloody, they grimaced, stepped apart and wearily saluted each other.

Anananki turned and handed his sword to his backguard Shem-esh-a, who was carefully watching the opposing forces. Behind him he was aware that his twin was handing her sword to her backguard, Ninurtan. Anananki and Shem-esh-a shared their feelings of pain as she put an arm around his shoulders. For nigh on a thousand years as he and Ninurtan had called each other Brother, Šem-eš-a and his twin had called each other Sister, yet now each was bitterly opposed to the other.

As the boys' awareness returned to the hotel room, the cold draught of a premonition swept through Qwelby as he realised he knew those warriors by other names. But who were they?

'Shee-ite! That was something else!' Hannu declared. 'My mind was going two ways. I was thrilled being you in the fighting, and Tullia, err...'

Qwelby knew what Hannu was feeling and thumped him.

'Dammit, Qwelby. It was your thoughts!' Hannu gave his friend a hard thump.

Qwelby blushed and the boys laughed.

'Why were you using such primitive weapons?'

'If we'd used what we had during the Space Wars, we'd have

killed thousands and destroyed the big island in the ocean you call the Atlantic. That was one of our main bases. A ladder-like bridge to where we also lived in higher dimensions.'

'Well. Use similar when you go back'

Qwelby stared, then started laughing. 'Oh Lamaannu, you truly are the genius to my fool. Yes, with changes. What you call Sci-Fi.' He pulled his friend into a big hug. 'I love you lots, Lamaannu.'

The following morning Qwelby left by the window and waited out of sight on Savannoisenpalku to be picked up. They returned the car early to a sleepy attendant who, mentally helped by Qwelby, saw the appropriate number plates. Seats were available for all three on the early flight to Siilinjärvi. Qwelby's Tuesday flight to Helsinki made a short stop-over at Jyväskylä and booking staff made notes allowing him to board there.

While they were waiting to be called for their flight, Hannu asked about the patterns Qwelby had sent to the Russians' minds. His compiler unable to find the words, Qwelby drew a picture and an excited Hannu used his virtual screen to display a glorious Technicolor picture of fractal images, known as Mandelbrot.

'Yes. Those patterns are like a picture of the quantum world. Are there underneath everything, both in nature and we make. So that pattern worked on Russians' minds as they were expecting a quiet day. No listening, we staying in chalet all day, so they not concerned.'

Qwelby had been on tenterhooks since arriving at the airport and heaved a sigh of relief when not only did the plane take off without him being apprehended, but there was no-one on board they recognised or who was taking a special interest in him. He closed his eyes and tried to sort through his turbulent emotions, especially the increasingly confusing ones for Tullia. As he went through the events of the last few days he became aware of a core of steel that was growing in him and, when he looked back on the shooting, satisfaction at what he'd done and that he'd not seriously hurt either of the Americans. He was comfortable with the idea of being a Warrior. For himself and his twin.

Hannu was wondering what Qwelby's life on Earth must be like. He leant back in his seat, trying to imagine how it would be if he arrived in a country of brown people and they hated him just because he was white. He couldn't do it. It was all just too weird.

Sensing his friend's discomfort, Qwelby took Hannu's hand in his, slipping into his friend's mind as he did so and sending images of the fight in the Kalahari, how his friend had helped with Qwelby's subsequent Awakening as a male and last night had saved his life. Mentally and emotionally Qwelby told Hannu that he was not a BestAzuranFriend, but a real BestFriend. Esting relationships just happened. No-one knew how Life made Its choices. He asked Hannu to accept that Life had chosen the Azuran to be Qwelby's elderest and that meant they had to remain in contact – somehow.

'You Tazian,' Qwelby said when he received a faint picture of a snowman, referring to the first time the two boys had seen each other.

CHAPTER 39

JENNI

SIILINJÄRVI-FINLAND

As soon as they had bought their plane tickets, all three used Hannu's phone. Mrs Rahkamo called her husband and Elsa Korpijaakko, and Hannu called Anita. Qwelby opted to send what he hoped were intriguing texts to Jenni and Oona.

When they arrived in Siilinjärvi, Elsa explained that Johan, her husband, was out at his usual Sunday game of Rink Bandy, a form of Ice Hockey played on a skating rink, and he always stayed for a drink afterwards.

It was so obvious from the air of excitement that the two boys were keen to tell Jenni and Riku of their adventures so, with a smile to Seija, Elsa told the youngsters to take their sandwiches and drinks upstairs whilst the two women had a quiet chat.

As the four reached the landing, Jenni made a "lips are sealed" gesture to Riku, her brother, took Qwelby's hand and pulled him into her room.

'I missed you,' Qwelby said as Jenni said, 'I thought I'd never see you again.' They put down the plates and glasses, flung their arms around each other and kissed, hungrily. Jenni's hands reached under his t-shirt and she stroked his velvet-like skin. Qwelby started to purr.

'I couldn't stop thinking about you,' she said. 'And that night. Wondering if....' She stopped talking as Qwelby's tongue slid between her lips and he remembered Viivi's lesson.

Later, cuddled up in his arms she said: 'Your mysterious text. Tell me.'

Having experienced Hannu's jealousy over the relationship that had developed between Anita and himself, Qwelby had thought carefully about what not to tell Jenni or Oona and had marshalled his story in his mind. Deliberately modulating his voice and letting his thoughts drift into Jenni's mind, he took her to Lainio and slowly immersed her in his experiences.

A small corner of his mind was sad that, after two tendays of carefully choosing his words so as not to give himself away, he now found it easy to be "economical with the truth" as Hannu described it.

As they returned from Lainio, Jenni wrapped herself around him. 'I wasn't afraid during that fighting and shooting. You were there with me.'

Qwelby heaved a sigh of happiness. At times, Life was good. Very good.

The door opened a crack and Hannu said they were leaving.

A few minutes later everyone was gathered in the living room to say their goodbyes. Jenni was leaning her head against Qwelby's shoulder, the fingers of their two hands intertwined.

'You all right, Jenni?' Mrs Korpijaakko asked with a frown.

'Yeah.' She was happy, stupidly happy even though she'd never see him again – and didn't care. "I love you," he'd said as his rainbow eyes were twirling. 'I know,' she'd answered. And tears had flowed as she hugged the man she'd fallen in love with as she gave birth to him – four days and a lifetime ago.

Her mother shuddered at the faraway look in her daughter's eyes and the thought she had been kissing that...

'We went into space.' Qwelby said. 'Riding on a comet amongst the stars. Umm... It's err... special.'

'Too right,' Hannu said, excited that he was increasingly becoming an alien as he responded to Qwelby's mental nudge for help.

'He's an amazing story-teller,' Mrs Rahkamo said, remembering her visit to his homeworld.

CHAPTER 40

OONA

KOTOMÄKI-FINLAND

After the drive back home, the boys stayed in the house only long enough to say a quick hullo to Hannu's father, wash and change before stepping out through the back door into the falling snow.

Hannu looked up and down the deserted road, grabbed Qwelby by the arms and gave him a quick hard kiss, then thumped the surprised alien on the shoulder before disappearing in the snow to see Anita.

A grin slowly spread across Qwelby's face. He hadn't intended to kiss his friend that night in Lainio. He had needed to recognise what his WingRider had done – not merely taking command but risking more danger as he ensured the mission was completed. It was only as he'd grabbed Hannu and the heat had flowed that he knew he was to deliver a WarriorKiss. As he touched his tingling lips he knew there had been more in that first kiss. An offering made and now accepted. Of course, idiot! BestFriends, properly cemented. For ever.

After a few minutes of steady walking and keeping a lookout for anyone following, he saw Oona standing in the doorway of the now closed jewellery shop she'd specified in her text.

'You taste of strawberries.'

'My lip-gloss.'

'Café?'

'Oh no. My home.' Oona explained that her parents were dining with friends in Jyväskylä and her brother was out with his girlfriend. As previously arranged, she herself had gone out with a group of girls, then left them pleading a tummy upset. They had to go to her home because she didn't want her parents to hear that she'd been seen with him.

'I'm sorry. It's not just you, it's any boy. They're control freaks. It's why I had to go out with friends. They won't let me stay at home by myself. I don't even have a boyfriend. The only boys I go out with are when I'm with the group you've been skiing with. I know what my parents think and it's humiliating.'

'Our day together?'

'I said I was with the group as usual.'

'If not safe for you, I not come,' Qwelby said, admiring his selflessness.

'Oh no, I want to see you. And the text you sent me. You've got to tell me what happened.'

The day of her intended skiing lesson they had spent far more time talking, drinking hot chocolate and eventually holding hands and gazing into each other's eyes than skiing. As the day progressed, Oona had left behind her schoolgirl self and become a mature young woman on her first real date, unaware of Qwelby's equal innocence as he had told her about himself.

She didn't know if she'd fallen in love with the tall handsome alien. What she had felt was his sadness and a need to comfort him. Their passionate kissing that day had ended all too quickly. She wanted more – and to comfort him.

The snow was falling heavily and the streets were deserted. Once inside the rear porch, Oona removed her outer clothing, revealing a soft pink blouse and deep rose leggings. 'Keep your outer clothes on, just in case my brother comes home early. I know my parents won't. Unless anything goes wrong,' she added, suddenly feeling frightened.

'I leave by window,' Qwelby said, with a grin.

'My room's upstairs.'

'I tall. I hang by fingers.'

'Oh, you do this with all the girls you meet,' Oona flashed back in a snarky tone.

'No. Only with twin,' he replied with a laugh.

'Oh.' Oona felt silly.

'We get into lots of trouble. She always blames me.'

Oona saw mischief in his eyes. I bet she's right, she thought as she smiled.

As soon as they were in Oona's room Qwelby unlocked the window, opened it and looked out. The path around the house had been cleared of snow. As long as he was careful there wouldn't be any sign of his departure. Closing but not locking the window he turned back into the room.

'I was so happy when you called me,' Oona said. 'Throwing you out. I thought you'd think. I don't know...'

He grinned, she blushed and they kissed.

'Ouch. Your coat's cold.'

As Qwelby removed his outer clothing Oona froze in panic as he stripped down to shorts and a t-shirt. What had she done inviting this big strong man into her bedroom? 'Is that what you always wear?' she asked in an unsteady voice.

'Yes. Your houses always too hot.'

'Oh.' Once again she felt silly as she remembered that was all he'd worn when inside on New Year's Eve.

'You all right?'

Feeling protective arms around her and sensing a soft and caring energy, Oona relaxed and rested her head against his chest. 'Mpf,' she mumbled, then pulled her head back and looked up at him. Their lips met.

Eventually, she pulled away. 'Now. That text. I want to know what that was all about.'

Sitting on her bed, Qwelby thoughtwrapped her into a visit to Lainio and his adventures.

When they returned and he opened his eyes, Oona was cuddled up to him. She was very cuddly. She lifted her head and looked at him. She was cute.

'I was so frightened with all that fighting. But I'm all right now.'

Rosy cheeks, bright blue eyes, moist pink lips tasting of strawberry...

Qwelby's mind and emotions were in a whirl as he later let himself out of the back door into the cold night. Wenkosi butterflies were descending from their chrysalises on the Planar trees. Their long silk threads, stronger than titanium, were reflecting the blazing sunlight in thousands of rainbows.

High above the trees, the Screechers were circling. One after another the jet black birds, symbiotic protectors of the Wenkosi, folded their wings and plummeted down, the screeching sound produced by air flowing through holes in their beaks scaring away the smaller birds wanting to dine on the butterflies.

I must be living in the ninth dimension?

Slowly, the Wenkosi threads gave way to falling snow, the sun to the moon and stars in the night sky. He had to leave. Still in a state of euphoria, he started walking. How could he have said to Oona that he loved her when he'd said that to Jenni? He'd not been able to say to Viivi the words she'd said girls liked to hear. He had wanted to say something genuine because the feeling had been there. Was still there. Life had come full circle. Oona, Jenni, Viivi, Jenni, Oona. And he did love them. Three very special girls who'd helped him do more than just grow up. He thoughtsent more than thanks to Viivi for how much she had taught him in guiding him through his initiation.

Viivi was enjoying a relaxing drink in her apartment when there was a tingling in her head and a memory of an impossible night. Sipping her glass of Maali, Viivi toasted the velvet-skinned boy-man and felt an increase in her warm glow.

Qwelby was stunned. He'd received a warm sensation in his mind from Viivi - impossible for an Azuran to do that! He recalled the warm glow that had surrounded her aura. And Hannu. His Azuran friend had become good at mental communication. And he did love Hannu. And Hannu - well, he thumps me just like Tullia does! And that kiss? Qwelby threw back his head and laughed. Love! TransDimensional SupraPersonal Activation of more of their DNA - Quantum Awakening for the Azurii!

And why not? He'd discovered that the Azurii really were human. The big difference was that they had only two strands of DNA whereas the Tazii had three; and their long lost Aurigan ancestors had had all twelve fully functioning. Strong emotions consistently held, regular concentrated meditation - imagining and imaging, believing - all influenced human DNA. Hannu's girlfriend, Anita, had told him that only about twenty percent of Azuran DNA was working, so a lot was available to be Awakened. He mentally capitalised the word as what had happened to Hannu and Viivi was like a birthing. He guessed the same must have happened for Oona and especially Jenni as she had guided him through his second Awakening.

As he recommenced walking, thoughts ran through his mind of the possibility of mental contact when back on Vertazia. It might be possible when he and Tullia were together and the increased quantum energy they could generate. Tullia. Tomorrow he was on his way to meet the most special girl in his life. He loved her. But it was different.

'Ohhh? Young QeïchâKaïgii?'

The voice was becoming more irritating with its incomprehensible symbols. Dismissing it, he smiled at the thought

215

of kissing Tullia. He was a warrior – in a different way! He would give her a proper kiss. She'd be horrified and would give him a real hard thump. Oh, how he missed her and all the fun they had together.

CHAPTER 41

REPLACEMENTS

LAINIO-FINLAND

It was the early hours of Sunday morning before the Russians received a reply from Lubyanka Square. The Ministry of State Security had awarded jurisdiction to the SVR. Extraction to take place on Monday evening. A later message instructed them to go to the airport in Kittilä to meet the plane carrying the two replacement agents from the SVR. They were to brief them on the plane to avoid the two pairs being seen together. Nicolai and Ivanova were to be debriefed on the plane as they returned to Moscow.

It was mid-morning when, having bid farewell to Nicolai and Ivanova, Maija returned to her room to await a call from them with the names of their replacements from their Foreign Intelligence Service. Instead, Nicolai called to say that the SVR agents had not been on the plane. He and Ivanova had been ordered to return to Moscow as planned and the SVR agents would now arrive late that night. With two SUPO colleagues and the new CIA agents also not due to arrive until late, Maija heaved a sigh of relief and looked forward to a relaxing day.

Earlier, over breakfast, Viivi had explained to Maija that, as that day's scheduled events were repeats of those that both boys had already been on and all three were booked on Monday's whole day Husky Drive, Qwelby had told her that Mrs Rahkamo had declared Sunday to be a day of rest. They were to stay in whilst she cooked and, he'd added with a laugh, do homework. Hannu had promised his father to keep up with the schoolwork that his girlfriend was emailing to him.

Viivi yawned. 'Sorry. Didn't get to sleep until early this morning.' She'd spent most of the night reliving her time with Qwelby. Had she really gone to another world and met his twin? And how was it that she thought she'd briefly been with his twin amongst a group of slender, dark-skinned girls? None of it was possible. Yet she had vividly experienced all of it.

Eventually, she had decided that as the young man had been very real and his differences definitely made him the alien he claimed to be, she wasn't going to spoil what was likely to be the most magical experience of her life by saying the rest hadn't been real. Noticing Maija looking at her, she blushed.

Remembering her own long gone teenage years, Maija had smiled and relaxed.

Late that night when Maija settled down with the six agents for a joint briefing in the Russians' chalet, she threw the proverbial cat amongst the pigeons by suggesting that the whole operation be cancelled, apart from her own people ensuring Qwelby left the country. Miska Metsälä, the SUPO agent who'd lost Romain in Geneva, had picked him up on his return. The Professor had spent a long time in Dr Keskinen's house, following which, passenger manifests had shown Romain booked onto that evening's flight to Helsinki.

Metsälä had used his initiative and phoned the hotel where the Professor had stayed previously, and it had been confirmed that a reservation had been made in Romain's name for two nights. Metsälä had then spoken to a young receptionist he'd cultivated in the hotel in Jyväskylä who said she'd overheard Romain talking to the manager about his sightseeing plans for the next few days.

Both Americans and Russians shrugged their shoulders and agreed they would continue with their surveillance until the boy was safely away.

Maija went on to comment that she'd not seen the boy or either of the others that day, which accorded with what Viivi had said, and that their car was still parked where it had been since the day of arrival. Lights could be seen faintly through the thick curtains of the living room and the kitchen blinds.

It was very late by the time the Americans and Maija left the Russians' chalet. It was only a few minutes later that the Americans were knocking on the Russians' back door and were advised that the Russians knew all their listening devices had been disabled and were not surprised to hear that none of the Americans' were working either.

The Americans returned to their chalet and advised Langley of their discovery. The response was swift. The Russians were not to be trusted. They could easily have nullified the Americans' transmitters, leaving their own functioning. Neither were the Finnish authorities to be trusted. Once Qwelby had passed through security at the airport there was nothing to stop the Finns taking him away. That was not to be allowed to happen. Extraction was to take place that night. Timings to be advised. As a back up, more agents were being sent to Jyväskylä and Helsinki.

Fifteen minutes later Langley advised that the StealthCopter was airborne. The agents looked at their watches. With the X5S maintaining radio silence, Langley was monitoring progress via satellite. The next alert would be in about one hour's time when one agent would keep the Russians company, whilst the other drove the boy to the predetermined location where the XS5 would land. Both agents ran a final check on guns and night vision equipment.

Although they had made the customary derogative remarks about the operatives from their despised rivals in the FSB, the two agents from the SVR, posing as yet another holiday couple, were relieved to discover that the Americans were similarly handicapped. Armed with the detailed map prepared by Nicolai and Ivanova, together with the latest satellite photographs, the two Russians set out to explore the whole area and plan the following night's extraction. The MSG General briefing them had made it very clear – the whole operation was to be conducted with the minimum of fuss, which meant the initial "lifting" was to be by car and the StealthCopter kept well away from the Snow Village.

CHAPTER 42

SHAMED

VERTAZIA

Ceegren's announcement on his previous visit to IndluKoba, the Custodians' Headquarters, that he was bringing his acolyte with him to attend to his personal needs, had not been well received and the Apprentices' resentment and jealousy had been obvious. Responding to that discontent, an out of touch Hosting Coordinator had attempted to humiliate Xaala by allocating her to the Junior Servitors' dormitory. There, Xaala had discovered the Juniors were being bullied and reported to Ceegren.

The Arch Custodian had been furious. The Juniors' supervisor had been dismissed and the short period suspension meted out to the two bullying Apprentices meant it was unlikely that either would ever become Custodians. On this visit, it was clear to Xaala that she was detested.

On her second afternoon, the WellBeing Provider summoned Xaala and told her that Chief Readjuster Dryddnaa had requested a massage.

'My Teacher must have recommended me,' a sweet Xaala said as she feigned pleasant surprise, happily twisting the knife in the disgruntled Provider by making it clear how highly the Arch Custodian valued her personal services.

Carrying her case of essential oils and crystals, Xaala arrived at the appointed time and was greeted by Dryddnaa also wearing the light robe of neutronfibre that was appropriate for an energy massage. The colourscopes on the walls of the spacious room were of gently moving pastel colours, adding to the relaxing feel provided by the scents of cinnamon and camomile.

Apart from indicating that the room was mentashielded as normal for a person of her status, the Chief Readjuster gave no indication that she was expecting anything other than a massage. Assuming she was being tested, Xaala stilled her nerves and proceeded.

When the massage had been completed, Xaala went into the ample bathroom to wash and energy cleanse her hands. As with Ceegren, the energy cleansing took time due to the strong energies she'd been handling. When she returned she found Dryddnaa had changed into a RelaxRobe of a pale sky blue across which small clouds gently floated.

'You wish to talk with me,' the Chief Readjuster said, gesturing to a RelaxChair close to her own.

'Yes. Thank you,' Xaala replied, not sure whether she was relieved that the message delivered by Khalen, a Junior Servitor, had been understood, or.... Too late. Sitting down, blushing furiously and having to honestly answer Dryddnaa's perceptive questions, she explained why she had not been able to call for help to prevent the twins reconnecting.

Dryddnaa was unable to reprimand the young woman. Not only had Xaala so well concealed her existential dilemma that the potential difficulties had not been foreseen, it was her failure to act that was bringing The Chief Readjuster back into the Dance of Discovery.

'I have been mollifying your Teacher,' Dryddnaa said with a wry smile. 'You are so proficient at what you do that we, *principally he* expected too much from you.'

Xaala bit her lip *I overestimated my Self* and ducked her head.

Insûmâne – Blame has no place in Life.

Xaala, her mouth dry, looked back at the Chief Readjuster *Acceptance* and nodded.

'I will make arrangements for Rulcas to come here and you will supervise.' *Being kind and considerate.*

To that MUUD...!?

Redeem yourself – with Ceegren.

Xaala allowed herself an impudent grunt of acknowledgment and a flash of her eyes.

'And, my dear *feisty bitchling* you may speak with me whenever you want. With or without providing a massage.'

Liking the image Dryddnaa had sent of a "feisty bitchling" and the accompanying sense of being admitted as a junior partner, Xaala lowered her lashes as she inclined her head in acknowledgment.

Back in her room, Xaala wryly smiled at the Supervisor's quarters she'd been allocated and the much appreciated privacy they afforded. She was happy she had no immediate duties because she needed to carefully analyse the interplay with the powerful Chief Readjuster.

When Xaala had gone, Dryddnaa relaxed with the satisfaction that Xaala's failure and being sent to work at IndluKoba had at last provided the catalyst for getting Rulcas close to the twins' friends. Having met the youth twice more she'd found there was a lot more to him than she had expected of any MUUD. During the last meeting he had disabused her of her two plans for getting him close to the twins' friends, then gone on to explain why they were not going to accept Xaala as an ally but would accept him.

His being labelled as a MUUD was a serious misdescription perpetrated not just by the several Junior Readjusters who'd worked with him but also their supervisors. That meant a complete overhaul of her own profession when she became Arch Readjuster.

One more reason why she had to succeed with her plans. She'd seen flashes of steel in the feisty bitchling. Could she turn her? What a coup!

Rulcas had agreed with her plan of sending him to IndluKoba to train as a Servitor, ostensibly as a trial for helping MUUDs. He'd learn a lot about a way of life he'd not experienced, then after a couple of days he would cause trouble and be thrown out. The problem they had to solve was why he should go to the twins' family rather than back home or to his father who lived with the Shakazii. Piloting her personal, four-seater isotor back home after that discussion, Dryddnaa had felt as if she'd attended a seminar on deception – as a student!

She now had the perfect answer. She would persuade the Servitor Supervisor to accept Rulcas with Xaala being responsible for him. When he left, he would go to the twins' family with useful information and a key contact – The Arch Custodian's own acolyte. With a spy at Lungunu, Dryddnaa would become indispensible to Ceegren.

Two days ago she had satisfied herself that she was able to provide total quarantine in all areas for the twins. She had not immediately mentioned that to Ceegren as he would have seen it as a challenge to his plans. Following the twins reconnecting, he had been relieved to hear her news. A delicate lowering of her long eyelashes had indicated her support for him and once again offered the prospect of an eventual mentameld. She knew he would not have believed her if that had meant anything other than if and when he was successful in his aims.

Deception. A new word was coming into existence in the Tazian language.

Whilst plans on Vertazia were going well, those on Earth were not. A by now very frustrated Colonel at Hohn was advising Langley of that night's operation being aborted. An engine warning light on the XS5 meant it had had to return when it was part way along the

Gulf of Bothnia. Inspection showed that repair was essential and would not be completed before dawn. 'At least this is better than Eagle Claw,' she said to her second in command. 'This time I do have the spares.'

CHAPTER 43

TRIUMPH!

KOTOMÄKI-FINLAND

After Qwelby had left Kotomäki, Mrs Keskinen had declined Romain's request to arrange a meeting with her husband, saying that he was working long hours at the Institute. Having heard from Erki on Sunday evening that all three had returned, Romain again telephoned. This time he spoke with Dr Keskinen, who agreed to a meeting later that evening.

Romain was surprised to discover that the boy was present together with the Doctor's daughter. After talking about the trip to Lainio, the boy seemed to relax and Romain approached the situation head-on. He explained exactly why he believed Qwelby to be from not merely another planet, but a parallel world, and was delighted when, although denying that, the boy was clearly taken aback.

Romain went on to set out why he was the only person in the whole world who might be able to help. He showed Keskinen the many printouts he had brought with him from his laboratory. Using the GlobeSynch he repeated the three dimensional display he'd created in his hotel room. Faced with the evidence, Keskinen confessed that Qwelby came from another dimension.

Betrayal! Qwelby felt as though he'd been punched in the stomach.

'Father. How could you? You promised!'

'It's for the best, Anita. I warned you his story would come out at some time.'

'But...'

'Enough!' Keskinen turned back to Romain and said the knowledge that Qwelby had displayed whilst they had worked together trying to make contact with Vertazia had convinced him that Qwelby was what he said.

'Qwelby,' Keskinen said, turning to the youth. 'You've heard what we've said and you know I've not been successful with any of my ideas. The Professor is the only person who can help you.'

'But, Dad, please. Now Qwelby's here, he can help you. He knows what to do.'

Keskinen shook his head as he continued talking to Qwelby. 'With Russian and American agents following you, you should go to Raiatea as soon as possible. It's...'

'NO! You're wrong. He belongs here.'

'Enough, Anita! Go to your room.'

'I hate you!' His daughter stormed out of the room and into the kitchen, slamming the door behind her.

Her father followed her, opened the kitchen door and stood there looking at his daughter sobbing her heart out in her mother's arms.

Romain took the opportunity to speak to a very unhappy Qwelby, who decided he had to say something. Being careful to keep his voice neutral and not thoughtwrap the Professor, he told the story of his arrival and gave a very brief summary of recent events.

The manager of his hotel had mentioned to Romain that there had been another set of EM disturbances on the third of January, but they had not been nearly as strong as those on 27 December and had affected a much smaller area. When the Professor asked what Qwelby was doing that day he was intrigued when told that the alien had been seriously ill. Had the disturbances been caused by the boy's unconscious seeking contact with his homeworld? Romain was going to have to be very careful how he proceeded and hope that the nervous system of the human-looking boy was very similar to that of a human, so that his GlobeSynch would be able to keep the alien subdued as long as was necessary.

Viljo sat down and listened, from time to time nodding confirmation to Romain. Feeling raw from the spat with his daughter he made no comment about Qwelby's failure to mention Tullia.

By the time Qwelby had finished speaking, Romain was delighted. He'd been right to try that experiment and his judgement had been confirmed. No sense of the mind control he feared, just a powerful personality, and he'd met plenty of people like that in his life. He didn't show his frustration when he accepted that the youth needed time overnight to think it all through. As he left, he reminded Qwelby to use his friend's mobile for a secure call.

'I will think about everything, Doctor Keskinen,' Qwelby said as he got to his feet. He paused and looked towards the kitchen door. 'Please say goodnight to Anita for me.'

Back home, Qwelby explained to the family what had happened and went to his room. A quick flick to his twin's corner of his mind told him she was there, but there was no response. Communication was still difficult. Controlling his frustration that for reasons he didn't understand, the slow vibrations of the third dimension were causing problems even after their full-on reconnection, he undressed and put on what Anita's mother had made. Wearing what he thought of as a Bushman's loinskin, he lit a candle to represent a fire, sat in the lotus position and thought of the baby Horned Snow Owl.

Tullia was soon there. They linked minds and enjoyed a few happy moments of being one. Qwelby then sent a stream of images about Romain and his activities, finishing with the offer to take Qwelby to his laboratory on an island. He added his strong feelings that Romain was not being completely open, that there was a dark twist inside him and he was very reluctant to go with him. Romain did not know of Tullia.

He was happy when Tullia agreed to her existence being kept secret for the time being and reluctantly accepted that by going to the island he would be safely in one place for long enough for them to make plans for reaching their friends in order to go home. Worried about all the travelling she was going to have to do, he tried to persuade her to stay with her tribe whilst, now they were reunited, they tried to contact their friends and plan how to return home. She demurred, insisting she had a plan.

Hannu arrived a little later, saying he'd phoned a tearful Anita who'd fled to her room, locked herself in and refused to come out. Qwelby consoled Hannu with what he knew of Anita's feelings for him and his own experiences of the times when he and Tullia had their spats – and later made up.

Sharing everything, they agreed they both had the emotions of normal human boys. The key difference being that Qwelby was born easily able to develop many "special" attributes, whereas Azurii had to work hard to develop just one. 'As you are doing, my elderest and BestFriend,' Qwelby happily assured Hannu.

Ah! Qwelby owed Hannu a lot for having been a great elderest and had just seen one area where he was able to offer a return of energy. He didn't know why he lowered his voice as he spoke of what he'd learnt. It just seemed right.

'I knew you'd done more than just snog Viivi!' Hannu exclaimed.

'Just over two tendays on Earth has changed me big-time,' Qwelby continued. 'The fights, the healing, shooting the Americans, the deception, and along with all that, the friendship of your group of mates and.' He grinned. 'Girls. I'm not a Warrior as in my fantasies, but strong and confident and ready to find Kaigii, go home and expose the evil in our world.' With what he had said hanging in the air and mocking him, Qwelby was content for Hannu to have the last words.

'I've changed. A lot. Less than two weeks since I had a fireside seat to that fight in the Kalahari. And now five days of us being together and,' he exhaled, heavily, 'I see things that aren't possible, hear your voice in my head and err, Tullia...!' Hannu blushed.

Qwelby thumped his friend and they laughed.

Romain drove back to his hotel, mentally replaying what had been said. Very satisfactory, except for one worm in the apple. However much Keskinen had supported Romain's reasoning and encouraged the youth, the Professor was not convinced that Qwelby would agree to accompany him to Raiatea. Romain was used to dealing with energy and had sensed an odd energy when, having quite reasonably said that he needed time to think, the youth had promised an answer by two o'clock the following afternoon.

The story of all the people who had followed the boy to Lainio was alarming. Romain dared not wait. Taking a deep breath he handed over control to his alter ego, Rekkr Reginsen. With the last shred of regret that the way ahead was now both difficult and dangerous, he had a final discussion with Franz, who confirmed that all was in place to collect and deliver "a package." Romain telephoned Erki and they arranged to meet, the youth indicating a discrete location on the edge of Kotomäki.

When Erki left Romain's car he had money safely stowed in a pocket and an unsettled feeling in his stomach. The man he had just spoken with was very different from the Professor of their previous meetings. And he had no doubt that the promise of what would befall him should he betray the trust now placed in him would be kept. He dared not tell Lokir in advance. But what could his boss in the shady underworld that Erki liked so much say, when Erki offered a useful contact much higher up in their dark World?

CHAPTER 44

A DOCTOR CALLS

THE KALAHARI

It was late in the afternoon when a little convoy ceased jolting along the sandy track and came to a halt at the edge of a large clearing in the bush, fringed by a long stand of trees. Frank climbed down from the first of three Landcruisers and called out to the others to take a break, but not to start unpacking as he had to go and speak with the San. The scene immediately became colourful as the students piled out wearing shorts or knee length skirts, a variety of lightweight tops and sandals.

Frank, middle aged, tall and solidly built, had spent his whole life in Africa and a large part of it working on game reserves, as had Lishi his wife. Blending in with the bush, he was wearing khaki cargo pants, a pale green shirt, a faded, once dark green gilet and scuffed boots. Unnecessarily, he signalled to his wife that he was going to check on using the campsite. Like her husband, Lishi was accustomed to blending into the background. Today she was wearing a long skirt in a gentle pattern of browns and dark greens but had treated herself to an orange sweater, over which her long golden brown hair hung in the pony tail she wore for travelling.

As Frank approached the entry to the settlement he saw Ghadi and Kotuma approaching. They exchanged greetings and hugged one another. As they did so a few other Meera walked up to say hello. This was their first visit this season. Although Ghadi was always happy for him to use the unofficial camp site, out of courtesy, Frank spoke with him before starting to unload. Agreement confirmed, Frank promised to return with his wife as soon as the camp had been set up.

Returning to the group he found that, as usual, Lishi and Kemah, their half San assistant, had already opened up the trailer that provided the kitchen. Well wrapped up in dark clothes against the chilly evening, Kemah was a slim one metre ninety tall. Most San were small in stature but Nature seemed to enjoy confounding scientists as many of the children of a San and other African pairing easily outstripped both parents in height. Given the go-ahead, Kemah lit a fire whilst the fifteen research students unloaded and erected tents, installed bedding rolls and made preparations for the night. Chatting happily about the day's events, Lishi and Frank continued to prepare the kitchen layout.

The main ingredients for the evening meal had been cooked the night before. As soon as Kemah had the fire going, he put the pot containing the curry on the grill to heat through and added a pot of water for the rice. A simple but tasty meal that was easy to prepare. Always important if there were delays in the journey and they did not arrive at a campsite until after seven when it would be pitch dark.

The kitchen area ready and the campers capable of preparing themselves for a stay of a few days, Frank and Lishi set off to talk with their Meera hosts. Old friends stretching back over many years, as usual they exchanged greetings and caught up on the news since their last visit, which all took longer than the business arrangements which were swiftly settled. Frank's plan of starting the discussion groups at nine was vetoed by the Meera who said it was still much too cold that early in the morning. A start at ten was agreed.

Frank and Lishi then returned to their own camp to find all

were settled around the fire with drinks in hand. Before they had left the last town they had stocked up with beer, wine and spirits for the cold nights around the camp fire. Lishi checked the curry and rice and then went to the back of her Landcruiser to make further preparations.

Frank explained the arrangements for the following day. Thinking of them as "students" was somewhat of a misnomer. Ranging in age from thirty-five to seventy, all were professionals following a variety of different careers. Their common interest was to understand the way of life that had enabled the San to survive for over seventy thousand years and how each one of them might be able to apply some of that in their careers in the so-called "civilised" world.

A sudden cry, a yell, a crash and startled faces swung around to see Lishi on her back with something large on top of her. As people rushed to help they saw it was the refrigerator. Lishi's face looked pale and drawn. Frank reached her first and enveloped the fridge in his arms. Even with his strength he could not lift it. A second pair of hands reached out to help. Danny, mid forties, tall and strongly built lifted the refrigerator off with Frank and set it down alongside.

The words: *What on earth were you doing?'* froze in Frank's mouth and all that came out was a cry of: 'LISHI!' He looked at the shape of her two hands with horror, bent backwards. Surely both were broken at the wrist?

The nearest medical care was several hours drive away. Ghadi was one of the most experienced and powerful San healers Frank had ever met. Lishi was the cook for the whole party, while they were camping for over two weeks in the wild. Too many worries were rushing through Frank's mind! After a career in game reserves he was not unused to dealing with injuries but was happy to move aside as Becky came to inspect his wife.

In her mid thirties and a nursing Sister working in A&E at a major hospital, Becky quickly agreed with Frank that Lishi's wrists were severely sprained and possibly broken. Marianne, a tall and silver haired anthropologist, brought the first aid kit and Becky started treatment.

Danny suggested something strong might be welcome and a few moments later Marianne was holding a glass of rum and coke to Lishi's lips. She did not mind the few drips down her chin as she swallowed gratefully, the liquor warming and easing her tensions.

Having finished treating one hand, Becky moved to the other. The conversations around the camp fire were stilled as they heard Kemah calling: 'Mr Frrrank.'

Frank looked up in surprise as, unasked, Kemah had run off to the village and returned with Ghadi, Kotuma, Xameb, a tall woman with a strange face and a little girl he remembered seeing on previous visits. Frank wanted to get Lishi to hospital as soon as possible but was in a dilemma when Ghadi, known as Two Powers because of his almost unique healing abilities, asked to examine Lishi and said that Tyua'llia had strong healing powers, having saved the lives of one of their own and also a police sergeant.

Reluctantly, Frank moved aside and, in turn, Ghadi and Tyua'llia very gently let each of Lishi's hands rest on their own. A conversation slowly developed between all the Meera. After a time Ghadi explained. Lishi's wrists were broken and there were other injuries: torn ligaments and muscles and serious bruising, including at the base of her spine where she'd fallen badly. Chest and stomach, nasty bruising but nothing broken.

Ghadi offered to have Lishi taken to the village for the night where Tu would care for her and preparations would be made for healing dances the following evening. Becky objected. Lishi's injuries were too severe. Proper setting of the bones was urgent and she wanted x-rays and even scans for possible internal injuries from the heavy refrigerator landing on her.

A hand gently rested on her shoulder. Turning her head, Becky was sucked into a pair of highly slanted eyes. Bright blue ovals with large purple orbs that seemed to be gently rotating.

'Rest. Heal,' Tullia said in her limited English as she slid an image into Becky's mind. The soft smile from starlight sparkling off white teeth in the sunburnt face enveloped Becky in reassurance. The tall and gently imposing doctor was right.

'Lishi is deep in shock,' Becky said, turning to Frank. 'A long journey will make everything worse. Now, she needs to rest. Tomorrow morning for the hospital and X-rays.'

'Yes. Long day. Need rest,' Lishi said, as Frank opened his mouth to object.

As the tribe's chief returned to the village to arrange for a stretcher, Frank looked around, thinking of what had to be done for the rest of the night. Catching his eye, Sylvia told him that dinner was ready. He grunted and everyone settled down to eat. Taking his plate to sit by Lishi, he found that in those few moments Tyua'llia had taken Kotuma's place and Lishi was resting against the woman described as a healer.

When Frank had finished eating, Lishi asked for another rum and coke.

'Only five,' Tullia said softly, looking at her hands as her sixth, Aurigan finger disappeared. Memories of previous healings cascaded through her mind. Pretending to be an Azuran without energy controls, a young Qwelby had badly injured himself.

"He needs to learn from a period of pain and discomfort," their mother had said when Tullia had asked why she had not been allowed to completely heal him. She had not been allowed to completely heal the deep cut in Xashee's thigh, later discovering that he was proud to bear the faint scar as a mark of having saved her life when she'd fallen over the cliff edge.

For Lishi, the immediate danger had passed. All bleeding had stopped and the bones had been reset correctly. Yet there was a lot more to be done. As the energy of Tullia's Uddîsû, Rrîltallâ, withdrew, it seemed to the young woman that her heroine had stroked her hair as though saying "Well done." Yet there was a lot

235

more to do. *Why?* Tullia asked, and was frustrated when the only reply was a sympathetic smile in her mind.

Frank knelt down beside Lishi with her drink. 'The pain's almost gone,' she said in a surprised tone. Frank grunted. His mind was racing. There were too many thoughts of the future crying for attention. For a few minutes he had not been in command and that felt very strange.

Kemah had gone off to fetch the healers without being asked. The girl, Tsetsana he'd discovered her name, had helped Kemah sort out dinner. Tyua'llia had been healing his wife. He felt left out yet at the same time it all felt good. A little voice at the back of his mind seemed to whisper: '*Remember, this is the Africa you know and love.*'

Four young men arrived with a stretcher. As with almost everything the San did, scarcely a word was spoken, no sense of hurry, but it was only a matter of moments before Lishi had been gently loaded onto the stretcher and carried back to the village where she was made comfortable in the second guest hut. After talking with Ghadi, Frank settled down beside his wife, until, tired after a long day's travelling, she was soon asleep.

CHAPTER 45

PLAYING CATCH-UP

LAINIO-FINLAND

All the agents were up early on Monday morning, especially the two Finns who were staying at a hotel in Kittilä and to whom Maija had given strict instructions not only to watch the other agents, but also to ensure the latter did no more than observe. Three men were watching the chalet, three women were being briefed for the Sleigh Ride, waiting for their "husbands" to join them. Time for the ride to get underway and no sign of their target and his friends. Suspicions aroused, Viivi was summoned to bring keys. No answer to the knocking on the door and the chalet was found to be empty, but the hired car was still there.

A flurry of phone calls and it was soon established that all three had flown to Siilinjärvi on that morning's early flight. An insistent Maija eventually established that the car hire company's records indicating Mrs Rahkamo had returned her car, were correct. Except that it had been fitted with the number plates of another, identical model that was due to be returned later that day. A check of engine numbers was the final confirmation that it was the vehicle in the car park at Lainio.

The Russians were furious, blaming FSB incompetence and wanting Qwelby held by the police on suspicion of being an illegal immigrant before he had the chance to disappear. A vigorous argument ensued with the Americans who explained that they wanted Qwelby free to move around in the hope that he was going to lead them to what had to be his contact in Helsinki.

Leaving the chalet, Maija telephoned her Director and once again suggested the youth be arrested as the best way out of a tricky situation. Furthermore, she strongly suspected the Americans' opposition to his being held by the police was because they intended to extract him. Last night the SUPO chief had felt obliged to allow time for the new SVR agents to be in place. Now, he requested an urgent meeting with the Interior Minister.

When the news reached Hohn, the colonel walked down the length of the C17 and stood with a grim smile on her lips, looking at the oil pump that had caused the X5S to return the previous night. She nodded to it and called her team together for a briefing.

Later, when a Finnish Air Force jet was on its way to Siilinjärvi with SUPO Deputy Director Maija and all six agents aboard, a message was received diverting the flight to Jyväskylä and advising that Qwelby's arrest had been authorised. The Americans were furious. Their target would be in police custody by the time they reached Kotomäki and they had no illusions as to which country had the greater leverage with the Finnish government.

Urgent coded messages were exchanged with ground control at Hohn Air Base. The jet that had delivered the replacement CIA agents to Kittilä and was now carrying the rest of their team from Hohn, was also diverted to Jyväskylä. The Colonel's instructions to her team aboard the jet were clear. Qwelby was to be secured before the police had him locked in a cell. The StealthCopter would be airborne as soon as it was dark and there had better be no more mistakes!

CHAPTER 46

FAREWELL

KOTOMÄKI-FINLAND

Early Monday morning Qwelby kept his promise and walked with Hannu to meet Anita. They said tearful farewells. 'I'm heartswarmed by both of you,' Qwelby said. 'More. I make new word. I'm heartsfilled. I love you both.' They shared a three way hug. 'Think of me and Kaigii. Try to reach us. One day...'

Holding hands, they walked to the stop for the school bus where Qwelby said goodbye to his other friends and shared a long kiss with Oona, who didn't care that everyone saw her tears.

Back in the Rahkamos' house Qwelby told Seija that he was going to honour his promise to Professor Romain to think over his offer of going to Raiatea and was going to do that whilst skiing at Muurame. He was going to take the shuttle bus so that, whatever he decided, he'd be back in plenty of time to catch or cancel the afternoon flight to Helsinki.

'What about those people who are following you?'

Qwelby tilted his head to one side as he thought of explanations involving perturbations in the quantum field. 'Thoughts are like a snowfall, Aunt Seija. All looks the same. But each flake is different. I will recognise them. Hannu tells me word is "signature".'

Given the order to arrest Qwelby as an illegal immigrant, Sergeant Sjöström changed into civilian clothes and knocked on the Rahkamos' front door, whilst a uniformed constable parked a discreet distance from the house where he was able to watch the back door.

Pia felt uncomfortable lying to Mrs Rahkamo when she explained that she only needed a quick word with the youth. The report of the incident on New Year's Eve had eventually reached the bureaucrats in their offices who had asked a couple of questions. Having accepted Mrs Rahkamo's offer to telephone when Qwelby returned from Muurame, she told the constable to keep watch on the back door, because that was the one anyone with skis would use. She then drove to the ski resort, parked discreetly and stationed herself under cover, where she was able to watch the bus stop and several of the runs.

CHAPTER 47

BREAKFAST

THE KALAHARI

Frank awoke with a start. It was dawn! Last night he'd fallen fast asleep as soon as his head had touched the pillow. Looking out, he could see Kemah already moving round the campsite in the faint tinges of first light.

The campsite was on one side of a gently sloping valley. To the left, the summit was a hundred or so metres away. The sun would rise over there. To the right, several hundred metres away, the San village was on the top of the opposite rise, screened from sight by Acacia trees. The tents and the three Landcruisers formed an arc facing towards the sunrise.

Frank clambered out of the tent. Two kettles were already heating on the grill. The next priority was to open the kitchen trailer and get out the large thermos flasks, cups and drink-making equipment. That done, he sat down by Kemah while they watched the flames flicker and crackle and waited for the water to boil. Whilst Kemah spoke English as well as more than one San language, he was most fluent in Afrikaans. They were using that as they discussed the plans for the day.

They were facing the tents. It was Frank's favourite part of the day. There was light in the sky for a good half an hour before the sun actually rose over the crest just behind them. He enjoyed watching the first rays strike the tops of the trees and then, like a beam from a yellowy orange searchlight, move down the trunks until it struck the tents. As the shadow of the vanishing night ran across the ground and the fire was bathed in sunlight that was for him, the signal for the start of the day.

The first kettle boiled, Kemah poured water into the thermoses, refilled the kettle and put it back on the grill. As he did so, he asked, 'A large saucepan of water for the milimili?'

'Yes please, Kemah,' a gentle, musical voice said.

The two men looked up, surprised to see Tyua'llia and Tsetsana. Their approach across the soft sand had been completely masked by the various noises around the campsite as people were waking in their tents, greeting each other and the new day. Frank was again lost for words. An uncomfortable feeling for him.

'Lishi tell me,' Tullia explained. 'I like African porridge.'

Tullia smiled shyly at Kemah. Although when not working with Frank or Lishi, Kemah lived in town and considered himself very modern, nevertheless he was half San and fully African. The combination of Tullia as a beautiful young woman of marriageable age and what he had been told was a Daughter of Nananana was overpowering.

Kemah filled the usual saucepan with water and set it to heat. Tullia and Tsetsana started looking around the kitchen trailer and fired a series of questions at Kemah as to where things were. He joined them and amidst questions and chatter the campers rose to the sound of giggles from the kitchen area.

Frank lent back in his chair. He had lived and worked all his life in Africa. He loved the people. He loved the San and was doing everything he could to support them, yet he was still discovering new things. Last night, this morning, Kemah's reaction. Kemah never did anything without checking either with himself or Lishi. He was surprised when he realised that the strange looking girl was fluently speaking Meera.

Frank shook his head in wonderment. Somehow, he was not in charge again. He realised with a shock that he had not thought any more about taking Lishi to the hospital. The westernised part of his mind started to tell him off for not having that plan, for not having rushed off to see how Lishi was, although she would probably be fast asleep, and for not having any thought of her when Tullia arrived and said Lishi had told her how to make milimili! The African part of his mind told him to relax. Over the years he had learnt to trust the San. If anything was not right with Lishi he would have been told immediately.

He took a deep breath and decided that a nice cold beer would be more settling than a cup of coffee. He settled back with his beer, relaxed and exchanged greetings with the folk as they came out of their tents, yawned, disappeared behind the trees and returned to sit around the fire.

'Everything as usual,' Frank announced. 'Hot water is on the table. All the breakfast stuff is there. If you want anything ask.... the kitchen staff.' He grinned. Finishing his beer, he got up from the camp chair and turned towards the trio in the kitchen area. 'I'm going to see how Lishi is. Look after the happy campers.'

'Yes, Mr Frrrank,' all three said together and giggled.

Frank made his way to the village, shaking his head. Kemah, twenty three years old, mature and reliable, was acting like a schoolboy. No, he corrected himself, he was acting more like a schoolgirl! That brought a smile to his face. He would be able to greet Lishi with a little story she would find amusing.

Arriving at the village, Frank greeted the Meera as he walked to the guest hut. Deena was sitting outside and gestured for him to enter. He found Lishi looking very comfortable and relaxed on a pile of blankets. One of the things he loved about her was her mass of golden brown hair that reached down to past her shoulders. Just now it was spread over the pillow looking like a halo. Squatting down beside her, he gently kissed her forehead as they exchanged their usual morning greetings. 'You look well.'

'I feel good.'

'Pain?'

'No. Just awareness of injury.'

'Hospital?' Frank was surprised at himself. He had asked rather than stated.

Lishi gently shook her head and looked searchingly at Frank's face. 'I don't think so. Everything feels alright. Tyua'llia says everything is in its right place and healing is proceeding slowly.' She hurriedly added, 'Ghadi and Tu agree.'

Frank sat there looking at Lishi. Who is this strange girl? What powers does she have? Ghadi says everything is alright. That, I can trust. 'You must have been awake early this morning?'

'A call of nature. I found Tyua'llia curled up on the floor. She helped me and we started talking. Without thinking, I mentioned the difficulty that you would have at the campsite without me there to prepare breakfast. Well...' Lishi raised her bandaged hands in a gesture of "you know the rest."

'Is there anything you'd like right now?'

'A cup of Rooibush tea,' she replied with a smile. It was her usual morning drink.

Frank rose and went to fetch tea bags from the camp site. As he strode across the little valley he was aware that Lishi had not told him everything, something else was going on. He firmly locked away all such thoughts and turned his mind to concentrating on the plans for the morning.

Looking into Tyua'llia's eyes Lishi had sensed that there was a lot to discover. She had thought of borrowing the young woman for the rest of the journey to cook and do the many other jobs that she herself could no longer do. She would keep that thought to herself for a while. She had been married to Frank for over thirty years and she knew exactly how to turn his "no" into a "maybe" and then a "yes."

Frank's immediate concern was catering for much more than breakfast. As he walked through the tents he was greeted by a very homely situation that looked almost like every other morning. A group of contented people sitting around the fire with a woman bending over a pot of bubbling milimili and scooping it into bowls. The difference was that the bending figure was Tyua'llia and the bowls were being held by Tsetsana.

As Frank announced that Lishi was recovering and had agreed to go to the hospital when she felt well enough to travel, Becky wondered why she had felt so confident in what she had said the previous evening. About to say she wanted to visit Lishi and check on the dressings, intending to persuade her to agree to go to the hospital that day, she caught sight of Tyua'llia looking at her.

Turning to smile her thanks for what the tall young woman had done, once again she found herself embraced by a pair of slowly twirling, purple eyes. Snowy white teeth smiled reassurance from a sunburnt face. The doctor was right. Healing was taking place and there was no need for a visit to the hospital. Becky nodded and continued with her breakfast. She'd check on the dressings later.

Slipping into the woman's mind without permission was wrong. This time Tullia squared the intrusion with Lishi's insistence that morning that she was not going to hospital unless it became essential.

It was only when back home and telling her friends of the adventures on her study trip that Becky thought back to the evening of Lishi's accident and wondered about the doctor. She was to reason that Frank must have used his Satellite phone to call the hospital, the doctor had driven out and stayed overnight. Images blurred in her memory and she found herself unable to recall any more about the doctor than teeth sparkling out of a sunburnt face and unusual purple eyes. When her friends teased her lack of detailed recollection, Becky happily answered, 'That's Africa. The magic of a different world.'

It was late morning by the time Frank had finished with business. After a meeting with the students to outline the day's plans he'd taken them to the village and seen them settled in their individual groups: researchers and Meera working together on the chosen projects.

He made his way to the guest hut to find Lishi sitting outside, holding court as it were. She was seated on blankets and propped up by cushions, resting easily against the fence that marked that particular guest area. Sitting next to her was Tu, a very old and accomplished healer, Tullia and Tsetsana. Tu spoke quietly in Meera and everyone laughed. Frank raised an eyebrow.

'Tu said: "Lion comes to check his lionesses are doing what is required",' Lishi explained.

Frank felt slightly affronted that they should think he was like a real lion, doing nothing other than order the women around. Yet at the same time his male ego was stroked by the thought they saw him as the king of the beasts. Before he could say anything, Lishi continued.

'Tu has checked my dressings. They're all right. Everything is sorted for meals for the next few days. Tyua'llia knows what to do and Xameb has agreed to Tsetsana helping.' She smiled. 'It seems we get one, we get the other.'

Frank knew he was being manipulated. Perhaps that was the price the lion had to pay for the privilege of having a pride of lionesses! Not wanting to give away his understanding he adopted his usual reply in such situations and merely grunted.

'Frank. I want, I need to return to the campsite. I want to be there with you. If I am there I can supervise the cooking.' She lifted a hand a little way. 'No, Frank. I need to do this. Take my mind off how useless I am. Besides which, I do have my reputation to maintain.' She was referring to the praise she always received for the excellent meals she prepared, cooking over an open wood fire in the middle of the desert.

As Frank sat down, Tsetsana got up and ran off, returning a few moments later with Xameb and Roland, one of the researchers. Frank was surprised to see the seventy year old therapist with his strange beliefs about what he called the quantum world.

'Tyua'llia has a story to tell and Xameb suggested that Roland should also hear it,' Lishi explained.

Frank totally accepted the San had their beliefs, but why an apparently intelligent man like Roland had learnt Afrikaans in order to discuss them with the Shaman, Frank couldn't get his head around.

Tullia switched on her compiler and told her story in Afrikaans.

There was a long silence when she'd finished, eventually broken by Xameb mentioning Tullia's need to get to the Republic of South Africa to meet Siboniso, the pre-eminent of all Shamans, who Xameb had said was the best person to help her reach her twin.

Roland had so many questions he wanted to ask that he said nothing. Frank ignored all the strange nonsense. The situation was clear. They were due to stay with the Meera for several more days. Danny drove his own Range Rover at home so, if Lishi was unable to drive when it was time to leave, Danny could drive her Landcruiser. As to the girl's wanting a free ride. He'd talk to Xameb later in private, ignore all her rubbish and explain the practical reasons that made it impossible to take her with them. 'The others mustn't know,' he said. 'They'll never concentrate on the project they're here for.'

'I have thought of that,' Xameb said and gestured to Tullia.

'I will not use my compiler but speak my own words. I like that as Tazii use fewer words.' She switched off her compiler and continued speaking in Afrikaans. 'Tazii not tell lies. I speak little English. Speak little truths. That hurt little. I come from far away. Learn Meera. San my family. My tribe speak Tazian. All look like me, like tribes of red skinned San. All is true.'

'Kemah?' Frank asked.

'He accepts Tyua'llia as a daughter of the Goddess Nananana. Naturally she has to invent a story to keep that secret from people who are not San,' Xameb replied reassuringly.

Tullia pointed to the sun. 'Prepare meal,' she said and she and Tsetsana got up and headed for the campsite.

Frank watched them go, turned to his wife and shrugged his shoulders. He allowed himself an inner smile at the thought that there was something to be said for having a pride of lionesses. Well, one lioness and two working cubs.

CHAPTER 48

CONFESSION

VERTAZIA

Since Yarannah, their mother, had had a change of heart concerning the attempts to rescue the twins, Tamina and Wrenden were keeping their parents updated with progress.

Now, seven days after the embargo on contact, the youngsters waited until their mother had gone out before asking to talk with their father. Jailandur was hoping his daughter might at last explain why over recent days she had become more moody and uncommunicative. Wanting to encourage her, he thoughtsent instructions to his study to provide a conducive environment.

He wished he'd not done that when the room darkened and the walls turned into a series of tall arches, admittedly beautifully proportioned, but in dark and foreboding colours highlighted by vivid splashes of more shades of red and orange than he'd ever seen before. As the children entered, the dark atmosphere eased a little as the vivid splashes reformed by highlighting the curving frames of the arches and a strong musky perfume filled the air.

'I have a story to tell, Dad. And Eeky has a right to know.'

Her father raised his eyebrows.

'I've got into the SubNet and done a deal in the Shadow Market.'

'Way to go, Sis!'

'I was surprised how easily I was admitted. I know I've acquired a lot of energy credits from all the approval I've received as the principal dancer of my troupe, but I had no idea how much I'm admired and,' she fixed her father with a look, 'far more relevant in the SubNet, for my displays of what is really Aurigan Unarmed Combat.'

Jailandur nodded. *You are a star pupil.*

'The more difficult it became to find anyone who would help, the more determined I became to find the truth about the Uddîšû.'

Jailandur grunted. *I hoped you would not need to do this until after you had achieved your adulthood.*

'I was eventually directed to someone who might help. What she wanted in return... Well. She asked for a Fire Lady. And got one. Full on, living fiery salamanders.'

'Already?!' Jailandur's eyebrows almost disappeared into his hair. *Are you all right?*

Managing. 'The night of the firefight on Earth gave me a big boost.'

'You were awesome, Sis!'

'You too, Eeky.'

'So?' their father asked.

Tamina explained about the incident with her flaming eyes and added: 'News of that whisked through the SubNet in nanoseconds so there was a MegaTie-In for the dealing.'

'Ah.' A soft gasp escaped Tamina's lips and all three turned their heads. Standing alongside the customary Living Statue of The Explorer was a new statue. Tall, copper-hued skin with her overlarge, steely green orbs set in exceptionally slanted yellow ovals. A high collared and snug fitting dress of flaming salamanders emphasised her overlarge breasts. Each of her bare arms was entwined by a golden salamander and the panels of the skirt parted to reveal the long and perfectly toned legs of a dancer. The ends of two long plaited ropes of golden tinted hair could be seen curling at her hips, gently moving as if alive. Beautiful she was not, yet desirable she was, once the onlooker accepted the steely blue-grey shadings in her energy field.

'Léshmîrâ,' all three whispered, and a wry smile crossed Tamina's lips as she acknowledged the steel that had been present in her when she'd danced in the Shadow Market.

'Welcome,' Tamina said. Her mouth dropped open and her eyes went round as, although the Living Statue did not move, she felt herself being embraced and kissed as her whole Form was filled with love for the Gift of Life she had courageously offered. Emboldened, Tamina pulled her shoulders back and sat proudly upright.

'I danced and they got a lot more than just a Fire Lady. I was in a different world. I was on the HomeSphere. I found new moves. Exciting. Stimulating. More than one man tried to dance with me. I. Well. I hurled them from me. They'd invaded my space and...'

'Unstructured!' Jailandur shook his head in dismay.

Ooooh, no. We were L'Entangled. Welcome, Daughter. The Living Statue's warm purring words sent a shiver down each man's spine as they felt wrapped in the embrace of a SabreTooth who was toying with the idea of snacking on them.

With fire burning in every cell of her body, Tamina was gaping open-mouthed at her heroine. She knew of the marvellous Living Entanglement whereby it was as if the superpositioning across dimensions collapsed and a Tazian became the Uddîšû. That only happened much later in life when that person had become an Elder, or even not until they were a Venerable. She heard a rich chuckle in her mind.

Tamina knew what she'd felt as she'd danced and had assumed it was the high energy of the Tie-In, not daring to think that she had been even briefly L'Entangled. To discover that not only had she been but, by being called "Daughter", the Uddîšû was confirming that was permanent, left her shaking with the awesomeness of what she had achieved, while her mind was full of questions.

The answer came in a montage of time-spanning images showing how the Tazii had lost energy and drive and, wrapped in fear, were heading towards extinction. But there was hope from the energies of youth through the SubNet Kulture, yet that was stifled at the adulthood ceremonies; and those adults who felt differently were constrained from acting by the pervasive negativity of the majority of Tazii.

It is your strength, passion and commitment that led you to find your inheritance; to serve, as I did, Léshmîrâ thought spoke. *The Twins need you, Daughter. Being L'Entangled, I am also your Attribute. Theirs are a Dragon and a Winged Unicorn.*

Be strong for your sister, Adventurer. Recall the firefight. I am your Attribute.

Both youngsters nodded as they grasped how difficult it had to be for the twins with animal Attributes.

Stunned by the depth of feeling in those words and intrigued that his hero, usually referred to as The Explorer, had chosen to address him as Adventurer, Wrenden reached out a hand to his sister. He was not sure whether he was offering support or wanting to feel that somewhere inside her was still the big bossy sister he'd always known. As she took his hand, he felt her asking for his understanding. He grinned. "Why not" never made it to thoughtspeak. *You got it, Sis.*

'What I did circled back to me in... difficult imagery.' Her mouth gone dry, Tamina wetted her lips, her now soft eyes begging for understanding. 'My reputation's been made and I've been given the KultureName of TamLâš'tûn.'

'Tamina, The Ultimate Dealer. Which can be interpreted in different ways,' Jailandur translated the Ancient Aurigan.

'The woman who'd offered to deal, truthdealt.' *Had she not...!* Tamina contained herself and went on to explain all she'd learnt about Léshmîrâ Kûsheÿnÿ, watching the Uddîšû nodding and feeling the shocks run through her young brother as he picked up on the hints of Death and tightened his grip on her hand.

'An Uddîšû cannot be denied.' *You know that, Dad!* Tamina challenged.

'I did everything possible to persuade your mother to put aside all her negative thoughts and not to think about the Uddîšû at all. As you have discovered, the Uddîšû, which are in essence the ten principal Archetypes that colour our whole race, thrive on energy.'

'Why not Aurigan twelve, Dad?'

'Many guesses about that, son. But no-one knows. As I was saying, an Uddîšû thrives on any energy, good or bad. With the quantum world permeating the whole of existence, that inevitably operates on our Forms and increases the strength of the relevant genes. That's why the Attributes tend to follow the gender.'

Yeah, Eeky. Tamina squeezed her brother's hand in support of his inheritance of Explorer, Adventurer and Trickster, and sent him and their father an image of a powerful and brave young man fighting alongside Qwelby in the Kalahari.

Aw, gee, Sis!

'We always wanted a daughter and a son. Your mother was trying to do her best for you. She feared you would go through the same wild post Awakening as she had done.'

'Mother?!'

Jailandur nodded. 'The stronger the Uddîšû genes, the stronger the L'Entanglement may be.'

Fear not, Daughter, I am with you. By rejecting me, your mother brought on her suffering.

Knowing how proud his father was of the strong genes that descended the male line, Wrenden stared at the Living Staue of his hero and felt his face turn red hot as he remembered how disappointed he'd been to discover his Attribute was only a man.

The Explorer smiled. *Hold strong, my Adventurer. We are needed.*

There was a long silence. Aware of Wrenden's churning emotions, sister and father waited for him to speak. As he drew on her support, Tamina saw images rising through his mind. His actions on the night of the firefight; when she'd saved him from drowning in the river of lava as they rescued Qwelby from the Pit of Despair; further back in time when they'd almost lost both their lives trying to prevent Qwelby leaving Vertazia.

Wrenden took a deep breath as he looked at his hero, Ngélûzhrâ Khèrñîszón, and reminded himself of his middle name of Ngé'zânâ, his entitlement as he bore strong genes of The Explorer, Adventurer and Trickster. He turned to look at his sister's shining face, the appeal in her overlarge, emerald green orbs and the bright reds, oranges and yellows of her aura.

'I will never discover Azura Yezi,' he said quietly referring to the fact that it had been The Explorer, who seventy-five thousand years ago had found the planet that had later become the two parallel worlds. 'Qwelby is not the Dragon Lord and you are not Léshmîrâ Kûsheÿnÿ.' He grinned. 'But, Blazing Novas, Sis, a flaming-eyed Fire Lady. Best be careful of the tricks we pull on you when Qwelby's back!'

Tamina and Jailandur stared at him for a moment and then burst out laughing. Brother and sister hugged, then parted. Jailandur hugged his son, stood back and held him at arms length. 'How did you become so old and wise?' he asked.

'Why not?' Ecky grinned, all three laughed, the dark colours lightened and the shades of red and orange and yellow framing the arches softened as more colours of the rainbow seeped into the room.

The Living Statues were smiling and nodding their heads. Tamina gave her brother a long look, decided that ruffling his hair was not appropriate and put her arm around his shoulders. He slipped his around her waist. *SisBro,* they shared and grinned.

CHAPTER 49

LOST

KOTOMÄKI-FINLAND

Late Monday afternoon the nine people squashed into Chief Inspector Penti Harju's office in Kotomäki were bemused by Sergeant Sjöström's report that the youth everyone knew as Qwelby had vanished. The only positive information came from Hannu and Anita, who she had found at the girl's home. Their two mothers had been about to telephone hospitals and injury clinics.

The youngsters had said that as they reached Hannu's home on the way back from school they'd been approached by a local youth, Erki, and a big man dressed all in black and wearing dark shades. Speaking with a German accent, the man had told them that Qwelby had been injured whilst skiing, taken to hospital and was insisting on having two items – a Globe and a satchel. When the kids said they'd take them, Erki had grabbed hold of Anita and the man had become threatening, saying if Hannu did as he was told, "Little Miss Precious won't get hurt."

The man had accompanied Hannu into his home. As they'd come back outside, with the man carrying the Globe and the satchel, a large black SUV had driven up. Erki had let go of Anita and accompanied the man to the vehicle, where both had got in and the car had driven away.

All the rest was negative. Qwelby had not boarded the flight to Helsinki, nor been seen at the airport. None of the local hospitals or injury clinics had any record either of his being treated or a call for an ambulance and Erki was not at home.

Since none of their additional agents had arrived before Qwelby's flight had left Jyväskylä, it was with clear consciences that both the Americans and the Russians denied that either they or another of their country's services had effected a kidnapping.

Maija switched off the microphone of the ComsUnit sitting in the middle of the table, pointed to the link in her right ear and held up a hand to still further conversation. All the others heard was a series of "Yeses", "Confirmeds" and, finally, "Agreed."

'Due to pressure from both your countries' Ambassadors, photographs and a description of Qwelby are being sent to all ports, airports and border crossings,' she announced. 'He is to be taken to Ratakatu for questioning. That will include representatives from both your countries.'

It was not until much later when a check on departures showed that the Professor had not boarded that evening's flight to Helsinki, yet his car had been returned to the hire agency at the advised time, that the agents realised they had been the victims of a carefully orchestrated deception. There was a flurry of recriminations and debate as to whether Romain was part of the deception and had carefully laid a false trail. Eventually, the Russians revealed the almost certain answer.

Moscow Centre, as the headquarters of the old KGB and now the Ministry of State Security was known, advised that an old file that had not yet been computerised had been unearthed. It concerned two former Stasi agents now living in Geneva under new identities: Franz Shosta and Pierre Kovich. They were proprietors of an establishment well known to the Swiss police – Bar Minge. Romain was noted as having visited that during his time working at CERN, and Franz Shosta had spent several months on Raiatea during the construction of the laboratory complex.

Too late, questions were asked about Metsälä's accident whilst tailing Romain. Shortly before full daylight he had been involved in a minor collision. Both the tourist whose fault it was and his wife had been very apologetic. They were driving a hire car and had made a great fuss over the formalities of exchanging names, addresses and insurance company details, all eventually proving to be false. By the time Metsälä was able to continue, Romain was long gone. The police had been asked to keep a look out for the car, advise SUPO headquarters if seen and follow discreetly until relieved. There had been no sighting. Now, photographs and a description of Romain were also sent to all ports, airports and border crossings and his passport details logged into the surveillance systems.

In the Mendeleev Bar not far from Dzerzhinsky, Feodor Ivanovich Demidov, an old man and former FSB clerk, and Andrei Petrovic Kurochkin, a young man and once hopeful SVR agent, were sitting far apart at separate tables, morosely staring into their beers. Unaware of their unfortunate connection in creating the misnamed Kwilby file, each was wondering how to explain their sudden dismissal from the security services – Feodor Ivanovich to his wife, Andrei Petrovic to his parents. Russian bureaucracy was no different from any other. When scapegoats had to be found, it was always the people at the bottom.

CHAPTER 50

HEALING DANCE

THE KALAHARI

The research party's second evening meal was prepared under Lishi's personal direction from her seat on a wooden chair the San had made for her that was well padded with blankets and pillows.

A short while after Tullia and Tsetsana had cleared away, washed up and returned to their own duties in the village, O'wa, Ghadi's young son, arrived with a group of men bringing long poles. O'wa said that the village was ready for the study party and the men would carry Lishi on her chair.

A few minutes later the researchers reached the ceremonial area where a fire had largely burnt down to a large bed of bright coals. The Meera had left open a small section of their circle around the fire. Set in a wide V shape facing the fire were two large tree trunks for the visitors to sit on or lean against. Lishi was amongst the Meera to the students' right, with Tullia and Tu seated on either side of her.

When his party was settled, Frank walked over to stand before them. 'What you will see tonight is a traditional Meera healing ceremony. It is similar amongst all the San tribes, although each tribe will have its own variations. Healing will be given to many people, including yourselves. The San have no musical instruments.

The women will clap. Sometimes in complicated patterns. It is very important you do not think of yourselves merely as onlookers. That is not the San way. Please join in the clapping.'

Around the fire with its leaping and crackling flames several men were dancing. They were wearing only loinskins, bead necklaces and headbands. Most of them carried thin sticks, like staffs of office. Bands of large seed pods were strapped around their lower legs, the seeds inside them rattling as they moved.

Dancing was small steps more like stamping, with the rattles going all the time in rhythm with the clapping and all against a background of the bright colours the women were wearing. Soon everyone including the students were clapping and swaying to the rhythms that were occasionally punctuated by off-beat clapping that added to the hypnotic quality.

Soon, sweat was running down the dancers' bodies, turning them shining golden brown in the firelight. Women called out loud cries, the energy increased and the dancing healers left the circle to lay their hands on Meera and students alike. Or they would stand in front of a person, crying out words in their own language. Each healer felt the power of the universe flowing into them from their ancestors.

The hand clapping and the cries of the women became louder and more vigorous. To the students joining in, it seemed to go on forever. Pulled into the hypnotic state, they were entranced. Stopping his dancing for a moment, Ghadi turned to face the fire, raised his arms in the air and called out passionately in his own language, then danced again.

O'wa walked across to speak to Frank, who nodded, then beckoned to the party to leave. The researchers walked back to their camp with hardly a word spoken.

CHAPTER 51

PROGRESS

VERTAZIA

On the evening of their sixth day of visiting different colleges, the youngsters gathered at Lungunu to discuss progress and then went down to the gatherroom to happily share with the adults that their plan was working. A lot of youngsters of all ages from Wrenden's thirteen onwards were interested in their ideas. Not surprisingly, the strongest interest was amongst the Shakazii, the most liberal group of all the Tazii.

The adults were impressed by the fact that many of the older and Awakened youths were suggesting that if there was sufficient support, the idea of Tazian society moving towards a more liberal approach to Life might one day be floated through the MentaNet.

That was great, but too far in the future. The more they talked, the more dark colours were flaring through Tamina's energy field as she struggled to control her frustration.

Tell them, Sis.

No!

Yes! Your aura. He sent an image of flames out of control.

Oh, Kh.... Shit and double shit! She dug her nails into her knees, took a deep breath and gave her brother a wry smile. *Why not?*

Attagirl, Boots!

Tamina was encouraged when the Living Statue of her Heroine appeared as she started to explain what she had learnt of the Uddîšû, keeping it superficial. Or she tried to as, surprising everyone, Shimara wanted to know more.

Keeping to euphemisms, Tamina explained what she knew behind the epithets of Reconciler, Befriender and DeathDealer, until Shimara with tears in her eyes let go Pelnak's hand, stood up, hugged and kissed Tamina. 'Our shield,' she said, thoughtsharing an image of an orb of salamanders surrounding herself, Pelnak and Wrenden. They all felt the tension easing from the tall young woman who was discovering that what she saw as the negative power of her Heroine was already being used for good.

As the youngsters left and the throughway returned to being part of the wall, Mizena spoke. 'That young woman has more courage than all of us together. She puts me, the twins' mother, to shame! No inhibitions were applied to any of us at Adulthood. We will follow the path the youngsters have chosen. It will be a lot harder for us but it's the least we can do.'

The adults agreed that doing that was not going against the collective decision. They were not even trying to change it as overtly as the youngsters were. Rather, their approach had to be on an intellectual level of theoretical discussion.

Mandara and Lellia privately shared troubled thoughts. They both held important places in Tazian society and were only a few years short of becoming Venerables. Using CuSho when approval had been withheld had been completely in defiance of Tazian norms. The objections which had run throughout the MentaNet had now reduced to mutterings, but how far could they go without damaging Tazian society and weakening their authority within the Spiral Assembly?

'I spoke with Tamina's mother the other day,' Lellia said as discussion finished. 'I know that Yarannah hates the Uddîšû inheritance and her ancestors who ensured the genes were strong.

But to refuse to discuss that with her daughter, especially during the crucial period of her Awakening, that is totally irresponsible.'

The epithet of DeathDealer hung in all their minds.

'I will do what I can for her,' she added.

Outside the gatherroom, Wrenden put a finger to his forehead indicating total mental shutdown, then made a waving motion with his fingers as he looked at Shimara and Pelnak, who understood he meant them to go to the Stroems. He turned to his sister and jerked his head in the direction of Mandara's laboratory and CuSho. All four made the XOÑOX symbol before heading off to their destinations.

There was a mixture of frustration and consolation when they gathered in the shielded room in their suite. Frustration that neither the Stroems nor CuSho had provided any information about timimg. Consolation that the messages were still positive.

'You know what?' Pelnak said. *Wait, I'm thinking.* 'The Stroems, CuSho, they're not going out trying to reach the twins. The information is coming to them. Trying to reach the twins through Óweppâ isn't working. What if we wait for them to reach us through our Talisman?'

'Like their colours changed, telling us they'd reconnected?' Wrenden asked.

'Better than that,' Shimara said. 'We do the empty mind type meditation and see if we "hear" anything.'

They looked at one another and shook their heads. Too tired right then, they agreed to meditate on their together-at-Lungunu days.

Until the formal ceremony of adulthood at the end of the second Era, age twenty counting by the traditional Tazian base twelve, the thoughts of youngsters made little impression on the MentaNet. It was this that had allowed the creation of the SubNet Kulture and its hazy interface with the Shadow Market. As both had grown slowly over the millennia, as with many other aspects of Tazian life, the new energies had been accommodated with very little discussion.

A distinct irony was that support for the Shadow Market came from many who should have been opposed to it, such as the more extremist Kumelanii who wanted to acquire goods and services otherwise unobtainable in their self-imposed enclaves.

Although they had not long been members of the SubNet, the twins were well known for their many appearances in LiveShows. The violence used in preventing them, not just from returning home, but from restoring the mental connection so vital to all Tazii, had rapidly become a cause for concern for many teenagers.

As Tamina had discovered to her surprise, she was already known and admired for her beautifully choreographed performances of Aurigan Martial Arts. The MegaTie-In for her Dealing had sent her popularity sweeping through the SubNet – along with her Kulture name. Seen as the leading youngster in the attempts to rescue the twins, she became a focus of interest. That spread to Wrenden as the SubNet took on board his part in the rescue attempts, his youth – well below that for admission to the SubNet – and his Uddîšû.

Of all the youngsters' four hero/ines, Explorer, as discoverer of the planet, was the most famous and also the most publicly acceptable. Even the UnicornRider healers were tinged with the memories they stirred of the long centuries of the Space Wars.

The discussions that the BestFriends initiated in various colleges were eagerly taken up and rapidly spread to other colleges. With so much interest by so many youngsters, signs of disturbance inevitably became apparent in the MentaNet. But by that time it was swamped by so much discussion, debate and mounting disagreement that the new small eddies were ignored.

Ceegren was to bitterly regret his failure to realise that, as the energies originated with youngsters, what he'd dismissed as a small particle was the indicator of a whole wave. He was to try to console himself with the thought that no-one could have foretold the dramatic change to the Tazian way of life that the twins' return was to bring about, harnessing the hitherto dormant energy sediment that was belatedly recognised as a youth Kulture at odds with Tazian Culture.

CHAPTER 52

A TRUCE

VERTAZIA

Two days after Dryddnaa's discussion with Xaala, Rulcas was installed at IndluKoba as a trainee Servitor, to much disgust and a "Serve the Ice Bitch right," from all the staff.

The MentaNet was abuzz as news spread about the twins' reconnection. Ceegren's pride and need to appear omniscient meant that the true reason for the failure to prevent that was concealed with... the truth... that they had moved with such quiet subtlety, typical of devious Azurii, that their mutual searching had not been discovered until it was too late to prevent their complete reconnection.

IndluKoba was a substantial estate providing facilities for rest, relaxation and study, providing enjoyable holidays primarily for the more traditional Tazii. In addition to the guests using the extensive facilities, more Custodians than usual were now staying in the large and separate area of buildings and gardens reserved for them. News rapidly spread of the efficacy of Xaala's massages of all forms.

Guests speaking with the tall girl with the glowing energy field and exceptional tunic, passed on compliments, for she was a mine of information concerning the True Aurigan Teachings and always willing to make an extra effort, especially for youngsters. Xaala was genuinely happy to help and enjoyed the mental gnashing of teeth she heard from staff at all levels.

When Rulcas arrived, Xaala's refusal to wait on Apprentices, as was part of a Servitor's training, was supported by Dryddnaa. If the Chief Readjuster's experiment was to succeed, the MUUD had to meet guests including Junior Custodians. To everyone's horror, Rulcas even accompanied Xaala when she attended distinguished members of the Spiral Assembly.

Dryddnaa and Xaala, the latter saying she was acting on Ceegren's behalf but without having told her teacher, had both promised Rulcas that if they were successful in their aims, he would be sent to live with his father in Tembakatii, the Shakazii homeland. Determined that was going to happen, Rulcas was biding his time as he got to know Xaala and discovered a side of Tazian life so different even from his earlier life amongst mainstream Tazii, that he needed to work out how to manipulate everything to his advantage.

After two days working together, during which Xaala held back on mental barbs and Rulcas bit his tongue, each had gained a grudging respect for the other. On the evening of the second day, a pair of Senior Apprentices several years older than Xaala jostled Rulcas in a corridor and tightbanded insulting remarks at him.

Denigrating Xaala in their minds, they had overlooked her schooling by the Arch Custodian. They discovered their stupidity as Xaala's mental riposte blasted them against the wall, leaving Rulcas standing with his fists raised.

'Hey. No need for that. I can look arter meself.'

'And get yourself dismissed. DeadMind.'

'Watch it. Bitch,' Rulcas spat out as he clenched his fists at the deadly insult.

Xaala froze. Shades! I've messed up bigtime with my Teacher, if I screw up with Dryddnaa... Get a grip! 'You call me "Tich"?' *Ratfink.*

'Might a done.' *MindJerker.*

'Right then, "Lofty",' *ShortArse.*

Rulcas gave her a long, appraising look, letting her know what was in his mind. He grinned as he saw her stiffen and blush, satisfied he'd found a weak spot in the mindjerkng Ice Bitch. Mind you... Back to business. 'You'll do. "Titch".'

'Up yours, "Lofty".' Wondering where on 'Tazia that had come from, Xaala grinned. 'Tripped, didn't they,' she said, as they walked away side by side, leaving the Apprentices groaning with pain.

More than just a truce had been declared. They both knew Rulcas had a lot to lose if they failed to work together and that gave her a hold over him. He wanted to find out what she hoped to gain and how to use that against her.

CHAPTER 53

DISGRUNTLED

AMERICA

Qwelby woke to the pleasant sensation of cool air from the open window bringing the smell of pine trees and the snarling cry of what sounded like a large wildcat. He was tired and aching but at least the woozy feeling he'd been experiencing for several days was a lot less.

As Qwelby looked around it dawned on him that he was not on Romain's island but at his American home, where he'd been brought the previous evening. He settled into his deep breathing routine, the woozy feeling lessened and his mind slowly cleared. He thought back. His last clear memory was telling Mrs Rahkamo he was going to Muurame to ski.

A series of images tumbled through his mind. Erki apologising and himself agreeing to a race "To put it all behind them." Almost at the end of the black run, two men standing by a stretcher. No-one on it. A trap. A brief fight and a sharp pain in his neck. Finding himself on a stretcher in an ambulance with his feet and hands tied and a gag in his mouth. Romain and a big burly man with a thick head of dark hair. Pleading for his Globe and his satchell, Fill Me.

A long journey in chains. But they were not like he'd seen on television – the restraints around his wrists and ankles were nicely padded leather cuffs. A cargo ship. A night crossing. A motel. A succession of airports and airplanes and nights in hotels. There had been no more drugs since the first injection but Romain's GlobeSynch had been present for most of the time the Professor had been talking.

A natural need forced Qwelby out of bed and into the bathroom. As he stepped back into the corridor he remembered Romain saying that there was a swimming pool. He opened the back door, stopped and stared.

Having arrived in the dark the previous night, he had no idea of the scenery except that they had driven high up into the mountains. The beauty of what he was now seeing took his breath away. Rich green meadow sloped down to the Santa Ana river tumbling over its rocky bed. On the other side of the valley, the forest covered mountain led his gaze up to the bright blue sky, streaked with a few clouds. There, above the mountain's summit, wings flapping, a bird was hovering. A bird of prey, watching. Silently, it dived down behind the trees.

Once again he was thirteen years old and with his twin watching three dragons circle around a hill until, screeching, they dived down out of sight. His great aunt, the daughter of Mandara and Lellia, had explained the incident as a practice for an event, leaving the twins to infer a future Shakazii festival. Two tendays ago he had recalled the situation and had been certain that was not the complete truth, but that dragons and riders had been hunting.

'Idiot! She did not lie, a festival is what Tullia and I inferred. The "event" was a real hunt. But Tazii do not hunt for fun. So. For what were they practising?' He had scarcely started to build one of his and his twin's problem solving pyramids when he shuddered as a fractal image appeared in his mind and the truth unfolded as the pathways blossomed with colour.

What he had discerned about the dark reality of hidden life on Vertazia was true. Deceit, outright lies, abuse, depression, fear and even hatred – all were so extensively and forcefully denied and repressed that those energies were being manifested as monsters akin to those that had attacked himself and Tullia the first time they'd attempted to reconnect. That fighting had taken place in higher dimensions. What he had sensed as evil on Vertazia was in fact present on the planet, pushed outside the areas covered by the MentaNet and physically in-formed in the fifth dimension.

He leant against the wall of the log cabin as he understood the real reason for the Tazii denying DragonRiders and their Dragons. Admitting not just their existence but the need for their work would mean acknowledging why – and the shifting colours in the fractal image revealed to him the darkness due to fear that surrounded Readjusters as a result of the often distorted adjustments they forced into people's minds.

He smiled grimly. He had no problem with fighting monstrosities when back on Vertazia. The Tazii creating them would be hurt, but it was not going to be like directly attacking fellow Tazii intending to harm them.

He felt sick as he understood why Winged Unicorns were almost never seen or talked about – the symbiotic relationship between them and Dragons. Well. When he and Tullia were united and back on Vertazia, there was a mountain of distrust to climb and they were going to need their four BestFriends in XOÑOX more than ever before. And Dragons and Unicorns, together with the high-tech weapons he was thinking about.

A quick look at the pool to measure its depth and he dived in, swam a few lengths and was pulling himself out as Romain came out onto the patio.

'Winter pale,' Qwelby said as he pointed at his torso. 'Need sun!'

'Breakfast in half an hour?'

'Kabona. Thank you.'

Qwelby settled himself on a sun lounger, closed his eyes and felt the tanning heat soak into his body as it also added to his low Solar Energy Quotient. Well, Professor, you have done me a favour. I was a fool to think I could travel the world on Hannu's doctored passport. If I'd tried, I'd probably already be lying on a dissecting table. Now I know all the procedures and have a genuine passport to use. Tullia will not know all that about travelling so I must go to her.

That decision brought up a very basic understanding that nothing ever happened by chance, no event was ever random, but always in-formed by the totality of the preceding data. Fine in laboratory experiments but difficult if not impossible to discern in the affairs of humans. Which meant that his and Tullia's departure from Vertazia was a consequence of preceding events, as also was their being apart physically and mentally. He heaved a deep sigh as he felt his body, mind and Self relax. He'd been so caught up in living on Earth and fearful of being captured that he'd drifted away from the very fundamental quantum nature of Life.

Preceding? Several flashbacks to the Space Wars, yet also once very briefly to Auriga over one hundred and fifteen thousand years ago. He shook his head. Too complicated. I'm only fifteen and a quarter, seventeen and a half in Earth years, and not a scientist like Dad or Great-Great Uncle Mandara. Whatever. I'm in the here-and-now. I dare not become trapped on that island, which means I must escape from here as soon as possible. And that means finding where Romain has hidden my passport and my satchel, Fill Me, and all about my surroundings.

Twenty-five minutes later he nodded to himself at Romain's caution as he realised that his clothes must have been removed whilst he slept. He was wearing only a towel around his waist when he entered the main living room of Romain's holiday cabin with its kitchen cum dining area. Furnished in what he was to discover was the rustic style typical of the Angelus Oaks area of the San Bernardino Mountains, the large log cabin was fitted with all modern conveniences including the obligatory heated swimming pool, sauna and cold dip.

'Robe too small to go on my shoulders,' was Qwelby's reply to Romain's raised eyebrows as he looked at the towel.

'Ah. Of course. Yours need cleaning. But I'll bring them.'

Dressed and seated a few minutes later, Qwelby was tucking into a very late breakfast of muffins, jam, cheeses, fruit and fruit juice when there was a knock at the door.

'Please,' Romain said, coffee mug in hand and tilting his head towards the door.

Qwelby opened it and stood staring. Although, during their long journey, Romain had shown him videos of Shoshones with their reddish-brown skin and black hair, he was totally thrown by being face to face with two women who, at a quick glance, could be mistaken for small Tazii.

Wearing a dark green coat over a voluminous dress in shades of brown and red, the short and plump woman was obviously the mother Romain had told him about. The tall young woman of average build in jeans, boots and with long black hair falling over her brown leather jacket, the daughter. His memory flashed up their names: Mother, Haiwee; daughter, Kimama.

Prompted by Romain, Qwelby invited them in and bumbled through a few words in French and Finnish before sorting his compiler into English. The amused look on the girl's face and her soft smile totally threw him. Since his hormones had awakened, girls had become different. Skiing, skating, in the games arcade, he'd just talked about what they were doing, but, now, here... He knew he was blushing as he stepped aside and closed the door.

Romain invited Haiwee to sit at the table, leaving Kimama to put away the shopping. Wherever Qwelby stood, he was in the wrong place. He desperately wanted to say something. Anything except yet another 'Sorry,' for being in the way, until an amused Kimama gently steered him to sit at the table. He felt his face go red as the smell of her perfume invoked happy memories.

When the unpacking had finished, Romain asked Kimama to join them at the table and explained who his guest was.

For centuries Raiatea had been on major shipping routes and Qwelby's parents were two of the many inhabitants who were a mixture of several races. Qwelby had been born on the island and his parents had moved to Europe shortly after his birth. He was Dr Tyler Jefferson's first cousin once removed and they were using the friendly terms of "nephew" and "uncle." Qwelby was an accomplished science student and his family had agreed that he should accept the Professor's offer to continue to pursue his studies whilst working in the laboratory.

The Professor then outlined to Qwelby the arrangements for the next few days. Romain was going to spend two or three days at the University in Los Angeles where he lectured. Because Haiwee's husband needed care, she was going to return home and Kimama would stay to look after Qwelby.

Maska, the nephew of the chief of the tribe, was going to take Qwelby walking the following day. Haiwee was now going to drive into Colton to buy a change of clothing for Qwelby, suitable for the comparatively mild weather in California. Because Qwelby was so tall, Haiwee told her daughter to measure him, much to his embarrassment and Kimama's amusement as she wielded the tape measure.

Whilst travelling, Qwelby had been able to be himself for most of the journey. Only on disembarking at JFK had he had to tell a little part of his new story. Now he was faced with having to live out being a French speaking Raiatean. His compiler had easily learnt the language from CDs, but living out yet another lie... How long could he keep up the pretence, especially with Kimama's dark eyes examining him, the curiosity in her aura easy to read and his two hearts beating fast?

He went to the bathroom and splashed cold water on his face and looked at himself in the mirror as he tried to visualise his twin. Her life seemed so different from his, amongst people who looked so similar to small Tazii. He had to get to her! He was certain they could live with the Bushmen. Forever if need be. It would be very different, but... as long as they were together, anything was possible. 'ANYTHING,' he said softly as he capitalised the word.

Romain left after a late lunch, leaving a discomforted Qwelby struggling with embarrassment as he talked with Kimama. Using his compiler in ThirdMode prevented him from accidently revealing more than he wished. But by not offering answers and leaving him to use the limited English he had learnt personally, he was too often stumbling over his words and blushing furiously.

He was relieved when there was a knock at the door and Kimama admitted Maska. Looking to be in his late twenties, tall, with long black hair falling over his shoulders and with the same red colouration to his suntan, he also looked almost Tazian. When Maska suggested a walk to explore the immediate area around the cabin, Kimama decided to join them.

Maska talked about the area and its inhabitants. Qwelby let his thoughts drift and more than once was pulled back to the present by a sharp tingle as Kimama's guiding hand steered him back onto the path. A smiled thank you and he felt his face heating up under her smile.

Later and shortly after a delicious dinner cooked by Kimama, the time differences caught up with Qwelby. He sagged in his chair, apologised and was in bed and fast asleep within a few minutes, too tired to try and contact his twin.

CHAPTER 54

TO THE FARM

VERTAZIA

From her meetings with Rulcas and Xaala, both individually and together, Dryddnaa was happy with Rulcas' changing aura and thoughts showing that he had come to look forward to his times with her. She was relieved that in spite of the tension between the youngsters, in public they were working well together. She'd not yet dealt with the strong criticism of Xaala's action in the incident in the corridor. Now she'd been given a serious complaint to deal with.

Expecting to be by himself, Rulcas was startled to see Xaala when he entered Dryddnaa's room. He went on the defensive and refused to speak.

'All right,' Dryddnaa said. 'I'll tell you what I've been told. Then you talk. Agreed?'

Rulcas nodded, preferring that to the alternative of mental persuasion.

'You hit a Senior Apprentice in the stomach, then several times around the head and body. You were about to jump on him when others pulled you back.'

'Thas a lie!'

'You're saying you didn't hit him?'

'No! Course I did. 'e were so tall I couldna reach 'im. I ad ter belt 'im in the guts ter bring 'im darn to my level. Then I giv 'im what 'e deserved. I weren't going to jump on 'im when 'e were darn... didn' need ter, did I!' He deliberately laid it on thickly.

'Why did you hit him?'

He looked uncomfortable. He'd not told Xaala the whole truth. 'Swhat he said about 'Er.' The two women heard the capitalisation.

'What?'

Rulcas shook his head.

Dryddnaa tilted her head to one side and raised an eyebrow.

Rulcas grimaced. He knew that look from the Junior Readjusters who had been sent to "help" him adjust. Totally unfair mental interference followed.

Rulcas glanced at Xaala and "heard" *Please.* He was shaken. She didn't want him to be forced. He looked back at Dryddnaa who was sitting back in her chair and no longer giving him that look. Shades-be-cursed, they're both being nice to me!

'That shitty little git used a word in that fancy tonal language I can't talk.'

'Aurigan.'

'Yeah. Wot 'e said was dead disgustin. I know what youse lot thinks of us. But yer 'ouldn't catch none of us doin nuffin like that.' He looked at Xaala and shook his head, telling her not to mindsearch him. *Why I do protect her when it's about time she lived in the real world?*

'I'll deal with that apprentice,' Dryddnaa said in a firm voice. 'And we will turn this to our advantage,' she added with a smile, carefully shielding a smug feeling that her plans were working to perfection. 'When that Apprentice's punishment is announced: Rulcas, you listen to the words people are saying, Xaala, their thoughts. We'll discover who our friends are and who are not.'

People like me, Rulcas thought to himself, we can't do their mindjerking stuff but we do read faces and body language and them better than energy fields. These two can mind control me, but they're not. Especially "She," as he thought of the Chief Readjuster, who was the only adult in his life who had ever treated him nicely, apart from his Da – and he'd left home. It's a Baryon game. I'm the downquark between two upquarks. By The Shades, I'll make sure when this is all over I'll be a blazing upquark! His attention came back to the room and the end of what Dryddnaa had been saying.

'… retributive action. Including you, Xaala, for the excessive force you used in the corridor. Two day's hard work on the farm.'

Rulcas managed not to laugh that that was She's idea of punishment. Out in the open air, something real to do and time away from the arselicking Servitors and the Custodians looking at him like a piece of shit.

When the youngsters had left, Dryddnaa toasted her scheming with a glass of AppleWine. She sighed deeply. If all went to plan, the twins would come back, Ceegren would be forced to act and she would replace him and then Rulcas' usefulness would be over. More than that. The amount of interference within his mind would mean he'd be seriously damaged and so compromised that he'd not be welcome amongst Kumelanii or Shakazii. The kindest course was inevitable – incarnation rescheduling.

As to MUUDs in general, she mused. They've been badly stereotyped. In my young days I was just as blind, accepting perceived dogma. When I have the power I will not be bringing the liberal-minded Shakazii "into the fold", as Ceegren wants, but getting the rigidly traditionalist Kumelanii "out" into the mainstream of Tazian life.

"Both?" Rulcas' question slipped out from her memory. She now knew that Xaala had been to see Rulcas before her own first visit. At the time she'd thought his question a little odd, but had accepted what she now saw as a slip smartly covered up. She replayed the fight on Earth, carefully examining the colours in all the auras. After a long time she let out a sigh and leant back in her chair as she flicked her fingers for the HouseCarl to refill her glass.

Plain as the rings around Companion! She named the planet the Azurii called Saturn. Before she was Awakened, Xaala wanted to be a boy. She'd intended to go to the girl twin, hoping to take her out of the picture. I thrust her against the boy and of course her emotions responded. Tall, handsome, well-built with a powerful Attribute. A hero in the making. What a role model! Now she's Awakened, he's double the attraction.

So the cunning bitchling wants him to return without his twin. Thus she can satisfy Ceegren who fears the twins together. Me? Well, doubtless she'd claim she did her best, but.... Dryddnaa shook her head. Devoted to and doubtless programmed by Ceegren, there's no way that feisty young woman can remain after I've taken charge. In fact, she needs to be put out of the situation sooner rather than later.

Dryddnaa swirled the pale green liquid around the glass and drank, savouring the exquisite taste of her favourite vintage as she allowed herself to experience a moment's sadness. At least Rulcas' Soul will understand that it achieved more with a short incarnation than most Souls do over a long one. As to Xaala. Mentally she shrugged. A comment to the Arch Custodian that I deeply regret having to make and she suffers the price for her duplicity and overreaching herself. Fire ran though Dryddnaa's veins as the Uddîsû ran her tongue around her lips.

CHAPTER 55

ESCAPE

AMERICA

By the time Qwelby awoke the following morning, Romain had
already left for the University. Shortly after finishing what Kimama
said the Professor termed a "Full English" breakfast, Maska arrived
on his motorcycle, bringing the clothes that Haiwee had purchased.
Whilst Qwelby dressed, Kimama loaded a backpack for him with
a groundsheet, waterproof, food and drink.

Yesterday, Qwelby had answered questions about himself.
Today was his turn, asking about the area and the First People,
as Maska said the Native Americans described themselves. By the
time they returned from their walk in the mountains, Qwelby's
trainers and socks were soaked from the afternoon's downpour.
From their conversation about how the First People had been
treated by white people, he was certain that the local tribes would
help him to evade capture by a white man. Best of all there was
what Maska called a "Sovereign Area" which was not part of the
USA. Qwelby took that to mean a different country where white
people could not follow him.

Whilst the three of them were eating dinner, Romain
telephoned and said he was going to stay overnight at the University
and be back early the next morning. Maska left soon after dinner

and Qwelby was happy to dry the dishes as Kimama washed them, delaying the awkward moment when they would finally sit down together.

He was becoming increasingly uncomfortable about her interest in him, his feelings for her and his deceit. "Being economical with the truth" as Hannu described it, was hurting him. He was lying about himself and pretending to be happy with going to work with the Professor, when he was planning to escape.

His discomfiture was compounded by the times he almost forgot that she was not Tazian, when he had to fight hard against the urge to slip into her mind and thoughtwrap her into a visit to his home. Having to turn attention away from himself, he asked questions and discovered the big cat he'd heard on his first morning was called a Cougar, or Mountain Lion, Doyadukubichi' in Shoshone.

Kimama's name translated as Butterfly. When she explained what a butterfly was, Qwelby said: 'We name "Gaashêzavezz" SunshineBringer. I like better sound of Butterfly. Beautiful like you.'

Entranced by his twinkling eyes and embarrassed by the warmth in his voice, Kimama muttered an embarrassed, 'Thank you,' and suggested it was time for bed and locked up. Qwelby was both disappointed and relieved as his impending betrayal of her trust was weighing heavily on him.

He was unable to get through to his twin's busy mind, as always incorrectly ascribing the difficulty to the slow vibrations of the third dimension. Setting his internal alarm for just after midnight, he settled down to sleep,

Waking, Qwelby carefully mentasearched Kimama. As expected, she was fast asleep. Gently, he added a reinforcement before getting out of bed and dressing. Checking the doors, he found they were locked and there was no sign of the keys or the mobile phone. The waterproof and his trainers and socks were now dry.

He put them in the backpack together with the ground sheet, his newly washed shirt, socks and boxers, then added food and drink, the Globe and his satchel Fill Me.

There was a desk with a computer in the living room. The top drawer was locked. The next one down revealed a treasure of small items, including what he later discovered were called paperclips. Smiling, he took one and bent it into a new shape. Kneeling, he leant his forehead against the drawer front and slid the clip into the small lock. Applying gently pressure he hummed, the clip glowed and - click! The lock turned, he opened the drawer and found his passport. He closed the drawer, deliberately leaving it unlocked.

Taking a deep breath, he slipped back into Kimama's mind and once again reinforced her sleep. Easing the door open, he crept to her bedside where he removed her phone and a key. Back in the living room he was about to remove the battery from her mobile when he froze.

'Labirden Xzarze!' he muttered under his breath. 'Where have I been?! Hannu and...' A series of images parade before him. Hannu and Anita washing and bandaging him the night they'd captured the thieves along with what had become his group of friends. Oona cuddling up to him on the sofa. Oona with his first real kiss. Jenni warding him through his second Awakening. Viivi! Then Jenni and Oona. He sat down. How could he have... not forgotten, but let all them drift from his mind? Each one so important. Years of growing up condensed into a few weeks. "Alien" Azurii, each of them as human as any Tazian!

Qwelby switched on the mobile, waited for it to power up, asked politely to have access and left a video message on Hannu's mobile. He'd been kidnapped, was escaping and please remember his Turkish story. He sent similar video messages to Oona, Jenni and Viivi, finishing each with 'I love you.'

His hearts thudding, he sat down to collect himself, asked the phone to delete all record of the message so as to protect Kimama, then switched off and hid the battery behind a cushion on the armchair where Kimama had been sitting, half hoping she would find it in the morning. He left the phone on the table. A few minutes later he locked the back door and slipped the key though the small bathroom window.

The woods smelt fresh from the earlier rain. The sky was clear with the first fine crescent of a new moon. As he adjusted his vision, the stars provided enough light for him to make out the path he'd already walked. The air was chilly, he was well wrapped and a fast pace kept him warm without needing to light his inner fire.

It had not been difficult the previous evening for Qwelby to mentasuade Maska into producing a map and showing Qwelby where they'd walked and where his tribe and other neighbouring tribes lived. Qwelby kept to his plan and walked steadily for three hours until the path degraded and it was too dangerous to go on in the dark. Using groundsheet and waterproof as a mattress, he settled down for a light supper. Whatever nerves he had about sleeping in the open, his body was so tired after the fast pace he had set that he fell into a deep sleep.

CHAPTER 56

PURPLE FRUIT

VERTAZIA

Although below average height, Rulcas was solidly built and used to hard physical work. With of all the years Xaala had spent trying to develop a boy's muscular body and working on Ceegren's farm, she was equally strong. In the fresh air and the warm sunshine of the more southerly latitude, working outdoors had been a pleasure. With no guests to be served and by themselves with only the occasional scrutiny from a distance, they had talked about their very different lives, slowly opening up to each other.

It had started by Rulcas questioning Xaala about her life and training as a way of seeking to understand the attitudes around IndluKoba. Somewhat reticent, Xaala had talked about a girlfriend's strict Traditionalist family and the obsession the parents had about her brother developing the Uddîsû genes to the maximum. Rulcas had made disparaging comments about the whole situation and described the brother as the worst sort of blinkered nerd and added a few other words that had expanded Xaala's vocabulary.

Rulcas had told her about the claustrophobic feel of living in an area of Extreme Traditionalists who forever preached the True Teachings yet condoned the widespread abuse. That was

283

never discussed with the Junior, and in his opinion unskilled, Readjusters who pretended to want to help youngsters adjust to Tazian values. At first disbelieving, searching his mind, a shocked Xaala finally accepted he was truthspeaking on both counts.

Their discoveries were such a revelation that they surprised the farm manager by working much later than required and had completed his proposed two day schedule in one day. For the youngsters it had been a mixture of each trying to outdo the other and wanting to continue talking in a part of the estate clear from mental surveillance. As strong as she was, Xaala would never have been able to cope with the gossip and innuendo if they spent time together in a shielded room. They returned from their first day, equals at work, dirty, exhausted, wiser and wanting to discover more.

Late that evening, clean and fed and with a big grin on his face, Rulcas settled into the Supervisor's room he'd been given - there was no way the Servitors had been prepared to accept him in one of their dormitories. Dryddnaa had summoned him and discussed the day. He'd said that he was building a good relationship with Xaala and she was beginning to trust him.

Letting go the overstatement of a "good relationship," Dryddnaa was complimentary about what he was doing. She'd gone on to say that his acumen had proved that she was right that the way youngsters like him had been treated for far too many years was wrong. She was looking forward to continuing to work positively with him. He trusted his ability to read people's faces and body language more than minds and aura and, in spite of a lifetime's accumulation of cynicism, believed her.

He didn't say he was doing his best to open Xaala's eyes to the dark world of suppression and ignorance and "turn her".

Xaala was in a sombre frame of mind. The friend's brother she'd described had been her own. As she'd talked about him she'd seen herself in a different light. Helped by Rulcas' disparaging comments about him she'd started to question aspects of herself and, a treachery that left her shaking and the colourscopes on the wall swirling in disorganised patterns, some of the teachings of her beloved Ceegren.

Again competing, Rulcas and Xaala worked hard during their second day of farm punishment. Talking more deeply than the previous day, their respect for each other increased. Xaala learnt to appreciate Rulcas' instinctual intelligence, and Rulcas her readiness to look outside herself.

Once again they worked longer than required. As the sun was setting they wandered along the edge of the orchard, Rulcas steering them to a stand of tall and slender PurpleFruit Trees. Xaala loved the fruits that her grandmother baked into her favourite cakes.

Rulcas issued a challenge. Climbing trees was "inappropriate behaviour" but Xaala wasn't going to be outdone by a MUUD! She watched as he wrapped arms and legs around the oddly gnarled trunk and shimmied up. She followed suit on a neighbouring tree, ruefully acknowledging that her developing girl's Form was not suited to that method.

As she pulled herself up onto the lowest branch, she heard the farm manager ordering them to get down. As Rulcas carried on climbing, Xaala "heard" his *Girls!* and said, 'Fuck you,' to her sickeningly goody, goody, late brother and continued climbing.

Reaching the highest levels they worked their ways along the dangerously dipping branches until they reached the big juicy bunches at the ends. Xaala was having more fun than she could remember. Danger? Not really. Although she'd never climbed a tree before, she was supremely confident in her ability to apply her skills to any situation.

The sun sank and Xaala heard a quickly repressed cry from Rulcas as a wakening NightSnipper dived at him. Carefully protecting her big bunch of fruit, she dropped through the branches whilst Rulcas waved his arms as more birds flapped around him.

Steadying herself amidst the shelter of the thick leaves, she sent forth a mentaformed image of a bright red Aigiiele, scattering the birds attacking Rulcas and allowing him to scramble down into the protection of the leaves.

He might have beaten her in climbing, but Xaala was down first, effortlessly dropping the long way from the lowest branch as he slid down the trunk. She threw her head back to drink in the evening's rainstorm, happily adding getting soaked to her list of enjoyable misdemeanours.

Combining their differing skills, the two miscreants dodged the angry manager with his bright lights and sensors, but not without getting covered in mud from a dive to the ground. Squelching through muddy puddles they munched the berries on their way back. Theoretically aware of the danger of eating them raw, Xaala was not going to be outdone by a mere boy – and one half her size.

As with all Tazii, she totally subscribed to Tazian non-discrimination on any grounds, but as with all pre-adults, not when it came to boys and girls. If she couldn't be a boy, then she'd be better than any of them, besides which, she did inhabit a girl's Form.

As they neared the Custodians' buildings, they were a long way from a staff entrance where it was possible to shower and change into clean tunics kept for situations such as they were in. Happily enjoying her first acts of rebellion, Xaala steered them over a colour-sparkling bridge that extravagantly arced over a bubbling stream into one of the Custodians' private areas, and straight towards what looked like a solid wall.

She thoughtsent and the throughway irised open onto the corridor leading directly to their rooms in the Supervisors' quarters. With her arm around Rulcas' shoulders and his around her waist, they stepped right into the path of the Arch Custodian and two guests.

All three were wearing the long colourful robes of Venerables. As it had been a business meeting, the robes had been put on over their normal clothes and thus were szeamed closed. Ceegren was wearing sea green with the bands of his Guilds around the hem of the robe and the long ends of his sleeves. Purple for Custodians, dark blue for Readjusters, yellow for Teachers and an affectation, a narrow lilac band for Arkaanas. Only one rank signature was ever displayed. For Ceegren that meant either side of the purple band flowed two thin streams of rainbow-coloured kuznii.

Next to him, the woman's robe was cobalt blue with the yellow of a Teacher. Her bands were edged with two thin flowing streams of silver photons indicating her to be a Senior. At her side was a Farmer in a russet robe with bands of dark brown, also edged with two thin flowing streams of silver photons.

Behind them, the doors of the room they had left had closed, the rich living wood set in the peaceful pastel colourscopes on the walls adding to an already impressive scene.

Xaala and Rulcas became horribly aware of how they looked. Dirty, wet, dishevelled and dripping mud onto the soft green moss of the floor.

Peering around the corner from the corridor was Khalen, one of the Junior Servitors who Xaala had saved from bullying. He had seen the two of them approaching the building and run to warn them to go to the staff entrance. Later he was to tell Xaala that he had felt as though he was in a HoloWrapper Adventure – waiting for an explosion to come. He was right.

Ceegren was not a happy man. Knowledge of the twins' reconnection had caused a variety of doubts and worries to flow through the MentaNet. Trying to prevent the twins from achieving mental reunification and abandoning them on Earth went against the Tazian way of life. Discoverers ought to be working on a way to get them back home. Healers ought to be devising an inoculation against the Violence Virus. Readjusters or Harmonisers should be preparing a place of quarantine.

Even many Traditionalists, who strongly feared any connection with Earth and its inhabitants, shared the underlying view that decisions had been made in haste and needed to be rethought in a calm atmosphere.

Trying to defuse the situation, Ceegren had been having regular meetings with senior members of the various Guilds who also were members of the Spiral Assembly. He had just finished a successful discussion with two more.

In addition to the mud, Xaala's crop-top and hotpants were covered with purple splodges. Rulcas' shorts and t-shirt were brown with slime from his slide down the wet tree trunk.

Expressions of disgust and dismay sprang from the lips of all three Venerables, most forcibly from Ceegren who was not only shocked but deeply affronted by his acolyte – and the stink. He said so forcibly.

'Shocked 'cos I been working hard with a MUUD? Doin' a proper job. Disc... disc.' Xaala hiccupped. 'Findin' out what life's about for the likes of 'im.'

'Enough! Go to your rooms,' Ceegren swept his arm in a gesture of dismissal, darkening the colourscopes on the walls.

'Why d'you want me to work with 'im if you don't want me to learn. Eh?' Xaala burped and a piece of mud dropped from her hand as she belatedly covered her mouth. 'Manners, trianners, proton... what?' As she turned to Rulcas for how to finish the slang expression, four Senior Apprentices arrived, thoughtsummoned by Ceegren.

''Sall right. I'm goin.' Xaala pouted and wiped the back of her hand across her chin where fruit juice was trickling down.

'Isolation,' Ceegren growled, ordering her to be locked in a totally shielded room, cutting her off from all mental contact.

Bet you'd like to know that little shit wants the twins to come back. Six years with Ceegren and Xaala was able to securely tightband her thoughts to him without any physical contact. She stumbled and the corridor darkened even more as she was hit by her Teacher's mental growl. The two girl Apprentices accompanying her smiled at each other. Smiles that were not nice as they enjoyed the sight of the "MUUD-loving IceBitch" in trouble.

Ceegren flicked his fingers at Rulcas as he thoughtsent commands to the two tall Apprentices standing by the youth. Sensibly, but with regret, Rulcas did not speak and walked to his room.

As he stepped, fully clothed, into the neutron shower, he was smiling. The PurpleFruits were large and soft. In the centre was a small chewy kernel that provided an enticing and fast acting chemical. He'd not let her see that he'd been palming most of his kernels. He was only a little tipsy. She had eaten all hers and was drunk.

Clean, he stopped the neutron shower, stripped and threw his clothes into the bedroom. Turning on the water, he luxuriated, not understanding why water for showers and baths was so restricted where he lived. Thinking of Xaala locked in a basement room and deprived of her much vaunted mental contact, for a brief moment he felt sorry for her. Her friend's brother? Nah. She was talking about her brother – and herself. Sad bitch. Needs to wake up. Yet...

CHAPTER 57

FREEDOM

VERTAZIA

Rulcas had finished eating by the time that Dryddnaa summoned him.

'What The Shades were you doing?!' Dryddnaa roared at him as he entered her room. The mental blast knocked him back toward the throughway, the iris remorphing into a concave SoftPad as he slammed into it. Wearing a shimmering RelaxRobe that made him think of a sunkissed waterfall, Dryddnaa beckoned him forward and gestured for him to sit on the floor, winked, slowly and deliberately, then questioned him.

He admitted that climbing the trees and eating the fruit had been his idea. The two days had been a competition. He was then verbally and mentally roasted. 'Destroying all we are trying to achieve. Yes, we, not just for you but for all youngsters like you.' She went on speaking as he cringed. 'For the damage you've done to that sweet, young acolyte, so important not just to the Arch Custodian but all of us.' Eventually, she eased up and winked again. Rulcas pushed up to be on his hands and knees, mentally aching like never before.

Slowly he took in the room. Between the guest suites he attended and coming here several times, he'd become accustomed to what he thought of as a Sci-Fi effect. Something he'd only ever seen in the TriDs of the ancient days on Auriga. But tonight was something special. She was mad at him, but the walls had become thick, floor length curtains in a variety of soft shades evoking a warm spring day. Rather than sky, the ceiling was a deep sunlit pool set in a wood. Right. Her words. PlayActing for... Memories. Mine if I'm searched. Hers for when she's talking to people.

Spring this far south meant the days were almost hot but the evenings were chilly. To one side of the room a large, open fire was burning with green and blue tinged flames. Dryddnaa gestured, the flames sprang up and a figure stepped out of them. A tall woman with copper-hued skin and overlarge, steely green orbs set in exceptionally slanted yellow ovals. A high collared dress of swirling reds and oranges left her arms bare and emphasised her well developed bust. Golden serpents coiled around each of her upper arms.

As she walked towards him, the panels of the skirt swirled to reveal the long and muscular legs of a dancer. The neckline was split almost to her waist and in the narrow gap he saw a dagger with a long thin blade hanging from her necklace. He did not think her beautiful. In fact, the steely blue-grey shadings in her energy field were frightening. The ends of two long plaited ropes of golden tinted hair could be seen curling at her hips, gently moving as if alive.

He knew Dryddnaa carried the genes of "Reconciler" but did not know whether he was seeing a LivingStatue or her Attribute. Either way he recognised DeathDealer. He was being tested. He took a deep breath.

'Her likes the twins.'

DeathDealer raised an eyebrow.

'A lot. S'good for us.'

DeathDealer stroked her stiletto.

'Like's one best.' He swallowed. 'I'll find out.'

DeathDealer's smile did not reach her eyes.

Betray your new friend? Dryddnaa checked on what Xaala had said was his increasing ability.

Deal's a deal.

Dryddnaa's smile was genuine. She gestured, the air shimmered, Léshmîrâ stepped back into the flames and disappeared. A cold draft swept through Rulcas' mind as what had happened since the flames sprang up was buried deep in the area of his mind that she controlled. The flames settled back down.

'Be careful,' Dryddnaa said as the throughway irised open.

Aware that her diatribe had all been PlayActing and she trusted him, Rulcas nodded, winked and gave her a cheeky grin.

Early the next morning, hiding on the edge of the woods by IndluKoba, Rulcas was on tenterhooks. During his time on the farm with Xaala, she had been honest about what she had done when they had struck their agreement. As she had locked their secret deep in his mind she had also set a limited MindWipe. If anyone succeeded in breaching the shielded area, everything in it would be erased from his memory. Collateral damage was a possibility.

He knew Dryddnaa had also locked their secret in his mind and assumed she had also set a MindWipe. Both women had complete deniability – as long as their much stronger Privacy Shields were never breached.

During their second afternoon on the farm he'd agreed with Xaala to leave IndluKoba and be taken to meet the twins' friends. It had been a massive leap of faith to allow her to use his mind to set that up.

Midnight was a key moment in the planet's daily energy cycle. A by then sober Xaala had strained every mental synapse, slipped from her prison and carefully made her way to Rulcas' room. There, once again she had used his now slumbering mind for cover as she opened a channel and received final details of the arrangements. Sighing with relief, she had awoken her "mate" and told him he was to be picked up by a twistor shortly after dawn.

He had surprised Xaala by displaying his ability with the room controls. They showed that he had left the previous evening as soon as he'd returned from his meeting with Dryddnaa. There was no record of her entrance, nor would there be of her exit. It had been a big decision for the ever wary gang leader to trust a "Mind Jerking Ice Bitch" and he had wanted to show Xaala that he had a few tricks up his sleeve.

Inwardly in turmoil, yet surprised at how much she was stimulated by the seeds of ice and fire growing within by playing such a dangerous game, Xaala had slipped back into isolation.

Rulcas knew how mentally superior to him were Xaala and Dryddnaa. If they were playing him for a fool, he was lost. But why would they? If each was trying to use him against the other? Well. That was a game he would play and enjoy, especially Xaala's gratitude if he ensured she won.

He was still uncertain about which of them wanted exactly what as far as the twins were concerned. He was certain that Dryddnaa genuinely wanted them both back on Vertazia, but not so sure if she really wanted them healed of the Violence Virus.

As for Xaala? The kid was definitely confused. If he knew anything about girls, and he reckoned he did, she'd been badly thrown by her Awakening. And that was being compounded by their odd... Yeah... "Friendship" was the right word. She was torn every which way and that made her easy to manipulate.

Rulcas' mind pinged and he thoughtsent a shout of relief. The twistor to take him to the twins' home of Siyataka was nearing.

CHAPTER 58

MISTAKES

AMERICA

Waking with the dawn, Qwelby splashed a little water on his face, ate and drank sparingly and set off. From all that Maska had said about the tracking skills of what he called the "Old Uns," Qwelby was banking on his early start getting him to the nearest Kumayaay settlement. He was hoping that whoever followed him would have split motives: track him, but not too fast, allowing him to reach the tribal homelands of the Kumeyaay who would shield him against Native Americans who were acting for Romain, a white man.

He would ask for shelter as soon as he arrived. If he was wrong, then he would make for the coast using all his Tazian skills to avoid capture. He had to get to his twin and that had to be done now, before he was trapped on what looked to be a tiny island.

Late morning and he was hearing bird calls that, somehow, were different. It slowly dawned on him that the cries were being made by humans, behind him and at times to his left, at other times to his right. From his fast pace on a mild day he had already stripped down to a t-shirt and his new walking shorts. He pressed on as fast as possible, the calls now tracking him left and right and with a different cadence.

He pushed through bushes into a clearing. And stopped. Three

Shoshone were standing on the opposite side. A slim man with two big built youths either side. The man lifted his head and sent out a warbling sound, answered from close behind by a series of yips. A few minutes later three more youths entered the clearing, forming a circle around Qwelby.

The discussion was brief. The Shoshone were to take him back to Romain. Qwelby was not going to do that. Two youths grabbed his arms and a fight erupted. Reeling back from a blow that nearly ruined his manhood, Qwelby had a moment to undo the straps and let his backpack drop to the ground. Accepting that the fighting was going to be dirty, he leapt into the fray, furious, as much at himself for having misjudged the distance and more so for how he'd misjudged the Shoshone.

He twirled and twisted, punched and kicked, hurled a youth to the ground over his shoulder and tipped another backwards by his swinging foot. He was a Warrior and was fighting like one. He felled a third youth as the others got to their feet. The slender man stood watching with his arms folded. A kick in the back almost sent Qwelby sprawling. He saved himself by seizing a youth by his arm and swinging him around to crash into another attacker, wrenching the arm as he did so and hearing the scrunch of dislocation and a cry of pain.

'One down, four to go,' he muttered to himself.

Someone landed on his back. Qwelby spun around and crashed backwards into a tree. The grip around his neck slackened and he threw the youth over his shoulder into another tree, hearing a satisfying crack of skull on wood. A foot swinging to his face was perfect. He ducked, grabbed, twisted and stepped over the leg as the youth crashed to the ground – and wrenched, hearing a scream and the sound of bones breaking.

'Two left,' he muttered.

The sight of the large knives they produced was the last straw. He raised his Attribute. Swore as he realised the dragon was not working in the third dimension, then felt the energy surge through his body. He roared a challenge, saw the youths take a pace back – and stopped as the image of punching Erki in the face flashed before his eyes and he heard the words that voice had spoken in his mind.

Fighting as his Warrior Self he'd badly injured two if not three youths. His whole body quivered as he fought for control. He'd been intending to terminate their LifeLines! Death, as the Azurii termed it.

He put out his hands palms facing the two youths and looked at the man as he said. 'No fight. Go back.' His voice was harsh and with no hint of his usual musicality.

There was a standoff as Qwelby refused to turn his back on the youths and demanded they put their knives away.

Dropping his shorts as ordered by the man to prevent him running or kicking, he felt his hands being pulled behind his back and his wrists tied together.

Another standoff occurred as Qwelby said he was a proficient healer and offered, then urged to be allowed to set the dislocated shoulder and help the youth with the broken leg. As the slim man looked directly into his eyes, Qwelby saw he was an "Old Un."

'I Haiah. You call Raven,' the man said as he gestured with his hand above his eyes as if searching from a great height.

'Qwelby. Means...' How to reduce the Aurigan influences in his proper name to one, inaccurate, word? 'Key,' he said. After Qwelby answered his questions, the man gave his orders. Qwelby stepped out of his shorts and his belt used to bind his feet. His hands were untied and the youth with the dislocated shoulder brought to him. Qwelby told Haiah how the youth needed to be held.

After carefully exploring the damage, with a steady pull and a scream, Qwelby reset the shoulder, then watched as the six fingers of his two hands slid through the joint. 'Be sore for several days. Support with sling. Drink water from clean springs,' Qwelby said as he sat back on his haunches.

The youth grudgingly acknowledged that his shoulder was sore, that he could move it and it certainly felt better than before. Haiah knew what had to be done for the other youth and straightened the leg as for a splint. When Qwelby had been brought over, he slipped his vision inside the leg and started humming energy as once again two hands with six fingers mended broken blood vessels and...

'Body not accept healing,' Qwelby said in surprise as he sat back. 'No bleeding now. Bones in correct positions but very... loose. Hospital urgent. Bandages and splints.' He made an apologetic gesture to Haiah, who said that he and two youths would carry him to the nearest settlement where there was a first aid station. The other two were to take Qwelby back.

Whilst Haiah watched, a length of rope was produced and used to tie Qwelby's hands in front, leaving a long lead. A slight tilt of the head, a raised eyebrow and an almost unnoticeable shrug was Haiah's response to Qwelby's protests at the bondage. A piece was cut from the lead and Qwelby's ankles were tied again, this time allowing him to walk. His belt and shorts were stuffed into his backpack

After a quick sip of water, Haiah and his group set off whilst Qwelby's captors sat down to eat and drink. That finished, they announced they were going to teach him a lesson he would never forget and set about kicking him all over. Slipping into their minds he was repulsed by their intense anger. Unable to defend himself physically or mentally, Qwelby tried to ride with the blows. A boot swung towards his face. He grabbed it with his bound hands and toppled the youth, only to receive a reinvigorated kicking as he curled up into a ball and tried to build his energy shield.

When they eventually set off, having strapped his backpack onto him, the youths took great delight in telling Qwelby how stupid he'd been to think he might reach the Kumeyaay settlement before he was found. They knew from the walk he'd been on with Maska where he had to be heading and they knew the woods better than any ignorant "Slit Eyes." They laughed at his thought that the Kumeyaay would take him in as "Another Darkie." They were paler than a white man with a suntan!

As they travelled, his captors became subdued and even stopped the occasional tugs on the rope that had been making him stumble and fall. Qwelby knew something was wrong but was unable to read their minds. The kicking had been vicious and his energies were fully committed to healing the serious injuries.

When his little remaining food and water was gone, the youths did not share any of theirs. He went hungry and drank from the occasional stream.

They had indeed taught him a lesson he would not forget. He had to learn to fight well in the third dimension. He would study Tai Chi and, at least for the time being, would accept what appeared to be "Warrior memories" of Aurigan unarmed combat.

Qwelby had travelled a long way before being caught and no matter how often his captors tugged his lead, he was in no state to walk fast. So it was that for a second night they settled down to sleep in the woods. Qwelby had never felt so miserable in his whole life. Exhausted and in continual pain, his thoughts did not have the power to reach Tullia. Yet all he thought of was his twin and being together. He had comforted her that night she'd been in prison and he needed comfort now. He, a proud warrior needing solace! Idiot. Pathetic, useless idiot! 'I do need you,' he whispered in his despair.

CHAPTER 59

KIMAMA

AMERICA

The sun was dropping close to the tops of the trees by the time that Qwelby, stumbling, aching and with wrists and ankles burning was jerked through the trees to find himself at the edge of the clearing around Romain's cabin. As his captors stopped, Qwelby dropped to his knees and bent over as he rested his hands on the ground.

He lifted his head at the sound of footsteps and voices. Coming out of the cabin were Romain and a tall old Shoshone of proud bearing. Qwelby was to discover he was the tribe's chief, Mumbichi, Grey Owl. They were followed by Maska, Haiwee and to Qwelby's embarrassment, Kimama.

Romain had been seething ever since discovering Qwelby's escape. Now he was furious at the state he was in. His request had been for Qwelby to be brought back unharmed or, if reluctant, for him to be summoned to talk to the young man.

Calming Romain and all the exclamations being made by the others, Mumbichi requested explanations. 'Speak English so all understand,' he ordered as the youths started in their own language.

They were eager to explain how they had tracked their target. 'Haiah,' Grey Owl added disparagingly. They glossed over Qwelby's "surrender" and went on to describe in conflicting and confusing detail a much longer fight, dwelling on the injuries Qwelby had caused. All the time Grey Owl was aware of the occasions when Qwelby shook his head, but also nodded at the injuries he'd caused. The youth with the dislocated shoulder had to confess to the healing, then blamed Qwelby for failing to heal his friend with the broken leg.

'No,' Haiah said to everyone's surprise as he stepped from the trees. He nodded to the chief as he indicated with his hand that he'd been listening from inside the wood. Receiving permission to his next gesture, Haiah walked over to Qwelby, untied the rope around his wrists, removed the back pack and stripped him to the waist. Gasps and exclamations greeted the sight of the whole of Qwelby's torso as well as his legs covered with mottled bruises.

The chief's thundering voice reduced the youths to their knees and their confession as to the beating they'd given him and, prompted by Haiah, that Qwelby had offered to fight no more and return. It took all the chief's power to still the uproar.

Romain had told Kimama that Qwelby's mind had been damaged from a severe accident and he was being taken back to Raiatea to recover. She had known him for two days, a lovely, innocent, gentle young man. Now she learnt that he was a fighter – with conscience and honour. He stank of sweat, urine and faeces and she saw him broken and destroyed. As much as she felt pity for him, anger welled up in her at how he had been so brutally treated. In response to her gesture, Grey Owl nodded and she knelt and untied the rope around Qwelby's legs.

'Sorry,' Qwelby said as he leant on her for support as she took him into the cabin and on into the bathroom. He slumped to the floor of the shower. Kimama found a stool, helped him to stand and gave him a: "What am I going to do with you" look, he recognised. Then, just like Tullia when she cared for him when he'd been stupid, which brought tears to his eyes, she pulled down

300

his boxers, sat him on the stool, stepped back and took a long look at him. He made what he hoped was an apologetic gesture and saw her shake her head. He heard Tullia saying, "LAIM boy!"

Since his accident, Kimama had often helped her mother with her father. This... forlorn little boy needed her help. She knew he liked her but he had kept a respectful distance while they'd been together, locked her in safely and...

'You guessed I'd look there for the battery?'

He shrugged and avoided her gaze. 'Not want you not to have mobile.'

'Right.' Mind made up, she stripped down to her undies and started to wash him. As he was pulled forwards and slumped over, then pushed back against the shower wall, there was the faintest smile on his face and occasional soft murmurs. He saw her kneel down and look into his eyes as she continued washing.

'You have a sister.'

He nodded before his brain engaged.

'An older sister,' she said.

He stared at her as thoughts tumbled through his mind. He'd wanted to keep knowledge of Tullia away from Romain. He'd never thought of a simple, well not really even a lie. Tullia was older than him and annoyingly acted like a big sister. He smiled and nodded.

Kimama asked and Qwelby answered and soon his voice took on its usual rich, musical baritone as Kimama was taken for a brief meeting with Tullia in the fields and hills of his farm home.

'You love her a lot.'

'Yes. Except when she bosses me about.'

'I expect you deserve it.'

'I do!' Qwelby laughed.

Kimama's heart went out to the... handsome young man so badly missing his beautiful sister. Grabbing all the towels in the bathroom, she led Qwelby into his bedroom, made him stand while she dried his back then let him collapse onto the bed where she continued to dry him. A rumble started at the back of his throat. 'SunshineBringer,' he murmured.

The musical voice, the pink tongue that flicked across those dark red lips. She lowered her head.

Liking the new taste of her lips, Qwelby responded and soon the sound of his purring deepened.

'He's sleeping like a baby,' Kimama announced later when she joined the others in the living room. Seeing the quizzical looks, she added that she'd learnt all about his older sister, how much he loved her and how he wanted to be with her again.

'Where?' Romain asked, unable to stop himself from leaning forward.

'Back home. Wherever that is. Didn't say.'

'He's lived in so many places the last few years, I guess he doesn't really know where home is,' Romain replied smoothly as his momentary panic disappeared.

Qwelby awoke feeling thirsty and hungry. He'd not eaten for two days nor had anything to drink since early morning, and had fallen asleep before Kimama had left the room. He went to get out of bed, groaned and fell back.

Moments later the door opened and Kimama entered. Qwelby explained his needs and a few minutes later the young woman returned with a tray bearing a mixture of snacks and a large jug of fruit juice. Putting it on the bedside cabinet, she helped Qwelby sit up and then sat on the side of the bed holding the tray.

When he'd finished eating and drinking and Kimama had put the tray down, he took her hand, looked into her deep brown eyes and gently slid further into her mind as he found permissions granted. He sighed with relief. 'You have Old Wisdom.'

Kimama nodded. 'All my people do.'

'I give lot of time, thoughts, energy to fear. I was afraid to be captured and cut open. My plan to get money to travel to Tullia.

A big fear. Make a mistake and be captured. I was followed by bad people. More fear. I had forgotten what lies beneath the quantum world, what my people call The Great Ocean, on which our consciousness acts. I was conscious of all my fears, so... like a mirror...'

'Reflected back to you.'

'The men who beat me...'

'You walk close with Great Spirit for lesson to come soon and strong.'

Qwelby's eyes shone as tears started. 'You understand. More. You know.'

Kimama nodded. 'When white men came to this country they said we were ignorant savages because we believed in what you say and we saw how what we call The Great Spirit works. I seek for an answer and I find it in the gnarled trunk of a tree. So I say, "The tree speaks to me." The tree does not use words and the answer is only for me in that moment. Inside me is the answer and that tree, or perhaps the flight of a bird or the murmuring sound of a stream opens my way to the answer.'

Qwelby reached out, took hold of her other hand and stared into the depths of her rich brown eyes. Time stood still as a kaleidoscope of images flashed through his mind. "Lectures" from their mother when he and Tullia misbehaved badly; their long discussions with Gallia, their Great-Great-Aunt Lellia, about how consciousness impacted on The Great Ocean; "talking" with the transdimensional Stroems. Through his hands came the beautiful sensation of the way Kimama's people understood, knew, lived in and with The Great Spirit.

In his mind he laughed at the prospect of "talking" with a tree - yet what was the difference between that and the Stroems "talking" through the swirls and colours and images of their energy fields? Dark and monstrous images invaded him and he shuddered as he understood, was seared by the pain of knowing, how much insidious darkness inside his own people filled his world to create the monsters the dragons destroyed and now the evil, pure evil, being unleashed on himself and his beloved twin!

He became aware of strong caring energy flowing into him. 'SunshineBringer, Butterfly, bring me lesson. I had forgotten way of Life and made bad things happen to me.' He grinned. 'And nice ones.' He pulled her closer, their lips met, her arms went around him and he started to purr as she stroked him.

Kimama broke away from the kiss and moved her lips to his ear. 'Be healed Doyadukubichi', my Purring Cougar.'

Later, when she returned to the living room and said he was once again fast asleep, Kimama told Romain of their conversation – leaving the Professor happy that he was going to be able to work with the alien at the cutting edge of quantum science. An area denied by many mainstream scientists still terrified of the word and concepts implied in what they saw as the totally discredited idea of an "ether" or "æther" underlying the whole of the physical world.

CHAPTER 60

RULCAS ARRIVES

VERTAZIA

Having been told by Siyataka, the twins' family home, that the twins' parents were at the home of the twins' Great-Great Uncle and Aunt, it was mid morning by the time a delighted Rulcas was dropped off outside Lungunu. Delighted because his father had flown the twistor.

His father had first asked then tried to persuade his son to go back with him to Tembakatii, but Rulcas had heard his own voice say: "Shit, Da, I'd like nottin' better. But I'm in the Deal of a Lifetime and gotta see it through."

Although he had intended to continue with his plan to go to the twins' friends, it had been a shaken youth who had discovered just how strongly set in him were the imperatives of his bargains when, for a moment, he'd been tempted to go with his Da. A large snake had curled around him, its tongue flickering threateningly by his eyes. And a long stiletto had hung in front of him, framed by a deeply plunging neckline the red of the dress which had turned into a drop of blood at the knife's point.

Now, nervously, he faced twelve people in Lungunu's main gatherroom. Lellia having asked Cook for refreshments, Mizena had suggested that Cook, along with her three assistants, should also be present.

305

A brief exchange between Lellia and House as Rulcas was met at the front door had resulted in House changing the décor of the gatherroom to suit what was perceived of the young lad's feelings. The floor was soft green grass, the walls a series of widely spaced and gently fluting stone columns rising from low stone walls. The view in between the columns was the fields and woods that surrounded Lungunu accompanied by gentle smells of freshly mown grass and flowers. In the far distance a dragon and a winged unicorn were flying side by side and soft horn fluting music was just discernable.

Rulcas had become accustomed to what he thought of as the Sci-Fi effects at IndluKoba. Here he was unsure. Was this an attempt at welcoming him or lulling him into false sense of security? He'd have been more at home in a smaller room with plain walls and none of the fancy stuff favoured by the MindJerkers. 'I'm here to help youse,' Rulcas said as he settled into a comfortable armchair. 'Youse'll want to mindsearch me,' he added almost belligerently.

'No,' Lellia said. 'Later, if we need. And only if you agree.'

Rulcas had not become a successful trader and the Proton of his gang without learning to know truthspeak when he heard it. Relaxing a little and more as he continued speaking, he told his story. He started at the age of seven when his father had left to go and live with the Shakazii and his mother had taken him from their home with mainstream Tazii to live in an area of Extreme Traditionalists. Although he resented his father for leaving home, he had been a good father and had just reconfirmed the agreement that they had made, without telling Rulcas' mother, for Rulcas to go and live with his father when Rulcas became an adult and was able to choose for himself.

What followed had been an unfortunate yet classic version of the eighth phase of an Era, usually first experienced during the second Era at the age of nineteen. Change. Letting go of "the old" and bringing in "the new", at the same time starting to form partnerships.

He hated being referred to as a MUUD. His first seven years had given him a normal and full Tazian start in life unlike, as he had discovered, children born in the Extremist enclaves. Initially, he'd learnt a lot from the kids he mixed with. His greater abilities and small size had resulted in bullying, forcing him to work out and stand up for himself. He'd learnt and applied his skills. By his twelfth rebirthday when his father presented him with a really good solid Torc, he was running a small gang supplying goods that were difficult to get hold of in an Extremist area.

He'd been surprised to discover that the world of energy exchange did not differentiate. He provided goods that people wanted and in return gained energy credits. By his fourteenth rebirthday he had widened the area he covered and ensured exclusivity, initially enforcing that by himself. As both the area and the size of his gang had increased, enforcement was taken over by selected "associates".

By the age of sixteen he'd earned a reputation as a hard bargainer and fair trader and, amongst other supplies, had acquired a reputation for good quality copies of illegally made TriDs of the Space Wars, together with reluctant respect from adults who especially valued his ability to provide forbidden strong alcohol. By then it was well established that protection from the dark side of Extremist ways was provided for all the kids who worked for him – and that extended well beyond his close associates.

That "understanding" was rigidly enforced. Not only were adult MUUDs incapable of countering the sharp energies of a group of highly motivated teenagers, the underlying energy balance was in favour of the ideal of Tazian harmony and thus did not upset the MentaNet. And the adults had no-one to whom they could complain!

As the meaning of the abuses that Rulcas was talking about became clear, Pelnak led a distressed Shimara out of the gatherroom, followed by Cook and her assistants. None of them able to contemplate the awfulness that Rulcas was hinting at.

Tamina firmly gripped Wrenden's hand, sending him strong energies of support. Turning to his sister he saw her eyes harden as her usually bright green orbs took on a steely look. *Thanks, Sis.*

We got you, Bro.

We? Khuy! She means and Léshmîrâ. His head reeled as he was back outside Qwelby's Pit of Despair, his sister following his plea to show her love for their BestFriend. *Partners, Sis.*

'Protection?' Mizena asked.

Rulcas considered the twins' mother. She had been the only person not shocked by his comments about the abuses perpetrated on youngsters. Well trained by Xaala, he thoughtsent her an offer to a limited mentasearch and nodded as he felt a gentle coolness in his mind, leaving him to choose how far to let her search.

'I an' a few mates 'as a word.' He was deliberately emphasising the rough side of his nature. He'd noticed the physical exchange between brother and sister, liked them both, admired their guts as a pair of MindJerkers and decided they had to know him if he was going to work with them. At the back of his mind he was already thinking of how to fit them into his gang. 'Arter that we summons one o' them shrinks. 'Im or 'Er what we's spoken to blabs like a nucleus shedding neutrons.'

'Cured?' Mizena asked.

'Sometimes. Usually choose Outlander.'

Everyone looked disgusted and puzzled. The results of being "Cured" were well known. A Tazian was turned into little more than an unthinking automaton. But "Outlander"?

'We'll explain later,' Mizena said with a nod to Rulcas. 'Please continue.'

Surprised by how aware she was and feeling very comfortable with the warm energy of the person who he saw as the most important one present, Rulcas explained why he wanted to help. He saw the twins as rebels who he would recruit to help him shine the light into the dark underbelly of living, he refused to call it "life", amongst the Extremists. His time amongst what he saw as the excesses at IndluKoba had been a final eye-opener and he had his friendship with the Arch Custodian's acolyte to offer. 'A pair of kuznii. Each of us matter and anti-matter. We repel and attract. Might be useful.'

His listeners saw that with the background he'd described it was not surprising that he'd Awakened a lot earlier than normal. His lack of mental skills meant that as he took them deeper into his story and his personal feelings, his enjoyment of his successes was easily perceived without the need for any searching. Honouring what Lellia had said, they were unaware of his thoughts about Xaala and Tullia, nor of the boundaries of the deeply concealed areas set by both Xaala and Dryddnaa.

His listeners thoughtshared and agreed.

'Thank you, Rulcas,' Mizena said. 'You are welcome to stay for the time being. Lungunu will ready a room for you. Whether or not you are invited to join the youngsters in this, their suite, is a decision for them to make when they get to know you.'

Wrenden winked as he nudged his sister. His Trickster genes had already taken a liking to the lad.

Rulcas nodded, content that all had gone well.

'I must make it clear that our whole object is to get my children back – and then help them readjust to Tazian life. When that's happened, who knows?'

'Of course.' Rulcas agreed. Unaware as were all the others that it was Vertazia that was going to have to adjust when the twins returned.

CHAPTER 61

APOLOGY

AMERICA

Qwelby awoke late, aching all over, far worse than after any of his other fights. He wanted to stay in bed. The prospect of facing his stupidity... he remembered having invented a Warrior Oath... rolled over and buried his face in the pillow. How could he have been so arrogant! He had totally misjudged the situation for an escape and betrayed his thinking to Romain. Worse. He was going to have to confess to his twin.

Taking several deep breaths he steadied himself and reached out for her. She was there but not available to mentalink. With a feeling of relief he sent her an image of an island, aware that the surrounding dark energies would tell her it had not been a simple choice.

Washed and dressed and with his head hanging down he walked into the living room where Kimama was preparing his breakfast. There was a long silence as he lifted his head enough to look at the Professor.

'Yesterday, you confirmed you had said you would return with me, knowing that meant coming to Raiatea,' Romain said.

'Yes.' Qwelby put his left hand on his right heart. 'I promise I not run away and go to your Island home.' He dropped his hand to his side.

'You betrayed my trust, so why should I believe you?'

Qwelby placed his right, warrior hand, over his left heart. 'Promise made. I Tazian. Cannot break.'

Romain gave him a long hard look. 'We'll talk later.'

Qwelby dropped his hand to his side and made his way to the table.

Seated in an armchair, lost in his own thoughts and thinking through his plans, Romain did not notice the youngsters' smiles and touching as Kimama put breakfast on the table and sat alongside Qwelby with a mug of coffee.

When Qwelby had finished eating, Romain took the alien into his room, closed the door and interrogated him. Qwelby had thought of all the reasons he might give for running away and had decided to keep it very simple.

He lived on a large farm set in wide open countryside. Raiatea looked very small. Exaggerating, he said no larger than his family's two farms. Driving up from Los Angeles and then the walks with Maska, he'd fallen in love with the great open spaces, the woods and the Shoshone.

As to science and Romain's fluke accident, the Azurii were so far behind anything on Vertazia that the Professor could not help. Now, he had made a promise. Given the nature of Vertazian life at the quantum level he was bound to honour that.

Romain was in two minds over his idea of having the youth medically examined at the University. Physical confirmation that his physiology was so different that he had to be an alien conflicted with wanting the boy safely secured on his island as soon as possible. If there was definite proof – the problem of how to keep that secret tipped the balance. The Professor told Qwelby to pack and gestured to Kimama to watch the youth whilst he did his own packing.

Following Qwelby into his room, Kimama quietly closed the door.

'Like a dragonette, you uplifted me when I was down. You live in my two hearts, Butterfly,' Qwelby said after a final kiss.

311

'And you in mine, Dekonogi'a Doyadukubichi'. My Purring Cougar.'

Standing in the doorway and holding one hand high in salute as she watched Qwelby being driven away, Kimama put her other hand on her heart. She'd been attracted to him the first time she'd met him, the big handsome shy man who needed looking after. Caring for him yesterday she knew she'd fallen in love with him. Later, she'd told him so. He'd fallen asleep without saying anything. He hadn't needed to. His eyes had said it all.

Savouring his last words as the car disappeared from view she let herself sink into the warm glow inside. No matter how ridiculous it was, she did love him. A warrior with a gentle heart.

Outside the Uturoa airport on Raiatea, Qwelby was introduced to nineteen-year-old Jean-Marie, one of the housekeeper's children. As they drove along the spine road up the mountain the whole of the western side of the island was laid out for him, ringed with the lights of its narrow coastal strip. Above, was the great dome of the star filled sky.

Romain turned off the air-conditioning and opened the windows. Along with the heat that assailed Qwelby came a tantalising mixture of smells and, as the four by four climbed higher, a cooler airflow. He reached out to the land, the trees and the buzzing insects. Perhaps his twin was right, not about Romain, but waiting here for her to join him, when they would escape. After all that had happened over the last three tendays he needed time to relax – and sunbathe!

Romain smiled as he heard a contented sigh from the back seat. He had been very circumspect with his researches at the University. What he had hoped might be true from the comment made during that dinner some years ago had turned out to be so. He settled back and enjoyed the drive. The youth was here and he had exactly the hold over his assistants he wanted. A hold to be revealed only if and when he judged necessary.

'Proud of you, Reginsen!'

312

CHAPTER 62

DEEP MIND

VERTAZIA

Ceegren had apologised about the PurpleFruit incident and persuaded the two accompanying Venerables to say nothing, explaining that it had been an experiment that had got out of hand yet had produced satisfactory results in several directions. Xaala had followed that up by apologising at personal meetings with each Venerable. Staying at IngluKoba, each had accepted an offer of her renowned skills at energy massage, and reported back to Ceegren that they considered the incident very satisfactorily closed.

Now Ceegren was more than content. Over two tendays had passed since the successful intervention, or Battle of the Desert as the fight that had prevented the twins reconnecting was known throughout the SubNet, and all reverberations caused by the violence had died away. Just over a tenday since the twins had mentally reconnected and there had been no evidence of them impacting on Vertazia. All was calm and, in typical Tazian manner, the problem was sliding ever further down the levels of conscious awareness towards the bottom of the MentaNet. There, along with many unresolved issues, it was adding to a deep, dark and increasingly troubled layer.

Like the sediment at the bottom of a river that is spread across the land when the river overflows, that collection of millennia's worth of suppression was manifesting in increasing numbers of inhuman forms. The warnings and pleas of the DragonRiders who kept those monstrosities safely away from inhabited areas continued to be met with patronising attitudes. They were overstating the situation and the cause had nothing to do with the Tazii, rather it was an indication of how the violence of the Azurii was slipping through space-time rifts.

In addition, Ceegren was well pleased that Xaala was at last showing the character he needed for a youth leader. She was totally devoted to him and that made his next step easy. As he schooled her in a new set of interpersonal skills, consciously steering her to meet all his needs, he inserted totally concealed commands in her Deep Memory to execute a permanent solution to the twins' situation, knowing that had to be on Earth. And soon.

CHAPTER 63

A NEW HOME

RΛIΛTEΛ

When they reached the laboratory that was Romain's home, they were met at the entrance on a ridge just below the top of the mountain by Hokuao, the housekeeper. After the long and tiring journey all Qwelby wanted to do was to soak in a hot bath and go to sleep. Romain was happy to agree and Hokuao took him down in the lift to the first floor, explaining the unusual numbering system whereby the top floor was number four as the Professor did not want to think of himself as working in the basement.

He was shown into a large bed-sitting room with a king sized bed and all the furniture required for a long stay, everything made in local woods including various thicknesses of bamboo. The wooded floor was a rich golden brown. One complete wall was made of glass doors. The other three walls were in varying shades of green, highlighted with a few yellow flowers. There was also a neat bathroom and a kitchenette. After a brief explanation of the controls in the suite, including how to change the amount and colour of light coming in through the securaglass doors, he was left to settle in.

Minutes later he was dozing off in the bath, too tired to try to reach his twin.

Awaking the following morning he lay there, gathering his thoughts. Although kidnapped and, he supposed, a prisoner, at last he was safe from pursuit! He was drained, physically, emotionally and psychically. It was all he could do to open the glass doors and almost stagger across to the right hand end of the swimming pool, descend the steps and float, gazing up at the clear blue sky.

After a while and having drifted to the other end, he heaved himself out and wandered to the railings where he admired the beauty of the lagoon some seven hundred metres below and then across the Pacific Ocean to the far distant horizon.

Turning to face the building he saw that the front was almost entirely made of glass. The windows and doors of all four floors were in varying shades of green, the supporting structure in shades of brown and the dark blue-grey of the mountain rock. The whole edifice was crowned by a large conservatory that ran across most of its width but was not apparent to anyone entering the top floor.

To his right, a table and chairs were set. Beyond them steps led up to a small balcony which he was to discover led to the domestic staff accommodation and main kitchen. Romain was to explain later that the whole building was his own design, the securaglass in the windows being one of his many inventions. From inside it provided a completely clear view with solar filtering as necessary. All the roofs were covered with solar panels. The back-up generators had never been needed.

Qwelby noticed a pair of sun loungers off to the left. Too lazy to walk that far he flopped onto a metal framed chair, comfortably padded with bright cushions. Heavy eyelids half closed his eyes.

A pair of feet came into view, followed by brown legs, leading to a short cobalt blue skirt topped by a blue and white short sleeved blouse. Qwelby opened his eyes and gaped at... Tullia? No. A younger version before she'd lost her teenyfat. Slowly his mind cleared and he took in the pink colouration to the girl's dark skin, high cheekbones and almond shaped eyes with lovely brown irises. Her cheeks were bright red.

'Oh. Err. Ah. I am sorry,' he stammered an apology in French for staring.

'Good morning mister Qwelby. I am Angélique. Enjoy your breakfast.' She put a loaded tray on the table.

'Please. Join me.'

'But no. I am sorry. I must prepare lunch.' She smiled and glanced towards the sun. 'After I clear away,' she added as he made a moue of disappointment. The few staff had all been instructed to take excellent care of the special guest. And he was handsome. The alarm in the kitchen had chimed as he'd opened the doors onto the patio and she'd got a good look at him as she'd made the coffee. And now – those eyes!

When Angélique had finished clearing away after the three scientists had finished their lunch, she looked out of her window and saw Qwelby flaked out, face down on one of the loungers in the blazing sun. His dark brown face turned towards her emphasised his pale reddish-brown body.

A few minutes later after a question and a smile, she started to apply her own Raiatean Tropic Dark oil to his back. 'The Professor says to tell you to rest today and tomorrow and please to meet him midmorning the following day. Doctor Miki will come for you.'

'Mmmpf.'

Hearing a very gentle purring as she applied the oil over his back, she continued down his legs. About to ask if he wanted to turn over, she noticed the purring had stopped and he was fast asleep. She placed the flask of oil in the shade by his head and took his breakfast tray back to the kitchen. She should have been in college that morning but her young brother had been unwell and she'd volunteered to cover for her mother, rather than have to take her brother to the doctor. Her mother had understood!

The following morning Qwelby sent his twin a series of images, confirming he was on the Professor's island, a darkness he would explain when they were together, that he was waiting for her and had information to help her journey. He finished with images of him shrugging his shoulders and a smile. The big smile that he received in return was accompanied by a sense of relief that he was all right and a reassurance that she was being helped with the journey. The complex sending in the third dimension had drained all his energy and he dozed for a while.

After his swim he took the DVD player that Anita had given him out of his satchel, Fill Me. He smiled as he caressed the shades of pink, remembering he'd said that, as it was special to her, it was special to him – and Hannu's scratchy reaction, which he'd not then understood to be jealousy.

He set it to play the Tai Chi DVD. As he followed the movements he found himself sinking into memories of watching Tamina performing Extended BodyDance, then being sucked back into a more aggressive format he'd previously known.

'Breakfast. QwelbySan.'

Focussing, he saw Hokuao with a smile on her face. 'Kabona. KulaLlaka,' he instinctively replied in Tazian as he made a deep bow as befitted a respected lady. Why I do this?

'Ahhhh. QeïchâKaïgïi. Such memories.'

'You should speak with Miki Sensei. The doctor does something similar.'

Qwelby tucked into his breakfast feeling excited. The movements had been both exhilarating and calming. He was going to enjoy his new morning routine – and in such beautiful surroundings.

CHAPTER 64

LIONESTA

THE KALAHARI

Tullia had never worked so hard in her life - and was loving it. Although communication with her twin required intense concentration and only lasted for a short time, they had reconnected and she was whole.

They'd made a connection a few days ago. He'd been unhappy and feeling trapped on a small island. She knew where he was. The images of the great American continent confirmed what Xameb had said, that because of the snow where Qwelby was, he thought her twin had to be at the very southern end of that great land mass. Comments that Lishi had made had given her hope that Mr Frank would take her with them on the next part of their journey. Although that was still several days away, after two tendays of uncertainty and with her connection with her twin restored, waiting wasn't a big problem. Moreover, it was giving her plenty of time to work hard and make herself indispensable to the research group.

She was busy from dawn until late at night. Her Awakening and the subsequent events had changed everything. She had her duties as a woman of the tribe and, now that Tsetsana was apprentice to Xameb, Tullia had taken over her responsibilities for the family, including sharing those for the grandparents.

Using her compiler in second mode, Tullia was partaking in both morning and afternoon study sessions, learning, translating and exulting in her new life of service, seeing it as a Tazian energy exchange towards all the Meera had done for her. The Meera were awake well before the study party and ate their evening meal earlier, leaving Tullia time to run back and forth, joining Tsetsana where, under Lishi's direction, they helped prepare and lay out the cold lunches and the hot evening meals. Afterwards, Tsetsana would return to lessons with Xameb whilst Tullia remained to clear away, wash up and join in the conversation.

Kemah was in his element and enjoying it to the full. Two young women with whom to chat and some gentle teasing from Lishi. Happy that at last she was a woman, Tsetsana was enjoying the obvious attention of a tall and handsome young man. Tullia was surprised at the openness of the comments that the Meera exchanged and giggled at some of them. She knew she blushed like mad when Kemah directed a comment at her. She tried to copy Tsetsana and make the right responses and guessed she had not done too badly when her friend giggled.

Tullia divided her evenings between discussions with Roland and returning to her family fire, when H'ani asked her to walk with him. She was amused by her own nervous and eager anticipation at having to wait for him to ask. He was a nice and gentle young man and she enjoyed the kissing and cuddling. Her newly energised hormones were urging her on, yet deep inside something was stopping her. There was an unsettling energy she wasn't ready to explore.

For her discussions with Roland she switched her compiler to full mode and talked with him in Afrikaans about her home, friends and the science of both worlds. It was whilst telling the story of her arrival that she discovered mistakes her compiler had made in learning Meera. She laughed as she discovered that the Meera words it had translated as Planetary Ambassador actually meant Sun Goddess.

'Poor girl,' she said in a sympathetic tone. 'All she wanted was to be accepted as a teenager.' Then added with a smile, 'And now I am one.'

It was during one of their discussions about life on Vertazia that Tullia grabbed his arm, her eyes shining. 'Thank you, Uncle Roland. You have answered a big question. A big problem.'

'Me?'

She grinned. 'Yes. By asking detail about the MentaNet and me being here in the Kalahari, I realised where I will be able to train my healers for the fighting to come. And Qwelby his Warriors. We think of the MentaNet as covering the planet. Well, it does, but it depends on where people are living. So there are... blank areas. Below the Great Lake that you call the Mediterranean Sea, we have a continent wide savannah, then like bands right across what you call Africa, mountains covered by forests and great rivers, then deserts and bush like this, finally a mixture of hills and savannahs. No Tazii live in the forests or the bush. So no MentaNet.'

'What about aerial surveillance?'

'Dragons!'

'Dragons?'

'Yes. They do breathe fire but they also... we say breathe but it's actually projecting, a range of mental energies. A few Dragons flying can provide a sort of dome of cover, making it look as though the land below is well, normal, unchanged, and prevents our thoughts from spreading out.'

With her Moon Day behind her and now fulfilling a woman's duties, continuing to share a hut with other young women and working with the researchers, Tullia was Meera. At the same time the tribe accepted the duality of their Goddess. Whilst her womanhood was dedicated to her twin, a God in her own world, she had selected H'ani for company on Earth. The women's fear of her had disappeared to be replaced by the normal feelings of jealousy from the young men for H'ani's success, together with admiration for his daring in risking the anger of a Dragon God.

As Tullia's post Awakening awareness continued to increase, it suited her to reassure H'ani that he was safe from any acts of revenge by her twin God – as long as she retained her virginity. She thoughtsent Qwelby a big exclamation mark and apology for that useful deception.

Although Tsetsana had built a tiny hut alongside Xameb's home, he had given her permission to spend her nights in the hut that Ungka and Ishe shared, along with Tullia and the two other young women from the Moon Day. Becoming the Shaman's acolyte with her own hut had set Tsetsana even further apart than had her friendship with Tullia. Spending her nights with the others in obvious celebration of her womanhood eased her passage into the new and demanding period of her life,

Xameb's motives had been professional as well as social. He was aware of how Tsetsana's skills had grown from being so close to Tullia and the repeated mental contact enfolded in their love for each other. He had started her training far too late and she needed every assistance that could be provided if she was to develop her full potential.

He had no idea of how rapidly his apprentice was to blossom and how soon she was going to need the tribe's support.

Lishi had settled into a very comfortable existence, accepting her physical limitations but nevertheless still fully in charge of the kitchen. She was happy to share with her assistants the compliments for the flow of excellent meals prepared under her instruction.

'I don't do a single thing,' Frank said on the last evening. He turned to his wife, with Roland sitting on her other side. 'I don't have to make any decisions. You have all the meals planned. Kemah knows what to do, yet from the permanent grin on his face is clearly happy being bossed about by Tyua'llia and Tsetsana.' Frank shook his head in wonderment.

'Truly a lion heading his pride,' Lishi quipped.

Frank laughed. He had felt affronted the first time he had been likened to a lion sitting back and watching his lionesses doing all the work. Now, it felt good.

'Why don't we take her with us?' Lishi asked, switching to Afrikaans.

Tullia had her back to them as she was washing up. Hearing them switch languages she focussed her hearing. Although Lishi demolished all the reasons her husband had given Xameb as to why that was not possible, it was clear he still had reservations.

A can was popped open. Surprised, Frank turned to a smiling Tullia who had dropped to her knees as she offered him a can of beer. Hoping to cover up that she had been listening, she spoke in English as she said, 'Lioness look after lion.' She did not flutter her eyelashes but she could not help her eyes shining with hope and an involuntary flicker of her bright pink tongue wetting her dry lips.

Frank spluttered, Roland hid his laugh with a cough, Kemah hid his smile behind his hands and Lishi burst out laughing. Tullia remained on her knees, puzzled at the reaction.

'Not a lioness, Tullia. Possibly a cub but...' Lishi was unable to stop laughing.

'How about Lionesta?' Roland suggested. 'I'm playing with the Italian language. Lioness for a lady lion and then 'esta' meaning younger.'

Understanding what she had inadvertently suggested, Tullia grimaced, then checked she had understood. Pointing at Frank, then Lishi, then herself she said, 'Lion, Lioness and... Lionesta?'

Frank took a long drink of cold beer. 'Hihhh.' He saw from the looks on the students' faces they had clearly understood what was going on. He grunted. 'Lionesta comes with us...'

Whatever else he was going to say was cut off by a happy squeal of delight from Tullia as she flung her arms around him and kissed him on both cheeks. 'Thank you, Mr Frrrank.'

'And I expect all my beers to be cold,' he added, trying to sound stern but only succeeding in making Tullia giggle as she added, 'Yes, Mr Frrrank.'

Frank walked over to the group around the fire and explained that, as they had participated in a second evening of healing dances, for their last night the Meera were going to share stories from their lives.

A concerned Tullia went to speak with Xameb, who explained that there would not be anything special from their history, but general teachings such as portraying a leopard with her cubs hunting an ibex. He went on to say that no-one who was not San would ever be told of who she was. If necessary, she would always be described as a member of one of the red-skinned tribes, searching for the places where her ancestors had lived. Obviously it was up to her to seek a promise of secrecy from Frank, Lishi and Roland.

Just before she entered the hut for a last night with the girls she went to Qwelby's corner of his mind. When she found a miserable sensation so small she was unable to link, she sent him a big, twinly hug.

CHAPTER 65

OUT OF SIGHT

THE KALAHARI

The day of departure dawned. Tullia had spent the previous evening saying her tearful goodbyes, being inundated with home-made presents and left speechless by Xashee's shy offering. She was sad that Kou-'ke had again avoided her, as she had done since the Moon Day and that Xashee had never mentioned her name since that day nor asked her to walk with him.

Mandingwe and N!Obile were making eyes at him, intending to progress further when the weather was warm enough for a Melon Dance. Last night they'd told her that the one she'd participated in had been set up especially for the young women to find out more about her. It had been like setting a leopard amongst monkeys, they had said, giggling with mischief.

Yet there was joy. During a farewell night with her group of girlfriends, Ungka and Ishe had invited Mandingwe and N!Obile to join them in a hut-sharing group. All four had then said to Tsetsana that they knew how having become the Shaman's apprentice was setting her apart, and offered friendship and a welcome to their hut at any time. A delighted Tullia said nothing about having seen H'ani's face dance before her eyes as they'd been talking.

Breakfast finished, Tullia was learning how to fold and pack tents and where everything was stored in and on the various vehicles and trailers. Xameb had allowed Tsetsana to help her special friend for the last time. Too small to lift the heavy tent rolls and having learnt how the stowing was done, Tsetsana scampered up the built-on ladder and packed the top of Kemah's cruiser as Tullia threw the rolls up. When everything was loaded and they were ready to leave, Frank called everyone together for a last talk before they went up to the village to say their farewells.

Apart from Roland who knew the truth, the students had accepted that Tullia was a member of a very small and unusual red-skinned San tribe.

Frank explained that in all her travels she had lost her identity card. It was extremely unlikely that there would be any passport checks but, if there were, then everyone had to ignore her, not talk to her or about her as she sought to blend in.

Earl and Pamela, two of the research students, started to object.

'You volunteering to do all the cooking and washing-up for another week?' Lishi firmly challenged. 'Three meals a day for eighteen people?'

They did not reply.

When the party reached the village, Tullia could not help bursting into tears as her adoptive family approached and she knelt down and hugged the children. Xashee? What to say? She was Meera. Yes. But she was also an alien. A Sun Goddess! Standing up, she took his head in her hands and kissed him, full on the lips. It was a long and firm kiss as, having been granted permission by his Inner Self, she infused him with dragon-warrior energies, unaware of being surrounded by a shimmering golden haze.

Stepping back, she became aware of ululating and shouts of joy and smiled. Her people had understood that it was no lover's kiss but that of a Goddess.

Frank seized the moment to direct everyone back to the campsite and climb aboard the vehicles.

326

Moments later, they set off amidst much waving and cries of farewell. Frank was in the lead with Roland having pride of place in the passenger seat. Danny followed, driving Lishi's Landcruiser with her sitting alongside. Bringing up the rear as usual, Kemah signalled to Tullia to come to him. She remained standing on the top of the rise, pointed towards the track and set off in that direction, walking with long strides.

Her timing was perfect. As Kemah reached the track Tullia opened the passenger door and swung onto the seat. She turned to him as she put on her seat belt, her face shiny with tears. 'I keep promise to Sah. I no run away. I walk to Cruiser.' She sat back in her seat and relaxed. Not being in the front vehicle there was no need to concentrate on the sandy track.

Having started her journey to her twin and then, somehow, on to their home on Vertazia, she began sorting through her memories of all she had learnt on Earth. She found pleasure in those areas she saw she would be able to use on Vertazia. Then she started wondering about odd aspects, such as tracking animals or driving on sandy tracks, that carried an energy of importance yet, surely, were irrelevant to life on Vertazia?

'Patience. Young QeïchâKaïgii.'

The convoy travelled for hours along a gentle upwards incline, a thick sand road where it appeared the crest of the hill was always a couple of kilometres ahead. Yet each time they reached some marker such as a lone tree, there was another crest a couple of kilometres ahead, then again and again.

Each time the convoy came to a gate, Tullia leapt out, ran to the front, opened the gate and then closed it when Kemah's vehicle and trailer were through. She needed to be with Kemah and talking Meera without using her compiler as she immersed herself in her role of an unusually large Bushman.

CHAPTER 66

DANCE OF DISCOVERY DEEPENS

VERTAZIA

Dryddnaa was very happy. Rulcas was firmly established with the twins' family and friends. Unnoticed, she regularly slipped into his mind. Their frequent meetings as she passed on information to Ceegren was involving her more in his plans. She was also steadily bringing Xaala in to be a junior partner in their enterprise to see the twins return and, if their DNA had degraded, to have them healed. And from the girl's carefully phrased comments, Dryddnaa was learning more about the Arch Custodian's long term thinking that he was not revealing to the Chief Readjuster.

Obviously aware of the line of communication, Xaala explained to Dryddnaa why she had not inserted an entry in Rulcas' mind to allow her to interrogate him when, during their brief time together, she had been helping him to develop his rudimentary mental skills. If she had done that it would have been a betrayal of their odd friendship – akin to the betrayals she had experienced from her parents.

Her inner confusion increased as, continuing to play her double game, she met regularly with Dryddnaa. Meetings encouraged by Ceegren who realised that his acolyte needed a woman with whom to discuss the pressures of her emerging womanhood. And who better than the Chief Readjuster, both for Xaala personally and for her to report back their conversations to him? A third player had entered the increasingly dangerous Dance of Discovery

Xaala slowly opened up about personal issues. Finding Dryddnaa a warm and friendly confidant their conversations were how she imagined they would be with a girlfriend. After their times together, Xaala deepsearched her mind and always found it clear of any attempted interference.

As a friendship developed, Xaala, who was still uncertain about whether she wanted both twins to return, or only one, and if so which, found the confidence to explore that, obliquely. She confessed to her confusion over her feelings for them.

'Very understandable,' Dryddnaa replied. 'From what I've seen on TriD of their LiveShows, she is beautiful, he is handsome. Imagine how much more dynamic they will be when they are Awakened. And the residual energies from the time of their reconnection indicate they are, and powerfully so. Identical twins. I think if you like one, you have to like the other.'

Xaala grimaced. *Of Course!*

Dryddnaa smiled as she slid feelings of reassurance into Xaala's mind. 'These two or three phases of this Era are your time to explore your developing genes. Remember. Whilst pair-bonding is the norm, whichever way that is, it is not at all uncommon for tri-bonds to be just as successful.'

Xaala had a lot to think about and no time to explore her new impulses. Fortunately, the demands of the intense training with Ceegren were leaving her without the energy to explore.

CHAPTER 67

PASSPORTS PLEASE!

THE KALAHARI

It was not long after the little convoy had turned onto the blacktop that it reached one of the many Veterinary control checkpoints spread throughout Botswana and Namibia since the 1960s, where they pulled into a parking bay on the right hand side of the road. Everybody got out and, as forewarned by Frank, were required to produce any and all footwear packed in their luggage. Frank attempted a pleasant conversation with the sergeant in charge, only to meet with a rebuff. She was almost aggressive in her tone of voice, sneering at a bunch of sightseers and frowning as she stared at Earl.

'I'm not San. I'm Jamaican,' Earl said in an almost angry tone of voice.

Discussions with the San and around the camp fire at night had ranged far and wide. Earl had heard the stories of slavery not being introduced by whites but already being practised by Arabs and by Africans on other Africans. Roland had mentioned what he had seen of former slave camps and the terrible conditions that had existed in Sierra Leone, where Africans had willingly seized their own kind and sold them to the slave traders.

Earl had been brought up to believe that slavery was a white

330

invention and most certainly and correctly had heard many and terrible stories of the atrocities inflicted on black slaves by white people. He had also experienced the discrimination meted out to his kind by the whites in Great Britain, the so-called Mother Country.

He had become increasingly critical of the San during his time with them. He seemed to be almost personally affronted by their lack of rebellion against what had been imposed on them by the British and now by their own government and people and far worse, the white South Africans who had exterminated all San in that country. He had taken part in protests in England against the treatment accorded to West Indians and non-white immigrants in general. For him, his time in Africa was an uncomfortable eye-opener to the fact that discrimination was not just by whites against non-whites, but also by blacks against blacks.

He did not want the sympathy and understanding of the white people he was mixing with. He wanted to be able to rail against them and release his anger at his pain and hurt. Instead, he had turned on the Meera, wanting to instil into them his own hatred of the white, oppressing races. For reasons he could not explain, Tullia was far too much for him to take on board in any way and Roland just a typical old white fool trying to pretend that his ridiculous beliefs had any basis in something he called quantum science.

The sergeant was on edge and Frank was worried. They had passed through the checkpoint several days previously when the same Herero had been in charge, so he knew it was not because of himself and his party. He became aware of an altercation between Earl and one of the policemen, not helped by the fact that the tall officer towered over the comparatively diminutive West Indian. It was something about smoking. The policeman was being polite. For some reason that did not suit the sergeant. Curtly, she ordered suitcases to be unloaded and opened for inspection.

Frank sought to protest and was surprised by the vehemence

only partly held in check as she responded. He realised with a shock that from scarcely under six foot tall, he was still having to look up at her. Fortunately, as the result of years of being ready for misadventure, all personal baggage had been loaded last and was easily accessible. Nevertheless, it took a long time to get the bags for eighteen people out, opened and inspected. Inevitably a pair of shoes was found - Earl's. He hadn't worn them, was his explanation.

The sergeant was angry which was made worse by Earl trying to persuade her that as a fellow black, there was no problem. He was badly mistaken. He was not even African. To her he was just another rich tourist "trying it on."

Although Frank considered he had been reasonable in the way he had approached her, the sergeant had seen it differently. In her eyes the way he had spoken marked him as a typical white colonialist. She had had enough, this was her country and these tourists had better know it.

'Passports!' was her peremptory command.

Chaos and confusion, the students were trying to repack their suitcases, put them back in the trucks and remember where they had stored passports against this eventuality.

Lishi knew that in due course she would have to get out and walk through the disinfectant trough at the other side of the road and had been leaving getting out of the cruiser to the last moment. Now, in spite of her two bandaged wrists she was ordered out. Roland swiftly moved to the door, helped her out and led her to stand by Tullia along with himself and Kemah.

Earl continuing to object, expecting better treatment in a country run by fellow blacks as he was calling them, only further increased the sergeant's irritation. Pamela was whinging. The plump middle aged woman had moaned constantly throughout the trip, making everyone wonder why she'd signed up. In trying to calm her down, Lishi only focused attention on her, which was exactly what Pamela wanted.

'Earl going on like this is not going to help us get the girl through,' Pamela moaned.

With all the disturbance, Tullia was fearing discovery and starting to panic which was destabilising her energy field.

Hands were held out, papers examined and passed back. The tall policeman was not paying particular attention. He knew Frank and Lishi by sight and had seen this group come through several days ago. It was a boring job in the scorching sun. A woman with a round face and dark hair, a passport photograph that looked similar. A tall man with a mass of white hair and blue eyes matching his passport photograph. He moved on. A brown hand, Botswana identification papers, a face that matched the photo. Again he moved on.

The Herero sergeant was standing back, observing. They were under orders to look for a San male charged with having murdered his wife in a drunken rage. He had been captured in the bush a couple of weeks ago and had escaped. Sadly, such a murder amongst the San living in the shanty towns was not unusual, but escape was unheard of. That marked him as a dangerous man. She was on edge. These tourists were a nuisance and she wanted them gone.

Tullia noticed an energy of uncertainty run through the tall sergeant's aura and watched nervously as she instructed the two policemen to collect all the passports and identification papers and take them to the table. She watched as they counted them, eighteen. Then the policewoman ordered the group into line and counted them. Tullia tried her best to be inconspicuous. Shrinking inside herself, her brown face surrounded by the hood of a faded grey sweater, eyes downcast, submissive, of no importance and sinking into HideNSeek mode.

Kemah was beckoned forward. The sergeant took time checking his papers, looked searchingly at him, returned the papers and motioned him to one side.

Out of the corner of her eye Tullia saw the sergeant looking along the group, her eyes stopping on Earl. With a grimace, she started to open the passports, then stopped and looked up with a frown. Hadn't she seen another brown face? No more Botswana papers. She rifled through the passports looking for an identity card. Nothing.

'You.' Tullia saw the woman point at her and beckon her forward.

As she moved she saw Frank step forward and start to speak. One of the policemen stopped him, putting an arm across his chest. She saw Frank's energy field swirl with anger but quieten as he held himself in check.

Tullia was desperately trying not to burst into tears as she explained all about her life and upbringing with the Meera, earning the wrath of the sergeant as she spoke mainly in Meera, interspersed with a few words in Afrikaans.

Finally, Frank was summoned to explain. He had had time to think, cool his temper and realise that there had to be something very serious going in the background to have so alarmed the sergeant. Effusive he never was, but he tried his best with his apologies for not having checked that his new assistant had her identity card with her.

The sergeant did not hear it that way. She saw and heard a typical middle-aged white colonialist with a South African accent telling her what to do.

Frank was able to point to Lishi's wounds and explain perfectly truthfully why Tullia was with them and that he had recruited her from the village where they had been staying. Identity cards were held by the chief and only handed out on the rare occasion an individual travelled far from the village.

In spite of her antagonism, the sergeant's anger and suspicions slowly drained away. The story was all too believable and in her mind indicated the over-weaning pride and insolence of a white man who still thought he ruled Africa, and the inbred stupidity of the San who were no better than cattle. Even cattle provided food to eat!

Now, Tullia had become just a damned nuisance. She was not a man, she was not the murderer. But she was without her papers. She would show the whites and the annoying black man who was not African, just who was in charge in Africa. The girl would be held for identification. The downside was that could take for ever. The girl would have to be fed and guarded in case, like the animal she was, she slipped away.

The Herero had heard too many stories about the San and their skills in the bush. Naturally, she'd heard of the army officer who hadn't noticed as his revolver was taken by that very murderer. She pushed all those thoughts to the back of her mind. Right now all she wanted to do was to get rid of the annoying tourists and their vehicles. Get them out of sight and she would deal with the latest problem. First, she gave some severe warnings to Frank.

Inside, he was boiling mad at the treatment and also angry with himself for having allowed Tullia to come, knowing there was the chance that this might happen.

Lishi had spoken to calm him down and Roland had tried to help by reassuring him in his calm and steady way that, after a month with the Meera, Tullia was as much a Bushman as they.

There was nothing Frank could do. He held his peace as the sergeant berated him, suppressing his anger as he comforted himself with the thought that, if Roland was correct, there might be a surprise in store for the policewoman.

The drivers took the Landcruisers and trailers through the disinfectant dip whilst, led by Lishi, all the others crossed the road and walked through the foot baths, carefully ensuring the soles of all their shoes and sandals were well trodden into the disinfectant.

As everyone was climbing back into the vehicles, Lishi spoke quietly to Roland. 'When we arrived there were three San women at the side by the footbaths. Their duty is to replenish the disinfectant. Just after we arrived I saw one of them heading back towards that village where we stopped at the tourist shop.' She gestured with her head.

Roland turned to look back down the road. They could just see what looked like the beginning of a group of people walking along the road towards them. He turned to Lishi and raised an eyebrow.

'I think they may have recognised a daughter of Nananana,' she said with a smile. 'I don't know what will happen to Tullia, but I think she will be looked after.'

'When I was talking with her about her lack of papers, I gave her an envelope containing a map I'd bought from the shop and marked on it where we are going, some money and my business card with the number of your satellite phone,' Roland said. 'Who knows?'

A short distance along the road Frank pulled onto the side and the convoy drew to a halt. As he got down he waved his hands in the direction of the bush. Those who needed to, disappeared. Standing downwind, three of the group gratefully lit up their cigarettes.

As the group reassembled Frank decided to take the bull by the horns. 'I think we could have got through that. Or rather we could have got our young assistant through had we all pulled together as a team.' He focused his attention on Earl and Pamela. Both started to speak.

'Don't.' He cut them off curtly. 'You have come out here to learn. The San have been here for seventy thousand years. They have survived amongst some of the harshest conditions known to mankind. They have done that by pulling together as a team. They are managing to survive with all the things that have changed for them so rapidly in the last few decades. You have seen a traditional old-style village. Most of them live in shanty towns like the one we visited this morning, yet they still survive.

'As we were leaving, Lishi pointed out to me a group of San approaching from that village. They do not know Tullia, but the women at the fence have seen her as San. They will do what they can to look after one of their own.'

336

He looked around the group of people catching as many eyes as he could. 'I would hope that to us, "one of our own" means a member of the human race.' He paused, aware of the uncomfortable atmosphere that had been created. Changing tone he spoke again.

'Across the road there.' All heads turned as he pointed. 'This side of that double fence lies our track down to the Saltpans. Remember, when we pitch camp tonight, Tullia will not be with us to help.' He pointedly addressed his last few words to Earl and Pamela with a glare that kept both their mouths shut.

'Now, before we move on, there was something seriously wrong back there. I did manage to discover from the San women at the side that the man from their shanty village who murdered his wife has escaped and the police are on the lookout for him. That was our misfortune. Now I want to look through the vehicles before we set off. We could run into deep sand and I want to ensure that all the baggage has been properly stored away.' He jerked his head towards Kemah and they moved to the rear of Kemah's Landcruiser as Frank looked at his watch.

'That inspection's delayed us and we're running late but we'll repack the bags. I want the loads evenly distributed,' Frank explained in a gruff voice.

Kemah nodded. He understood. Frank was hoping the police would let Tullia go, she would slip through the fences and be waiting for them some way down the track.

When all had been sorted and Frank could delay no longer, the convoy set off, heading south for Makgadikgadi.

They were making good time when Frank saw deep sand ahead and shifted gear. The sand was deeper than expected. He felt the softness as the Cruiser rode onto it and changed gear as the wheels started to spin. Another change but to no avail. The wheels were spinning too much and Frank brought his vehicle to a stop before it sank too far. Although it had been three years since he had driven along that particular track in a lighter vehicle, he was sure the sand had never been that deep.

The situation was not difficult. They would dig down until the bedrock was reached, the wheels would grip and all would be well. It was the time lost that was annoying. Spades were unpacked and digging started.

And continued.

It did not take long before it was clear that the sand was too deep. Frank pulled out a depth rod, similar to those used by mountain rescue teams to plumb the snow and drove it in.

'Much too deep. The rock bed's shifted. No way can we dig this out. We'll need to back up the other Cruisers then use the one Danny's driving to winch the trailer back, then do the same with my Cruiser. The only map of the area is this satellite map. It's provided by people like myself regularly travelling the sand ways. There's no information about this problem, nor any alternative route.'

At Frank's request, Roland walked further along the track, plumbing the depth whilst Frank organised the others to guide the trailer as Kemah careful reversed his Cruiser. Roland returned a few minutes later to say that the bedrock plummeted down until it was deeper than the pole for about ten metres, then reached the surface shortly after that. A lot later Frank was to discover that where they were, the sand was over seven metres deep and the rock bed had shifted in several more places further ahead.

It was mid-afternoon before everything had been done and all three Cruisers with their trailers were back beyond the turn-off. Kemah had walked down it and reported that it was not just a short loop around that particular sand patch. Worse, it appeared to drift further to the left away from the main track and there was no sign of any place to pitch camp. Everyone was exhausted. Frank wanted a clear run in daylight on the new track and it was agreed to make camp where they were and make an early start the following morning.

CHAPTER 68

PRISONER

THE KALAHARI

It was mid morning when Inspector Modisakgosi finished a pleasant meeting with a charming lady detective who'd travelled from her office in the capital of Gaborone in search of a missing husband. From a desk drawer he took the file he'd slipped into it when she'd arrived and noticed a pile of circulars. The date of the top one told him they were very old. Anything important and there'd have been another, now dealt with.

As he tidied them into a neat stack for shredding, the bottom one slipped to the floor. Two dates underneath the heading caught his attention. He flicked his fingers across the monitor screen and, yes, there they were, in the file on that girl with the purple eyes. No arrest warrants had come from Namibia or anywhere else and with the inevitable disturbances that occurred as the tourist season got underway, she'd slipped his mind.

He read the fax reporting the near accidents that had occurred to two airplanes on dates that exactly matched with those in the girl's file: her date of arrival in the village and when there had been some weird disturbance over the Tsodilo hills at the time she'd been on the top of them. He'd known there was something strange about her. There had not been any earthquake the day the station had been wrecked and how had she lifted that solid iron door? Now he wondered about electronic warfare and Kaigii, no witchdoctor's evil spirit, but – what was it called – her controller?

'Ditau!' he shouted, as he grabbed the keys to the Land Rover. 'Going to the Research Village,' he called out to the duty sergeant as he almost ran from the building.

At the Veterinary post, Tullia remained sitting inside what was now a tent, the previously open long side having been closed, leaving only the end facing the road open. She'd tried to call her twin but he was fast asleep. She was sitting bolt upright, her nails digging into her palms as she tried to control her panic.

That day in the bush my captor said that he'd die if he was put in a metal box. Any Bushman would. Not just a Bushman. I'd die if they lock me away in that prison cell. What am I doing here? I'm not a hornsfluting Goddess or a Bushman. I'm an alien on a strange world. I want to be with Kaigii! I want to go home! Her nails drew blood as she forced down the tears.

She became aware of noises outside. Voices, sounding like a lot of people. The policeman guarding her got up and went out of the tent to help his colleagues. She heard orders being given, but in spite of the efforts of the police to keep them back, San were just flowing around them – men, women and children all heading for her. Their energies were... warm, accepting and... honouring?

Self conscious, she stood up and without thinking ran her hands through her hair. Lit by a beam of sunlight through a tear in the roof, green lights flickered all along her thick black tresses and she heard murmurs, once again acknowledging her as a Goddess and a daughter of Nananana. She grimaced. A young child giggled and then looked stunned as though expecting to be struck by a bolt of lightning. Tullia laughed and the sound of violins and clarinets rang throughout the tent.

A steady stream of San continued to enter the compound. The police had never experienced anything like it. The San were always totally well behaved and always did as they were told. In fact they were so docile it was unbelievable. The sergeant was uncertain. Should she call for reinforcements? To do what? If she had to admit she could not control a few of the despised Bushmen she would forever be a laughing stock amongst her colleagues. And, anyway, what was the harm? They were only talking to another of their people. She turned to the constables. 'Get in there and watch her. Make sure she does not get away.'

After a while as people started to leave the tent, the sergeant stopped one of the older men and asked what was going on.

'A daughter in trouble.'

There was no answer when she asked why so many had come. Two trucks arrived at the crossing and she checked them through, noting that on the opposite side of the road the San women were operating the foot dips as usual.

Eventually, when the last of the Bushmen had drifted away back towards their shanty town, the sergeant walked in under the awning where the girl was slumped across the table with the hood of her jumper once again pulled up over her head. As she approached on the opposite side of the table, she knew something was wrong. Previously, the girl had sat erect, quietly self-assured, a proud bearing like a fellow Herero.

The sergeant prodded her prisoner's arm. The girl drew back. The ends of small fingers appeared from a sleeve. With a horrible premonition, the sergeant leapt to her feet sending her canvas chair crashing to the ground behind her, bent over the table, grabbed the girl's arms and pulled her up. It was not her prisoner!

Furious, she hauled the girl across the table, sending it crashing to the ground. The girl was wearing the same clothes as the big one had been. Ripping the hoodie off over her head the sergeant discovered several layers of thick clothing that had made the skinny little thing seem a lot bigger.

Tsetsana stood there, meek and mild, eyes lowered, waiting for the blows. With a roar of rage the sergeant turned to the side and

341

slammed both fists down on the other trestle table, collapsing it to the ground. She bent down, picked it up and hurled it across the compound, swearing and shouting at the two constables who had let themselves be so easily tricked.

'They'll have taken her to the village,' the tall constable suggested, not daring to look his sergeant in the eye.

The sergeant narrowed her eyes as she studied him. He was right. There was no police vehicle at the checkpoint. The crossing had to be manned. By the time a constable walked to the village, the girl would not be there. She would have disappeared into the bush and only emerge after the police had left. She swore. Still, it saved her the trouble of making a report and, better still, she did not have to lose one of the constables from crossing duty to guard a prisoner.

Aware of their failure, the two constables waited for the sergeant's final words. They knew her temper and could handle that. It was the punishment that would follow that had them trembling. Would she report them? What would the Inspector say or, worse, do? They continued to wait.

'Identity card,' the sergeant snapped.

Fumbling through all her layers of clothing whilst the big Herero stood, impatiently tapping her right boot on the ground, Tsetsana eventually produced the document and handed it over.

'Research Village,' the sergeant snarled, robbed of another victim. She returned the card and dragged Tsetsana outside. 'Get outta my sight!' she roared as she kicked Tsetsana in her well clothed backside and had the satisfaction of seeing the girl sprawl in the sand.

'Seventeen tourists and one Motswanan male crossed the border,' she said as she turned to the constables. 'That's all!'

'Yes, Sah!' they chorused

The sergeant narrowed her eyes. Were they smiling at her? She, a proud Herero, making a mistake in front of the Batswana! 'If I ever hear a different story, your lives will not be worth living!'

'Yes, Sah,' they said in sober tones.

Tullia had stood gawping, unable to believe her eyes as Tsetsana had appeared through the crowd.

'Make nice place between tent rolls on top of last truck,' Tsetsana explained. 'No one see me.'

Tullia bent down and picked the small woman up in a bear hug, laughing at her BestFriend's audacity. 'Why?' she asked as she sat down and let go of Tsetsana.

'!Gei-!Ku'ma must be with the !Kwe-!ku'gn. Know you not have papers.'

'If I not arrested?'

'Stay on top.'

Knowing that healing in its widest meaning was a key to her future as a Sangoma, last night Tullia had infused Tsetsana with Rrîltallâ's energy. Remembering her tribe's acceptance when she'd kissed Xashee, Tullia slipped inside her BestFriend's mind. Receiving permission from the woman's Inner Self, she drew energy from a sleeping twin and kissed Tsetsana full on the lips as she infused her with dragon-warrior energy, again unaware of the golden haze shimmering around them. Easing back and enjoying the look of amazement on Tsetsana's face, Tullia became aware of the soft murmurings of acceptance for the young Sangoma.

'Twana-Udada. Enabawena liziyoritwimiti,' Tullia said in her rich contralto, then translated into Meera. 'Little-Sister. You live in my two hearts.'

After a long silence, Tsetsana took a deep breath and shook herself as she came back into the present. 'You go. I take your place.'

Tullia's protest was stopped as several women said they would look after Little-Sister.

As Tsetsana put on the several garments that the San passed to her, a dazed Tullia handed over her hoodie, sweater and tracker bottoms. Staying seated so as to remain out of sight of the police, Tullia pulled herself together and thanked the San in Meera,

Afrikaans and finally in her musical Tazian, her big smile again making the children laugh.

Crawling out of the back of the tent and checking that no police were in sight, hearts beating so loudly she was sure the noise must be heard, Tullia had made her way downhill to the nearest clump of bushes and settled down to recover. Her training took over.

She'd been growing ever since she'd arrived on Earth and that had accelerated after her Awakening. When she'd grown out of her khaki shorts she'd been offered a dark green skirt. Shortening it to mid thigh had given her enough material to add two panels to make it go round her hips and also make two pockets and several belt loops.

She'd made a new tank top by using two t-shirts. Even though faded, the green and red stood out against the browns of the bush, as did the dark green skirt. She smiled that she was on the way to her twin whilst wearing his favourite colours.

She stripped down to her skirtlet, which she'd worn under all her clothes to help anchor her in her pretence at being a Bushman, apologised to Thathuma, her beautiful necklace, as she slipped its shiny links over her head and put the necklace in one of the pockets of her skirt. Checking that the only people who might see her move were the San returning to their village, she crawled a lot further downhill and settled close to the fence, behind a larger clump of bushes from where she was still able to watch the police compound.

She watched as Tsetsana was kicked to the ground and the police walked to the near side of the crossing. The ground sloped heavily and they soon disappeared from sight. Why are they not searching for me? Tsetsana must have told them I'd gone to the village. Or. From all I've heard. Well. I'm just another despised San. She snorted her disgust and then stifled a laugh. A few minutes ago I was a terrified alien. Now I'm an unwanted Bushman!

With a sigh of relief she saw Tsetsana pick herself up and walk towards the opposite side of the crossing, heading for the women who'd said they would take her to their village for the night. As she disappeared from view, Tullia felt alone and abandoned. She tensed her muscles and started to rise to run after her BestFriend. An image of the prison cell flashed before her and she dropped back down.

NO! My Little-Sister was prepared to go to prison, be locked in a dark cell and die, because.... she loves me and my twin. I owe it to her to get to him.

I'm not a Bushman. What I heard some of the young women say. They're right. Compared to them I am big and clumsy and with an ugly face. But they took me in, adopted me into their tribe and gave me a new family. I owe it to all of them. I WILL survive.

She took a deep breath and looked down at the "V" of her loinskin with the intertwined letters Q & T. We are one. Remembering how much stronger she'd been when that night in prison Qwelby had wrapped her in his big strong arms, she smiled, curled up into a ball and fell asleep in what was for her the hot sun.

CHAPTER 69

LAUNCH

VERTAZIA

There was an atmosphere of tense expectation throughout Lungunu. Everyone was working so hard in their various ways that there was a constant demand for food and drink and the soothing of tired and troubled minds. The growing of crops and husbanding of animals, fish and birds, the supply of food, its preparation and serving were all handled with respect as part of the Aurigan legacy of wholeness. In addition, all Cooks prepared their own ingredients, restorative drinks and ointments, learning to allow those caring energies to flow through their hands and, where required, into people. Busy all the time in all areas, all four Cooks were happy key players in the enterprise and an integral part of what had become The Lungunu Family.

It was a tenday since the adults had started talking with other adults about the twins' situation and Vertazia's responses. Building upon the threads of discontent running through the MentaNet was a very slow progress, hampered by their having to devote a large part of their time to their commitments to the planet, especially Mizena. As overseer of two large estates, she was responsible for the supply of a vast range of foods to the Tazii. Having only recently finished supervising final preparations for the nesting season, she was now heavily engaged with preparation for the lambing season.

The four BestFriends had plunged vigorously into their new routine and their days at colleges were continually bringing more youngsters into a planetary wide support group. Tamina spent a lot of time in the Shadow Market and SubNet Kulture. Emboldened by her KultureName of TamLâŝ'tûn – Tamina, The Ultimate Dealer – she was revelling in the demand for her new style of performances.

Traditional dances rapidly changed into Aurigan Martial Arts then into a Fire Lady morphing into swirling salamanders. Hints of darkness and even brief glimpses of DeathDealer heightened the viewers' experiences. Threading through all her performances was the message of gathering enough youthful energy to demand a change to the oppression that was denying the twins a return home. Many were inspired and support groups arose throughout the SubNet. Putting aside conventional mental and electronic means of sharing, youngsters created a new SubKulture and enjoyed the excitement of meeting secretly in groups in out-of-the-way places – but always establishing a link into the Kulture and TamLâŝ'tûn's performances.

Whether at Lungunu or their home, Tamina had come to rely on "Her Eeky" for his stalwart support. She did not speak to him of her issues. Just cuddled up to him when he listened, held and comforted her as if he were her older brother. A lot later they agreed that it had been much better for both of them that he had not been able to understand the drives, pressures and tempestuous emotions that had been besieging her.

Lellia had been true to her word. Unable to discuss matters with her own mother, Tamina had accepted the offer from Aunt Gallia, as the BestFriends called the Elder, with relief. She explained that she had always loved Tullia, but now she was Awakened and knew through Óweppâ that the twins also were Awakened she was very confused about the strength of her love for both of them.

347

It seemed to be the same. She wasn't ready to explore that. Just needed someone to know. Someone who'd understand and who she trusted.

Her real issue was that she was uncomfortable with what she was doing. And that was strongest regarding her unAwakened brother. He hero worshipped Qwelby, was looking to her as a sort of elderest and she felt she was failing him by not living up to some standard or other. And that meant she must be failing Tullia who was her youngerest. Yet it was her love for all three and her commitment to the six of them who made up XOÑOX that was driving her performances and wild dances. And she knew that her increasing reputation was an important part of the growth of the teenage "Twins Come Home" movement.

Confessing all that, Tamina had ruefully acknowledged that she needed Aunt Gallia's reminder of the holographic nature of the cosmos, where each tiniest part was a representation of the whole. And that actions were not the key, but deep emotions were and where there was action, the emotions that prompted those. She had been so focussed on what she was doing in the physical world that she had forgotten the power of the non-physical that permeated everything.

Lellia had talked of The Great Ocean underlying the Cosmic Hologram. Acting on that hologram, Tamina's powerful love had to be reaching the twins, as well as being a part of her energies that were reaching out through her actions in support of them and their return.

Tamina had spoken about the time just over a tenday ago when she'd explained what she'd discovered about the Uddîšû, and been forced to say more than she wanted by shy Shimara. The fifteen-year-old had hugged and kissed Tamina, saying 'Our shield,' and thoughtshared an image of an orb of salamanders protecting them all. When Lellia had made a "That says it all" gesture, tears had come to Tamina's eyes as she remembered nearly a moon ago when Shimmy had offered to be sisters. She acknowledged that

348

the young girl had more inner strength than people recognised, yet she had doubted that. Thanking Aunt Lellia for the insight and opening herself to Shimmy's strength, both through the subtlety of the non-physical and by talking with her, Tamina had plunged ever more vigorously into the SubNet Kulture, setting aside for later consideration her confusion over her feelings for the twins.

Mizena had become comfortable with her regular checks on her children's energy quotients because the news of what had to be their healthy state – energy growth equivalent to their attending college almost every single day – was heartening news for everyone and a constant reminder of their Aurigan heritage.

Whilst the family and friends were breakfasting, Lungunu shivered as the Stroems SuperXzyled so heavily that Lellia called Lift for an emergency trip.

Lift arrived. Well it had to be because what else could it be? They were looking at a vertical oblong box of dark wood, the side facing them had a strange pattern of bronze coloured metal grills, which turned out to be a pair of doors as they creakingly slid apart. Above the doors was a semi-circle bearing a series of names and a large pointer – which was resting on "Breakfast Room".

'Going up,' Lift announced in a posh voice. 'Elder Lellia and StroemFriends to Stroem Cavern. Then going down. Keepers to the laboratory.' Jerking and creaking the doors closed, the pointer moved to "Stroem Cavern" and Lift appeared to rise through the ceiling.

'What was that!?' Mizena asked as Lift departed.

Looking embarrassed, Mandara and Shandur shrugged apologetically. 'Been researching conditions on Earth,' her husband said.

'Testing my translators,' Mandara added, trying not to look like a naughty schoolboy.

It was not long before Lift returned Lellia and the four BestFriends to the main gatherroom where the others were waiting. Lift departed and Lellia gestured to the youngsters to sit as she seated herself by her husband.

'The Stroems have shown us that a key opportunity will exist,' Shimara said, blushing at having been chosen as spokesperson. 'As we understand it, there's a point in space-time-consciousness where several tides will harmonise. Amongst them are a purple and lilac, and a red and green.'

'The twins' colours,' Mizena and Shandur said together.

'CuSho said we must leave as soon as we've prepared for a long journey,' Wrenden said.

'And we must take Óweppâ, our Talisman, with us,' Tamina added.

'This is all so vague,' Mizena protested.

'Natural when dealing with dimensional discontinuity,' Lellia replied. 'And it's not just the Stroems here. Their colourswirling showed that all six Stroems have been involved in discovering that point in the Cosmic Hologram.'

An intense thoughtshare by the adults was followed by Lellia returning to the Stroems to continue orchestrating the balance of all six and the two men exploring with CuSho what alterations were necessary for a long trip. Mizena discussed with Tamina and Wrenden what provisions they wanted, then the two Keepers joined the discussions with CuSho.

Lellia kept to herself the sense that as all six Stroems had been involved, the matter was crucial to the Vertazia-Azura link and "long" almost certainly applied all three aspects of space-time-consciousness. Later, she shared with her husband that amongst the swirlings were colours confirming their speculations. Each twin was experiencing temporal discontinuity.

The changes to CuSho's Tazian room were soon completed. Having transweaved, Shandur returned with Jailandur and Yarannah. With hugs and kisses all around and tears from Yarannah and Mizena, Tamina and Wrenden assumed their posts as Keepers and CuSho departed.

Rulcas was no longer a mere gang leader, he had become the Boss, the Proton. His early years amongst mainstream Tazii had given him an edge over his less mentally skilled associates, but now he was well out of his comfort zone. Lungunu was full of thoughts that for him were an indecipherable cacophony. The imperatives to advise Dryddnaa and Xaala of what was happening were pressing on him, but he feared discovery.

Swept along with all the action he managed to be by himself for long enough to thoughtsend Dryddnaa the simple alert they'd agreed. Seconds later a cool breeze wafted through his mind as she extracted the memory he'd encapsulated. He sent his other alert to Xaala. Again, the memory was extracted.

Once again Lungunu drew in all five wings and hunkered down as, Xzyling exuberantly, the Stroems completed the defences by smearing the outside with a camouflage pattern of Xzyliment.

Rulcas had been at Lungunu for five days and as yet no decision had yet been made about his having a mini apartment within the XOÑOX suite. Thus he did not have to feign either his surprise or his delight when Pelnak and Shimara asked him to join them to provide supporting meditations from the comfort of their gatherroom.

CHAPTER 70

HIDENSEEK

THE KALAHARI

A chill woke Tullia up, leaving her feeling unsettled. She'd been in a beautiful dreamstate, curled up in her twin's arms with her head resting on his well-developed chest. And in love with him! Why had her unconscious shown her such a ridiculously impossible future!?

The bottom edge of the sun had already slipped below the horizon. Time to act. H'ani had shyly offered her a farewell present of a small, serrated knife in a sheath he'd made for it, explaining that it had two narrow slots in the back so it could hang, as it now did, from one of the side ties of her skirtlet. Keeping a careful watch, she cut branches and then dug for maramas. She ate one and stuffed the others in the pockets of her skirt. Using the belt she made her clothes and digging sticks into a neat bundle.

The sun set and the millions of stars in the Milky Way lit the bush clearly as she made her way to the fence and listened for the electricity flowing through the single wire. Crouched low so the wire was level with her ear, she followed the fence further downhill. Her luck was in. After a few hundred metres the sound stopped. During the journey, Kemah had told her that was not an unusual occurrence as cattle liked rubbing against the wire for the sensation it gave them.

She pushed her clothes through the space between wires, adroitly slid over, gathered all her clothes and walked to the next fence. Kemah had explained that there were two fences because a Kudu could easily leap a single fence of almost three metres and the space between them was the roadway for the maintenance vehicles.

In the still night air she could hear the electricity gently humming. She loped along for a few hundred metres before deciding that she was losing too much time. Carefully inspecting the fence she found the largest space between wires. Undoing her bundle, she placed her clothes on the wire and cautiously slid over it.

Checking that her necklace, the tubers and the precious package that Roland had given her were safely stored in the pockets, she retied her bundle, located the Southern Cross as a reassuring check and set off at a steady run. She was hoping that Roland would manage to persuade Mr Frank to wait for her. If not, then she must carry on south, cross the border, and with the help of her twin's energy, find Siboniso, who Xameb had said was the most powerful Shaman in all of southern Africa.

The sand of the tyre tracks was too deep to run on, but the ground was reasonably firm in the centre. Navigation was not necessary as the track was straight as an arrow all the way alongside the fence.

The faint smile on her face at the idea she was running towards her twin was wiped off when the quiet of the night was broken by the sound of an engine behind her. She turned and watched. The vehicle was a long way behind but it took only a few seconds before the bright lights told her it was driving along the same track. So, not a maintenance vehicle. The police? Why now? Once again an image of the prison cell flashed before her eyes and she shivered.

Taking a few deep breaths, she ran her hands over her tiny skirtlet, reminding herself of all she'd learnt with the Meera. 'Tyua'llia Rrîl'zânâ Mizenatyr. !Gei-!Ku'ma. Now is the time for you to really become a Bushman.'

353

She turned and ran, watching the ground and using her Kuzwayo, her seventh sense, to keep a check on the vehicle. It was being driven fast. Much faster than Ditau had driven the light Land Rover. The police were anxious to catch her! Had they tortured Tsetsana into telling them where she'd gone? Easing her pace she felt for her BestFriend and smiled as she sensed a proud and relaxed young woman, safe and unharmed.

Thanking his good sense for having spent part of his small budget on extra satellite phones, whilst Ditau had driven fast back to the main road from the Research Village, Inspector Modisakgosi had called the Veterinary crossing. He'd exploded when the segeant had to tell him that the girl had been arrested but allowed to escape. His subsequent orders had been simple. The night relief for the crossing was about to arrive. In the Landcruiser were a sergeant and two constables. With little traffic at night, the relief sergeant was to operate the crossing and the others were to pursue and capture the girl, now wanted as a possible security threat.

The lights were coming closer. Too close. Tullia dived off the track and dodged between the bushes. This was a game reserve. No-one lived here and the area was much wilder than where she'd been living. Although slowing her movement, the closely packed bushes provided excellent cover and there were no tracks for vehicles.

She settled down behind a clump of low acacias. Lowering her head she looked up through her now very long, curved eyelashes. She had grown in so many ways since her Awakenings and they provided excellent shielding for her bright eyes. She watched as the half truck rocketed past and disappeared over the next downward curve. She ate one of the maramas as she watched it drive on for a long way. It stopped and the lights were extinguished.

Game on! She made her way back to the track and ran. Tazian against Azurii. This was easy!

Bright lights dazzled her. Shocked, she stopped. The lights were a little to the left. She threw herself down and crawled as fast as possible through the bush, wincing as the thorns slashed her flesh. The lights swung around. Stupid! Stupid! Stupid! she berated herself for underestimating the Azurii. They had pulled the cruiser off the track and hidden it behind a clump of acacias. The lights had come from higher up than normal headlights.

Hearing doors open and shut then the sound of voices followed by movement, she stopped and focussed her senses. Two lights were still swinging around covering the area where she was and she heard three people moving. HideNSeek! No Tazian game but deadly consequences if they locked her away in that prison.

She focussed into her Kore and drew together her Tazian skills and Bushman training. She thought for a moment and decided not to draw on her twin's energy. She had to do this herself. As her breathing and pulse rate settled down she observed that there was a somewhat haphazard pattern to the swinging lights. Peering through the bushes she saw the three searchers clearly silhouetted against the billions of stars. In the still night the noise of their clothes catching on the thorns was so loud she did not even need to see them. Each time the lights swung away from her, she moved as silently as possible.

Slowly, ever so slowly, she moved back and to the left then swung around in a long arc to get close to the track. It took ages as the lights were now swinging across a much wider area and the police had both switched on their own torches and widened the area of the search, calling out to each other and cursing as each time they thought they'd found her, but hadn't.

The thick bush that slowed the searchers and made them so noisy was great for her concealment, but terrible for the number of long sharp thorns cutting her flesh. She grimaced at the thought that without clothes to catch and jerk the bushes, at least she wasn't making any noise.

She heard a discussion start. Whether to continue searching or drive further on and try again and, if necessary, keep that going until daylight when a helicopter would be used.

Why am I so important? Blazing Novas! Surely they cannot know what I am?! Think, Tullia, think. The cruiser. Without that they are helpless. She slipped into her memories of riding with Kemah and Constable Ditau and all the questions they'd answered. She knew what to do. Could she? She had to. She'd have only one chance. Failure was not an option.

Although the night was cold she was sweating and the smell of the lovely mixtures of the bush was now spoilt by the acrid tang of her fear. Again gritting her teeth against the pain, she crawled silently to the edge of the track well in front of the cruiser. She lay down on the soft sand, easing the tension in her muscles and softy moaning into the back of her wrist as she let out the pent-up pain from so many cuts.

On all fours she crawled to the front of the cruiser. Facing away from her, two men were standing in the back, operating the searchlights mounted on the cab. They were talking quietly. Putting down her bundle of clothes she crawled to the driver's door. With the truck facing downhill, that was shielded from the searchers out in the bush. She stood, peered in and saw the key fob sitting in a depression in the centre console.

She reached up and grasped the door handle.

'I need a pee,' a voice above her said. The man moved, the truck dipped slightly and Tullia opened the door. She heard and felt the man walk to the back of the truck and stop. The truck bounced slightly as he jumped down and she slipped into the cab, keeping the door a crack open. She heard the expected mixture of sounds and waited, poised. The truck dipped again as the man grabbed the back. As he hauled himself over the tailgate, Tullia, key fob in hand, was out of the cab in a flash and stood flat against the side of the truck, a hand on the door.

'Needed that,' the same voice said.

Tullia slowly took her hand away from the door and scuttled into the cover of the thick bushes lining the road, picked up her bundle and breathed easily. The thick covering that had concealed the cruiser did the same for her as, crouching low, she made her way down the edge of the track.

Far enough away, there was no point in continuing to be careful. She stepped onto the centre of the track and sprinted. Seconds later a searchlight beam lit her up. Shouts and swearing, the sounds of people crashing through the bush and more swearing as thorns ripped clothes and flesh. Doors slamming.

Silence.

Tullia smiled and heaved a sigh of relief as she eased back into a steady run.

Moments later a howl of anger carried across the still night air, followed by a string of curses. Tullia recognised the sergeant's voice threatening all sorts of dire consequences when she was finally caught. Holding in her mind the image her twin had sent of the island and setting a mental reminder to listen out for a whirlybird at daybreak, she continued at her steady pace.

Thinking of her twin and the island and home, her thoughts turned to Tamina. Oh, how she longed to share girly stuff with her Elderest, now woman to woman. Share what she'd discovered of Aurigan Self Defence, her fight with that slender Tazian girl and new dance rhythms. Happy thoughts powered her long legs as she ran on

and on

and on.

Modisakgosi's immediate reaction when he answered the Sat Phone was anger and frustration, followed by a moment's sympathy for the sergeant. She was overbearing and annoying but a good officer, and he knew she would take it hard at being outwitted. 'I'll send Ditau with the spare key in the morning. Sorry. It's the best I can do. You know how short staffed we are.'

'Yes. Sir. The helicopter.'

'Yes, sergeant, of course. I'll keep you posted if there are any changes.'

'Yes. Goodnight. Sir.'

357

CHAPTER 71

SO NEAR

THE KALAHARI

Frank and Kemah were up as the first tints of pale blue started to spread across the sky. By the time it was light the students had been woken and breakfast was ready. Earl had been quiet since the incident at the Veterinary post and even Pamela was too tired to whinge.

The meal finished, working in pairs as usual, everything was soon stowed on board and the campsite cleared. Marianne walked back to the top of the nearest rise so as to look along to the next false summit. She walked back, shaking her head.

Frank looked at Lishi. She smiled sadly. She knew how fond he had grown of his Lionesta and felt bad about abandoning her, although there was no more he could have done. He signalled to Kemah and Danny and they started up their vehicles. Frank's own sounded rough, running unevenly. He revved the engine but it did not improve.

Tullia saw the first fingers of light starting to spear the sky to her left. The sun edged over the horizon and lit the track a long way ahead. There was no campsite to be seen. Despair flooded her and she collapsed. She ate the last of her precious supply of tubers as

358

she examined the track, confirming what she knew, that heavy vehicles had passed by only a few hours ago.

Aching all over, she got up and forced herself on. She had to reach them before they moved on as it would take at least two days hard travelling to reach their next campsite. And would they still be there when she arrived?

She was staggering. The sun was heating up and sweat was trickling into her eyes, making everything blurred. She heard a noise, stopped walking and listened. It was an engine. Then another and a third. They were leaving! In despair, she forced herself into a pathetic run, pleading with the Multiverse to let them be close so she'd see them past the next dip.

'Damn! Engine trouble. That's the last thing I want,' Frank said, switching off the engine and signalling to the others. Out of the cab, he lifted the bonnet up and he and Danny looked it over.

'Can't be the carburettor. That's been serviced recently,' Frank said.

They started the engine again and agreed, the next likely cause was the spark plugs.

'Spare set?' Danny asked, as Frank killed the engine and got down.

'Of course,' Frank replied, indignantly.

Tullia heard the engines stop. Then one started up again. It did that a couple more times then stopped. Something was wrong. She had hope. Tears of exhaustion filled her eyes. Along with the sweat, her vision was blurring even more. The bright white sand of the tyre tracks, the dark of the bushes and trees, she staggered on, pleading with the Multiverse to help her.

Her thighs and calves were aching brutally. Her bare feet hurt from several cuts and the many cuts all over her body were stinging from the sweat dripping into them. For a third time she missed her footing on the centre of the track and fell, sprawling full length.

Weeping, too tired to brush the sand off, she pulled herself upright and limped on.

Modisakgosi looked at his watch. It was time to telephone again. He'd arrived early at the station and spoken to Ditau as soon as the young constable arrived, sending him off to rescue the sergeant and her team. He'd typed up his report and, as required during last night's telephone call to the Air Support Branch in Gaborone, followed that up by emailing a formal request for the helicopter.

The "Squirrel", as it was named, was equipped with day and night tracking that even a Bushman would not be able to evade. The duty sergeant was apologetic in explaining that there had been several requests for the few choppers and the Inspector's was one of those awaiting a decision. Modisakgosi put the phone down with mixed feelings.

His daughter was happy there was to be no circumcision. He'd not had to say anything. His wife had meekly accepted the wish of an extraterrestrial – as she and his daughter believed his erstwhile prisoner to be. Modisakgosi would be very happy if the girl was not caught for, if she were and thus proved not to be an ET, then the arguments at home about his daughter's circumcision would start up again.

The third spark plug was surprisingly blackened compared to the previous two. Frank shrugged and they replaced it with a new one. The engine fired and ran sweetly. As Danny closed the bonnet Frank got down from the cab and signalled to everyone to climb back on board. He got back into his cab with a grim look on his face.

Roland nodded a silent acknowledgment that Tullia still had not reached them.

With a last moment's hesitation, Frank engaged the gears and pulled away, concerned about how far along the side track the sand was going to support the heavy Cruisers.

Tullia heard an engine start up, then it sounded louder and faster. She was in despair and without even the mental strength to plead with the Multiverse.

Then a second engine started and a third. Finally, they were leaving! She was so close. She wanted to call out but her mouth was dry and she had no strength.

Loud sounds, odd hooting sounds she'd never heard before. Elephants? Surely not, but what? They sounded like a warning, an emergency. Was she going out of her mind? Blinded by sweat in her eyes, she staggered on. A dark shape appeared in front of her. She was going to crash into a tree. She stumbled to the side.

It moved.

A tree that moved. She was delirious. She crashed into it.

'Tyua'llia!'

Uh...?

The tree put its branches around her. They were soft.

'Tyua'llia.'

'Kemah?'

She sagged against him and was lowered to the ground. She tried to wipe her eyes with the back of her hands, looked up into his grinning face and smiled.

Scarcely had Frank finished changing up through the gears than there had come a blast of horns from behind. Looking in his wing mirror he'd seen Kemah flashing his lights. With a curse at more delay, he'd pulled to a halt and swung out of the cab to hear voices shouting. 'She's here!' 'Tullia!' As Frank reached the back of the last Cruiser he saw his Lionesta stagger along the track and fall into Kemah's arms.

'My Africa!' Frank said in a tone of wonder as he thought about all the things that had conspired to delay them.

'Water!' Frank shouted as he strode through the students, knelt by Tullia and saw a weary smile on her sweat soaked face.

'Sorry I'm late Mr Frrrank,' she croaked.

'I wasn't planning on an early start anyway,' he said in a gruff voice as Roland knelt down with a bottle of water in his hand.

Tullia eased herself into a more comfortable position in Kemah's arms as she took the bottle and drank little sips.

Kemah helped her to her feet and led her into the shade of his cruiser and propped her up against the front. Marianne arrived carrying a plate of bread, meat and cheese. She was followed by Becky. 'You're so badly cut?' the nurse said.

'Bush too thick. Police noisy. Cover my noise,' she said as Becky went to her Cruiser and returned with a black sack containing Tullia's few possessions. 'Is true what girls tell me. Good part of living in Research Village,' she said as she took out a towel, flannel and soap, thanked Danny for another bottle of water and quickly washed herself. Dry, she was stopped from dressing by Becky who insisted on wiping antiseptic over the myriad of cuts as various people explained what had happened to delay them.

Drink and food consumed, Tullia put on her skirt and tank top. 'I see new track?'

Frank looked at her bright twirling eyes, felt his head nod and shrugged his shoulders at his wife. This young woman was not one of their daughters, but... He accompanied Tullia and Kemah along the side track for a lot further than he'd previously gone. He looked at Kemah, raising his eyebrows.

'Bushman,' the half San said.

As she knelt for the third time to examine the tracks, Tullia grinned with pleasure. Yeah. And a Tazian with a boy twin to get the best of. 'Light vehicle. If weather conditions same. Long time. Five days.' She looked up at Frank. 'Good track. Sand deep but okay for heavy trucks.' She shrugged her shoulders. 'I feel. Like day with Ditau,' she added, referring to the time she'd detected deep sand that had not been obvious from the tyre tracks. 'Keep steady speed. No stop.'

Having used the depth rod in an earlier section of the track, Frank was again impressed by Tullia's skills. Explaining why he agreed with her observation about speed, he was rewarded by a beaming smile and sparkling eyes and the weird sensation that he was looking at a happy young child. As he ordered everyone back on board he decided to have her in his cab rather than in the last cruiser with Kemah.

Soon, Tullia's eyes were glazing over from the warm comfort of the cab. She remembered Kemah had told her that when he was not driving he sometimes rode scout on top. Before Roland had time to stop her, she climbed onto the seat, slipped out of the window and up onto the roof where she settled herself amongst all the gear that was stored on the roof rack.

In response to Frank's bark of surprise, her voice floated down. 'Kemah tell me this.'

Frank was muttering about what he would do to Kemah when they next stopped when Tullia called out, 'I have good view and I safe.'

Frank was wondering what he could do. He did not want to stop because the sand was quite deep and he needed to keep the whole convoy moving at just the right speed. He did not want to shout her down into the cab while they were moving.

'Track fork right. Two hundred paces,' Tullia called down. 'Narrow but looks good,' she added as they got closer.

There was silence as they arrived at the fork and Frank carefully swung onto the new track. After a few minutes he breathed a sigh of relief as he discovered the sand was shallower. He checked his wing mirrors to ensure that the rest of the convoy had followed safely.

Frank relaxed as he realised that his scout high above the cabin was an excellent spotter. Not only was she regularly calling out the depth of the sand far ahead, from time to time she also called out and pointed in the direction of kudu, ostrich or some other animal or bird for the group to photograph through the open windows – made possible as this was not a game reserve with dangerous animals such as big cats around. Or Tullia would not have been allowed to stay on top!

Eventually, they rejoined the main track and Tullia slid in through the window. 'Not cross with Kemah,' she said looking at Frank, made her eyes go round and fluttered her very long lashes whilst giving him a cheeky grin. 'I do good?'

'Ptah!' Frank spluttered. 'Not cross Kemah and you do good.' He shook his head in amusement, happily recalling the times when his own daughters had done similar things.

A few moments later Tullia's head was resting on Roland's shoulder as she fell fast asleep.

CHAPTER 72

SHARING

RΛIΛTEΛ

On Saturday, following Miki's advice to use his own sitting room on the top floor, Romain introduced Qwelby to his doctoral assistants: the doll-like Japanese-American, Miki Tamagusuku-Jefferson in her late thirties and her older, well-built Jamaican-American husband, Tyler Jefferson. Miki's dark skin and the red tint to Tyler's dark brown colour from a Native American ancestor made Qwelby feel very comfortable.

Wanting to help Qwelby feel relaxed and settle in to "returning home" all three were wearing typical Raiatean clothes. Miki, a multi patterned knee length dress in soft peach on cream; the men conventional slacks with brightly patterned short sleeved tops; Romain's was a series of green and olive vines on a cream background, Tyler a swirling pattern in orange and white.

Using his compiler in what he thought of as its second mode – translating the French into Tazian and suggesting answers – gave Qwelby time to think through what he was going to say in the limited French he had personally learnt during the journey. He spent Saturday and Sunday talking about Vertazia, his home, family and friends and especially about Tullia, his older sister who was still at home. Making her some eighteen months older, he gave her birthday as the same as Tamina's and described the two girls as being like twins. Along with mentioning the not-twins of Pelnak and Shimara, that was intended to cover any slips he might make if he referred to Tullia as his twin.

Romain agreed with Qwelby that the youth should reassure his friends in Finland that all was well and repeat their need to keep his identity secret. Miki set up a series of links so that the communication could not be traced back to Raiatea. Qwelby sent another series of video messages, saying he was now safe and happily settled and to remember his Turkish story as it was still very important to keep his real identity secret. Knowing Hannu had taken lots of videos of the Snow Village, he added with a smile that where they'd been was no longer a secret.

'He thinks HoloBlitz is great,' Qwelby said. 'So realistic how the holograms project from the phone.'

Romain smiled as he nodded to Miki. 'One of our rewarding inventions.'

The following two days were spent in one of the conference rooms on the third floor as Qwelby explained the basics of Tazian science and inevitably learnt a lot about Azuran knowledge and theories. Wanting to have what Hannu had described whilst teaching Qwelby how to play cards as "An ace up the sleeve," Qwelby continued to keep secret the existence of his compiler, this time speaking fluent Finnish. Romain explained that they would speak English as that was used extensively for science and mathematics. A computer was used to provide real-time translation and Qwelby was happy to explain that his rapid learning of English was due to having learnt a little in Finland, the syntax and grammatical construction being very similar to his own language and an excellent memory.

With mounting excitement the scientists listened to the alien's explanation of what the Tazii considered to be the fundamental particle of all existence, the Kwozakubezeninii – shortened to kuznii, as being half matter and half anti-matter held in dynamic

366

balance by Shadow Energy, which the scientists interpreted to mean Dark Energy. They saw that as an answer to the question of what "physical particle" lay under the quantum world, as far too many quantum particles were still being discovered for them to obey one of the fundamental principles of the basic structure of the Universe – simplicity.

All four were in agreement over the existence and function of what the Azuran scientists termed the unified field and the Tazii the Great Ocean in intentional-ising the quantum field which then in-formed the physical world.

They saw his journey across dimensions, spending what had turned out to be seven days spread throughout the cosmos as uncountable "bits" of pure information, not only as a major proof of information = matter = energy and a confirmation of holographic in-formation theory, but also confirmation of the principles of matter transport – the teleportation beloved by science fiction fans.

Late afternoon on the fourth day when the discussion had turned to successes Earth scientists were having with the transmission of data on photons, Qwelby commented that the Tazii used dynamic nonlocality to effect matter transport, what they termed TransWeaving.

'Entanglement?' Tyler asked.

Qwelby raised his eyebrows.

'A pair or more of, say, photons, linked across a distance. The one changing when the other does,' Romain explained.

'Yes. As you step through the Deconstruction Field, a plane of light, photons, transfers the "bits" of your information to a subsystem of photonic clusters. That cluster is then projected onto the photon group in the transmitter, and the cluster, those "bits" of you, appears instantaneously in the linked photon group in the assembly grid in the receiver.'

'For a racc you say also uses energy as a sort of currency, that must cost a lot,' Tyler commented.

Qwelby nodded.

The scientists well knew that although nonlocality, or entanglement, was part of Einstein's' theories and he had denied it, calling it "Fuzzy action at a distance," nowadays the "transmission" of data from one entangled photon to another was a common laboratory experiment, right up to the "sending" of pure minerals such as diamond crystals. But human beings, and whilst moving...

'Qwelby looks very tired,' Miki said. 'I'm sure he needs a rest.' He nodded, and Miki continued by proposing a programme for the future. Qwelby would have a late breakfast and join the scientists after their mid-morning break, discussion to continue through a working lunch and then Qwelby to have the afternoon free to swim and sunbathe before a pre-dinner session, which would finish about seven as it became dark. Enthusiastic about sunbathing, Qwelby just managed to stop short of saying he needed to catch-up with his twin's summer colour.

The scientists were only too happy for Qwelby to leave so as to start exploring the thoughts that were on their minds. The fourth neutrino that Romain had discovered, which they had used in the experiment that had brought Qwelby to Earth, and was, like all "particles," paired with its anti-particle but unique because the two parts were pair-bonded. Could it be split and used in a similar power-generating manner to the kuznii? Could they be used for what Qwelby described as dynamic nonlocality to develop their previous experiments to provide a means of matter relocation on Earth? And then the next stage. Could such a device be combined with the rhythmic entrainment that was keeping the alien stable in the third dimension to create an inter-dimensional transport to reach into his world in the fifth dimension?

It was late when they eventually retired with minds full of challenging questions, thoughts of all the experiments to come and the possibilities of great fame and fortune.

After his dip in the pool on Wednesday morning, Hokuao served Qwelby his usual breakfast. He wasn't really hungry for all the cheese, cold meats, bread, honey, jam and fruit. He buttered some of the freshly baked French baton, added jam and munched away as he reviewed progress.

He was aware of the scientists' frustration and from Tyler a mixture of dislike and disbelief. Qwelby had not been able to do more than explain basic principles, all too often ending up saying that for specific details they'd have to ask his father or Great-Great Uncle Mandara.

What Tyler would not accept was what Qwelby referred to as the fourth dimension being consciousness or super-consciousness. Nor that Qwelby was not able to thought communicate with home because it was only possible to reach out beyond the slow vibrations of the third dimension in dreams and meditation. Tyler had been seriously discomforted when Qwelby had thoughtwrapped the scientists into their first visit to Vertazia and had refused to "listen" to any more, instead having to rely on his wife's reports.

The discussions were useful to Qwelby from two different perspectives. Tyler accepted the existence of the unified field but saw it as doing no more than in-form the physical world and was uncomfortable with Qwelby referring to it as the Great Ocean. Romain was prepared to explore any theory if it might show him a way to prove the existence of other dimensions. Miki was very interested in pursuing the non-physical or esoteric implications of the Great Ocean. That was just what Qwelby wanted. A different focus by each member of the three person partnership that he might be able to manipulate to his advantage.

And Qwelby was confirmed in his initial opinion that there was no way that Romain and his colleagues were able to help him return home. Now, he had to wait for Tullia to arrive – when they would leave the island. How? He needed to visit the town and the port. Hiding away on a ship seemed the obvious choice.

Surprised, he looked at his empty plate, laughed and thought of the afternoon when Angélle, as he had taken to calling her, would come up and they'd spend time together until it was time for his second session with the scientists.

He was worried about the faint image in the Kalahari that Romain had shown him and which had appeared on the professor's detector screens at the same time as the large disturbance when he'd arrived in Finland. Romain had been pressing him to explain.

It was too small to be Tullia, yet that's where she was. In desperation he'd offered the suggestion of the Unidirectional Transweave Projector, saying it had been in his satchel but he'd not seen it since leaving Vertazia. Both statements were true but omitted the fact that he had taken it out of Fill Me when he and Tullia had used it to escape from the stairwell and ended up on the top of a Bell Tower. It had proved to be a disastrous mistake as the Professor was now planning a trip to Botswana. After his kidnapping, Qwelby had become obsessed with keeping Tullia's presence on Earth a secret from Romain and the others. It was like a safety net and he was desperately searching for something to say to stop Romain travelling to the Kalahari and finding his twin.

CHAPTER 13

SALT PANS

THE KALAHARI

The convoy was making good progress when the land changed with a speed that was startling. It was as though an architect had drawn a line straight across it. They drove out of the bush and onto a flat, green savannah which stretched as far as the eye could see in every direction. There were no bushes but a few trees looking as though artistically placed around the landscape. Frank slowed to a halt and declared a lunch break.

Tullia grunted as she got down from the cab and steadied herself against it for a moment.

'No work for you now,' Roland said.

'Lion need Lionesta,' she said with a cheeky grin.

With the kitchen trailer secured and its side dropped down, cutlery and food were rapidly spread around and everyone started to tuck in. Frank explained that the stop needed to be very short because they'd lost so much time and he was concerned about getting to the Saltpans before the sun set.

Shortly after the convoy restarted, and almost as abruptly as before, the landscape changed again. The trees were gone and the grass had become much longer, growing in thick, heavy clumps. The Landcruisers slowed and had to wind their way around now

371

clearly defined sand paths. The sun was drawing close to the horizon and Frank was concerned. Finding a stretch of hard sand, he drew the convoy to a halt. 'Devil's must,' he muttered to Roland as he got out of the cab and walked back to speak to Tullia who had returned to being with Kemah. 'Will you come and scout for me again? I need your keen eyes looking ahead.'

With a big grin, Tullia dropped from the cab and followed Frank to his Cruiser while he explained what she was to look for, then pointed out the more secure way up the fitted ladder at the back. Satisfied that she was safe on the top, he climbed in, closed the door and the convoy set off.

'The edges of the Saltpans are very varied,' Frank explained to Roland. 'We could drive for a long time following this path, yet there may be places to the left or right where we can camp for the night. Up on top, Tullia can see over the grassy hillocks.'

The lower rim of the sun was just touching the horizon when Tullia called out she could see an open stretch of sand. She answered Frank's questions, he slowed and turned the cruiser onto the high terrain. The vehicle lived up to its reputation and steadily forged ahead, lurching left and right as it pulled its trailer across the rough, heavily clumped grass. The others followed. Sure enough it was only a few minutes drive before they reached a spit of sand that had lanced deeply into the surrounding grasslands.

Soon all three vehicles were on the flat. When they'd stopped for lunch, Frank had spoken with Lishi, Kemah and Danny. They'd all agreed that if they found a spur of sand whilst it was light, they would drive fast out onto the Pans. It would be dark by the time they stopped but with the lights of the three Cruisers, an onboard generator and their own torches, pitching camp in the dark would not be a problem.

As the last vestiges of light left the sky, Frank's arm circling outside the cab signalled to laager for the night and the three vehicles came to a halt in a neat semi-circle.

Lishi smiled as she watched Tullia work with Kemah to stabilise the kitchen trailer, open it up and take out a can of beer which she carried to Frank and offered to him with a little curtsy.

Coming up by her side Marianne spoke softly. 'I showed her how to do that. She asked me what was appropriate for a Lionesta and her Lion.' Smile gone, Marianne asked, 'Will she ever get back home, do you think?'

'If last night is anything to go by, then I think she will be able to slip across the border,' was all Lishi had time to say as Tullia walked up and proffered a can of beer.

'Tullia,' Lishi stopped the girl as she started to turn away. 'No more work for you tonight. Rest. And that's an order,' she said with a smile.

Later, around the camp fire, the meal finished, Frank explained all about the salt flats, their history and their extent. After a brief discussion as to who was committed to getting up in time to watch the sun rise, a hardy group set out their chairs before they all retired for the night.

Tullia awoke whilst it was still dark and lay in her comfortable bed in the back of a Cruiser, thinking. Decision made, she got up, put on her loinskin and necklace, grabbed a blanket as she slipped out of the tailgate and padded her way to Roland's tent. A few minutes later she had him seated on a blanket, facing due East.

'You must be freezing,' he said as she removed the blanket from around her shoulders and offered it to him.

'I Tazian. Make inner fire. And Bushman. Honour sun.'

Roland nodded. He'd learnt from her that each Bushman greeted the sun of a new day in their own way, often making the slightest of nods towards it as they kissed the back of a thumb.

'Xameb tell me. This very special place. When sky right you see whole world as picture upside down in big circle.' She thought about switching on her compiler and decided against it. She liked speaking with Tazian economy of words. 'Bushmen here since

373

time began. Sun only rise because they greet it. When no more Bushmen. Sun not need to rise.'

She paused and looked down into Roland's eyes. They had talked a lot about science, quantum science, superconsciousness and the differences between their worlds. She knew he did not agree with what she was now saying. For this brief period of her life she was a Bushman and not a Tazian. She saw Roland slowly nod his head, acknowledging that she was in a different time-and-space. Quantized.

She sat down. 'Hold my hand,' she commanded in a soft voice and turned them back to face the East. The sky lightened. The first rays of the sun caught thin wisps of cloud, turning them into varying hues of salmon pink. The very sky itself greeted the watchers by spreading a thin band of clouds as far as they could see from left to right just above the horizon, catching and reflecting the sun's rays.

Slowly, the massive yellow orb of the sun rose, turning orange as it progressed, momentarily red and then its deep bright shining yellowy orange. In front of them there were no shadows. There was nothing between the watchers and the edge of the world as the sun majestically climbed up the horizon.

Roland was in two places at once. Watching the magnificence of the sunrise and being drawn into the world of a Bushman. Time shifted and he was taken forward – days, months, years, centuries into the future. Nothing changed. Every morning the sun rose over the edge of the world and in return for the homage of a multitude of "Original People" it blessed the whole world with its life giving warmth.

'My sister, Šem-eš-a, with her salamanders,' Tullia said in a voice that seemed to echo from the beginning of time. 'She was not pleased when you mortals changed her name to Shamash and worshipped her as a male God. Neither was I, Zeyusa, to be called Zeus and made father of the Gods.'

Powerful energies were flowing from Tullia's hand through

the whole of Roland's body. From the side, he could just see that her purple orbs had turned to gold and her usually blue ovals had become purple, all limned in silver. Roland, whose lifelong studies into quantum and esoteric sciences had brought him to the conclusion that they were merely using different language to express the same underlying concepts, felt himself suspended in time and space as a series of images flashed by of what humans called Gods and Goddesses, psychologists called Archetypes, and Tullia, her people, the original Auriganii.

'Ereshkiegal to Pluto, Tiamat to Neptune,' he whispered, and was bathed in Tullia's smile as she turned to him and nodded. He remained staring into her eyes until she shook her head, let go his hand and got to her feet as her eyes returned to normal. 'I wish I here for solstice. Think how powerful.'

Roland frowned as he remembered discussions they'd had. 'A week before your arrival on Earth.'

'No. I left Vertazia day before winter solstice.'

A confused conversation followed until Roland established that Tullia's home was a little north and west of the mountains that were at the top of what the Tazii called "The Boot" – Italy. With a look of horror on her face, Tullia accepted that winter at their home meant summer where she now was, yet it was nearly four tendays after the winter solstice.

'I never go home!' she wailed.

'No,' Roland said firmly. 'You've been with your twin, wherever he is, and he and your friends have been here in the Kalahari. Not in the body. All of that was in the mind, or through dimensional travel.'

Tullia nodded. 'I never thought. I never... Xameb said Kaigii must be in very south of America where is winter.' She shook her head. 'I not want be Goddess. I want be young girl. Have home here. Be Bushman. Foolish child! I make like a NullPoint and live inside a bubble.' Calming herself, she took a deep breath. 'Tazii say: "Inside every genius a fool. Inside every fool a genius." Life's balance. Like the kuznii. Half matter, half anti-matter.'

'It takes a wise woman to know when she is a fool.'

Tullia threw back her head and laughed. 'Thank you Uncle Roland... Ah!' She clutched her head. 'Time difference is why hard to thoughtspeak twin. Thoughts are in fourth dimension of consciousness. Not third. Knew something wrong but not what.'

A rumbling sound as of muted thunder ran across the sands in front of the watchers. Tullia gripped Roland's hand as the ground shook and a hundred paces away the air shimmered as a waterfall appeared. Impossibly, the waterfall wrapped around itself and a shape slowly emerged. Squarish and off white, door and windows shifting, merging, darkening as behind a cloud of mist it appeared to finally become – a Botswanan hut?

It was built in traditional style with a thatched roof and walls of interwoven branches daubed with dried mud, but this one had an arched doorway with round windows either side and, curving over the doorway in a shimmering rainbow of colours was a name, Nuuskierige Winkel.

'Curious Shop,' Tullia translated the Afrikaans, remembered what Tamina had said during the night of the firefight and squealed in disbelief.

The mist cleared and two tall dark-skinned figures could be seen waving through the door's window.

Tullia was jumping up and down, shrieking like a young child, then calling out words in her rich, musical contralto that no one could understand. She ran towards the building. The door opened and she stepped inside. Her shout of joy was clearly heard back at the campsite where the others had been gathering around the fire that Kemah had just lit.

His legs stiff from having sat cross-legged for so long, Roland eased himself onto his feet. Tullia appeared in the doorway, calling to him and waving him on. He walked over, stepped inside and stopped in surprise when he saw two young people looking similar to Tullia, yet dressed as Bushmen.

Tullia introduced Tamina and Wrenden, then ran out saying she would be back in a moment.

Later, Roland was cross with himself that, facing two more aliens and with all the questions in his mind, all he asked was why they were dressed as Bushmen. He saw the logic in the technical energy based answer delivered in a beautiful singing voice and at the same time translated into English in his head.

Tullia ran back in, clutching her spear and an out of place, black plastic waste sack. She dropped them on the floor of hard packed earth.

'I still have your package, Roland,' she said as she gave him a big hug and a kiss.

'Good,' was all he could say, sad that he was about to say goodbye to a girl who for a few days had felt as if she was one of the younger generation in his family and, just like them, one of his teachers.

Tamina spoke a liquid musical language.

'Must go. Temporal discontinuity,' Tullia translated. 'Wrong solstice!' Like Xameb, Roland had been an uncle for her. Well, she was no longer a girl but a woman, a Quantum Woman. She put her hands either side of his head and gave him a long kiss on his forehead. Stepping back, she grinned as she saw the amazed look in his blue eyes.

Speechless, a dazed Roland left the building to what sounded like a happy scene from an opera. 'They're leaving,' he called out as he walked away, stopped and turned back to see Tullia standing behind the closed door and waving. He held a hand up and watched as the building slowly shimmered into invisibility as if retreating behind a waterfall. As it finally vanished there was a clap like thunder and a strong gust of wind which threw dust across the saltpans.

Together with the others he walked to where the building had been and they examined the depression made in the ground by the walls. 'It was a lot larger inside than this,' he said in a perplexed voice. He felt both elated and heart broken. Elated because Tullia had been rescued by her own people. Heart broken because there was so much more of her world, their ways, beliefs, power of thought and imagination that he wanted to hear about.

'I guess we've just seen the Vertazian Travelling Embassy,' he commented. Banal, stupid, unnecessary? It helped him break free of the spell that had descended upon him as Tullia had led him out of his tent. Yet the spell was to remain, deep inside and forever accessible.

Frank and Lishi sat in companionable silence for a time, watching the group as they breakfasted around the fire. 'I shall miss not having my Lionesta bring my cans of beer,' he said in a gruff voice.

PIRATES

IN-BETWEEN

Tamina issued rapid instructions to Tullia as CuSho left the SaltPans. 'Be very careful where you sit because your surroundings will change as we move. The safest place is there, by the two shimmering columns. Do not come close to this throughway. And you must not come through it until we are safely back on Vertazia. Eeky and I will go into the other room and explain more.'

She turned, grabbed hold of her brother who was still gazing at Tullia as though unable to believe they'd finally found her, pushed him through the waterfall door and followed into the Tazian room.

'This throughway acts like a biological computer,' a now naked Wrenden explained to an amazed Tullia as he stepped into a pair of ragged blue jeans and pulled on a green sweatshirt with the words "LONG BEACH VIKINGS" on the front. 'Latest Terran fashion,' he added, grinning.

'The waterfall changes us when we come through into the Terran shop and gives us appropriate clothes. Well.' Thinking of Finland, Tamina grimaced. 'What It thinks is appropriate.

She let her SalaSuit slide up her Form and partially close the front szeame. The bright orange and red Salamander Suit had been a gift from her father after he'd learnt that she had become L'Entangled with what was no longer the Uddîšû, but now her Uddîšû. It was similar to a BodyDance suit, more sentient and capable of containing her hair and extruding a hood complete with protective face cover.

'When we get back home it will change you into your normal vibrations of the fifth dimension. We'll explain more as we travel.'

Tullia opened her black sack and dressed once again in her dark green skirt and red and blue tank top. 'Made these myself. The people I was living with are a lot smaller than Tazii.' She ran her fingers through her long hair and thanked her good fortune that she'd reverted to her normal hair style, removing the many beads the girls had added when they'd plaited it.

She settled herself comfortably and her friends started to explain what had been happening on Vertazia. Everything was complicated by their surroundings constantly changing. CuSho was having difficulty in maintaining the theme of a corner shop, changing between what It considered appropriate for being in an interplanetary shuttle craft, then a large aeroplane. Finally all movement ceased and the view through the windows was of the deck of a sailing ship on a vast ocean.

The shelves behind the shop counter and those in the windows were full of a contrasting mix of items. Jars of sweets stood alongside ski goggles, African statues, a host of models of the HomeSphere, Twistors, an Omnitor and anti-gravity toys, together with a plethora of objects demanding they be picked up and inspected.

Ranged around the room were skis and sticks, an African drum, a lifebelt with "TCH CuSho" in bright red letters and a partially dilated doorway that opened onto a view of a spaceman. Hanging on the walls and from the ceiling were more models of spaceships, aeroplanes and sailing ships, African shields and spears, knives, curved swords, a hat with an extravagant feather, frightening masks in bright colours and cute clocks with chirruping birds.

The floor finally stabilised as highly polished wooden planks. What had been a bed turned into a two-tier pair of bunks and a strange thing like a failed hammock on a wooden frame.

'That is a deck chair,' CuSho said in a huffy tone when Tullia complained at how uncomfortable it was, then piled pillows and a thick travelling rug on top of her.

Impossible without a face, but Tullia knew It was smiling. She'd met a TransSentient with a sense of humour! She threw the stuff aside, fell out of the deck chair and bumped into a wooden box on wheels, on top of which rested a long black metal tube, with the end nearest her rounded off. Thick ropes held the odd construction in place with the tube pointing out of a square hole in the wall.

'Never been like this before,' Tamina explained.

'I wish we were together,' Tullia said.

'Temporary stability exists,' CuSho said.

Wrenden and Tamina walked through the shimmering throughway and stood, gawping at the changes. Wrenden was wearing a long, dark blue coat with gold buttons and gold trim on the pockets and sleeve cuffs, a white silk shirt with ruffles all down the front which was tucked into baggy dark green trousers which, in turn, were tucked into a pair of brown boots with gold buckles. Under his coat a broad sash crossed his chest and a cutlass hung from his left hip. Everything was topped off by an extravagant hat with a wide brim, turned up on one side.

Tamina was wearing a cream blouse that was tied under her breasts leaving her midriff bare. Tight, yellow leggings finished just below the knee leaving her legs and feet bare. A bright green headscarf was tied around her head and an enormous pair of round gold earrings fell to her shoulders.

'What?!' All three exclaimed.

'Ah. Let me explain, m'dears.' A figure appeared from within the bifurcated column where the Keepers' two crystals pulsed.

'Jeffri??' Tamina and Wrenden queried.

'At your service, m'dears.' A short and somewhat round man with rosy cheeks, dressed as a ship's cook, stood there smiling. Under a once white apron he was wearing a red and white striped jumper over dingy brown trousers. His scruffy shoes sported bright gold buckles. A faded red cloth was wrapped around his head and a multi-coloured dragonette sat on his right shoulder.

'Qubits. Eight qubits,' the dragonette squawked.

Tullia made a faint squeaking sound and flopped back into the deck chair, a hand across her eyes.

'Jeffri!!' Tamina and Wrenden demanded.

'Tullia-twin,' Jeffri said. 'With the last set of upgrades to my, our, that is CuSho's programming, we all, that includes my two Keepers, agreed it would be user-friendly for me, that is CuSho, to have a more personal appearance. They, that is my Keepers, named me, that is Jeffri, as the personal interface.

'Given that our current situation is clearly in rebellion against the authorities on our homeworld, I, and the accoutrements applied to my Keepers are considered a best match. Namely, or, viz, taking images from the minds of my Keepers, well, that is to say, principally Keeper Wrenden's viewing of uncensored flikkers recorded by Mandara... err... Pirates.'

Wrenden roared with laughter. 'Ho! Ho! I'm a pirate captain.'

'WHAT. Am I?' Tamina asked.

'The cabin boy.'

Tullia and Wrenden stared at one another, turned, looked at Tamina and burst out laughing. Tamina stood with hands on hips, her fuming making her breathe heavily and her BestFriends laugh even more.

'It was very common in those days for girls to go to sea,' an affronted Jeffri explained. 'Unable to be sailors, they went disguised as cabin boys.'

'Boys!!' Exploding with laughter, Tullia fell out of the deck chair as Wrenden bent over, clutching his aching ribs.

'By All The Shades, CuSho!' Tamina stormed. 'What we haven't asked because of this crazy KiddyKartoon we're in is WHY we are still on Earth?'

'A multi-phasic, transdimensional disorientationflux is in operation. It forced me back from my original trajectory and now is preventing us leaving the third dimension,' Jeffri said as his image shimmered and he became tall and slim, now wearing a dark suit, pale pink shirt with matching handkerchief in his breast pocket, green patterned tie and black shoes – with buckles. There was an image of a small dragonette on his breast pocket.

'But we're on the ocean,' Tullia said. 'We must have gone somewhere as I was on the land when you picked me up.'

'Correct Tullia-twin. As we briefly moved through dimensions so the planet rotated underneath us, effectively moving us in a westerly direction.'

Tullia reached out and all three held hands and mindshared. 'Right, CuSho or Jeffri. We focus and establish a small degree of "lift-off", hold it there and, as the planet rotates, we go to the island of Raiatea where Kaigii is.'

Jeffri faded back into the control consol and a cool breeze slid though the youngsters' minds. Jeffri reappeared, still in his suit and looking grim.

'Possible. Will require intense concentration. Need Qwelby-twin to participate. Warning. Inevitable attempts at disruption with serious consequences to this Twins-Come-Home vehicle and sentient occupants.'

'Alternative?' Tamina asked.

'Remain in third dimension and sail all the way around America, through what my databanks indicate are called the "Roaring Forties" and the most hazardous nautical passage anywhere on Earth. Sorry. I do not believe I have the skills to navigate a seventeenth century sailing ship through those waters.' The dragonette reached up, took hold of the pocket handkerchief, wiped its eyes and blew its nose.

383

'A different ship,' Wrenden suggested.

'Regret no. Extracted consciousness parameters now set in sixth dimension.'

Tamina and Tullia mindshared. One with warrior genes, the other an albeit young but already powerful Fire Lady.

'Don't try to leave me out of this,' Wrenden said, guessing the thoughts going through their minds about a not-quite-fourteen-year-old boy. 'Adventurer, Explorer, Trickster. AND I've fought already!'

'There is another possible alternative,' Jeffri said. 'You are well provisioned. Wait it out here in the expectation that, eventually, the Spiral Assembly will agree to a compromise.'

Sister and brother shook their heads. Tullia nodded her agreement with them.

'Keepers. With the latest programming changes you initiated for being in your Forms, I remind you, as you have already experienced, only your clothing will change as you move between rooms. Tullia-twin, you must remain here in the Azuran room at all times.' Jeffri gave a little bow and merged back into the consol.

'Personal interface extrusion ends,' CuSho said.

Each youngster settled into the lotus position, mindshared and imaged Qwelby joining them. All three jerked as a connection was made, fine and faint, yet within, hot and strong and surprisingly full of reds and oranges. Tamina was at first embarrassed and then, like Tullia, puzzled because the colours were also attaching to Tullia.

The ship tilted, the cannon ran back a metre before the ropes held it fast and a dark cloud swept through the room, stinking of putrefaction. The youngsters scrambled to their feet as the cloud spread around. Wrenden drew his cutlass and slashed at the leading edge – which squealed, sank back and was followed by a dark pseudopod reaching out and wrapping around him, pinning his arms to his sides.

Tullia seized her spear and stabbed at the "arms".

Tamina invoked her Attribute which briefly flickered before vanishing and leaving her struggling in the grip of two more arms.

Slashing and stabbing, Wrenden and Tullia freed Tamina, the pseudopodia spurting vile black liquid that hissed before it vanished amid shrieks of pain, both from within the cloud and from the youngsters as drops of liquid burnt their skin.

BATTLE ROYAL

RAIATEA

On Thursday morning Qwelby asked for permission to visit the town. Romain had anticipated the request and agreed, subject to the alien wearing a tracker that had been made. Qwelby was fitted with a heavy metal bracelet which had an electronic lock and another lock operated by a small and specially shaped key. Romain demonstrated a simple sequence to trigger an emergency alarm.

Later that afternoon Angélique admired the bracelet and Qwelby showed her how to operate the alarm. He explained that it was in the very unlikely case of his having a black-out. Part of his cover story for being on Raiatea included the sun and sea air helping his recovery from a neurological imbalance.

That evening as usual Angélique served their meals last and they ate together on his patio. The Ice Bar had been special, but he'd been with another boy, inside and wrapped up well against the cold. Now he was sitting with a beautiful girl under millions of stars which were reaching down to where the moon was reflected in the great expanse of the ocean. The faintest hint of a warm breeze was bringing the smells of the sea and coast and making the candles in the jars on the table flicker. Qwelby was having to fight his pounding hearts and stirrings that demanded action.

Angélle was so like a young version of Tullia that she was not just a constant reminder of his twin, she'd become a copy in the here-and-now and that was so much stronger tonight. The stirrings when her gentle hands rubbed sun oil over him, tonight, the plunging neckline of the short red dress presenting teasing hints of her full breasts, so like his twin's. Her warm brown eyes inviting him to kiss those luscious lips. It was as though his twin was calling to him. Impossible! Kissing Angélle, it would be as if he were kissing his twin!

Seeing the look in Qwelby's sparkling eyes, Angélique was reminded of that morning's conversation with her best friend who'd asked her regular question about sun oil.

'I've told you,' her friend had said when Angélique made her standard reply. 'Any man who lets you spread oil all over his body every day, rolls onto his front and never tries anything on. He sure is gay.'

Angélique had shaken her head. 'No. The way he looks at me at times. I know what he's thinking. Then he goes all cold. He's playing with me and it's pissing me off.'

'You've told him about skinny-dipping. So. Ask him to join us. From how you've described him, Luc will be very happy to find he's gay.'

Determined to find out for herself, after clearing away all the meals she'd changed as usual, but tonight into her favourite red party dress. Self conscious because of what was in her mind, she'd added a large white Jasmine flower to make the daring neckline a little more modest. He was looking at her the way he so often did. She gritted her teeth and mentally dared him not to blank his eyes and shut her out.

'Will you take me skinny-dipping and for a look around the town?' Qwelby was surprised as he heard his words. He'd only meant to ask to visit the town.

'You want to see more of me?'

'Ah. No. We can just walk around town.'

'You don't want to see more of me?'

'I do.'

'Which bits do you want to see more of?' Leaning forward, Angélique widened her eyes, lowered her head and looked up at him from under her eyelashes, which she fluttered.

Tullia! He spluttered as he lowered his eyes and found his gaze riveted.

'Oh. Those bits!'

Qwelby's spluttering turned into choking. His body was on fire as his hormones urged him on. His emotions had been in a whirl since the first time he'd seen her. Only his eyes telling him he was looking at his twin stopped him from grabbing her each time she spread sun oil all over him.

He leapt to his feet, stripped, took three long strides to the pool and dived into the cool water. Reaching the steps at the far end he turned, swam back, turned and swam back again. Breathing heavily, he stopped, lifted his head above the water, shook his long hair – and stared at a small, piercingly bright light in his room that had not been visible from where he'd been sitting at the table. It had to be from the Globe. How long had it been shining? He heaved himself out and ran into his room. It was the Globe. The tiny light was in – Raiatea!

Memories raced though his mind. The firefight in the Kalahari. Words Wrenden had spoken – an EyeBox. He picked up Soloc and tilted it to align with his eyes. The colours changed to match them and it opened. This time the three coloured disks were glowing and steadily rotating backwards. With shaking hands he turned the inner dials until a set of Ancient Aurigan symbols locked in place.

'Tullia! She's coming!' he exclaimed to Angélique, now standing at his side.

'When?'

'Don't know. Never used this before.' He stared at Angélique. Tullia was coming. His twin. From the Kalahari. This lovely girl in front of him with her soft brown eyes and inviting lips. He felt his eyes soften and glow. 'Oh, Angélle. I am so stupid.' He swept her into a long and passionate embrace. His hearts pounded and he spread his wings.

Soloc chimed from in his hand behind her back. Fire lanced through his mind and he staggered. 'Attack!' he exclaimed. 'No fight here.' He grabbed the Globe and ran from the room as a wide-eyed Angélique fell back on the bed.

She'd kissed plenty of boys during her short holiday romances but she'd never been kissed like that. She'd read about it in books and giggled with her girlfriends at the ridiculous descriptions. But it was true. The stars had whirled around her. Who the hell was he?

'Urgh.' The silky material of her lovely dress was soaking wet. Without thinking, she pulled it over her head. He was naked! She took one of his Raiatean tops from the wardrobe, put it on, then ran to where he'd thrown his clothes. Picking them up, she followed a trail of water into the lift and out of the top floor via the main entrance.

He was across the track on the edge of the forest that covered the mountain. Practising his exercises. No. There was a difference. He flailed his arms, staggered back then charged forward and launched himself into a two-footed kick against – a tree? He'd gone mad!

For a moment he seemed to settle into his morning exercise routine, but again the movements were different. He was moving much faster and now looked to be imagining wielding two swords in a fight against invisible attackers. Her heart sank. This gorgeous hunk of man really was mad.

Ducking away, he turned, swung back, threw his arms in the air as he shouted then – stood there for an impossibly long moment as she stared at the three dark lines all down his back that had not been there before. He sank to the ground. She ran to him and found three deep gashes in his back, bleeding. She ran to

Romain's private entrance and urged him to come immediately, then ran back to Qwelby.

Believing the fight was going to be on the island, Qwelby had run out onto the mountain top to get away from dangerous proximity to the Professor's dimension seeking equipment. As he ran towards the shelter of the forest he slid from his Form. Not so! He was hurled half way back by some sort of moving wall, pinning him in the disorientating flux of the boundary of a singularity, part in and part out of both dimensions.

Defending himself from the wall's attacks, he thought about his Attribute. It did not work in the third dimension, but he was not totally in the third. He had one swift chance. Ducking away from a swinging claw he shouted 'Zhûkhorlânn', morphed into his dragon and rolled over on wooden planks as he entered the singularity of a NullPoint, the dragon disappeared and he was returned to his seventh dimension InForming Matrix – on a ship?

'A *Pirate Ship.*'

Disorientated and wondering about the name Jeffri that slid into his mind, he whirled round as a green and yellow striped Griffon bounded towards him. A knife appeared in Qwelby's hand as he swung to the right. The griffon ducked and slashed him with its sharp nails as Qwelby swung back to his left, the knife changing at his command into a longer sword that sliced the two heads from a serpent-tailed dog.

Ducking and rolling, Qwelby tumbled across the floor and stabbed upward into the Griffon's belly which dissolved in a shower of dark red spume, burning Qwelby where it struck him. He leapt to his feet as a large snake swept into the room and crashed into him, turning into a tall and slender Tazian girl in a jet black DarkSuit who dived through a door that turned into a waterfall, and attacked Tullia.

Springing to his twin's aid, Qwelby was dragged back by a long green tail lashing around his neck and thrusting him into the mêlée alongside his friends. Trading blows with a giant Ichthyocentaur, he threw quick glances towards his beloved twin and was puzzled. He recognised the girl from their previous encounters and knew her to be a good fighter, but she was armed only with a club and a small shield against Tullia's spear and a short, saw-toothed knife.

Xaala was fast and nimble and the more blows she landed on Tullia, the more the link between the twins was weakening.

'I must help Kaigii!' Qwelby called to his friends. He leapt over the Ichthyocentaur's slashing tail, dived under the pounding hooves and heard the pitiful scream as he slashed through the beast's belly. As the monstrosity exploded in a rain of burning black blood he threw himself through the waterfall.

Confusion! As his dragon had left, he'd appeared as he'd originally imaged himself, wearing a Warrior's skinergy suit made from the tiny dragonscales the babies shed as they grew. Why now was he dressed as an Azuran in a frilly shirt, breeches, knee boots and a stupid hat?

His hesitation was nearly fatal. As Xaala swung her club fast, he was slow to duck. The club caught his head a glancing blow and he saw Tullia's spear fly into... through the girl's arm as she screamed and disappeared, the pain snapping her back into her Form on Vertazia as Qwelby fell unconscious back into his Form on Raiatea. The twins' connection broken, CuSho dropped back to the third dimension and the first of many fights was over.

When he regained consciousness, Qwelby found himself in Angélique's arms as she was washing his cuts, Miki kneeling at her side with a medical kit. Having washed away the dirt and sweat and bathed his cuts with antiseptic, Angélique went to bandage the foul smelling gashes in his back.

'Leave to open air. Friendly organisms eat foulness.' Qwelby heard his voice say. How The Shades do I know that? Rrîltallâ – his twin's heroine? When Angélique tried to help him into his clothes, he shook his head. 'Be ripped. Get into cuts. You see my body. See wounds. Heal. But.' He managed a weak grin. 'Need protection. Have suede loinskin.'

Angélique looked pleadingly at Miki, who a while later returned with the briefs that Taimi Keskinen had made.

With the EyeBox kept under constant surveillance, by Angélique taking over when Qwelby slept, he was able to time his runs back into the forest to perfection. Now he knew what to look for, he was able to switch vision and see the faint shimmering of "the wall", the disorientation flux, call upon his dragon and soar through dimensions to join his twin and their friends as each armada of imaginary beasts was hurled at them.

Her arm healed, Xaala returned to the fray, each time eagerly anticipating fierce combat with Qwelby as she sought to disrupt the vital connection between the twins.

Now unfazed by his changes of clothing, as he returned this time, Qwelby threw himself into the Azuran room where Tullia and Xaala were exchanging blows, just as a banshee leapt on Tullia from behind, pinning her to the floor.

Momentarily distracted as he severed its head from its body, his guard against Xaala was down. Out of the corner of his eye he saw her neutron whip curling through the air. Although he flung his left arm up, even in the seventh dimension a DarkShield was taking too long to materialise. The whip hissed down the side of his body, burning him as the tip sliced through a Minotaur he'd not sensed behind him.

Xaala gave him a curt nod and a grim smile. *You're mine!*

Qwelby thoughtsent an image of him saluting her with his sword as he lashed out with a leather shrouded steel whip, wrapping it around her wrist and ripping the neutron whip from her hand. The jerk brought them crashing together, blood dripping from a slash across his belly from the knife that had appeared in her hand.

She'd been fast. He'd been slow. The knife could – should – have plunged into his belly. She'd turned it at the last nanosecond, she was that good. Her mind was closed but her eyes staring into his revealed confusion, death and...?

A flare of pain from his burning side broke the impasse as he groaned. The sharp edge of the knife drew another line of pain across his body. Gripping her knife hand, Qwelby slipped sideways, wrapped his other arm around her waist and fell backwards, hurling her over his head. He heard a thump, a muffled moan and watched his twin give the fallen girl a mighty kick to the side of her head – snapping her back into her Form on Vertazia.

Tullia put out a hand and helped her twin to his feet. A swift embrace. 'Miss you,' each of them said. ''Til next time,' Qwelby added, grimaced, slid back to his Form and staggered out of the forest to collapse in Angélique's arms.

The fighting continued on and off for three days. Each time the visitations from Vertazia ceased, CuSho sank back into the third dimension where it settled on the Pacific Ocean, Qwelby returned to his Form on Raiatea and Jeffri materialised.

Wearing a white coat over a grey suit and with the dragonette carrying his stethoscope, Jeffri examined the youngsters, then morphed into being a nurse in a smart green and white uniform. What was now Jeffria attended to their wounds, the dragonette flying back and forth with vials of TenderLovingCare and oils to rub on wounds from injured pride.

All the time the pirate ship was surrounded by the multiphasic flickering of the oppressive disorientationflux which was preventing activation of any Attributes.

Regularly checking the bright light on the Globe which remained centred on the island, Qwelby was slowly coming to understand the timing displayed by the EyeBox. The discs were always spinning slowly. Moving erratically, the dial had always rotated a lot more when he'd been on CuSho. He was certain it was counting down to arrival.

Angélique refused to leave Qwelby, nor let anyone else attend to him. For the entire three days she remained at the forest's edge, waiting for him to return from the fighting, washing him, cleaning his wounds and leaving open to the air the deep gashes that seemed to have been caused by the claws of a variety of animals. When he slept, she remained alongside, watching the discs in the EyeBox slowly rotating. She only slept when he awoke and ordered her to sleep, unable to resist the hypnotic colours in his beautiful eyes.

She longed to follow him into the forest and nurse his body. He forbade that, explaining that his Form was at the very edge of powerful and dangerous energies. He guessed that on the night of the firefight in the Kalahari, the Bushmen had been safe because that NullPoint had formed as a Bubble on Earth, providing a defensive screen to non-Tazii. Now, because of what was happening with CuSho, this Bubble was clearly reaching into other dimensions.

Miki explained that Qwelby lived in a fantasy world that his imagination made real in a way the scientists were trying to understand. Angélique smiled faintly and nodded. Doctor Miki was a lovely lady, but she was not Polynesian. Angélique knew Qwelby was empowered by Oro and was fighting the dark forces that had always tried to overcome the Gods of Raiatea. Forces that existed in another dimension, even though they made their effects felt on Earth.

The one kiss that had set her afire had been enough to tell her he was a real man. More – he was a warrior who wanted her – Angélle. She'd fancied him the first time she'd seen him. Since then she'd had plenty of opportunity to see that he was a man with an intriguing physiological difference. Now, she wanted to be his woman. She dismissed the head-shaking coming from the mind of a sixteen-year-old college student and part-time assistant housekeeper. This was neither the time nor the place for that child.

CHAPTER 76

ARRIVAL

IN-BETWEEN AND RAIATEA

CuSho had been continually transforming. All pretence of a corner shop was long gone and the youngsters were fighting on a full-blown pirate ship. As the twins maintained their connection, CuSho continued to skim the waves with Its energies a tiny fraction lifted out of the third dimension.

Fancy clothing had become a nuisance. Items were ripped and torn and got in the way. Coats swirling around, claws sinking into shirts and trousers, all unbalanced attacks or defences. Tamina and Wrenden had told Jeffri to stop CuSho making more changes and were now fighting in their own tight-fitting BodySuits.

Tullia's t-shirt had been ripped from her and she had cast aside what had become an irritating, torn skirt and was fighting in her loinskin. Feeling it swinging against her thighs was a lovely reminder of her time with the tribe and she drew on their strength as the motifs on the back and front were energising her through their symbols of her dedication to her twin and XOÑOX.

She wiped the back of her hand across her sweating brow as the Djinn she'd been fighting imploded into a spew of blood that hissed across her hand making her drop her cutlass. Through blurred vision she saw a large red form leap through the doorway.

It looked human, with a spiky tail and horns sticking out of its head. In one hand it held a three-pronged pitchfork.

Too exhausted to fight any more, panic ripped through her. In a confusing mix of imagery and with Thathuma, her Tazian necklace firmly grasped in her hand, she shouted. 'I Bushman! Hunter! Warrior!' Image-into-action had to work, or she was lost. Wrapping her hand around her purple crystal she cried out, 'Kanyisaya! Drakobata!' imploring her crystal to link her with the rich red of her twin's crystal. Strength flowed in and she reached out for a shining, two-handed sword hanging on the wall.

She heard a voice screaming 'Zeyusa!' Her voice! The bright red Demon sprang at her, the trident held high above its head was striking down for her body. She swung her sword and there was a mighty clang as the two met. Ducking, she pulled the sword away. Freed of restraint, the pitchfork shot over her shoulder and the Demon crashed into her, sending her swinging away. She continued to swing, bringing the heavy sword around until the blade cleaved into its arm. No more Demon but a middle-aged Tazian in the short robes of a Junior Custodian stood there, gawping at his half severed arm. A flash of light and the Tazian was gone.

Tullia reeled back against the wall of the shop, horrified. Until now all she'd destroyed had been fearsome mythical beasts. The worst she'd done in her fights with the tall, slender girl had been no more than in her fight with Kou-'ke. But this time she'd almost cut off the arm of a human being! No matter that it would be reattached or even regrown over several weeks. This was too much. Was it better to stop, return to the Kalahari to live physically apart from her beloved twin yet now with their full mental contact?

A great wave of energy engulfed her, wrapped around her and poured through every atom of her being. Such beautiful loving. Never before in all her life had she felt anything so strong.

'KAIGII!'

She opened to her twin totally and without reservation.

They flowed together, two-as-one, awesome in their renewed and now twice Awakened twinergy. All the fights on Earth had changed him, irrevocably. Added to the speed of his ordinary Tazian mental skills, he had become a skilful fighter. In a timeless moment of peace they shared a sparkling image of four hearts embracing each other. *I I love love you you!!*

A resounding crash ended the moment and Qwelby led them into becoming a pair of choreographed, ferocious, fighting dancers. Cutting, swerving, slicing, diving to the floor to hack at legs and feet, rolling back up to block swords and spears, slashing at arms and heads.

The fighting was not without cost to all the youngsters. Short periods of rest and sleep in between long periods of fighting were inadequate and all were reaching the end of their endurance. More and more often they were taking heavy blows to their faces, black eyes, cuts to lips and cheekbones, bleeding noses were commonplace. Blows to stomachs had them doubling up and rolling across the floor gasping for breath and puking. Slashing cuts were no longer shallow but opening flesh deep to the bone.

His frustration mounting as, along with the block on Attributes, he was unable to mentaform any of the weapons he remembered from the Space Wars or had used in Video Games, Qwelby was reduced to fighting with a sword in one hand and a dagger in the other. He was everywhere, aiding whichever of the others was most hard-pressed. Fighting on the Pirate Ship, he was inspired by his love for his twin. Recovering back on Earth, he was enfolded in Angélique's heartfelt caring.

All sensed the battle was reaching a peak. From the malformed beasts that poured over the starboard side it was clear that the strength of the Custodians was fading. The youngsters faced them in a line, the twins in the centre, flanked by Tamina on Tullia's left and Wrenden on Qwelby's right. Weak and unskilled though the beasts were, there were so many that the friends were outflanked and they were forced to fight back to back.

Wielding a two handed sword a deformed warrior rose up between Qwelby and Tullia. The twins hacked him down and grinned at each other, then were bumped from behind. 'Ninurtan!' he cried. 'Šem-eš-a!' He saw Tullia's eyes flare as she also recognised Wrenden and Tamina, fighting as their backguards as they had done thirteen thousand years ago – this time all together.

'QeïchâKaïgïï našgâde!!' 'Quantum Twins for all eternity!!' they roared, redoubled their assault on the enemy and soon the line of four had reformed, thinning the tide of creatures as cut and thrust, shriek and yell, the beasts vanished, spurting little of the black blood that hissed and burnt less than before.

'Hold the line!' Wrenden shouted and ran up the companionway onto the poop deck, where jolly-jack-tar Jeffri was struggling at the great wheel.

Pirate Captain Wrenden Njé'zânâ Jailandurkul braced his legs apart and looked down the length of the deck. 'CuSho! Load the starboard guns,' he commanded.

In a blur of movement the six cannons that were still on their mountings rolled backwards. Moving liked greased lightning, a barefoot Jeffri rammed wads of powder and balls down the tubes whilst the dragonette flew over his head screeching encouragement.

Half way up the companionway, Qwelby was hacking the heads off a Hydra as fast as they regrew.

Wrenden sliced the head off a Manticor as it crawled over the guardrail. 'Run out the guns!'

The cannons rolled forward.

Qwelby had almost retreated to the poop deck and ducked as a pterodactyl swooped overhead. Wrenden slashed a wing off the prehistoric monster and brought his sword swinging down. 'Fire!'

A rippling burst of noise, flames and smoke, thunderous crashing, yells and screams and a sickening smell of burning hung in the air.

Silence.

A ginormous crash shook the whole ship, sent the youngsters

sprawling to the deck and carried on reverberating for an age as the attackers' defensive shield was blasted out of existence, the fighting ceased and Qwelby was returned to his Form on Earth.

Silence.

The squawk of a lone gull.

The flapping of canvas and the creaking of timbers. The clatter and rumble of objects sliding across the ship's deck as she rolled. The soft shushing of the sea turning into the roaring of an angry ocean.

Tullia looked around. The deck was devoid of all life, apart from her two friends. Looking up, she saw the sails were in tatters, the foremast had gone and the mainmast was broken, the top half lying over the side. The carronades were scatted around the deck with their barrels split apart. As she scrambled to her feet and held out a hand to Tamina, the ship hurtled down the side of an enormous wave and the Unicorn figurehead at the bow plunged into the other side. The shock sent Wrenden tumbling down to the deck. Sea cascaded over them. The bow slowly climbed up and up, the water sweeping the youngsters, choking and spluttering, into a pile of arms and legs, down the companionway and below deck.

They struggled to separate themselves. Led by Wrenden, they clambered back up to the deck as the ship levelled out. Where was the sea? They rushed to the side. It was still there, a long, long way below.

'Avast there m'hearties,' Jeffri cried from the poop deck, now all a-glitter in a sumptuous yellow frock coat, white breeches and stockings, shiny black shoes with golden buckles and all crowned by a fore-and-aft hat, atop of which perched a dragonette. Its cry of 'Qubits. Eight qubits.' was snatched away by the wind.

'Land ho!' came a shout from above. Looking up the youngsters saw – a ragged and barefoot Jeffri? – in the crow's nest, a telescope in one hand and the other pointing ahead – to a bright green island. They were just about on a level with the tops of the trees on its highest peak.

'Now cruising at a height of three thousand, three hundred

feet,' Jeffri announced, clad in a light blue uniform with four gold rings at the sleeve-ends and a dragonette with spread wings on the breast pocket. The black shoes bore the inevitable gold buckles and this time he was wearing a sensible light blue cap, its peak edged in gold braid.

The youngsters clung to each other as the deck split down the middle and swung out sideways to form two wings and the stumps of the masts along with the tattered sails tried to pretend they were part of an airborne sailing-ship. As the youngsters fell towards the bilges, the Corner Shop reformed around them.

'All crew to the Azuran room and keep seat belts fastened until the sign is switched off.'

'Eh???'

'Hang on tight, chaps, we're in for a bumpy landing.' Jeffri was now wearing baggy breeches tucked into knee length boots and a leather hat with flapping earpieces. A pair of goggles hung around his neck. The dragonette was rapidly clawing his-her way inside Jeffri's leather flying jacket.

The glider, plane, ship or Corner Shop struck the tops of the trees and bounced over the edge of the mountain.

'Oops!'

'Personal interface extrusion ended,' CuSho announced as Jeffri somersaulted into the control console and the youngsters again ended up in a tangle of arms and legs.

The thundering broadside had shocked Qwelby back into his Form. Dizzy and disorientated, Angélique helped him sit down as he wandered out of the forest. An arm around his shoulder, a cold drink, a wet cloth wiped over his face, a smile and a quick kiss – Qwelby grinned and held out his hand for the EyeBox. Opening it, he stared, blinked and reached for the globe. 'They're landing!' he exclaimed as he pointed to its changed surface which was showing only the Island and a bright spot of light on the very edge of the coast down below the Laboratory home.

A few minutes later the Professor stopped his Ranger just off the edge of the coast road. Tired beyond belief from all the fighting and with blood trickling down his body from several deep wounds, Qwelby leant on Angélique as they got out and headed for what looked like a Raiatean shop, canted over at an angle several metres out into the lagoon. Tullia jumped out and started splashing her way through gentle waves, using her spear as a prop.

'Must go,' Tullia said as she reached her twin.

'Can't.' *Not yet.*

Tullia stared, uncomprehending.

'Tullia!' Tamina called. 'We must go. The flux is starting.'

'I love her.' *Please understand.* Qwelby was looking deep into his twin's eyes, reinforcing his plea.

'Qwelby!' Wrenden called, the urgency in his voice clear for all to hear.

Stunned. Shocked beyond belief. Exhausted. Hurting all over with violent spasms of pain racking her, Tullia collapsed to her knees then folded forward as Qwelby caught her.

'TWIIIINS!' Tamina yelled. 'NOW!'

Qwelby raised a hand. *Not coming. Not now. Can't.*

Glittering streams of light zipped around a typical Raiatean corner shop. CuSho rocked and swivelled as one end lifted off the shore. Moments later a black plastic waste sack was thrown out of the door. CuSho shimmered. A scrunching sound hurt the ears as It rotated on the rocks spraying water like a Catherine Wheel. The screeching of a thousand fingernails ripping down a hundred blackboards as a plume of water leapt into the air, drenching the three youngsters. When the water fell back – CuSho had gone.

Angélique helped Qwelby back to the Ranger whilst Romain and Tyler carried the unconscious Tullia and laid her down on a travelling rug in the large luggage compartment.

Tullia was soon set down on the King sized bed in Qwelby's room. Angélique helped an exhausted Qwelby to wash and dry, then the two of them did the same for the still unconscious Tullia.

Qwelby healed his twin's wounds as much as his depleted energies allowed, whilst Angélique bandaged the deeper cuts. Eventually, Qwelby's energies gave out and he meekly accepted Angélique's tender caring until he fell asleep, holding hands with his twin.

Angélique was in a whirl. She was tall and well-built. For the few moments she'd been standing next to Qwelby and his sister she'd felt small. Now she was looking at two young children, whose feet extended past the end of the bed. She closed her eyes. Over the last three days she'd regularly held in her arms a well-built young man, much taller than herself. She reopened her eyes and again saw two young children. Who the hell were they?

Various aunts had driven up to cover her normal duties. It was late, she was too tired to eat and was driven home. Even the dizzying round of questions to which there were no answers were unable to stop her mind constantly repeating his impossible words: "I love her."

CHAPTER 77

AFTERMATH

VERTAZIA

There was no further resistance to CuSho's return to Vertazia. The broadside had blasted the last of Ceegren's dwindling group of Custodians back into their aching Forms and the twins were reunited.

As Ceegren spread thoughts throughout the MentaNet, he needed more than his own silver tongue and golden mind to convince the Tazii that the three days of fighting had been essential for the preservation of the race.

He was a worried man. For a long time he had been subtly steering the race in what he saw as the right direction for the future that would see them united and positioned closer to the Traditionalist path. There, they would be without all the liberalisms and exceptions enjoyed by the Shakazii in their homelands of Tembakatii.

Now that plan was in danger and he was having to increasingly rely on Dryddnaa for support. Although that was forthcoming and unconditional, nevertheless it was subtly nuanced and a growing number of younger Custodians were attracted to her softer approach. She was positioning herself to survive if he should fail. But was that all?

Needing an upswell of support across the MentaNet for his actions, he decided the time had come to activate the many Tazii whose ceremonies he had attended since well before becoming Arch Custodian, and still continued to do so. In their minds he had deeply buried commands of devotion. Those were not directed to himself personally, as that would never work on Vertazia, but as being the embodiment of the True Aurigan Teachings.

He had made a serious mistake regarding Xaala. Previously, he'd always tutored boys. He'd never seen her as a growing woman nor, worse given that one of his careers had been as a Readjuster, considered how damaged she was from her family's treatment of her – and how much help she had failed to receive.

He thanked the Multiverse that the experiment with Rulcas had failed, as he had expected. His disruptive influence had gone and it was time he paid his acolyte special attention. Her changes following her Awakening meant that she was now perfect for what he had in mind.

Dryddnaa was cautiously satisfied with developments. Given the amount of violence perpetrated on the twins and the concern spreading throughout the MentaNet, there had been great demand for the services of Readjusters, primarily in their role as Counsellors. The old, and in Dryddnaa's opinion over-the-hill Arch Readjuster, had been only too happy to let Dryddnaa take the leading role in coordinating such services.

That had enabled Dryddnaa to increase her support from Readjusters of a more liberal persuasion. Her avowed aim was not to challenge the Arch Custodian, but to assist him with his aim of ending the divisions in Tazian society. Her supporters understood her carefully nuanced words. Instead of bringing the Shakazii "into the fold," the aim was to bring the Kumelanii "out" into more liberal ways.

She had good professional relationships with several current Discriminators and had maintained friendly contact with many former Discriminators whom she had treated in the past and who were now following other careers.

It was a very new profession that had only come into existence when Vertazia started to receive transmissions from Earth as they slipped through space-time rifts. Someone had to censor them and it was mainly Shakazii who were capable of coping with the violence and depravity – and then only for a few years at a time.

Events were moving fast and she believed them to be spiralling outwith Ceegren's ability to control. She needed to move equally fast in expanding her power base outside both the Custodians and her own profession – and with great care. The Dance of Discovery was entering a vital phase.

Xaala was all at tens and twelves. She'd fought well against Tullia who, in the third dimension, had been slower than the nimble Xaala in the seventh. Yet she had never been able to sever the link between the twins because of the blasted boy who'd kept on interfering. Oh, Xaala had enjoyed fighting him. In the seventh dimension they were well matched. But By All The Shades, he'd always bested her!

Either one of the twins would serve as a support for her to become the youth leader that Ceegren needed – and then for her to rule alongside him.

Once again she'd experienced the love the twins had for each other and now the love they shared with their friends. A love like that confirmed the conclusion she'd reached during her period of solitary punishment. Ceegren was wrong. Both twins had to return to Vertazia.

Her head spun, her stomach heaved, she fell to the ground on hands and knees and sicked her guts up. Sweat poured off her and the puking went on forever as her mind pulled her in one direction and her hearts in the other. Condemn the Abominations to the NoWhenWhere or ensure they returned?

Then her stomach flipped and her hearts thudded as she was

torn again. Satisfy both Ceegren, who feared the combined power of the twins, and Dryddnaa who wanted to show they could be healed, by bringing only one back? But which? The beautiful girl or the handsome boy. Whose love did she want most?

'*Your Master's,*' a voice whispered deep in the recesses of her mind.

AFTERMATH

LUNGUNU

Pelnak and Shimara had spent all three days of the on-off fighting supporting Tamina and Wrenden whilst they were fighting and snatching what sleep they could when they returned. Exhausted and totally disillusioned by the violence initiated from Vertazia, the not-twins were only too keen to return to their own homes. Their mothers, themselves twins, had been at Lungunu throughout the venture, helping care for all the children. With the deepest of regret they explained to the family that they were determined their children should suffer no more. They were to take no further part in any rescue attempts.

Before leaving, everyone assembled in the sombrely coloured main gatherroom where both youngsters paid tribute to Rulcas.

'We couldn't have stayed strong and committed without him,' Pelnak said.

'His strength and steadfastness of being there in support kept us going though all the terrible dark energies that repeatedly surrounded us,' Shimara added.

They said sad goodbyes with tears in their eyes as all the adults hugged and thanked them and said they understood their feelings and decision.

When the not-twins and their mothers had gone, Tamina and Wrenden were helped into the newly created Recovery Suite. Mizena's hearts were full of joy that her children were reunited and, tired beyond belief, was grateful for the help of her husband, Cook and the latter's young assistants as she administered to the youngsters.

Lellia returned to the StroemCavern whilst Mandara settled down for a long discussion with CuSho, helped by Jeffri now sporting a multi-toned, green and yellow, safari style trouser suit as homage to the Arch Discoverer. Perched on his shoulder, the dragonette tucked her-his head under a wing and snored gently.

Rulcas had shrugged off all offers of help, only wanting to be left alone and able to request anything he needed from House. He'd experienced a totally different aspect of Vertazia life and a strong energy bonding with the four BestFriends. He had a lot of thinking to do.

Tamina and Wrenden spent a day and a night at Lungunu, and although by no means fully recovered, went home the following morning after a late breakfast shared with Rulcas. There, the family settled down for the youngsters to tell their story. They had only just begun talking when Nariel, the house's central semisentient, announced that Readjusters were requesting landing permission.

'How long?' Jailandur asked.

'Hovering over docking bay.'

'What?'

'I have only just been contacted. The Isotor must had been in InvisMode.'

The four Tazii looked at each other, amazed – and very concerned.

'Confirmed,' Jailandur said as the family got up and headed for the main entrance.

As the front doors slid apart they saw the Isotor settling. This version was a medium sized transport. An aerodynamic lozenge with three short stubby "wings" at the back set at one hundred and twenty degrees to each other.

Any doubts they may have had about the official nature of the visit were dispelled as a door irised open and Lerinda stepped out onto the ring of light of a gravitrek.

Apart from her cream blouse she was dressed all in blue. A light blue jacket and midi length skirt with dark blue calf length boots. The Readjuster's dark blue cuffs and trim at the edge of her skirt were bordered by silver, indicating her new status as a Senior. She was accompanied by a much older Senior and a Junior.

Behind them were two Senior Persuaders. Their grey suits with trousers tucked into shiny black boots and the high black collars and black cuffs of their jackets all edged in silver created an oppressive atmosphere.

Wrenden and Tamina bridled at the Persuaders' black badges of a small round shield with a tiny, recumbent dragon. To them it was an insult to the boy they both loved, with his DragonRider genes.

'In the light of recent events, concern has been expressed regarding the development of your children, especially your youngest. Wrenden is to be taken for consideration.' Lerinda stated formally.

There was uproar.

'Yarannah!' Lerinda shouted above the noise. 'This is for the best. He must be set on the right path through to adulthood.' *Please understand. I have been forced to do this.*

Everyone was talking at once, red in the face. As the argument became increasingly heated, mental exchanges slipped from angry to downright insulting in a most unTazian manner. Two Junior Persuaders rode the gravitrek down from the Isotor.

'We can take the girl "for consideration" instead,' the older Senior Readjuster said, the euphemism clear in her vocalisation. *That vessel needs both Keepers to work.*

There was a stunned silence as Yarannah stared at Lerinda. *You promised you were acting as a friend and not officially!*

The older Senior smirked. She intensely disliked Lerinda with her pathetic liberal ideas and for sucking up to Dryddnaa.

'I was only taking advice in order to help your children,' Lerinda explained. *I was acting as a friend. I only sought Dryddnaa's advice to ensure the best for your children. She promised....*

'It is Chief Readjuster Dryddnaa's decision,' the older Senior said. She placed a hand on Lerinda's arm and tightbanded: *Stop snivelling!*

Jailandur grabbed hold of his daughter's arm as her Attribute started to materialise. *CONTROL! Please.*

'All right. I'll go,' Wrenden said, stepping forward.

'NO!' Tamina grabbed her brother's hand and pulled him behind her. 'I will go.' Struggling for control, her eyes were blazing at her mother, who staggered backwards as she covered her own eyes.

Njé'zânâ, Tamina thoughtspoke her brother and sent a picture of five protons and one quark.

Trickster. Gulp!

Pirate Captain and his Cabin Boy.

You got it, Boots.

Tamina heard the quaver in his thought and sent him a picture as the Captain ordering the guns to be run out and fired.

'I'll pack,' she said, turned and went into the house followed by the two Junior Persuaders.

After the Isotor had lifted off, Wrenden went to his room, seething. Their mother had betrayed them – deliberately. Her interest in what they'd been doing had only been to rat them out. And his father. Instead of coming with him to plan how to free Tamina, he was consoling his wife. *Labirden Xzarze. Adults. I'm never going to be one!*

Wrenden took a deep breath. Not only had he seen how shattered the not-twins were by their experience, their mothers had banned any further participation. XOÑOX was being torn apart. That left Rulcas. He didn't really know the lad, but he'd trust the not-twins' judgment, especially Shimara's. 'Right, mate, now you've really got to prove yourself.'

He changed back into his BodySuit. 'Njé'zânâ. Also Explorer and Adventurer,' he said to himself as he quietly left by the window, asking Nariel, the house semisentient, to silence the protest of the plants as he climbed down the trellis. He and Qwelby would never use a gravitrek. That was not part of a proper adventure. Besides which it used energy, an energy balance was required and all that would be in Nariel's log.

A few moments later he mounted his twistor and stroked it as he asked for silent mode, meaning concealment of all energy signatures. Against all Tazian rules and it had been he who had shown Qwelby how to make the adjustments, subject, of course, to the twistor agreeing. His seventh sense told him to fly at ground-hugging height and take the long way round through the hills to Lungunu. His care was rewarded when he saw an Isotor on the docking bay and slid behind one of the farm outbuildings where there was a cradle.

Patting his twistor as he dismounted, he scaled the back of the barn and peered over the rooftop from between a pair of exhaust stacks. He was in time to see a group of men and women departing as Mandara politely waved them off.

The Academy of Discoverers had a problem. The members opposed to Mandara wanted him removed from his post, but it was not possible to vote him out of office as he had not been voted in. The Pinnacle of any Guild or professional group simply emerged because, at that time they were clearly accepted as being the best person to meet all the requirements. The reports of what he had invented made all Discoverers want to see it. If the reports were true, not only was he still the Arch Discoverer, but the pre-eminent of all such since the passing of Aurigan times.

Thus three plus one members of the Technicians' Council and three plus one from the Collectors' Council had requested a meeting with Mandara to inspect the purported transdimensional vehicle. Sitting in the laboratory inside what looked like a typical Tazian corner shop, strewn with a multiplicity of items, some recognizable and others vaguely similar to Tazian artefacts, they had participated in a confusing discussion with, even more unbelievably, a TransSentient, in the form of a tall and well-blessed motherly Jeffria.

Jeffria's brightly patterned voluminous dress and large turban with its preening dragonette had added to the otherworldly sensation. Her sweet understanding smile, backed by CuSho's subtle energy waves, had reduced the Discoverers to a sense of being young children listening to a motherly Educationer who, of course, knew best.

Afterwards, none of the Discoverers were quite sure what they had learnt, except that all was well, nothing was anybody's fault and they were welcome to come to tea anytime they wished. Although it seemed that Jeffria preferred that to be at tea-time.

None of them had the answer to her question when one Discoverer later asked, 'What on 'Tazia are "CupCakes" and when is "tea-time"?'

The Discoverers had stood no more chance than a stream of protons in an accelerator. For centuries it was to be a matter for debate – had archetypal energies from Aurigan times combined to create a unique locus in space-time-consciousness? Or how else had all the circumstances come together at exactly the right moment to create a transdimensional rescue vehicle, unintentionally creating a TransSentient, on the way? The answer, of course, was that nothing was ever random. But the Tazii were humans and logic was very often an unsatisfactory answer, even for Discoverers.

Four family members on whom no inhibitions had been applied on achieving adulthood. Four youngsters with the sharp, penetrating energies of their second Eras, irrevocably committed to the twins, not merely through being BestFriends but also their group of XOÑOX and their Talisman. They included inheritors of strong genes of six of the great hero/ines of Aurigan Times. Lellia's Kûllokaremmâ the Mystic, Mandara's Lûzhrâzón Na'Ûkówÿz, the great scientist who had conceived the idea of the HomeSphere then steered it across galaxies, and arguably the four greatest of all: Dragon Kèhša, Unicorn Kèhša, Explorer, Reconciler.

It was either the greatest ever betrayal of Tazian values or the starting point of the Great Rebellion. Debates always reached the same conclusion – it was both.

In addition to all that had gone into Its creation and modification, CuSho had communed deeply with Its two Keepers, Tamina and Wrenden, and then participated in three days of intense fighting. It had been analysing, calculating and absorbing the multiplex energies flowing between the six BestFriends, Rulcas and Xaala.

Above all It had met the Quantum Twins and been immersed in the energies that flowed between them and between them and their BestFriends. It understood the word for that was love – and was aware of how powerful the energy was and how it was influencing both Rulcas and the puzzle that was Xaala.

Over the days that had become tendays then moons, Mizena had come to love Tamina and Wrenden almost as much as her own children, enabling CuSho to draw heavily on her powerful healer's energies when InForming Jeffria and providing answers to the Discoverers' questions.

Those Discoverers who were opposed to Mandara and the attempts to rescue the twins and who had not been at the meeting, were not satisfied with the report. A small cabal formed. They accepted that destruction of the vehicle would seriously damage the Keepers, even possibly terminate their Lifelines. It had to be rendered inoperative whilst safely respecting Tazian lifeforms. 'Take control, slide it through the sixth and lose it inbetween dimensions,' was the agreed solution.

They saw no serious difficulty in doing that. The vehicle could not be a TranSentient as that level of expertise had not existed on Vertazia for millennia. Jeffria was merely a basic TriD image controlled by Mandara. 'Sorted,' an elderly Discoverer said, proud to display his understanding of teenage slang.

When the Isotor departed, Wrenden asked his twistor to contact House and was invited in. When all were settled in the main gatherroom he explained what had happened at home.

Outraged by all the violence there had been, the adults were numb with shock at Wrenden's story. None of them had been able to discover any reason for what obviously was a great fear of the twins returning - except the story of the Violence Virus, which none of them believed.

'Us got thinking to do, mate,' Rulcas said as he got up and the two boys headed for the XOÑOX suite.

Rulcas had mentioned his connection with Xaala and how it had come about, but said nothing about their odd friendship or about her, other than that she had sympathy for the twins. 'Xaala must know. 'Er likes the twins,' he told Wrenden. 'Yet 'er's like a quark at the end of that Arch Custodian's superstring. I recons er'll tell me. Not 'ere.' He tapped the side of his head. 'Got to get to see 'er.'

Wrenden nodded. He was going to have to earn his "Trickster" epithet in earnest and in more ways than one. Oh how he wished Qwelby was there to help.

Mizena and Shandur were helpless as, with the collapse of the assault on CuSho, the Spiral Assembly had taken the step, unprecedented in all of Tazian history, of authorising a Gheas to be placed on them that prevented any more action on their part to recover their children.

Mandara and Lellia only just escaped the Gheas by reluctantly promising not to take any more action to recover their great great nephew and niece. The leading scientist of the period, Orchestrator of the First XzylStroem, Elderests and senior members of the Spiral Assembly, they were unable to escape the fact that their first duty was to the future of their race, and that meant fulfilling their responsibilities in order to maintain stability across the planet and the link with Azura.

Mizena openly wept in her husband's arms. Without Tamina, CuSho was out of action and the fate of her children now rested in the hands of Wrenden, the youngest of the BestFriends, and the unknown quantity that was Rulcas, a Mentally Underdeveloped Unstructured Degenerate. 'Supposedly,' she said to herself.

LOVE HURTS

RAIATEA

Qwelby awoke feeling... cold? The sun shining through the partially dimmed securaglass into his room showed him he was on Raiatea. He turned to his twin. She was the source of the cold? Ouch! His gentle probe into her mind struck... stone walls... walls of the prison he'd visited.

He got off the bed and stood breathing heavily as he looked at... a beautiful, cast-in-stone image of his twin. But it wasn't. The rise and fall of her chest and belly sent the message that it was his real, alive, Quantum Twin, wearing several bandages and bearing the marks of slowly healing cuts. Was she sleeping? Her eyes were closed but he thought not.

'I'm going for a swim, then my exercises,' he said. 'When I finish, Hokuao will serve breakfast on the patio.'

As he settled in his morning exercise routine, Tullia walked past him, devoid of any bandages. He stopped and watched as she dived into the pool. He was trembling. He'd never seen anyone's energy field so inundated with shades of black, grey and brown that seemed to be chasing the other colours and dulling them as they passed. It took a great effort of will to finish his routine then walk to the table as Hokuao arrived with breakfast for two.

Miki arrived as he ate and drank whilst Tullia continued to swim. 'Please bring your sister at the usual time,' the petite doctor said with a slight bow of her head. 'Today, in the Professor's quarters.'

Tullia only started her meal when Qwelby went into their room. He changed into his normal t-shirt and shorts and went to speak to his twin when she'd finished her meal. He took a pace back when she turned her face towards him and he saw her eyes – two completely grey ovals. 'The Professor who I thoughtsent you about has asked us to join him and his assistants at my usual time. In a few minutes.'

Tullia rose, walked into the room and went through to the bathroom. A long time later she emerged, having assiduously brushed her hair which now cascaded below her waist in thick waves. Opening the wardrobe and drawers, she found a short red skirt, matching red briefs and a top in two shades of green on white that would leave her arms and shoulders bare.

'I didn't know they were there,' Qwelby said. 'Hokuao, she's the housekeep and cook, must have bought them.'

Tulia's grey-eyed gaze swept over him, dismissing him and the clothes. She took the sheet from the bed and wrapped it around under her armpits, knotting at one side. She then buckled the belt from her skirt around her waist and pulled Thathuma, her Tazian necklace over the top of the sheet. Looking through all the presents she'd been given, she selected Xashee's. He'd worked on the head of the arrow he'd loosed at, but missed, the leopard, smoothing it into a perfect heart shape, then bored a tiny hole and added a plant-fibre loop, turning it into a necklace. She slipped it over her head, stroked the heart where it lay between her breasts, picked up her spear and jerked her head.

Qwelby opened the door to the corridor and watched her walk around the room and past him. His hearts were beating fast. He was looking at the most stunningly beautiful Denizen imaginable. A walking stone statue showing one long and shapely leg. That's my twin?!

417

In his suite, Romain greeted Tullia and introduced Tyler and Miki.

Tullia's eyes had turned from grey to violet, but still no purple orbs. She walked across to the windows and looked out over the Pacific Ocean. She was making a statement and drawing all eyes to her.

After a few moments she turned and spoke in a language neither Qwelby nor his compiler understood, at the same time thoughtspeaking him in Tazian. He had to translate. And he had to translate with total accuracy. His foreboding of retribution was immediately confirmed.

'I am Tyua'llia !Gei-!Ku'ma, Queen of the Red San. We are the last of the Tazii on this planet. Our home is with the Meera in the Land Of Great Thirst. I have crossed the sea to take him home. He is suffering from an extreme affliction of his mind.'

Tullia's eyes blazed and Qwelby jerked, grabbed his head and fell to his knees as a bolt from his twin struck his mind. Was he the only one who saw her spear turn into a long slender snake?

Over one metre ninety-five, well-built and looking every inch an imposing ruler, Tullia dwarfed even the tall Professor. Her purple orbs had returned to her eyes and from time to time her ovals flickered with bright colours as a torrent of questions bounced off her as if she were a stone statue. At last, there was silence. Tyler helped Qwelby to his feet.

'I shall rest,' Qwelby "translated".

Tullia walked to the door by which she'd entered from within the laboratory complex and stood, waiting, until Romain recovered his poise and opened it.

Qwelby noted the claw marks over her right shoulder were not healing as well as the other wounds he'd treated.

There was silence as the door closed, then Romain erupted in fury at Qwelby's deceit. The Professor slowly calmed as he accepted Qwelby's fear of her discovery stemmed from all he'd heard about the probable treatment of aliens. His emotions soon turned from

418

anger to excitement, an excitement that spread to Miki and even the doubting Tyler. Not only did they have two aliens to work with, if the boy was to be believed and that could soon be verified, they had a pair of fully functioning identical twins – Chimarae.

Miki nodded sombrely as Romain gave her the responsibility for softening Tullia's attitude. 'Hokuao may help as Tullia will need to talk with her about meals,' she suggested to approval from both Qwelby and Romain.

Qwelby told them the little he knew of Tullia's time in the Kalahari, CuSho and Jeffri and what was happening on Vertazia. 'As to her telling lies or being economical with the truth. All she said is, in her mind, true. "Queen of the Red San." She sees the San as our direct descendants, making us sort of like their ancestors. They gave her that title. She believes that my home is with her in the Kalahari. At least while we are on Earth. My affliction of mind. Refusing to get into CuSho and try to go home.'

The discussion had taken them well through their working lunch, during which Romain had agreed with Tullia's request, conveyed by Hokuao, to be allocated her own room.

As Qwelby arrived in his room he saw Tullia leave the patio and go into hers. All attempts at thought contact failed, her shield was complete. They had their own Privacy Shields but had never totally blocked the other. That was hurting him a lot and he knew she must also be in pain. How could loving Angélle be so wrong and hurt another – the person he loved most of all in two worlds? Yet that love was so different from what he felt for Angélle.

Wasn't it?

'Oh, young QeïchâKaïgïi…'

Cross with himself, Tullia and that voice, he stripped and plunged into the pool, then lay down on one of the loungers. What could he do? Wait and hope that as time passed she might open a tiny chink in her armour? Surely there was more? He'd ask Angélle. She was a woman. She'd know.

When Angélique arrived for their usual afternoon together,

she told him that her Mother had passed on the message that Tullia was not to be disturbed and her evening meal was to be delivered to her door to the corridor. All done by very clear sign language, she explained.

Qwelby said nothing about the mental commands Tullia would have issued.

CHAPTER 80

LOVING

RAIATEA

As usual when they finished the evening meal, Angélique cleared their table then brought down the trolley that cleared away the meal she'd served to the scientists. Back in the kitchen she looked out through the window at Qwelby slumped over the table with his head on his arms. A big, strong warrior. Yet at the same time a gentle soul and tonight, a little lost boy in pain. Her heart went out to him.

She'd already broken the golden rule for holiday romances that all the girls agreed on – she'd fallen in love with him. He'd said he loved her. Now he needed her. Well, there was no harm in giving him a comforting cuddle. Was there?

Qwelby looked up as he heard her footsteps and wondered why she hadn't changed out of her working clothes for their after dinner time. She walked up to his chair and held out a hand. As he took it, she pulled him up and led him across to the steps leading to the kitchen. The colours running through her energy field were a confusing mix. Did she want a kiss out of sight or was he to help with the washing up?

'You go first,' she said as they reached the bottom of the stairs. He gave her a puzzled look.

421

'You're not looking up my skirt,' she said as she pushed him.

'Oh. Just down your bits,' he said from atop the first step as he smiled at her. 'Ouch!' He grinned at the slap.

Inside the small apartment she led him through the kitchen-cum-diner to her bedroom.

'Your room is nice. I...'

'Shut up.'

She undid the buttons of his brightly coloured shirt and pushed it off his shoulders, put her arms around him, rested her head on his chest and sighed. Who is wanting the comforting cuddle? she asked herself as his arms came around her, he rested his head on the top of hers and she felt the beating of his two hearts.

Tullia's attitude was killing him, but Angélle. He loved her. He loved Tullia. They were different. As the tension drained out of him he gently lifted Angélique's head and their lips met. It started as the gentle kiss he'd intended, then his hearts were pounding and his head throbbing.

With Angélique wearing a tighter top than usual and with two buttons undone, tonight, he'd not been able to take his eyes off the sight of her full breasts. His hand slid around and cupped one. She gave a little sigh. After a while he started to undo the remaining buttons, then slipped a hand onto a bare breast and gently caressed it.

If she liked a boy, she let him fondle her breasts, but never do any more than that.

Moments later her blouse dropped to the floor. She put her arms back around him and rubbed her breasts over the velvet-like skin. She'd been imagining doing that ever since discovering how soft his skin was as she rubbed sun oil over him.

He lifted her head and they kissed. He teased her with his tongue. Her lips parted a little and his tongue slid inside. She gasped and became very aware of his hard masculinity pressing against her stomach. She went hot and wet. Oh God, he'll think I'm a tart and do this with all the boys I kiss.

Remember – nothing below the waist.

A few moments later her hands were gripping his hair as her feet meekly accepted being lifted out of her skirt and panties now lying on the floor.

'You are beautiful,' he said, looking up from where he was kneeling in front of her.

She was used to skinny-dipping with a group of girls and boys. Enjoyed being looked at. Now, surprisingly self-conscious, she pulled his head against her stomach. Moments later he threw his shorts and boxers to one side.

She gripped handfuls of hair at the back of his head, but failed to pull him away when his mouth encompassed a breast and she softy moaned as she again felt hot and wet. Oh God. No. Please!

With one swift movement he bent down, picked her up and then lay down alongside her on the bed. 'You are so beautiful,' he said as he gently caressed her.

She pulled his head to hers and kissed him, sliding her tongue into his mouth. Anything to stop him gazing at her with that look that was robbing her of all resistance.

His hand was gently caressing her breasts. She was on fire and didn't want him to stop... just yet.

His fingers traced a path down her body to her thigh.

She was going to pick his hand up and put it back on her breast. Her hand reached his and rested on it, now between her legs. Oh God. He'll know I'm a tart!

There wasn't much room on her single bed, so it felt right that as they moved her legs parted to give him the space to lie between them.

No sex.

Watching him climbing out of the pool that first morning, his long hair and the sunlight turning the water cascading off him into a multi-coloured waterfall, he'd looked like a god emerging from the ocean. She'd imagined being in his arms. Now she was, but much more intimately than... liar!

423

No sex. I've broken all my other rules but I'm not going to break that one. He's been slow and gentle. He'll stop when I ask. In a moment I'll put my hands on his shoulders and push him away. No need for words. He'll understand.

His mouth met hers. They kissed, gently. His tongue slid in between her willing lips. She moaned and arched her back – and found she was riding on the back of a dragon as they soared through space, out beyond the solar system and into the Milky Way.

The dragon disappeared and she wrapped her arms around her magic alien. Joined together as a fiery comet they plunged through a Black Hole into a new universe full of exploding suns, thundering lava flows and exultant cries.

There came a time of peace. He rolled them over and she was on top. If he thinks me a tart, I don't care. I'm his tart. She gazed into his eyes. Two ovals of total purple, full of millions of twirling stars. 'I love you.' She rested her head on his chest. 'You're mine. All mine,' she whispered to herself. She felt a gentle squeeze, gave a big sigh and fell asleep.

Qwelby opened his eyes to a window looking out onto the bright blue sky. A few moments of adjustment and he accepted it was late morning and he was in Angélle's room. She'd said there was no college today, so she'd offered to stay overnight and prepare all the meals for the day.

He looked down at their two bodies. With her head pillowed on his chest her face was not visible. With her long, black hair and brown body with its pinkish hue, she was Tazian. A beautiful, adorable Tazian and he was in love with her.

He watched as she rubbed her face against his chest, then her soft and wondering eyes looked up at his. He ran his fingers though her thick, Tazian hair.

She examined his chest. 'No bite marks,' she said. 'But I must have hurt you?'

'No. You set me on fire. But I hurt you.'

'No. Well, yes.' She placed her fingers on his lips as he started to speak. 'It was my first time.' She pressed with her fingers. 'And you set me on fire. Everywhere.'

'Ohh, Angélle. I love you so much.'

'Mpfh.' She snuggled into the place between his neck and shoulder. She'd broken every one of her rules, including the very final one – no sex without protection. She had a pack of condoms in the bottom drawer of her bedside cabinet and hadn't thought about them for one moment. Right then she didn't care, though there'd be hell to pay if ... 'Je t'aime. Mon vel-ours.' She stroked his chest. 'I love you. My velvet-bear.'

CHAPTER 81

AGONY

RAIATEA

A buzzer sounded in the kitchen, signalling time to prepare breakfast. Several minutes later Qwelby walked down the steps, watching Tullia swimming lengths of the pool. He was lost in the magic of being in love and the euphoria of a wonderful sharebonding. After a month and a half during which no one had read his aura he was blissfully unaware of the vibrant colours swirling through it, telegraphing both his feelings and what he had been doing.

Unbuttoning his shirt as he descended, he finished stripping as he reached the patio. Before he could dive into the pool, Tullia lifted herself out in one fluid movement. A deep honey-gold, reddish brown, the sunshine on the water cascading off her sparkled with thousands of diamond sharp, miniature rainbows. She was Beautiful. Magnificent. A veritable Uddîšû. His identical twin? Impossible!

'Ow!' he cried and staggered back at the force of her punch in his chest and another 'Ow!' as she hit him again. He caught her fists for the next two punches.

'Wha...?'

'You Shades fucking shit! More than four whole tendays apart and you don't welcome me. Not only that. You refuse to come home with me.'

'We were wounded and...'

'Don't lie to me! It's that fucking girl.'

'I...'

'I have a new family. Father, mother, brother and sisters. My Awakening was with ALL the women of my tribe. I had a knife fight to the death to earn my place. I was adopted into the whole tribe. I AM MEERA, a Bushman and a hunter. I gave all this up for you and what do you do, you...'

'I love...'

'And I love them. All of them. Four tendays building a life...'

Qwelby was overwhelmed by the pain behind her vituperative words and the flood of images and emotions she was pounding into him. Quantum Twins, she made them his images. He was sitting amongst a family around a tiny fire with two young children cuddled on his lap. His children. Their children. He saw blood trickling from two deep gashes across his belly and the spurts of blood from a girl's buttocks as he slashed with his knife. He commanded a Kudu to stop and slit its throat. He was stirred deep within as a mixture of faces of young women and men drifted past.

'...and you cannot give up even one girl! You betrayed me. Us. Everything!'

Qwelby cried out and collapsed, clutching himself where she'd kicked him. Slowly, the agony eased, his sight cleared and he saw Angélique at his side holding a glass of freshly made fruit juice. She helped him sit up and drink. Eventually, he managed to stagger to the table and sit down. By that time Tullia had finished eating and gone to her room.

Qwelby was late arriving at the second floor meeting room, the delay already explained by Angélique. No Tullia. A quarter of an hour later, still no Tullia. Having gone to fetch her, Miki returned to say that Tullia was going to spend the day meditating and did not want to be disturbed, even for food.

Qwelby suggested a new approach. Instead of him trying to explain Tazian science, why didn't he learn what they were doing and how. Then see if and how he was able to help them develop that to a stage where communication with Vertazia might be possible.

He explained Doctor Keskinen's idea of piggy-backing messages onto satellite broadcasts that his friends enjoyed. The "violent" KiddyKartoons for all, teenage fashion for the girls, science for Pelnak and the heavily censored adventure films that Wrenden liked. Romain agreed to the general idea and they worked through the afternoon as Qwelby tried to ignore his churning insides by burying himself in the challenge.

They took a break in the late afternoon. Qwelby went for a swim and lay on the lounger, soaking up the sun. Something was wrong. Although Tullia had shut him out, she had left what felt like a tiny light visible. It was both reassuring in that she was saying "I am here," and also intensely annoying as it was also saying "But you are not welcome." It was so delicate he had not been aware of it whilst working, but now... he felt around. It was not there. He searched. Nothing. He switched to HideNSeek mode and searched again. Nothing.

Concerned, he went to the patio doors to her room and "listened". Still nothing. Alarmed, he ran through his room and to the door from the corridor to her room, focused his hearing and listened. Again, nothing. The internal security of the modular system on that floor, only ever intended for guests, was simple voice recognition with a password if required.

Controlling his panic he modulated his voice and said 'Tullia.' The door remained shut. He thought and said, '!Gei-!Ku'ma.' About to hurl himself at the door, he stopped and relaxed. 'Tyua'llia.' The door clicked open and he breathed a sigh of relief at her choice of her Meera name. The suite was a duplicate of his.

A generous bedsitting room with a king sized bed, a bathroom and a tiny kitchenette. No Tullia. None of her possessions in the bathroom. No clothes anywhere. No spear!?

He ran into his room and stopped in horror, Soloc and the Globe were not on his bedside cabinet. He slid open the wardrobe door. The satchel, Fill Me, had gone. He sank onto the bed, his head in his hands. What had he done? Was being in love with Angélique so wrong? Where had his twin gone? And why had she switched into deep HideNSeek mode? They'd never been able to totally hide from each other. They'd always been able to retune their vibrations rapidly enough to sense the other. But this...

In a daze he walked to the pool and slowly submerged himself in the water.

A short while later a deeply unhappy Qwelby explained to the others what he had found and outlined what had happened that morning. His twin could be anywhere, but his worst guess was that she was intending to return to the Kalahari. Tyler said that was going to be very difficult as transport off the island was limited to the one airport at Uturoa and the ferry service from the terminal adjacent to the main port.

Romain had cultivated and maintained excellent relations with the island's administration. A telephone call and notices were issued for a watch to be kept for Tullia. The story being of a young woman who was suffering from post traumatic shock disorder and had been sent to Raiatea to recover. She was not to be approached but Romain was to be advised, when he and her uncle, Doctor Tyler Jefferson, would collect her.

Given the emotional state Qwelby was in, Romain was adamant in refusing his pleas to be allowed to go and search for his sister. He was supported by both Tyler and Miki that unobtrusive, passive surveillance by people Tullia did not know was far better – especially given what she was wearing.

Whilst the twins had been asleep, Hokuao had been asked to buy an outfit for Tullia. Guided by the ripped clothes in the bin liner and constrained by what was available for a very tall young woman, she had purchased the short bright red skirt and an off the shoulder top, patterned in shades of green on a white background. Although the Islanders were a tall race, at her height with thick black hair down to her waist and her perfectly proportioned figure, the others said that even hunched over and shading her eyes, Tullia was going to stand out wherever she went. Qwelby kept his doubts to himself.

Later that evening a telephone call advised that a woman answering Tullia's description had boarded the Hawaiki Nui. It had already left for Tahaa and would go on to Bora Bora and Huahine before returning to Raiatea the following afternoon.

By the time they retired for the night, they also knew she had not disembarked at Taha.

CHAPTER 82

REVENGE

RAIATEA

Qwelby threw himself into work the following day. He accepted that his twin was punishing him but he was not going to be sucked into her game by going down to the ferry terminal to meet her. She had walked into Uturoa, she could walk back.

As usual, Hokuao had served a working lunch and gone back home with Jean-Marie, who had brought Angélique with him. Qwelby was nervously waiting for a telephone call from the ferry terminal. When the call came it was to say that no-one answering Tullia's description had disembarked before the Hawaiki Nui departed. Half an hour later it was confirmed that she had not gone ashore at Bora Bora, nor was she on board.

'She must have got off before the ship left,' Qwelby said.

'No,' Angélique said. 'She is a striking woman. And with what she is wearing, men and woman will notice her.' Again Qwelby said nothing about the mental skills he and his twin possessed.

This time Romain accepted Qwelby's impassioned pleas and agreed to his searching the island – accompanied by Tyler. Miki suggested that Angélique should also go. As a local and a woman she was the best person to be asking questions.

The youngsters sat in the back seat as Tyler drove them into

431

town. They left him to move around a variety of cafés as they went into shop after shop.

Several hours later they had discovered Tullia's shopping spree, using Qwelby's money that he had stored in the satchel. She'd started in Le Fare de Claire Marché de Uturoa with a large pair of sunglasses. That was followed by a large shoulder bag, a smart pair of sandals, a large sunhat, a scarf, a headband and several pins and combs for her hair. It appeared that her final purchases had been a blouse in the same style that Hokuao had bought, this time in shades of lilacs, and a purple skirt. 'We shortened it for her,' the shop assistant in issa-de-mar said. 'It looked lovely on her long legs.'

Tyler suggested that Tullia had boarded the ferry in what Hokuao had provided, changed into what she had bought for herself, pinned most of her hair under the hat and left the ferry. Given the clear description of what she had been wearing when she'd left the laboratory complex, if anyone had noticed her after she'd changed, they'd not thought to mention it. Angélique shook her head but then had to admit that there was no other obvious explanation.

Tyler telephoned Romain and the authorities at the ports in Tahaa, Bora Bora and Huahine were given a new description and asked to question staff again. Angélique telephoned her brother to ask around his mates who worked at the port in Uturoa.

Qwelby explained that it all made sense as his favourite colours were red and green, whereas Tullia's were purple and lilac. His twin was kitting herself out at his expense, distancing herself from him and making him suffer from worry.

'A woman scorned,' Angélique said, giving Qwelby a sympathetic smile as she took hold of her man's hand.

Dripping with sweat as much from nervous tension as the double layer of the clothes she was wearing, Tullia sighed with relief as she leant back against the door she'd just closed. Trembling from two days of exploration, excitement, laying false trails and the danger of being discovered, she took a deep breath.

She'd been on Earth for more than four tendays. During all the time of that rollercoaster ride she'd been focussing on being reunited with the most important person in her life. The mental reconnection a moon ago had been amazing and so full of love that she'd happily shared that with her new girlfriends.

Kaigii had refused to leave the island – because he loved another girl. More than he loved her! That betrayal had blasted her world apart. He'd denied her and now with her mental lockdown she was denying him. Both hurt, physically, emotionally and mentally. Deep down inside, her very Self was screaming with pain.

She'd learnt about love after her two Awakenings. At last, she'd understood the meaning of the colours in the auras of Kou-'ke and Xashee – showing their love and desire for each other. Through her nights with the girls she'd experienced the flow of loving and the full passion of Ungka's desire.

Not content with the pain her twin had already caused, that morning as he'd left Angélique's apartment he'd deliberately stoked up his energy field to show his love and passion for her. Then the man-stealing bitch had followed him, their auras matching in a soul-sickening display of their togetherness. A togetherness that belonged to her! Tullia was bereft.

Hating Angélique, she understood how Kou-'ke had felt, and felt the same. She wanted revenge. And that was so totally unTazian that it piled more hurt on top of everything else. Her world was full of unbelievable pain, yet she knew her plans for revenge had to be working.

It was the first time she'd gone into total mental lockdown by herself. With her twin, yes. But by herself, never. The downside was that she no longer had any sense of how he was feeling. Yet, for this, after a whole lifetime of being inseparable – she knew – he'd be deep in The Shades.

Her initial intention had been to leave, hide and spy on the laboratory complex. To go outside she'd had to wear the clothes that Hokuao had bought. The next steps had unfolded as she'd gone through the day.

What had been available amongst the tribe had meant she'd ended up wearing red and green as she'd left the Kalahari. She'd been excited like a silly child that she was going to meet her twin wearing his two favourite colours. She understood why Hokuao had bought the clothes she had – but now she hated the colours.

Checking her reflection as she finished dressing, she was astonished. All she'd seen of herself since arriving on Earth was her face in an occasional reflection in a bowl of water. Having once used a bowl of water as Mirror, she automatically switched vision to see Image.

'Yeeow!' she squealed as a dark figure appeared, smoke swirling around and flames shooting through her energy field. Snapping back, she closed her eyes and took a few deep breaths. 'I look just like Kou-'ke.'

Steadying herself, she opened her eyes and looked in the mirror at what she knew to be a true reflection of a fifteen-year-old girl transformed into a mature young woman. All her teenyfat had gone, her hips had widened a little and her bust was more developed. She sighed. The Meera were right. She was a "Big Girl." With an embarrassed warmth inside, she understood why she'd received so many thoughts of admiration and desire.

'At least I am in proportion,' she said to her reflection. 'And okay when back home.'

Her eyes lingered on her well-toned legs. In proportion to her six foot five inches imperial, or one metre ninety-five, as the research students had measured her, their length was emphasised by the short skirt. 'Sorry, legs. I'll need to cover you up if I want to walk around and not be noticed.'

She walked into Uturoa, found a Bureau de Change, changed some of Qwelby's money and followed a pressing need to buy new clothes in her own favourite colours. The styles Hokuao had chosen were pretty and flattering and Tullia allowed her Tazian Self to honour the Raiatean by choosing the same. And that provided a new idea – to continue to be noticed. So she asked for the new purple skirt to be shortened.

A walk around the seafront and the ferry terminal gave Tullia an idea. Whilst shopping, she'd surreptitiously acquired some garments in the Mercato Coperto di Uturoa, leaving money to be found by a surprised stallholder. She'd not had any specific plan in mind – just the fact that she could disguise herself, Qwelby would never know what she was wearing and she could "disappear". Now, she'd board the ferry, change, get off and, unrecognisable, find a café where she'd sit down and make plans.

Clutching a brochure, smiling and thoughtsending to the crewman checking tickets, girl-in-a-purple-skirt boarded the ferry, sat down and calmed her racing hearts. She'd been ready to turn and run if challenged, but although Azuran minds were difficult to read, influencing them was easy.

Calmer, she joined the queue at the toilets and eventually was able to lock herself into a cubicle. Her hat, lilac top and purple skirt went into her large shoulder bag which she hung around her neck and then pulled the voluminous dress over it. It took time to arrange that to look right and add a turban. When she stepped out of the cubicle and looked at her reflection in a mirror she grimaced. "Big Girl" was now "Big-Big Woman." A deep breath and she nodded. She'd be noticed because of her height but, dressed like one of the large and gaily accoutred African tourists she'd seen, the disguise was perfect.

As she walked into a seating area she was shocked to discover the ship had left the terminal. Lost in concentration on getting her clothes right, and never having been on a ship on Earth before, she had not understood the meaning of the changes in sound and movement. She stood staring at Raiatea as it shrank into the distance.

Shaking her head, she pulled out of her daze and started

thinking. The assistant in issa-de-mar had given Tullia one of the shop's bags to contain the top and skirt she had changed out of. That added to her disguise by making her look like many other passengers, whilst it also served as her handbag.

Thanking the research students for teaching her to recognise letters and numbers, she slowly worked her way through the brochure, her compiler reading it back to her in English. The ship was going to stop at Tahaa, Bora Bora and Huahine before returning to Raiatea the following day. Goosebumps ran all though her insides as she accepted that she'd just entered a dangerous Dance of Discovery.

Discovering that many people on board were tourists taking the round trip as what they called a mini-cruise, Tullia relaxed and enjoyed the new experience of the voyage and the views of the islands. Late at night, along with most of the other passengers, she made herself comfortable and settled down to sleep. By the time the following day when she joined the many people disembarking at Raiatea, she was happy and relaxed, except for being desperate to get rid of the weight and discomfort of the shoulder bag hanging around her neck.

Walking across the ferry terminal she met a group of elderly American tourists who were delighted to tell the tall African, with an intriguing accent to her excellent English, all about the long cruise they were on, with their last stop at Tahaa before sailing back to Los Angeles. Smiling at the thought that she really could make her twin suffer, Tullia continued talking with the Americans as they walked to the entrance to the main port where she watched them pass through security.

A few minutes later, girl-in-a-purple-skirt walked from behind a stack of pallets at the back of a building as another group of tourists approached the main port entrance. Once through security, Tullia stopped to watch the men carrying supplies into the ship through a large loading bay. If she decided not to stay on the liner, that would provide a discreet exit.

The tourists had continued on board, leaving Tullia with the companionway all to herself. Half way up she heard a strange whistle, stopped, turned and waved to the stevedores. More whistles and comments followed as she made her way to the top. Smiling, she gave the young man and woman checking boarding passes a cabin number. Her smile increased as neither of them even glanced down at the brochure she was holding in place of a boarding pass.

Once inside the ship she collapsed against a wall in relief, soaked with sweat. That had been the most demanding performance of her life. Even with her lockdown, the tones of the stevedores' voices, the looks on their faces and a few gestures had bruised her emotionally more than the physical bruising she'd suffered from three days of fighting.

Calming herself, she walked along the passageway, looking for a toilet where she could sit down and think. 'It's worked,' she said softly. 'The little shit'll find out I've boarded. And I hope he hears how the men fancy me. Make him sick!' As it has done me.

Having managed the round trip on the Hawaiki Nui without any trouble, her self-confidence was high. The Americans had said the Cruise Liner made three more stops before docking in Los Angeles. She might get off at any or even all of them and ensure that girl-in-a-purple-skirt was seen. She could be anywhere. Remain on the liner. Get off and return on another sailing of the Hawaiki Nui. Find another ship – it had all been so easy. There would be pain, misery and doubt for that pathetic, immature, whelp of a brother – for as long as she wanted!

Not wanting the bother of changing clothes, Tullia pulled the brightly patterned dress over her head, added the turban, slung her shoulder bag over her shoulder and emerged from what she thought of as a dressing room and in character. Participating in LiveShows on Vertazia and sagas for the Meera, she easily slipped into her latest performance – a confused passenger speaking Afrikaans and Meera with only a little English.

Correcting Tullia's misunderstandings, a helpful stewardess provided all the information she needed as Tullia surfacesearched the woman's mind. A few minutes later, the door of an unoccupied cabin provided no challenge to Tullia's lock-picking skills. As her trembling eased, she stripped, showered and, confident she was not going to be discovered, sank back into her maelstrom of emotions.

Angélique's face slipped across her vision and plunged her even further into the darkest and blackest mood of her whole life. Not content with stealing her twin, the conniving bitch had what Tullia wanted – a big strong man. She wanted a man to whom to rail about the injustices of Life, hammer her fists on his chest and have him drive away the terrible demon she'd seen in Mirror.

Her hunter-warrior self sneered at the scared little girl inside who wanted to be wrapped in strong arms and be told that all was well.

When she finally fell asleep she was tormented by a succession of confusingly overlapping images full of death and destruction. The kudu with Angélique's face, Tullia eagerly drinking the metallic tasting blood. A series of images of brown buttocks, his and hers, blood trickling from deep gashes. Each new image revealing more and deeper cuts until rivers of blood flowed and she cackled with pleasure.

Kou-'ke spread-eagled on the ground with her twin's head on her body, a long knife tight against her loins. Then Kou-'ke's head on his body. Back and forth they went, yet there was never a sign of his manhood and the blood trickling along the ground slowly turned into a river. Each time she dropped to her knees to drink, she was stopped. Either Tsetsana appeared saying, 'You love him.' Or Ungka saying, 'I love you.' Tullia was left pounding her fists on the thick red sand as she again absorbed Ungka's love for her and tried to deny that was what she felt for her twin.

CHAPTER 83

CLAIMED

RAIATEA

Later that evening, Qwelby listened with increasing anxiety as Angélique took a phone call from her brother.

'Jean-Marie says that none of the guys he spoke to saw Tullia getting off the Hawaiki Nui when it returned, but one of them is certain he saw her today with a group of tourists about to enter the main Port itself.'

'How certain?'

'Very. She was head and shoulders above a group of mainly white people and, he thinks, possibly with a purple skirt.'

'Possibly?'

'She's got long legs.'

'Yeah.'

'And the other bits,' Angélique said cattily, hearing the feeling in Qwelby's one word.

'I prefer YOUR other bits.'

Angélique threw her arms around him. 'Sorry.'

Qwelby held her firmly against him as he infused her with his love and thanked Hannu and Anita for a valuable lesson about jealousy.

'She won't be able to get into that part of the port.' Angélique's voice was muffled by her head pressed against his chest. 'Security is good.' She looked up at him. 'I know. We try to get in to sneak aboard the big cruise ships.'

'What's a cruise ship?'

'It's a tourist ship. They go around, stopping at an island during the day and then sail at night.'

Qwelby remembered the big ship he'd seen and turned to look across the island to the port. It was no longer there. His eye was caught by a collection of bright lights out on the ocean. 'Is that it?'

'Yes. But she can't be on it.'

'Where goes it?' he asked in almost a whisper.

'That big one. Three islands, then back to Los Angeles. Where the Professor lectures.'

'Labirden Xzarze! I must speak to the Professor. I'll explain when I come back.'

When he returned he led Angélique into his room, sat her down and demonstrated how easy it was for him to fool her into believing that the blank piece of paper she'd carefully examined was a ferry ticket.

Since Tullia had arrived, everything had been a whirl. He'd wanted to tell Angélique the truth about himself and his twin the other night. Instead, they'd made love. Last night, too much had been going on and she'd gone home with her brother as usual. Now, he enfolded her in his arms and thoughtwrapped her into a visit to Vertazia.

When they returned, she melted in his arms. It had not taken her long to work out that, along with his obvious physical difference that was definitely not a defect, he had a big secret he was hiding. And that had been before the three days of fighting. He had made her a woman. Tonight she would show how much she loved him. 'Stay with me,' she said.

He understood, and they made love in his room, on Earth, whilst the moon and her cohort of stars remained firmly in the heavens, until the roaring ocean swept them away.

A lot later she lay on top of him, watching the bite marks on his chest slowly fade. 'There's an ancient tradition in these Islands. When a girl chooses a man to be her first, she may claim him. In my mind I chose you when I saw you emerging from the swimming pool your first day, looking like Tangaroa, the Sea God. It was a young girl's fantasy. You made it come true.' She took a deep breath. 'I claim you as my man. Until you return to your home.' Tears ran down her face.

His hearts in pain from the sadness in her eyes, his mind in a whirl with all the implications of "return home" and wondering what to say, Qwelby kissed the tears on her cheeks and once again found her fingers on his lips. He did not need to search her mind to understand. As he was her man, so she was his woman. "His woman!"

His hearts expanded until he was standing astride the island, holding her in his arms. Then he shrank as humility overcame him. How could she love him so much? She was so adorable, sweet, kind and understanding. How could he ever leave her – yet he had to. Tears pricked his eyes. 'Nous t'aimons. Mes coeurs et moi. We love you. My hearts and I.'

Angélique burst into tears. In her mind she'd become his woman as she nursed him through all the fighting then, for her, he'd confirmed that the first time they'd made love. Her sobbing eased as he gently stroked her. She managed a faint smile at his abuse of the French language and rested her head on the broad chest of her man. Her funny, alien War God with his exciting differences. One day he was going to leave. Until then, she was determined to enjoy every moment with him and try to help him become reconciled with his twin.

As they dressed a little later, Qwelby put on the suede briefs Taimi Keskinen had made for him. It was a small but important link with his twin and, daft as it seemed, he hoped that the energy that had been in their previous connections might find a chink in her mental armour.

Not wanting to make her feelings obvious to her brother, Angélique had previously insisted that Qwelby did not come up to the top floor to say their goodnights. Tonight, she accepted it when he said he wanted to come up and thank him. The sixteen-year-old college student would have her place tomorrow. Tonight, she was his woman and proud of her warrior man.

Looking up at Qwelby outside the main entrance, Jean-Marie said that on his way from home he'd stopped off to speak to a mate who worked in the Port's restricted area and had just finished his shift. 'Marc said he watched your sister go up the gangway, past the two guys checking boarding cards and then into the ship.'

'What was she wearing?'

Jean-Marie grinned. 'A purple belt.'

'Belt?'

'A very short skirt,' Angélique said, glaring at her brother.

'She really wants be noticed and send me message,' Qwelby ground out through clenched teeth.

The door to Romain's suite opened and the Professor stepped out to say that reports from Tahaa, Bora Bora and Huahine were equally negative of any sightings of "Lilac Woman", as they had been of "Green Woman". The liner's captain had denied that it was possible for anyone without a pass to board, especially someone as striking as had been described and had refused to have a search made. He had gone on to confirm that it was one of the regular luxury cruises, but due to labour problems at Tahaa, this time stopping only at Maupiti and Bora Bora before arriving in LA eleven days later.

Romain said he'd have calls made for people to check on Tullia's possible disembarkation at the two islands.

Qwelby believed Marc. His twin was on board the cruise ship. She had carefully planned the whole venture and by flaunting herself in a new outfit of her favourite colours made it clear she was rejecting him. She was on her way back to her tribe and her family and – stroking her heart shaped necklace had made it abundantly clear – her lover!

She Zeyusa and he Anananki. He'd never forgiven her betrayal for raising an army in an attempt to prevent him activating the great crystal sphere. Now, feeling his hearts crack at being deserted by the person he loved most in two worlds, he just managed to thank Romain and Jean-Marie and give Angélique a quick kiss before tearing across the track and plunging into the forest. Crashing through the trees he howled like a wild animal as with all his strength he thoughtspoke his twin to return.

'Look!' Angélique exclaimed, pointing up to the sky

'What?' 'Where?' the others asked.

'That rainbow. Shooting straight out into the stars.'

'For God's sake, now she's seeing things!' Tyler exclaimed in disgust.

'No.' Miki put a hand on the girl's arm.

'My man,' Angélique said.

'She sees what she sees,' Miki added as she looked up into the girl's unseeing eyes.

Angélique walked across the track and stood, waiting for Qwelby to return. She did not have long to wait.

CHAPTER 84

ORO FIGHTS PELE

RAIATEA

Xaala had finished her duties for the day and was in her room, once again struggling with her mental and emotional confusion. She jerked as she was struck by... the boy's call arcing out to his twin. Her DarkSuit was still moulding itself to her Form as she morphed into the eighth dimension, straddled her Attribute and hurtled across into the third dimension.

During three days of fighting she'd discovered that intense concentration on her seventh dimension club had made it an effective weapon against the girl's third dimension Form. The boy was not going to morph out of the third and leave his immobile Form as an easy second target. She'd had a chance with the Minotaur. That had been a matter of microns and nanoseconds. But, even though it would have been an unfortunate accident, Tullia would have seen and would never have forgiven her. Now there was no Ceegren to watch. No Custodians fighting alongside. She and him. Alone. She laughed as she mentaformed a flaming sword in one hand and a fiery shield in the other.

A mighty crash shook the ground, sent birds screeching into the sky and yelping wild dogs running across the track as Xaala slipped from her snake and flung herself at Qwelby.

Impossibly burnt by her slashing sword, Qwelby was forced back by the ferocity of her attack. He needed to morph – but – his Form. Love reached him. Strong and sure. Angélle. His Woman.

Running back, he pulled his brightly coloured Raiatean top over his head and threw it aside as he reached her. Noting her unseeing eyes as he undid his shorts, he felt a thud against a solid shielding at his back. He swung around and made out Xaala's faint image looking puzzled at the flaming sword stuck at the edge of a golden haze.

Angélle. Our love – Quantum Awakening. Qwelby smiled. But not for protection in another dimension. Entanglement? But how...? L'Entanglement with an Earth Goddess?

An energy shield like that from an Azuran? Xaala was thinking. Entangled? She searched Angélique and found the girl's thoughts contained surprisingly clear images of olden times. Myths. History. Aurigan roots of course. Even so, entanglement with an Azuran was impossible. Insufficient active DNA. But... An Image was there. Nāmaka. An Earth Sea Goddess... An Attribute? With power! What effect was the boy, and presumably the girl, having on the DNA of the Azurii?

Xaala was flung back as Qwelby, having let his Form fall at Angélique's feet and now equipped with a DarkShield and a DarkField projector, leapt at his stunned opponent. This time he was going to pin her to the ground and force answers out of her.

Her heart full to bursting from having protected Qwelby with her love, Angélique sat down and lifted his head onto her lap. His animal skin briefs were befitting for Oro and his otherwise naked body allowed her to see and treat any wounds he suffered in other dimensions. She lent over and kissed his forehead as he twitched and jerked. Truly, he was her man as she was his woman. More. His grin and flashing eyes were similar to the look on her brother's face when he was going in to bat. Her man was a warrior without malice. It was impossible, yet each time she saw a new part of him, she loved him even more.

Miki recognised the nature of the energy radiating from Angélique and bobbed her head in deference. Tyler shuddered at the remembrance that the old spelling of Ra'iatea that translated as "Far Away Heaven", was known as "Sacred Isle", where for hundreds of years human sacrifices had been made to Oro, the God of War.

Jean-Marie kissed the first two fingers of his right hand and with them gestured a circle in the direction of his young-sister-now-woman, then with a hand on his heart he inclined his head in the direction of the sounds of fierce fighting. After a moment, he turned, nodded to Romain, got into his truck and drove home with a heavy heart. He had not inherited his father's skills, Angelique had and Jean-Marie had seen enough to know his young sister was more than competently using them.

Miki looked at her husband and shook her head, turned to Romain and made a slight bow, then sat down beside Angélique. They looked up at the sound of whistling as a red crested A'a bird flew from the forest.

'Oro fights Pele,' Angélique announced in a voice full of pride at the bird's confirmation that her man was a living embodiment of the Polynesian God of War.

'You see, Angésan?' Miki asked, looking at the girl's still unseeing eyes.

'Through his eyes.'

Romain gestured to Tyler to join him where he had remained standing by his front door and led his assistant into the living room. The room stretched the full length of the apartment and they settled themselves by the window that overlooked the forest. Tyler's hands were shaking as he sipped from a glass containing a generous measure of the Professor's favourite Rémy Martin.

Like Miki, Romain was far more in touch with the energies of the Island than her husband. Sipping his brandy, the Professor was wondering what had happened to the sweet young girl he'd known for many years to cause her to refer to the alien, not as her

446

boyfriend, but as "My man." And why did she think he was Oro fighting the Fire Goddess?

'Two aliens fighting in another dimension,' Romain said. 'This isn't some weird trickery. They're doing it right there. In our back garden so to speak. We hear them and that girl even sees them. We must find his twin. Fully functioning Chimerae if he's to be believed. Think what we can do with the two of them working together!'

First, he had to get the girl back to Raiatea. A passport. Identical twins. A little adjustment to the boy's photo and 'Thank you the Shostakovich Brothers,' he murmured.

If she was unwilling? Romain swirled the brandy around his glass as he surrendered to Rekkr Reginsen, his alter ego. An accident. A medical condition. A tiny dart fired from a tube, everything made from the polymers he'd invented as part of creating his unique equipment. They would pass the security checks as integral components of a piece of equipment he was taking to the laboratory at the University where he lectured. The strong sedative distilled from a pretty plant that grew wild on the mountains.

Two doctors with a girl who had collapsed, the dark-skinned niece of the equally dark skinned Jamaican-American. Her passport presented. Seriously disturbed runaway liable to fainting fits. Convulsions? More dramatic and more obviously requiring urgent attention. A little research and he'd provide a suitable illness.

'I'll offer a reward for anyone who sees her at any of the islands, as long as that results in us finding her. If not seen there, you and I will fly to L.A. and meet her at the port.' He fixed Tyler with a determined look. 'She must not be allowed to escape. If she is not willing, there will be an unfortunate accident. No-one else must know of her and thus his existence. Not for a long time yet. Capisci.'

There was no question in Romain's final words and Tyler, who

447

loved American films, paled as he understood why his boss had switched to Italian for, "You understand."

Noting the look on his assistant's face, Romain leant forward. 'Do we need to have a little talk about your wife's Doctoral thesis?'

Comprehension slowly dawned and Tyler's face went ashen. At that time Miki had been very ill. By the time the misdiagnosis was confirmed and correct treatment was being given, it was too late. Desperate to have her Doctorate awarded before she died, not for herself but in return for all that her parents had sacrificed for her, Tyler had helped complete her thesis.

In the turmoil of believing himself about to be robbed of his love and his future wife, he'd been unable to think straight and had resorted to adapting sections from his own published work – badly it was now clear. If that were to be revealed, the light of his life would be stripped of her Doctorate. That would destroy her career and badly damage his own. Far worse, it would destroy her family. A family he loved and honoured as if his own.

Tyler took a large sip of brandy, licked his lips and shook his head. 'No need. I understand.' He emphasised the "I" – leaving Miki out of it – by placing his hand on his heart.

A smiling Romain sat back in his chair and sipped his brandy in a silent toast to himself. The trap had shut and Tyler was inside. Soon so would be the girl. Alien Chimerae! He almost dismissed the idea of Nobel Prizes, they would be insignificant compared to the other rewards that would flood in. A just recompense for so many years outside the mainstream scientific establishment.

Cave drawing 17,000 BCE of Shamans morphing into animals as they travel into the spirit world of other dimensions

CONTINUED IN

REBELLION

Discover more about The Twins, their world and the science background through their own website: www.quantumtwins.com and contact them by their email: twins@quantumtwins.com

THE AUTHOR

Postman, Milkman, Hotel Porter, Cub Scout Leader, TA Commission working with Army Cadets, twenty years in amateur theatre, twenty years member of the national Committee of his union representing HM Inspectors of Taxes. Oh and yes, a career in what was then the Inland Revenue. Now an Accountant and Tax Advisor as well as continuing to be a Counsellor, Astrologer and Medium (or channel as that is sometimes called).

Keen traveller who annoys waiters abroad by trying to speak Italian, French, German or a little Spanish, when they want to show off their command of English.

And most important of all, Husband, Father, Grandfather, Uncle & Great Uncle.

Lives with his wife, Olga, in Royal Sutton Coldfield in a house which together with the garden continue to provide challenges for his gardening and DIY skills (!)

Geoffrey's wide-ranging interests that provide him with some of the background that has helped him get to grips with what the Twins tell him, can be found at:

www.geoffarnold.co

and

www.dreamscapes.co.uk